The CALL of KERBEROS

Silus knelt beside the guard and prised the sword from his stiff fingers, passing the weapon to Katya before unsheathing his own blade.

"We may have to fight," Silus said. "There may be no other way to protect our child."

Katya nodded and kept a tight grip on Silus's hand as they ran towards the harbour.

The clash of weapons and the cries of the injured – both human and inhuman – were clearer now. Flames had started to spread to more of the buildings and, as Katya pulled Silus to a halt, they saw the roof of The Necromancer's Barge cave in. Someone flailed out of the building, a human torch that screamed so shrilly it could have been either a man or a woman. The blazing figure got only a few feet from the tavern before it keeled over in the street.

A hideous form emerged through the smoke shrouding the end of the street. Katya cried out as it put one huge, clawed foot on the skull of the burning corpse. The noise that echoed off the walls with a sharp, yet wet, report as it stamped down was not something they would ever forget.

WWW.ABADDONBOOKS.COM

An Abaddon Books™ Publication
www.abaddonbooks.com
abaddon@rebellion.co.uk

First published in 2010 by Abaddon Books™, Rebellion Intellectual
Property Limited, Riverside House, Osney Mead, Oxford, OX2 0ES, UK.

10 9 8 7 6 5 4 3 2 1

Editors: Rebecca Levene and Jennifer-Anne Hill
Cover: Mark Harrison
Design: Simon Parr & Luke Preece
Marketing and PR: Keith Richardson
Creative Director and CEO: Jason Kingsley
Chief Technical Officer: Chris Kingsley
Twilight of Kerberos™ created by Matthew Sprange and Jonathan
Oliver

ISBN: 978-1-906735-28-9

Printed in Denmark by Norhaven A/S

TWILIGHT of KERBEROS

The CALL of KERBEROS

JONATHAN OLIVER

Abaddon
Books

For Alison

For Everything

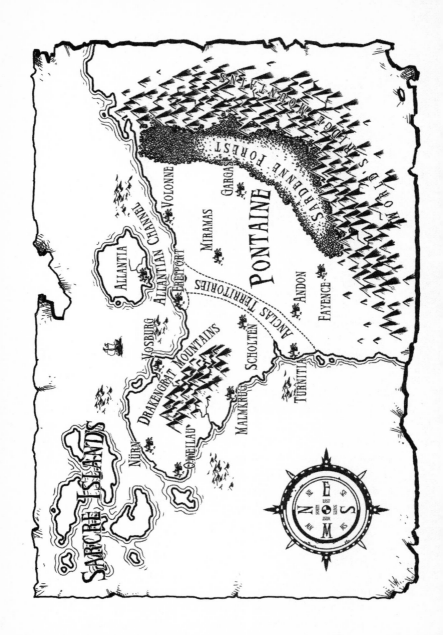

CHAPTER ONE

Stealing a ship from the harbour at Turnitia would have been an audacious enough task in itself, but stealing a vessel belonging to the Final Faith was another matter entirely. When Dunsany had first suggested it to Kelos he had stared blankly at him for a moment and then said: "Have you seen what they do to heretics? Have you seen the rather fetching collection of heretic skins Makennon keeps as mementos?"

Katherine Makennon was the flame-haired, hot-tempered, Anointed Lord; the leader of the Final Faith. A religious tyrant who kept a firm hand on her church and made sure that its message was heard by all, whether they wanted to listen or not.

"I may have no love for the Faith, Dunsany, but I rather value my fingernails."

"But we're in a perfect position to do this." Kelos said. "We have my contacts on Sarcre and a hiding place that's virtually impossible to find. Besides, who's in a better position to pull this off than the Chief Engineer and the Head Mage on the project?"

The designs for the ship had been found almost a year before in an elvish ruin near Freiport, by an adventurer called Kali Hooper. Hooper had been forced to part with her find once Makennon's people had got wind of the importance of the artefact. Ancient texts had spoken of the elves' mastery of the rough Twilight seas and of how they had ventured far beyond the Storm Wall and the Sarcre Islands but, until now, no reference had been found as to the design of their ships.

And just as Kali Hooper had been forced to part with her find, so Dunsany and Kelos had been forced to work for the Final Faith.

Dunsany had been working as a shipping engineer in Turnitia for the last ten years, before that he had been the Captain of a merchant vessel plying its trade between Sarcre and Allantia. He was a master of the rough seas that surrounded the peninsula and the ships he sailed, and later designed, were considered to be some of the finest in existence. When the Anclas Territories fell to Vos and the Final Faith tightened its grip on the city, Dunsany was the first person corralled into working for the church's naval division.

The second was Kelos.

With the subjugation of Turnitia, Kelos had considered fleeing across the border to Andon, but before he could act on his decision booted feet had kicked down his door and he had been dragged into the night.

Makennon had heard rumours of this powerful mage who worked his magic at the Turnitia docks; of how his wards protected the ships against the ravages of the sea and how his mastery of the elements had guided home many a battered vessel. It was true that his magic was no match for the angry waters beyond the Storm Wall but, even so, it was reckoned that his power was one of the main reasons Turnitia thrived as a harbour town.

When Dunsany had looked up from his diagrams one night to see Kelos standing over him, he had grinned and said: "What took you so long?"

So the two men applied themselves to whatever marine

problem Makennon threw their way; Dunsany maintaining the fleet and mapping routes while Kelos empowered the ships with his charms and wards. The crossed circle of the Final Faith soon became a familiar sight at the docks, as it was painted onto the ships preparing to bring indoctrination to Twilight's coastal towns.

As the Faith's power had grown, so Kelos and Dunsany's resentment had increased. It was true that they were spiritual men, to a certain degree, but they resented being forced along one path of belief. "All paths lead to Kerberos," Kelos's mother had once said. But if either Dunsany or Kelos dared mention the old ways, the penalty would be severe indeed and they'd soon be joining their ancestors.

And so they strengthened their comradeship in the hatred they held for the church and, with the discovery of the designs for the ship, that hatred soon found purpose.

It was called the *Llothriall* and it was a song ship. As Dunsany and Kelos had been presented with the ancient scrolls, detailing the schematics for the vessel, their awe had been palpable. Both men had heard of the song ships but neither had ever imagined they'd see the plans for such a vessel. Dunsany had never thought that a ship could be so beautiful, or so difficult to build. As he and Kelos had worked through the list of materials required they realised that the actual construction of the vessel would be the least part of the project.

The hull was to be composed primarily of a wood found only in the Drakengrat mountains. Even with their enchanted armour and cadre of mages, the detachment of men sent there suffered massive losses when a pride of shnarls smelt the human meat entering their territory. The pitch required to coat the hull had also been somewhat difficult to source, having to come – as it did – from the veins of the many-spiked, semi-sentient and highly poisonous spiritine tree. Twenty-five men were sent into the Sardenne and only five made it out. The fate they suffered, however, was as nothing compared to the torment experienced by the young men and women sent to steal the silk for the sails from the X'lcotl. All forty sent on that mission to the World's Ridge mountains returned, but their minds did not. Their consciousnesses remained with the X'lcotl – now a part of their web – and, as those strange creatures traversed the strands, the vibrations echoed out, inducing visions and delirium in the souls captured there. The shells of humans who sat and muttered in the padded cells of Scholten cathedral would die in time, and their bodies would return to the earth, but their souls would always be caught in that terrible web.

The heart of the *Llothriall* – the great gem whose magic powered the ship – was, thankfully, already in the possession of the Faith. The iridescent mineral had sat in Katherine Makennon's private quarters and had been used, variously, over the years as a footstool, a table and a support for a bookshelf. It was only after the discovery of the designs for the song ship that Makennon realised the worth of the artefact. Originally a general had found it in a field during the last war between Vos and Pontaine, and it had been presented to Makennon as a tribute. When Kelos told her what she had, Makennon's estimation of the general was greatly raised. If he had still been alive she may even have made him an Eminence.

The power within the gem required a key to unlock it, and that was where Emuel had come into the picture.

Elf magic was based on song and no human could achieve the pitch required to sing their spells. No normal human, at least.

Emuel had been the priest of a small parish near Nürn. He was the youngest priest in the Faith, at only twelve years old, and was utterly devoted to the church. Even through the soft, lilting tones of his voice he managed to communicate his passion and devotion to his congregation. His parishioners had often speculated as to whether elf blood ran in Emuel's veins, for he was unnaturally tall, unusually pale and unquestionably feminine. So it was that his was one of the first names put forward for the role of ship's eunuch; a role that he accepted demurely and gratefully. Once the surgeon's knives had ensured that the youthful pitch of Emuel's voice would remain, and the elven runes and songlines had been needled into his flesh, Kelos wondered whether that gratitude endured.

The *Llothriall's* construction was brought through suffering and loss and there was no limit to the number of men and women Katherine Makennon was willing to spend in building the Faith's flagship vessel. Unfortunately, there also seemed to be no limit to the amount of the faithful who were willing to give their lives to the cause. Dunsany and Kelos wouldn't have given their time so freely had it not been for the threat of certain heresies and indiscretions suddenly being 'remembered'. Even through their resentment, however, both men couldn't deny the majesty of what was taking shape at the Turnitia docks.

And it was partly because of that, and partly because of their hatred of the Final Faith and all it stood for, that they planned to steal the *Llothriall.*

"Makennon cannot be allowed to keep it," Dunsany said one evening when they were away from the ears of the Faithful. "It's bad enough that they use the regular ships to enforce their beliefs on the coastal towns, but the *Llothriall* can go further than them. Make no mistake, Makennon isn't planning some altruistic voyage of discovery. She's on a mission of religious conquest."

Kelos stared into the depths of his ale, behind him two sailors were beating a sea shanty into a broken piano. "No one's been beyond the Sarcre Islands and the Storm Wall before. No ship could survive those seas."

"The *Llothriall* can and just imagine what it may find."

"New lands."

"New people."

"New races with new ideologies. What do you think will happen, Dunsany, when those ideologies come up against the Final Faith?"

"What do you think?" Dunsany sighed and ran his fingers through his beard. "Gods, whatever happened to discovery for discovery's sake? Why does every pitsing artefact, every pitsing scroll and spell that's unearthed instantly become a weapon in somebody's war?"

"We could always run away to Allantia. Start up a small fishing concern. I could do cantrips for the locals."

Dunsany shook his head and smiled. "Or we could take Makennon's new toy away from her."

This time, when Kelos looked at him, Dunsany could see something like resolve in his eyes. "Discovery for discovery's sake?"

"Discovery for Discovery's sake," Dunsany confirmed, raising his tankard. "Cheers."

"Get down!"

Dunsany shoved Emuel and Kelos behind a crate as the guard rounded the hull of the vast ship. Beside him the eunuch whimpered, the strange runes and illustrations inked on his body glowing with a blue-black sheen in the Kerberos-lit dusk.

"Was it really necessary to bind him like that?" Kelos whispered, looking over at the shivering, tattooed eunuch.

"If he gets away we're buggered, you know that. No one else can sing to that gem and unlock the magic but him. Unless, that is, you'd like me to perform an impromptu operation on you right here?" Dunsany slowly unsheathed his dagger, a smile playing across his lips.

"No, no that's fine. *Really.*"

It didn't look like Emuel was going to make a break for it though. He'd been close to a state of catatonic shock ever since they had sprung him from his cell in the cathedral. All they had to do now was board the ship, make him sing and they were away.

"Gods Dunsany, are you sure that this is a good idea? I count three men with crossbows on the foremast and I wouldn't put it past Makennon to have a Shadowmage tucked in there somewhere."

"Well then, old friend," Dunsany said, putting an arm around Kelos's shoulder. "You'll just have to weave your own magic won't you? Now, keep Emuel quiet while I take care of this guard."

The guard was coming towards them again, having completed a circuit of the ship. Dunsany knelt down and loaded a quarrel into his crossbow. Slowly, he edged around the crate, carefully drawing a bead on the guard while keeping to the shadows. The weapon was custom made, expertly crafted, and the quarrel made almost no noise as it exited the crossbow and entered the throat of the man in the robes of a Final Faith guard. Dunsany briefly left cover to grab the corpse and pull it out of sight of the ship.

Emuel looked down at the pool of blood edging towards him from the body and, before Kelos had time to clamp his hand over his mouth, emitted a piercing shriek. Instantly there was movement on the foremast. Dunsany glared at Emuel and briefly considered cracking him round the head with the stock of his crossbow, but without the eunuch they weren't going anywhere.

"Kelos, remember that magic I mentioned? Well, now's the time."

Kelos closed his eyes, summoning the threads of elemental power. A coolness coursed through him as the pounding of waves thundered in his head. Beside him Emuel and Dunsany backed away as they tasted the tang of ozone that told them something big was about to happen.

Kelos stepped out of cover and raised his hands.

The ships in this part of the docks were already swaying drunkenly, the fierce power of the sea only slightly dissipated by the massive breakwaters, but the *Llothriall* now began to lurch even more than its neighbours. The guards in the foremast were having great difficulty in keeping their aim on the man who had emerged from the shadows below them. One let loose with his bow just as the boat lurched hard to starboard and the arrow sailed high into the night. A few almost found their target but Kelos didn't even flinch as the arrows thudded into the wood of the crate behind him. Instead, he concentrated on the great wheel of energy that spun through his mind. The sea surrounding the ship began to churn more furiously now and Kelos spat out the syllables that he had memorised five years before from a rare and mildewed book. For each guttural exclamation a thick rope of water erupted from the waves.

One of the guards dropped his weapon as a tentacle of water snaked around his neck. Hearing the snap of vertebrae his comrade started to scramble down the rigging, but before he could reach the deck he was thrown clear of the ship, crashing into the side of a warehouse. The last man was picked from the foremast, where he had been standing frozen in shock. His bow dropped from his numb fingers as an arm of living water encircled his waist. He looked down as the ship receded below him and then he was upside-down and the sea was rushing towards him.

Kelos lowered his hands and edged towards the dock wall but the guard didn't resurface. The tendrils of water fell, lifeless, and Dunsany and a shaken Emuel emerged from hiding.

"I think that you've found a new way to clear the decks. Don't suppose there's anything you can do for laughing boy here is there?" Kelos cast a silence spell on the eunuch. Emuel looked offended and opened his mouth, but his protest failed to emerge. "Thank the Gods for that. I didn't fancy boarding the *Llothriall* while he continued to scream the place down. Now, when we want you to sing, you'll sing okay? Kelos, lead the way."

On board, at the bottom of the steps leading below, they stopped in front of a door. Dunsany cocked his crossbow and put his ear to the wood. He was raising his arm to signal that it was safe for them to proceed when twelve inches of steel erupted from the door just by his nose. The sword was quickly withdrawn and the door burst open. Kelos flung his palms out and a fireball thudded into the chest of the man who emerged, launching him backwards down the corridor behind him.

Dunsany glanced back at his friend as he stepped over the felled guard.

"I'm warning you now that I can't keep this up for much longer," Kelos panted.

"Relax, we're almost there."

Two more short flights of steps and a long corridor led them to the heart of the ship. They stopped in front of a reinforced door, elvish script covering its surface. Kelos traced the design with his fingers, muttering something to himself. Eventually he stepped back and nodded. "That's the advantage of having designed the wards, I know how to counteract them. On three?" He drew a short sword.

"On three." Dunsany agreed, drawing his own blade.

As they charged into the room Kelos was flung against the ceiling. For a moment he thought that the boat had taken a massive hit, but then he saw the man in the corner, smiling as he weaved threads of magic, muttering strange syllables.

Kelos's windpipe started to constrict as the Shadowmage increased his hold. Below him, Dunsany was squaring off against the guards who stood in front of the magical gem that was the engine of the vessel. The stone, sitting in its housing of metal and wood, seemed to whisper to Kelos as he gasped for breath.

He watched as Dunsany swung at one of the guards. The man tumbled to the side to avoid the blow and Dunsany took the opportunity to fire a quarrel at the other guard.

When the quarrel entered his thigh, the man grunted and stepped back. However, the injury hadn't slowed him as he roared and shoulder charged Dunsany into the wall. The guard pushed his blade against Dunsany's throat but Dunsany gritted his teeth, reversed his grip on his sword and rammed the pommel into the base of the guard's neck. The man dropped and Kelos cried out a warning as the remaining guard stepped in to fill the gap.

Dunsany failed to fully evade the blow and the blade sliced into his cheek, flicking blood into his eyes. He staggered and almost tripped over Emuel, who was on the floor behind him, rocking back and forth. The guard took advantage of the stumble and swung again, this time nicking Dunsany's wrist, making him drop his sword. Dunsany raised his crossbow and fired. Kelos saw the mage in the corner blink and the quarrel turned to powder millimetres from the guard's face.

"I knew Makennon should never have trusted scum like you." The guard said, brushing dust from his jerkin. "If you ask me we didn't do enough in converting this shit hole you people call home. Unbelievers should have been put to the sword a long time ago."

Kelos continued to gasp for breath, barely conscious now. The stone was practically screaming into his head and, with a jolt of realisation, he realised what he must do.

He gestured with his right hand and cancelled the silence spell he had placed on Emuel.

"Sing Emuel! Sing or we'll all die!"

Emuel looked up at Kelos and, for a terrible moment, the mage thought that the eunuch was going to defy him. But then, he stood.

"That's it retard, sing a lament for the death of your friends." The guard raised his sword. The sound that emerged from Emuel, however, stayed his hand.

The room shivered as the song reached out to the gem. The magical energy traced veins of midnight-blue fire in the stone and all in the room felt the ship shudder as it responded to the song. The tattoos on Emuel's body flowed as the song possessed him.

The Shadowmage stepped into the centre of the room and Kelos could see a dark warning in his eyes. He could almost taste the magic flowing from the stone now and, concentrating, Kelos called forth a thread of that energy. The mage below him realised what was happening too late. He tried to finish Kelos with a word but, before he could utter the syllable, Kelos concentrated the thread of energy from the stone and blasted it into the Shadowmage. The room filled with a searing light as his body burned.

Kelos dropped to the floor and lashed out with his sword. The stunned guard didn't even feel the blade enter his belly. All he felt was the song and its ethereal cadence as it followed him into darkness.

Kelos put a hand on Emuel's shoulder. "You can stop now. It's over."

As the Turnitia docks fell away, Dunsany nervously scanned the shoreline.

"Don't worry," Kelos said. "I've cloaked the ship."

Dunsany turned to look at his friend. Wisps of arcane energy surrounded the mage in a dark amber corona.

"Shouldn't one of us be piloting this vessel?"

"Actually, I am. And have you noticed something *really* strange?"

"Apart from your new hair-do and ruddy orange glow?" Dunsany looked around him and had to admit that *everything* was really strange. The sails billowed with the wind and were utterly silent, the rainbow sheen of the X'lcotl silk moving like oil on water as it reflected back the soft light of Kerberos. Around them the ship thrummed with magical energy, veins of which ran through every part of the *Llothriall*. The vessel cut through the sea with a sureness and ease that Dunsany had never before witnessed in a ship. "We're so still."

"Indeed, the ship should be furiously pitching beneath our feet and we should be staggering around like two drunks at the end of a wedding party. Instead, we have this unnatural serenity. Deceptive really, as the power of the *Llothriall* is so vast that it should *feel* like something is happening. And it is, look back at Turnitia."

Dunsany turned. The coast was dwindling rapidly behind them, almost imperceptible through the spray and the mist. On any other ship it would have taken them most of a day to leave sight of the peninsula and, even then, they wouldn't have been able to venture too far from land due to the vicious and unpredictable currents that surrounded Twilight. But the *Llothriall* was not at all affected by the pitch of the waves. Instead, it seemed to skim across the surface.

"And this is the least of the ship's abilities," Kelos said. "Do you know, that it is actually capable of sailing under water? We must try that particular feature out some time."

"I'm glad that we took this away from the Faith," said Dunsany. "I just hope that this hiding place you have in mind is as good as you say."

"Oh yes. And, once we reach Sarcre itself I can introduce you to our crew."

"And do they know that they are going to be shipmates on this mighty vessel?"

"Well, not quite. But once they see the *Llothriall* they're not going to take much persuading. Talking of ship mates, where's Emuel?"

"All sung out. Sleeping soundly below. You think that boy's going to be a problem?"

"He's terrified of everything and he's too timid to be a threat. Anyway, there's no way for him to get back to Makennon now."

The sound of Katherine Makennon's rage was so great that the Eternal Choir almost stopped singing. The congregation who sat with bowed heads looked up from their prayers for a moment as they sensed the anger that flowed through the many halls, chambers and chapels of Scholten cathedral from Makennon's quarters. At his pulpit the Eminence's hand was momentarily stayed from making the sign of benediction.

In her private chamber Makennon stood over the priest who had delivered the news of the *Llothriall's* theft and, for the briefest of moments, considered having him excommunicated. But decisions driven by emotion were not becoming of a leader of Twilight's true faith. Seating herself once more Katherine resumed her air of authoritative calm.

"Why is it that Old Race secrets and artefacts have a habit of slipping out of our grasp? Don't these people realise that we are merely trying to use the knowledge of our ancestors to unite the peninsula and spread our message beyond civilisation?"

Around the room, the members of the Faithful looked at one another, wondering if an answer were required. One cleared his throat and seemed about to speak, but Makennon dismissed his words before he could form them with a wave of a hand.

"It was a rhetorical question Rudolph. I do not require your observations. However... do you know whether our guest has regained consciousness?"

"Our guest Anointed Lord?"

"Yes, the marine creature we recently acquired."

"Ah yes, I shall enquire right away."

"Thank you Rudolph."

Rudolph edged slowly from the room, making sure not to present his back to the Anointed Lord. Once beyond the chamber he descended through the many levels of Scholten until he was far below the foundations of the cathedral. In a corridor lined with cells he stopped at a particular door and slid back the viewing hatch. The stench that poured from the room beyond made him take a step back. For a moment he thought that the creature within had died, but then there was a wet sound as it left its water trough and approached the door.

"Prepare yourself to meet the Anointed Lord," Rudolph piously informed the prisoner.

He couldn't be sure but the sound that came in response sounded almost like a laugh.

CHAPTER TWO

The blast of spray and the wind in his face made Silus struggle for breath as he fought with the boom. The boat leaned hard to port. One of the morning's catch took advantage of the motion to leap free of its bucket and belly-flop on the deck, before the boat lurched again and sent the fish back into the sea.

"Alright, you can have that one," Silus shouted at the waves.

He lodged the catch bucket against a bench, wrapped his right hand in a rope, pulled hard and hauled the *Ocean Lily* back on course. There was a lull then and Silus took advantage of the brief respite to lash everything down. He looked up at the clouds and considered casting out one more time, but the flicker of lightning and the kiss of warm rain convinced him that he was done for the day.

The lights of Nürn shone weakly through the mist but Silus managed to guide his boat back by the light of the beacon that blazed on the farthest sea wall. People had already begun to gather at the harbour, hurrying to get the best of the catch.

Katya caught the rope that Silus threw to her and together they moored the boat.

"Any gemfish Silus?" called one of the punters.

"We'll get to the catch in just a moment. But first, a kiss for my wife."

Silus pulled Katya close and some of the cold of the morning dissipated as he was wrapped in her warmth. Smiling, he ran his hand over her belly and his touch was greeted by a slight nudge from within.

"A feisty wee one alright," Katya grinned. "I worry about you out there you know. How far out did you have to go today?"

"A bit too far to be honest and the catch isn't great either. I really don't understand why the shoals are sitting so far out." There was a tugging at his sleeve and Silus turned to see Mrs Greaves brandishing a couple of coppers at him. "Gemfish Mrs Greaves, yes gemfish! Well, there are three right here with your name on them."

Silus and Katya laid out the catch and all but two sold.

"Ooooh, seacrake for breakfast again. Truly we are spoiling ourselves." Katya said, tossing the sticky yellow tubes back into a basket after the crowd had dispersed. Silus put his arm around her and together they made their way through the precipitous Nürn streets to their home.

Silus and Katya had been married for almost three years. Both natives of Nürn they had met at one of the many festivals that dotted the local calendar. Katya had been immediately impressed with this softly spoken fisherman who – unlike some of the other locals – was not in the process of drinking himself into a coma or starting a fight.

On that day, as the sun had started to move out of the shadow of Kerberos, the two of them had broken away from the revellers and wandered down to the harbour.

Beyond the breakwaters the fierce sea churned, the foaming white tips of the waves catching the light of the new sun like cascading diamonds. Grinning, Silus helped Katya down into the

Ocean Lily and cast off. The roar of the sea quickly swallowed the sounds of the party as Silus began a familiar dance with the boom.

They crested a wave that seemed to climb forever and then Katya was screaming with delight as they hurtled down the swell.

"Hold on!" Silus shouted as the sail swung round and the *Ocean Lily* leaned hard into the curve of another wave.

Katya marvelled at the way this man fought the sea and didn't once flinch as it fought back. Silus never once lost his footing as he danced around the sail and he even had time to steal a kiss as the rope played through his hands.

The boat lurched again and the crest of a wave burst across the bow, soaking the two of them instantly. But Katya didn't mind and they laughed as they looked at each other through dripping fringes.

"I think that you're probably ready to give it a go now that you're a seasoned sailor." Silus said.

"More like a salted sailor! No, I'm happy to leave it to you, thank you."

"Come on, I'll show you how."

Katya scrambled across the deck to lean against Silus as he taught her the play and pull of the rope. The power of the wind frightened her a little as it sent them hurtling across the sea, but she found herself trusting him absolutely and relaxed as they guided the boat together.

"See? We'll make a fisherwoman of you yet."

"A fisherwoman? Oh thanks, that's very romantic."

Suddenly Katya couldn't feel Silus at her back or his pull on the rope. Then, he stepped in front of her and smiled.

"No hands!"

"Silus!"

"You can do it. Just play the ropes as I've shown you."

The only still point in her world was Silus as he stood with his arms folded, calmly riding the pitching deck. He nodded as she guided them into the wind, the *Ocean Lily* immediately bolting across the water. In the distance Katya could see the lights of Nürn as they tumbled around the horizon. The sails keened as the wind pushed against them. Katya began to relax, timing her turns so that the boat didn't keel over and capsize, learning when to play the rope out and when to reign it in. Soon she felt that the *Ocean Lily* had become a part of her.

"Superb!" Silus shouted. "I'll let you bring her in now. Change course for the shore."

Katya swung the boom around and it was immediately slapped back by the wind. She ducked as it narrowly missed her head, the rope whipping through her hands. Silus lost his footing as the deck slanted away beneath him and Katya watched as he fell towards the edge. She launched herself forwards – ducking the boom as it swung back round – and her hands closed on Silus's shirt just as his upper body crested the lip of the boat. Barely a metre from his head the black waters frothed angrily. It seemed that the boat was almost ninety degrees to the horizon now. Katya's arms burned with the effort of keeping Silus from toppling into the sea. She looked down and was astonished to see him laughing.

He grabbed her as the *Ocean Lily* crashed into a wave. Silus's lips met hers in the freezing water's embrace, and then they were through and Silus was scrambling across the deck to right the boat.

The horizon stabilised and Katya managed to struggle back to Silus's side.

"Did we just almost die?"

"Nah!" Silus said. "You have to be used to the randomness of the sea, that's all."

"How can you get used to randomness?"

"Good point. Okay, how about I show you something a lot more tranquil and just as beautiful?"

"Sail on."

The sun had fully left the shadow of Kerberos now and the day was already promising to be a hot one. They hugged the shoreline for a while before Silus angled them towards the mouth of a cavern that gaped in the side of a cliff. The sea was considerably calmer here and Silus had no problem in guiding the boat into darkness.

"Would you mind lighting those two lamps there? Otherwise the next few yards can be a little difficult to negotiate."

Katya lit the lamps as a light wind followed them into the cave. It was so quiet that all she could hear was the gentle wash of the sea and their breathing. The soft illumination coming from the boat showed walls glistening with veins of minerals and turquoise lichens. Above them she could hear the scrabble and twitter of small creatures and, as they passed beneath a stalactite – its tip almost scraping the top of the sails – she thought that she saw something slowly undulating upwards along its length.

The wind changed direction, coming from before them now. A warm breath from the depths, rich with the smell of wet stone and something sweeter, like cinnamon. The tunnel narrowed and Katya saw Silus's brow wrinkle as his concentration increased. She winced as the *Ocean Lily* scraped against the tunnel wall, but then they were through and the gloom surrounding them increased ten-fold.

Katya had never been in such darkness before and she felt a wave of panic begin to fizz through her nerves. She turned around, half expecting to find Silus gone. But he was still there, the rope now slack at his feet, the sails dead above him. He was looking past her into the depths of the subterranean night and he gestured for her to follow his gaze.

Ahead of them there was a... it was hard to tell and Katya screwed up her eyes as she tried to make it out. At first she thought that it was a glowing mist, but as they drew near she could hear the rush of water. Katya then realised that what she was looking at was a waterfall surrounding a wide shaft of brilliant light. The *Ocean Lily* glided through the shimmering curtain and into the familiar and comforting glow of Kerberos. Katya looked up to where a hole in the cavern roof seemed to cradle the azure disk, water cascading around its circumference. The boat came to rest and Silus gently fed out the anchor.

"Wow," Katya said. "Do you bring all your girlfriends here?"

"Believe it or not you're the first."

"What, the first girlfriend?" Katya smiled. "I'm sorry, I shouldn't tease. Anyway, you owe me one you know."

"What for?"

"For saving your life."

"Oh, I see. I owe you one what?"

"One of these."

Katya kissed him. She tasted of the sea and when Silus pulled away from the kiss he could see Kerberos reflected in her eyes.

"Do you ever wonder what it's like, up there?" Silus said, looking up at the azure planet.

"Well I don't suppose that we'll find out until we pass on and join our ancestors there. I do hope that you're not in any hurry."

"But what if we could go to Kerberos before that? I sometimes think that it's one vast ocean. You could sail forever on its azure seas. The marine creatures would be unlike anything you've ever seen and, beneath the waves, would be vast and ancient cities."

"You certainly can't take the sea out of the boy can you?"

"I'm from a long line of fishermen. Not very exciting really.

"The other night I dreamed that I was swimming down a great hall. It was dark, but on the walls I could see paintings of strange creatures. They stood on two legs and were covered in dark scales. Sharp spines ran up their backs to the top of their heads. Each finger ended in a wicked looking talon. And then I was at the end of the hall before a set of enormous doors. I reached up to open them and my hands were just like theirs." Silus's focused on Katya again, wrapping his arms around her. "Anyway, it was just a dream. Silly really."

"As long as you're not about to abduct me and take me to your underwater lair."

"Ah, well. Wouldn't you say that's sort of what this place is?"

That had been almost four years ago and Silus was still dreaming of Kerberos

In The Necromancer's Barge his stories and dreams were well known and when Silus came off the *Ocean Lily* he'd often share a tale or two over an ale or three.

That morning the seas had been calmer than usual but the catch hadn't improved and Silus was beginning to worry that if the fishing didn't pick up soon he was going to be out of a job. The drink was starting to take the edge off but he didn't want to get too deep into his cups, Katya would need a hand with some of the chores and he still had nets to mend. One more for the road, however, would do no harm.

Silus signalled to the landlord but another hand arrested his.

"Let me get this one friend."

The man sitting beside him was dressed in simple garb and appeared to be little older than Silus. He could remember having seen him in the tavern a couple of times before but didn't think that he was a local.

"Thank you. I'm sorry but I didn't catch your name. I'm Silus by the way."

"Yes, I know. Kelos." They shook hands. "I saw you out on the water. Can't be easy for you with conditions being what they are."

"It hasn't been easy, but it's not the sea that worries me so much as the lack of fish."

"You handle that boat of yours beautifully."

"Thank you. The *Ocean Lily* has been in my family a long time." The landlord placed two tumblers of liquor before them and Silus thanked Kelos again before knocking his back. "Haven't I seen you in here before?"

"A few times. I'm just passing through really."

"A trader?"

"I think that entrepreneur is a more fitting description."

They sat in silence for a while then. Beside themselves there were few customers in The Necromancer's Barge. There was a group of elderly men playing a game with woodrene bones and a stout woman busy with her knitting, a scrawny dog snoring at her feet. Despite the quietness of the bar, Kelos still looked nervously about before speaking again.

"Actually, I'm putting together an expedition and we're in need of strong, reliable men like yourself, who can handle themselves at sea."

"We?"

"My colleague and I. We are in possession of a unique vessel."

"And where is this expedition bound?"

"Beyond Twilight."

"Impossible. You won't get more than five miles off the peninsula before your ship is smashed to pieces. There's not a vessel on Twilight that could make it through the Storm Wall."

"As I said, we are in possession of a unique vessel."

Silus suddenly went cold as he realised who he may be speaking to. "You're Final Faith."

"Used to be."

In some ways this was even worse and it was now Silus's turn to look around nervously.

"Listen. Thanks but no thanks. You may think that Nürn is a small town and that we're comfortably far from Scholten, but even here you don't know who may be listening. There's no question of me joining your expedition. I have a pregnant wife at home and a livelihood to consider. You said that you were passing through Nürn? Well if I were you I'd *continue* to pass through, because any day now Makennon's Swords are going to catch up with you and I'd rather you were far away from my town when that day comes."

"Trust me, Makennon hasn't the first clue where to find us." Kelos took out a map and laid it on the bar. It showed the peninsula and was heavily annotated. "What do you think lies beyond these rough seas Silus?"

"I really don't know."

"But you want to, I can tell. They all know your stories here, those dreams of other places. What about making those dreams a reality? I know that you have a wife with child, but she'd be well looked after and you'd be paid handsomely for your time. Do you really want it to be Makennon who discovers new lands, only to bring them in line under the banner of her faith? If there's something out there to be discovered wouldn't you rather that it was people like ourselves doing the discovering, not those with a vested interest in spreading the 'word'?"

As a child Silus had often played with maps, adding in his own details, drawing in new islands, whole continents peopled with his imagination. His father had told him tales of the Old

Races and their mastery of the sea and Silus had wondered why humans hadn't achieved the same heights of naval prowess. They were the ones who ruled now after all, long since those strange beings had perished. Why couldn't they dominate and harness their world in the same way? Silus had been fishing and exploring the same stretch of coast ever since he was old enough to handle a boat and he often yearned to strike out far from shore and try his hand against the stormy waters beyond the horizon. He remembered that first time with Katya and how they had lain in each other's arms, looking up at Kerberos, imagining beyond Twilight, wanting to explore together.

"Look, I hardly know you." Silus said, folding the map and handing it back to Kelos. "Really, the dream is compelling but I'm sure it's just that. A dream."

"From what I've seen of you out on the water and what the good people of Nürn have already told me regarding your character, it would be a great shame if I couldn't tempt you to join us. However, the decision must not be forced. No doubt I shall see you around."

Silus watched Kelos walk away. The dog at the knitting woman's feet woke briefly to watch him go before returning to its snoring. The men playing the bones paused before the next throw. Then the ribs were rattling across the table once more as the door closed.

CHAPTER THREE

Querilous Fitch looked up as the prisoner was brought into the room. There was little natural light this deep in Scholten cathedral but what scant amount there was – funnelled by sun traps and mirrors – was more than enough to reveal the obscene form of the creature. Fitch grimaced at the smell and brought a pomander to his nose. The monster didn't even acknowledge his presence as it was chained in place.

Two of the attendants periodically doused the prisoner with water as a third was sent to request the pleasure of the Anointed Lord's company.

Fitch was well used to the torture and interrogation of human subjects but this was the first time that he had been requested to apply his technique to a member of an entirely different species.

He looked into the thing's eyes, hoping to at least catch some emotion, some strand of fear that he could later use. But there was nothing.

"You. Hand me that needlereed."

Fitch used the sharp implement to extract a blood sample, which he then smeared thinly across a sliver of highly polished metal. The blood was black with a strange blue sheen and it smelt of the sea.

Well, this is a challenge, Fitch considered. He wasn't entirely sure whether he was looking forward to it but he would certainly apply himself to the best of his ability.

The door to the cell opened and Katherine Makennon entered, a small retinue trailing respectfully in her wake.

"Querilous, I see that the prisoner has been prepared." She leaned in close to the creature, a cruel smile playing across her lips.

"Anointed Lord, can I perhaps ask where you attained this specimen?"

"It was apprehended at the Turnitia docks. Some of the thieves' guild were attempting a raid on a ship and this is what they met. I must say that even the city guard couldn't have done a better job in routing the rogues. They were hosing down the docks for days afterwards."

"But where does this thing come from, *originally*?"

"We don't know. But we're hoping that it will be able to use its knowledge of and affinity with the sea to help us locate the *Llothriall*."

"I can assure you, Anointed Lord, that I shall do my utmost to persuade the creature to be cooperative."

Fitch looked down at the thing that sat before him. Barbed spines ran from the small of its back to the top of its head and he examined these closely before signalling to one of his attendants to hand him a pair of heavy-duty clippers.

"I need to be certain that these sharp protuberances are non-venomous. One shouldn't take risks in working with an unfamiliar species."

As Fitch snipped the spines from its skull the howl of the creature was so loud that it rattled the instruments in their metal tray. The thing fought against its bonds for a moment but the collars and chains that restrained it only tightened in response.

Fitch waited until the creature had calmed before running his fingers over its scalp. The scales were cool to the touch and the tang of its alien thoughts flowed into him like incense. He lay his hands on the creature's skull, and then pushed against a slight resistance before his fingers sank into its mind.

"The prisoner should be ready for questioning now, Anointed Lord."

Makennon sat down and looked thoughtfully at the thing for a moment before proceeding.

"How many more of you are there?"

Fitch moved through the creature's mind, his eyes rolling back in their sockets as he went deeper.

He looked up and, far above him, saw the underside of rolling white breakers. A brilliant shoal of iridescent fish darted in front of him and when they parted he found himself surrounded by the creature's brethren. They were swimming down towards a great domed building. Entering it they left they filed into a huge circular chamber. They congregated before a dais on which stood one of their own.

"There are many more," Fitch said. "Hundreds."

"Can't it speak for itself?"

"Apologies Anointed Lord, this method is more direct and I don't think that the creature has an affinity with the human tongue."

"Very well," Makennon turned her attention back to the prisoner. It was breathing shallowly, wheezing gasps whistling through its many vicious teeth. "I think it needs dousing again." The attendants threw salt water over the creature and it seemed to recover slightly. "Now, why the attack on Turnitia? What possible interest can you have in Twilight when the whole of the ocean is your domain?"

Fitch's found himself standing closer to the dais. The creature that stood above him was aged and stooped. In one clawed hand it grasped a staff, inset in its tip was a scarlet jewel that shone with an inner light. The ancient one was telling its people of a battle to come and Fitch could feel the blood lust and joy move through the crowd as the thing's words inspired a dreadful passion.

"I believe that they mean to make war on us Anointed Lord."

"War? And how can you possibly hope to succeed when there are hundreds of you and thousands upon thousands of us?"

Sweat started to break out upon Fitch's brow and he could feel the resistance of the prisoner increasing as he probed even deeper.

And now he was on his own with the old one from the dais and the creature was showing him the pages of a book wrought entirely in metal. It moved its fingers across characters and diagrams but despite Fitch's concentration he could make no sense of the information. The thoughts that flowed into him began to cloud and Fitch pushed hard against the interference, his heart thumping heavily in his chest as his vision was obscured.

Out of the darkness emerged a single unblinking eye. Fitch was lost in the vastness of its pupil, around him he could sense an infinity of nothingness.

"Fitch?"

He couldn't feel anything. Not his fingers in the creature's thoughts, not even his own thoughts.

"*Fitch?*"

And then that great eye was speeding away from him and Fitch was falling at an astonishing speed. For a moment Kerberos hung before him and he had time to watch the flickering of lightning deep in its clouds, before he was slammed back into his body and sent flailing across the cell.

The creature snarled and snapped forward in its chains. Makennon felt a waft of its foul breath as it screamed.

"Your kind's days are numbered! The half-breed will father the new race and the Chadassa will stride through your land! The Great Flood is coming!"

Fitch raised himself, unsteadily, to his feet and reached for the instrument tray.

"The Land Walkers will lay waist to Twilight and break open the World's Ride mountains! The Great Fl — "

The creature slumped forward and Fitch threw the heavy, blunt instrument back into the tray.

"I cannot apologise enough, Anointed Lord. Its will was exceptionally strong."

"Querilous, how did it learn how to speak our language? And, more importantly, what is the Great Flood?"

CHAPTER FOUR

Beyond the Storm Wall, far and deep off the coast of Twilight, beneath waves that rose to the height of mountains before crashing into troughs so wide they could accommodate an entire fleet of ships, stood a city that no human eyes had ever seen.

Great structures of coral and mineral, fused together and roughly shaped, rose from the seabed. Vicious, many spiked towers were linked by archways, carved from rock and glittering with iridescent minerals. A wide avenue, illuminated by the glow of gelatinous octopus-like things staked at regular intervals, linked narrow streets and alleys. At one end of the city, before a series of rock shelves fell away into darkness, a great mound heaved and shuddered. Its surface looked like stone but moved like flesh. Fissures ran zig-zagging across it, occasionally emitting chinks of brilliant light, making the water around it boil briefly, before the mound settled back into a restless slumber.

No lights came from the buildings of this deep-water metropolis and the sea was quiet for miles around. Not even the leviathans, who had no natural predators, would swim these waters and the only marine life visible were the albino catfish that rooted in the muck of the bottom, occasionally regarding one another with blank – almost stupid – expressions before burying their blunt noses into the silt once more.

Along the central avenue the glowing things rose on their tethers as something approached from the south.

Its structure had no grace and no attempt had been made to streamline the craft or make it look functional. It looked like a barnacle encrusted boulder and it turned end over end, silently, as it made its way towards the city. As it drew close a hole opened up in the centre of the illuminated avenue and the craft descended into a wide, deep shaft. It passed through a shimmering circle of light and continued its descent into a vast hall.

Dark scaled creatures watched its approach as it drifted down towards a central podium, where it came to rest. The craft opened up like the petals of a flower, thick blue mucous oozing from its folds. The creature that stepped out was clearly of the same breed as those filling the hall, yet its flesh was pitted and scarred. The spines that ran from the top of its skull to the small of its back were faded at their tips. In its right hand the creature held a staff, a red gem embedded in its apex. This it raised to the audience and they responded with a cry, the joyous sound reaching him clearly through the water.

"Belck!"

Belck surveyed the ranks of creatures before him. He had led the Chadassa for thousands of years, taking on the staff from his father, who had inherited it from his father in turn.

"Broodkin, the time draws close. Our blood is strong in the half-breed's veins. It is his seed that will give rise to the Land Walkers and with them we shall take Twilight. The time of the Great Flood is almost upon us!"

The hall echoed with the sound of the creatures' praise. Around them lights danced on the many murals that decorated the hall. In one of these the Chadassa were depicted in battle, cutting down members of another marine race that looked not unlike themselves, in the background a city burned with spectral flames. Another mural depicted a huge, black disk. Its face was barely defined, only the stars that surrounded it picked it out of the blackness.

It was towards this scene that Belck now turned his gaze and, without his prompting, the gathered Chadassa joined him in chanting their creed.

"Beyond Kerberos he waits
He will come again
Beyond time and the stars he waits
He will come again
From the one Great Ocean he is formed
He will come again
He is the Great Ocean
He will come again."

"Broodkin he will indeed come again. Tonight the elders will join me and the ceremony of calling shall begin. For now, return to your nests and meditate upon the Great Ocean. Remember the songs of your ancestors and the stories of our many victories over the Calma. Prepare yourselves for the Great Flood." Belck raised his staff, the gem at its tip burning with a fierce scarlet light.

"He will come again!"

Belck, for all his posturing and pronouncements, had his doubts that 'He' would come again. In their many preparations and holy rites they had received no sign from their god. Even in his special place of meditation, among the deepest thermal vents, Belck had sensed nothing.

Rimbah had urged him to take heart. "If it is his will to be silent," Belck's advisor had said, "then it is his will."

But such cryptic words were of little comfort and did more to frustrate Belck than anything else. At times he had to restrain himself less he lash out at Rimbah. His father wouldn't have hesitated. In his day many were put to death with little more excuse than his displeasure.

Belck signalled to Rimbah to bring him his ceremonial garments. Sign or no sign they had a summoning to perform. As his advisor dressed him in the close-fitting raiment, Belck looked out over their city. From his vantage point he could see all the way down the central avenue to where the Queen slept.

He had personally supervised her cultivation, from lowly Chadassa maid to the great mound that he now surveyed. In the beginning she had fought as the caul had been formed around her, but Belck liked to think that she now lay in a state of contentment, cradled in the centre of that liquid warmth, listening to her own heartbeat amplified by the egg sacs that were growing around her.

Soon those sacs would team with new life when the half-breed became one with the Queen. From her would then come the Land Walkers, the new race, a mighty and unstoppable army. They would stride across Twilight, laying waste to the humankind until they came to the great mountains at the edge of the world. There they would call upon their god to break apart those ancient stones and reveal the heart of this world, bared for him to pour into it his very essence, this Great Flood leading into the reshaping of all reality to the glory of the Chadassa.

Through the window Belck could now see the approach of the elders as they swam into view. Quickly checking over his ceremonial garb, he swam out to join them.

Together they swam to the edge of the city where they followed the descent of the seabed as it shelved down, before dropping into the sheer sides of a trench. Standing on the edge of absolute darkness they acknowledged one another – "He is the Great Ocean," – before stepping off the edge.

Belck quickly lost his buoyancy as he emptied his air sacs. The others followed him down and, for a moment, he saw them suspended in a line before the darkness took them. Even though they could no longer see each other, Belck could feel the touch of their minds near him. It was easy to lose himself in those thoughts as the walls of the trench fell away and that was just what he did, becoming – together with the elders – one mind.

He is the Great Ocean.

They came to rest. Around them they could feel nothing, not even the touch of the water that should have been freezing cold this far down.

He is the Great Ocean.

The voice of their consciousness echoed out into infinity and the part of them that was Belck urged that formlessness to take shape.

Beyond time and the stars he waits.

Belck's doubts tinged their thoughts for a moment but the group consciousness drove them back, consuming them in the fierceness of its belief.

He will *come again.*

And with the disappearance of those doubts small points of light began to illuminate the darkness.

But they shone only for a moment before they began to wink out. However, the stars weren't going out, something was moving before them.

The great sphere was darker than the emptiness between the stars and, as they moved across its surface, the great depth of its blackness seemed to stare back at them like an unblinking eye.

Belck spoke for the gathered. "The half-breed has come of age and the Land Walkers will soon ravage Twilight. Your time is upon us. We call you forth to initiate the beginning of the Great Flood."

He is the Great Ocean.

There was the slightest movement across the sphere, as though a ripple were spreading through it, and then the stars were blurring as their God rushed past them. Belck joined with the others in revelling in the ecstasy of their God's wake.

Then the stars that surrounded them began to fade as they rose from their communion and through the depths of the trench, exultant that he had finally come amongst them.

CHAPTER FIVE

The room was thick with smoke and conspiracy. Heavy black curtains shut out the daylight and the men sitting around the table, whispering, looked up nervously every time someone passed by in the street outside.

When a rapping came at the door they fell into an immediate silence. Dunsany put his hand on the heavy bolt and his eye to the spyhole.

"It's okay. It's just Kelos."

A collective sigh of relief was breathed as the bedraggled looking mage was let into the house.

"Gods, the humidity of this place is insufferable!"

"Just wait till you see the thunderstorms they get here," Dunsany chuckled. "You'll think that Kerberos itself is being torn apart. Come, sit down. You look like a man in need of a drink."

"You're not wrong," said Kelos helping himself to a glass of flummox. "This constant back and forth between Sarcre and Nürn is beginning to age me, I'm telling you."

"How did the recruitment drive go today?"

"Not well. He's still not biting."

"And you're still getting this 'feeling' about him?"

"Oh yes, our boy is unusual alright. I don't know whether it's a latent magical ability or something else, but Silus certainly has talent. You should see how he handles a boat."

"Come on Kelos, there's surely nothing magical to that."

"But with Silus it's as if he has a sixth sense when it comes to the sea. Even if it takes three more weeks of persuasion I still think it's going to be worth having him on our crew. Speaking of recruiting I see that you've been doing some yourself."

"Ah yes, I'd forgotten that you had yet to meet our new colleagues."

"Let me be the first to say, Kelos, that it is an honour to be working with a mage of such power." The man who rose from his seat to thrust a bejewelled hand at Kelos staggered slightly, as though he had been on the flummox for quite some time. Kelos was bemused to be referred to as 'powerful' but also somewhat flattered. He had, after all, recently defeated a Shadowmage.

"The gentleman with the jewels is Father Maylan, an old friend of mine." Dunsany said.

"*Father* Maylan? *Father?*"

"Relax Kelos, Maylan has little affection for the faith he purportedly represents."

"Indeed," said Maylan, sitting back down and eyeing the contents of the flummox bottle. "I'm the Faith's token priest on Sarcre. Their *only* priest in fact. The church has very little real interest in the islands, but they can't be seen to be lax, so they 'converted' me and set me up as their Eminence here. Once a year I have to go to Scholten to maintain face, but it's all just a show. Not that Makennon knows that of course."

"I met Maylan back when I was plying the trade route between here and Allantia. In those days he was head Diviner of the Many Paths." Dunsany said.

"And to most of the locals I still am. But the crossed circle of the Faith is my mask now."

"No offence Maylan but do we really need a priest on board?" Kelos said.

"Actually, you'll find that Father Maylan has already proven himself invaluable. It was through him that I was introduced to the three gentlemen you see on your right."

The three gentlemen in question had the look of men who spent much of their time being blasted by the elements. Sun tanned to the point of burnt, with large, scarred and calloused hands, it was clear that they all shared the same profession. They squinted at Kelos through the smoke from thin, mean cheroots. He noticed that the same tattoo was inked upon the back of each of their left hands.

"Prison tattoos," Maylan said. "My friends here have spent time at the pleasure of Vos due to the nature of their export and import business."

"They're smugglers?" Kelos said.

"We prefer free traders," said the man in the middle of the group. "I'm Jacquinto. The man on my right is Ignacio, my brother, and on my left is Ioannis."

"They bring me a certain spice that is essential to divination." Maylan said.

"That and it gets you high as a woodrene." Ioannis grinned.

"The important thing is that they know how to handle themselves at sea." Dunsany said.

"Three smugglers and a priest." Kelos poured himself a glass of flummox. "Okay Dunsany, I'm sure you know what you're doing. Just give me a little more time with Silus."

"Excellent! Then we're most of the way there." Dunsany rose to his feet. "Gentlemen, charge your glasses. I propose a toast. To adventure and new horizons!"

Dunsany's grin fell as a thin, reedy voice came at them out of a dark corner of the room.

"They will walk beneath the waves and no man shall halt their march. Already their god stirs and from the dark night of infinity he shall come."

Jacquinto and his comrades were on their feet, blades in hands. Dunsany was just in time to stop the downward swing of Ioannis's attack.

"No!" The knife skittered across the room and Ioannis turned an angry glare on Dunsany. "No. It's okay. This is Emuel. He's with us."

"My Gods Dunsany, what is he?" Father Maylan said, eyeing the tattoos and elvish script that covered almost every inch of the eunuch.

"Emuel is the ship's eunuch. It is his song that empowers the *Llothriall.*"

"Dunsany, something's not right," Kelos said. "Look at his eyes."

Now that Emuel was fully revealed by the lamplight they could all see that his eyes were a deep violet. Kelos leaned in to take a closer look. Peering into the eunuch's eyes was like looking into the heart of a storm. Threads of energy sparked from his pupils and played across his eyelids.

"The Great Flood is coming."

"Kelos, snap him out of it!" Dunsany shouted.

Kelos gripped Emuel's arms and was shocked by how cold he felt. Ignoring his babble for a moment he felt for a way to break through the glamour. Looking deep into Emuel's eyes he spoke words of power, but they had no effect whatsoever and the magic that had taken him was starting to fill Kelos's head, making his skull ache.

"Nürn will fall. The half-breed will be theirs."

Kelos abandoned his attempt at magical defence and made to slap Emuel, but before the blow could connect the light faded from the eunuch's eyes and he dropped to the floor.

Kelos felt for a pulse. "He's alright. It seems to have left him now."

"What the hell was that about?" Ioannis said, retrieving his knife.

"It looked like possession to me." Kelos said.

"He said that Nürn will fall." Dunsany said, helping Kelos move Emuel to a chair. "Isn't that where Silus lives?

"Yes," Kelos said. "It is."

Silus had been thinking about his meeting with Kelos at The Necromancer's Barge all day and, that night, the strange man had even found his way into his Silus's dreams.

He had dreamt that Kelos had led him down to the harbour where a magnificent vessel was berthed. The ship shimmered with the light of Kerberos, the great azure orb seeming to lend its glow to every part of the vessel.

And then Silus was aboard and they were leaving the shore behind, though the prow of the ship pointed not towards the horizon, but towards Kerberos itself.

Soon they were flying above an endless sea of clouds and Silus leaned hard against the rail, trying to peer into the depth of Kerberos, only for a hard shove to send him spinning into the storm.

Katya had shaken him awake. "Silus, Silus stop it, you're screaming. What's the matter?"

After he had towelled the sweat from his body and calmed down, Silus told Katya about his meeting with Kelos. She had laughed over the implausibility of the venture that the man had proposed and, as the soft light of dawn crept into their room, Silus had to admit that it did now all seem somewhat fanciful.

Nevertheless, later that day, Silus stopped in at The Necromancer's Barge to see if the man had put in a reappearance. But there was just the usual crowd; drinkers coming in off night shifts or workers fortifying themselves for the day ahead.

Silus had stood in the *Ocean Lily* for a while then, reluctant to cast off into the fierce wind, knowing that today's catch would probably be worse than the last and that he and Katya would be eating seacrake again for supper. But the sea was a part of him, just as it had been a part of his father and his father before that. There would be hard times and bad days, but that was true of anything and when he and Katya's son or daughter came into the world, Silus wanted to have a trade that he could pass on.

The song of the waves, the gulls wheeling above, the whisper of the wind were all calling to him and so Silus played out the rope, swung the boom and faced the sea once more.

The *Ocean Lily* protested against every pitch and yawl and

twice Silus swore as the rope cut too quickly through his hands. The sails screeched with the force of the wind on them and he feared that the fabric would tear, leaving him unable to return to shore.

Eventually, though, he found the edge of the squall and the boat glided out onto calmer waters. He checked his nets and then made to drop anchor.

As soon as the weight left his hands and plunged into the water he knew that something was wrong. Silus had no time to react, however, as he was pitched over the side, his right foot having become caught up in the rapidly uncoiling rope.

He managed to resist the urge to gasp as the cold water hit him and he followed the anchor into the depths.

Silus could see nothing but a stream of bubbles and debris as he fought against the pull of the rope. There was a sudden tug and he found himself arcing over a rock surface. He struggled to grab handholds, trying to bring a halt to his descent, but succeeded only in scraping his face and palms. The sting of the saltwater in his wounds was immediate and he came to a stop, suspended upside down beneath the overhang of a rock shelf.

The worst thing that he could do, he realised, was panic but, even so, he felt a very real fear begin to buzz through his nerves as he struggled with the knot at his ankle. Taking a knife from his belt he jabbed at the tangle of rope but all he succeeded in doing was cutting his fingers and losing the blade to the sea.

Silus knew that he had only seconds before his oxygen-starved body forced him to take a breath and he drowned. But as he fought with his entanglement he began to realise that his chest wasn't burning with the need for air and, strangely, his vision was crystal clear. Down here, in the shadow of the rock shelf little light penetrated, but Silus could see everything with a startling clarity.

It was then that he looked round and saw that he was in even greater danger than he had first realised.

Their clawed feet dug into the seabed as they strode towards where he hung, kicking up clouds of sand. Silus estimated that there were at least twenty of them. At their head marched one more gnarled and misshapen than the rest, holding a staff half again as tall as itself, a scarlet gem burning malevolently at its tip. The creatures stood as tall as a man and were covered in scales that looked as though they could stop the sharpest of arrows. Great black eyes bulged from either side of narrow heads filled with hundreds of needle-like teeth. From the small of their backs to the top of their skulls ran a line of barbed spines that flexed with the movements of the current, as though they aided the creatures in sensing their environment.

Silus knew that even if he could sustain his held breath, when the monsters reached him he would be finished. His heart broke as he realised that he'd never see Katya again and that he'd never be a father to their unborn child. Closing his eyes he sent up a prayer to Kerberos, calling on his ancestors to either accept him with open arms or send their aid. When he opened his eyes again the creatures were moving below him and Silus braced himself for a slash from those wicked talons.

But the creatures continued to march on as though they hadn't seen him at all, and soon the last had passed beneath him.

And now fear really did begin to take hold because, watching the retreating backs of the creatures, Silus realised where they were heading.

They were marching towards Nürn.

Silus's fingers scrabbled again at the knot that ensnared his ankle. His lungs really were beginning to burn now and a lethargic weakness spread through his hands.

Suddenly his vision was obscured as shoal of brilliant and multi-coloured slivers of light engulfed him. *Gemfish*, he realised as they swirled around him, tickling him with flickers of their tails. Perhaps these were the emissaries of Kerberos, who were to escort him to his resting place amongst the clouds.

His stomach lurched as he dropped several feet. Silus realised then that he could move his ankle. He was free, the gemfish had chewed through the rope that had bound him.

His vision started to blur as he kicked for the surface and when he finally broke through the waves, the breath that he took seemed like it would go on forever.

Even though he wanted to do nothing more than lie on the deck of his boat and breathe in the fresh, cool air he knew that he had to alert Nürn to the danger that was heading their way.

Silus pulled up the rest of the anchor rope and set the boom. As the sails took the wind he just hoped that the *Ocean Lily* would prove to be quicker than the things that marched along the seabed below.

In the small barracks five of the Nürn guard were rolling woodrene bones. Already they had played six rounds of cards – in which one of them had lost almost a week's pay – and many more games of dice. This was the way it went most nights.

"You know what? I think that was my last throw," said Officer Stinton. "Besides, it's probably time that I went on patrol."

"And I think that it's probably time that you sat back down and gave me all your money." Officer Tolley said, leaning back in his chair and giving his friend a condescending smile. "Come on Stinton, don't be such a pussy just because you lost a couple of pieces."

"Yeah, we'll give you a chance to win it all back, honest." Officer Bardsley said, his gold tooth catching the light of the lamp as he smiled

"To be fair to Officer Stinton," said Officer Springer. "We do have a job to do."

"Yeah, and that job is to take Stinton's money and then go and get pissed." Office Mooney grinned, looking at the wealth that he had gathered that evening.

"Really, I'd love to be a further part of your games, but Nürn is not going to police itself."

As Officer Stinton left the barracks he could see someone running towards him. It was the fisherman, Silus, and he looked to be in some distress. Stinton made sure that his sword was secure and then went to meet the citizen.

"Ring the alarm bell now." Silus said as he struggled to regain his breath. "Summon every volunteer you can. We're under attack."

"Silus, calm down. Attack from *whom*?"

"From the sea. They're coming from the sea."

"Who are coming from the sea?"

But Officer Stinton's question went unanswered as Silus ran for home, and he was no closer to understanding whom their assailants were when they burst from the waves.

The alarm bell was ringing and, as Silus rushed Katya from their home, they could see a plume of smoke rising above the harbour.

The first body that they came across was Officer Springer's. He knelt on the cobbles as though in an act of penitence, his head on the ground turned at an angle that shouldn't have been possible. A shard of vertebrae protruded from the back of his neck. From the cracked stones of the road beneath him it looked like he'd fallen from a great height. It was almost as though he'd been thrown.

Silus knelt beside the fallen guard and prised the sword from his stiff fingers, passing the weapon to Katya before unsheathing his own blade.

"We may have to fight," Silus said. "There may be no other way to protect our child. We'll try and make it to the *Ocean Lily* and get to Vosburg. We'll make sure that you're safe there and then we'll get help."

Katya nodded and kept a tight grip on Silus's hand as they ran towards the harbour.

The clash of weapons and the cries of the injured – both human and inhuman – were clearer now. Flames had started to spread to more of the buildings and, as Katya pulled Silus to a halt, they saw the roof of The Necromancer's Barge cave in. Someone flailed out of the building, a human torch that screamed so shrilly it could have been either a man or a woman. The blazing figure got only a few feet from the tavern before it keeled over in the street and was still.

A hideous form emerged through the smoke shrouding the end of the street. Katya cried out as it put one huge, clawed foot on the skull of the burning corpse. The noise that echoed off the walls with a sharp, yet wet, report as it stamped down was not something they would ever forget.

"Stay close to me!" Silus shouted, raising his sword as the creature advanced.

His first blow skittered across the beast's scales, deflected by tough hide. As he moved in again, Katya swung her own blade at its ankles, but the creature stepped out of the arc of her attack and raked its claws across her face. Had she been a step closer Katya would have been blinded. Instead four wet, red lines opened up on her cheek.

On seeing his wife's injuries anger boiled up in Silus. With a yell he put all of his strength behind his next attack. He could see himself in the pitch-black orbs of the thing's eyes as he leaned in close, the tip of his blade catching in a gap between scales. For a second Silus thought that the flesh there was too tough to penetrate, but then there was a sound like lobster claws cracking and the creature howled in pain. But before he could withdraw his blade, Silus's head was caught in the creature's claws and he went over with it as it fell.

They landed heavily in the street, Silus sprawled across its body. Hot, sour breath blasted into his face as the creature increased its grip and began to speak.

The words were guttural, harsh and not in a language that he understood. Silus fought to pull away but the pressure on his skull increased. The pain that arced between his ears was worse than anything he had ever experienced and he let out a keening wail, not quite believing that such a sound could be coming from him. The darkness that crowded his vision streamed from the creature's eyes and into his. The thing's words were clearer now and, just before Katya plunged her sword into its left eye socket, two broke through Silus's darkening consciousness.

"Half-breed."

The creature's arms fell away, releasing Silus's head. Katya helped him to his feet and he staggered a little, almost losing his balance as he pulled his sword free of the corpse.

"Are you okay?" He said, seeing the blood running down Katya's face.

"For now, but if we stay here we'll die."

"I'm sure that the Nürn guard will have at least started to drive them back." But he wasn't, especially not when he remembered how Officer Springer had been kneeling in the road. "I love you Katya. We'll get through this. Come on, we don't have far to go."

It was hard to see what was going on as they emerged into the open space before the harbour. The smoke was so thick in places that it obscured the fighting and the glare from the flames made it difficult to make out much more than the gleam of steel and the shine of wet scales. Three of the Nürn guard were squaring up against one of the creatures beside a nearby warehouse. Silus saw the short work that was made of the men – their blood arcing high up the planks of the building – and prayed that the creature didn't turn their way.

It didn't. Instead it cocked its head to one side as though it were listening to something and then loped off into the smoke.

Silus pushed Katya to the ground as the whoosh of a blade cutting through the air came perilously close. But no attacker barrelled from the smoke and he saw only a confusion of shadows as they got to their feet.

One of the shadows stumbled into Katya and Silus was just in time to block the sword that swung towards his wife. Officer Stinton glared hatred at him before he realised that what he was seeing was not one of the demons from the sea.

Silus gently lowered Stinton's blade with the flat of his palm. "Easy. Easy. We're comrades not enemies."

The guard was covered in blood but most of it was not his own. The only wound that he seemed to have sustained was a long ragged gash on his left thigh. In his eyes, however, was a look that had gone beyond battle rage and into something that Silus didn't think the guard would ever recover from. He knew that look well. His uncle was a veteran of the last war between Vos and Pontaine and he had that self-same stare.

"Officer Stinton, we need to get to the *Ocean Lily*." Silus said. "There's no way that Nürn can hold out against these things. If we can get to Vosburg we can come back with reinforcements."

Officer Stinton didn't seem to be listening, unable to take his eyes off Katya. "I almost killed you."

"Samuel, it's fine." Katya put a hand on his shoulder. "You didn't know. But we need you now. All three of us."

The guard looked at the mound of her belly and, seeming to realise what a fragile position Katya was in, came back to them a little.

And then there was a sudden stench and the sound of scale on stone as four sea demons stepped out of the smoke to surround them.

Running at the creature nearest to Katya, Officer Stinton swung his sword, connecting with the thing's side and carving a gash that ran with oily, black blood.

The creature staggered into one of its comrades, but its reach was long and it tore into Stinton's sword arm. Despite his wounds the guard retaliating with a cry, hacking at the creature again and again until its guts were coiling down around its legs. Finally the pain overcame him and he dropped his weapon.

Katya stepped forward to finish the beast that had attacked Officer Stinton, ducking as it made a grab for her, driving her blade up into its throat.

Silus shot her a warning glance to stay out of reach as he took down another of the creatures. He was surprised at the ease with which it fell and he wondered why the guards hadn't had more success against the sea demons. As he squared up against another of them it seemed almost reluctant to strike, instead backing towards its brethren.

They showed no such reluctance when it came to Officer Stinton.

He tried to reach for his sword, but was stopped when a taloned fist punched deep into his sternum. He was dead before he hit the ground. Katya cried out and swung at the creature but overbalanced with her attack, and soon the thing stood looking down at her.

Silus was too slow to prevent his wife from being grabbed and now the fight was on a different footing. The two remaining creatures watched him, unblinking, making no move to finish what they had started. Around them the sounds of battle had stopped. The smoke was beginning to clear as a strong wind came in off the sea, revealing the smouldering ruins of buildings and corpses.

"Let her go!" Silus yelled. "I know that you can understand me, one of you spoke to me. I'm telling you to let her go!"

The sound of a staff tapping out a regular rhythm approached them as another of the sea demons stepped into view.

Though this one was larger than its brethren it was stooped, its hide was tarnished and encrusted in places with barnacles and other molluscs. One of its eyes was a milky white and scars criss-crossed its chest as though it had faced battle many times.

The creature approached Silus, laid a finger on his chest and regarded him intently with its one good eye.

"What are you?" Silus said.

"We are the Chadassa." The creature said. Its voice reminded Silus of the sea breaking on shingle. "I am Belck."

The thing gestured for Katya to be brought forward and crouched down before her, running its hands over her belly, making strange crooning noises at the back of its throat. Some of the molluscs clinging to its hide opened up at the sound of its pleasure. Katya tried to draw away from Belck's touch, but she stopped struggling when her arm was forced further up her back by the Chadassa restraining her.

Silus rushed Belck then, burning with the desire to cleave the creature's head from its body, but one gesture from Belck's hand halted the fisherman and another sent the sword tumbling from his grip.

As the aged sea demon straightened and turned to Silus, Katya spat at it. "You touch me like that again and I'll break your neck! Nobody but my husband touches me like that."

"This man is far more than just your husband. Our blood runs in his veins."

"Silus is nothing like you freaks. Trust me, when Vos finds out about your little invasion you're going to wish that you had never left the sea."

"Ah, but with the help of Silus we shall soon leave the sea behind anyway. All of Twilight shall be ours, and then shall come the time of the Great Flood."

"Listen," Silus said. "I don't know what you're talking about and I'm not about to help you. I've no idea who you think I am."

"No, you really don't do you? Allow me to offer an explanation."

Belck stepped in close to Silus. The light of Kerberos faded from the creature's eye as he watched, the darkness intensifying until it was all he could see.

And then Silus was looking back at Nürn, but it was not the place he knew. The church of the Final Faith did not dominate the town square here and the old stone forts that dotted the coast no longer looked so old. What had once been crumbling, lichen encrusted brick now looked almost newly laid.

Silus found himself standing by the rock pools not far from the harbour. In front of him a woman was collecting mussels. He called out to her but she didn't turn round.

Having filled her pail she turned to leave and, as she did, she failed to spot the thing curled within the deepest of the pools.

It rose up to meet her as her shadow fell over it.

The woman screamed and staggered back, dropping her pail as the creature forced her into the sea,

Silus didn't move but his point of view changed and he found himself following the Chadassa and the woman down beneath the waves.

She struggled in the creature's grip, thrashing like a caught fish, but the thing didn't let go. It swam with her into a dark gash in the seabed, before surfacing from a pool in the centre of a vast cave.

The woman was carried through an echoing darkness, illuminated by the glow of thousands of tiny thread-like worms which writhed over the cavern walls. Soon she stopped struggling and lay limply in the creature's arms. Her eyes spoke of the turmoil within, but she made no sound as the creature laid her on a bed of seaweed and cuttlefish bones.

The Chadassa tore the remains of the woman's clothes away and then unfolded itself and embraced her like an octopus cloaks its prey.

And now Silus saw her crawling from the sea, sobbing and naked. Blood trickled down her thighs.

And now he was watching her lying on a bed and he could feel her thoughts as she screamed and sweated, the nuns surrounding and fussing over her urging her to keep pushing. But she didn't want to push and she prayed for death rather than the chance to see whatever foul progeny would emerge from within her.

When the nun handed her the struggling, mewling thing, however, she didn't hesitate to hold it to her breast, overwhelmed with relief that this tiny creature was a he rather than an it. Silus sensed her fierce resolve as she swore to raise the child as her own, in defiance of that which had been done to her by the creature.

Silus blinked and he stood before Belck once more.

"Your ancestor," said Belck. "That child was your great great great grandfather. Our blood has been running in your veins for all these generations. Only now, however, has the line grown strong. You are special, Silus. You belong with us."

"You're lying." Katya said.

"No, and Silus knows that I am not."

Silus did indeed feel that what Belck had shown him was true.

"Come with us Silus."

Silus looked at Katya and saw something like despair in her eyes.

There was a thunderous bang and the air itself seemed to tear as Belck was sent tumbling across the ground. The Chadassa that had been restraining Katya roared in pain, flames erupting from its eye sockets as it cooked from within.

Silus looked round for the source of the conflagration and was stunned to see Kelos standing at the prow of a small boat, shrouded with arcane energy as it rushed towards the shore. Another burst of that energy erupted from Kelos's palm, hurtling into one of the Chadassa as it flung itself at the mage.

The creature turned into a fine mist before it could even reach him.

"Get in!" Kelos yelled.

Silus grabbed Katya's hand and they ran.

Behind them, Belck was raising himself to his feet. The gem at the tip of his staff began to glow as he brought it to bear and, at the same time, the ancient creature emitted a sound that made Silus's skull ache.

A line of fire tore through the air towards them, the intense heat from the attack singeing the hair on the backs of their heads as they tumbled into the boat. Once they were safely on board the boom swung of its own accord and the sails met the wind, pulling them quickly away from the shore.

Silus turned to see Belck watching and, even from this distance, he could see the reflection of the flames in the creature's one good eye as the town burned.

The prow of the boat was pointed towards the Sarcre Islands, and Kelos sped them across the water on channels of magic that left a glittering wake.

"Silus help me."

It was Katya. She was bent over, intense pain etched onto her face. Blood dotted the deck below her.

"Silus, I think I'm losing our child."

CHAPTER SIX

Katya awoke. Looking at the clock in the corner of the room she saw that it had only just gone eight in the morning, yet it was hot enough to be midday. She felt as though she had drifted through these last three days on Sarcre. Nightmares had painted the gaps between the moments of lucidity with lurid visions of sea creatures and screaming infants. Cradling her belly she was relieved to feel the curve of her flesh unchanged. When a kick responded to her touch she began to cry.

There was a knock on the door and Silus entered. Three days growth of stubble darkened his already swarthy features and his eyes spoke of a severe lack of sleep. For all that he still managed to show Katya a look of pure love. He kissed her and put a hand on her forehead.

"No fever it would seem. How are you feeling?"

"Better. I think we're okay now."

"Kelos and Father Maylan are mostly to thank for that. Do you feel well enough to join us for breakfast?"

"I think so."

Supported by Silus, Katya descended to the parlour. The men gathered around the table – variously eating, arguing and leafing through documents – were mostly unfamiliar to her, though she recognised Kelos as he helped Silus guide her to a chair.

"Why thank you gentlemen, you're awful kind to a cripple such as myself."

Kelos blushed. "I didn't for a moment mean to suggest... Why, I've seen you fight!"

"Sit down, I was joking. I can't thank you enough for all you've done for me. And I apologise for not recognizing you other gentlemen. The last time we met I was in a bit of a state."

Dunsany introduced Katya to the crew, each met her nod with a smile or a raised hand of greeting. Only Emuel didn't respond. He hadn't spoken to any of them since his vision. This was something that suited the men gathered around the table just fine. Their only hope was that when it came time to leave Sarcre, Emuel would rediscover his voice.

"Without you, Kelos, we would be dead." Silus said. "But now that Katya has recovered I think that it is time we thought about going home. Nürn will need our help to rebuild."

"I'm afraid that you'll find Nürn is beyond your help. I returned there myself just yesterday and it would seem that after you fled the creatures took their anger out on the rest of the town."

"Oh gods!" Katya's grief was sudden and bitter and made the room swim. She leaned into Silus and he put his arm around her. "What were those things?"

"I'm not sure," Kelos said, "but there were reports of similar creatures launching an attack on the Turnitia docks last month. There the devastation was on a much smaller scale however."

"And Nürn," Silus said. "What have they done to our town?" Kelos's grave look told him everything he needed to know. "*Everyone*?"

Kelos nodded. "As far as I could see."

Silus and Katya no longer had any family in Nürn. Silus's parents were both dead and Katya's mother lived on her own in Allantia. A severe and bitter split in the family meant that they hadn't spoken in years. However, the loss of their friends and colleagues in Nürn had utterly stunned them and, for a while, they stared at each other in incomprehension, until Silus's anger boiled over.

"But... What the hells *for*? Why did those things attack us?"

"I don't understand it myself, but when I rescued you it appeared that the creatures had come for you specifically."

"The thing with the staff called me 'half-breed.'"

Emuel let out a gasp at that and everybody turned to look at him. Though they were braced for a return of the eunuch's visions, none came.

"Yes, we have heard that term quite recently in fact." Father Maylan said, nervously eyeing Emuel.

"That tattooed retard practically gave us all a heart attack screaming about it." Jacquinto said.

"He does have a name!" Kelos snapped.

Jacquinto sneered but otherwise held his tongue.

"Have you any idea what the creature may have meant by 'half-breed'?" Kelos turned his attention back to Silus.

"It was just evil." Katya said. "Just a creature. It didn't make any sense."

"The thing showed me a vision. But it may mean nothing. It may just have been leading me along." Silus said.

"Even so," Dunsany said, "it was something important to them."

As Silus explained what the thing that called itself Belck had revealed to him, Katya looked at her husband in bemused horror. For the creature to have thought that Silus was one of them was just beyond ridiculous.

"I must say that it does seem unlikely." Kelos said. "For a start you display none of the traits of these Chadassa."

"Half man, half fish!" Ioannis laughed. "One tattooed maniac, a renegade priest, two ex-members of the Faith, a pregnant lady and us. Yup, this is far more entertaining than sneaking in crates of booze by dusk."

"Sorry, but you seem to be presuming that we're part of the crew." Silus said.

"As Kelos has already pointed out, Katya will be well looked after here on Sarcre and you will be paid handsomely for your time." Dunsany said. "Besides, it is likely that the first expedition will only be for about four weeks. After all, we don't know that there *is* anything beyond Twilight."

"Apart from sea demons." Kelos said.

"Dunsany, have you ever been married?" Katya said. She felt an anger that was threatening to unleash itself on the people surrounding her, but as she spoke to the sailor, her voice was calm and level.

"The sea is my mistress." Dunsany said.

"Your right hand is your mistress." Ignacio said and Ioannis slapped the table as he roared with laughter.

"You men are clearly a bunch of cretins!" Katya shouted. "What you are proposing is not going to be some jolly boy's outing, it is going to be your deaths. Firstly you have the Final Faith on your tail and, secondly, even if you do manage to make it beyond Twilight those sea demons are going to tear you apart."

"I would have to agree with my wife." Silus said. "This expedition, everything about it, sounds preposterous."

"Ah, but you have yet to see our unique ship." Dunsany said. "Did you know that it can actually sail *under* water?"

"For that matter I too have yet to see this ship." Father Maylan said. "In fact, we just have the words of yourself and Kelos regarding the pedigree of the *Llothriall.*"

"It better be as good as you say," Ioannis said. "For every day that we sit here talking about plans and theorising we are losing money."

"If you're going to sail away from all these problems, then you better have something that is nothing short of spectacular." Katya said.

"In that case – and to forestall further argument – I suggest that we all make a visit to the *Llothriall.*" Dunsany said. "Katya, can I persuade you to come along?"

Katya's gaze still burned with anger, but eventually she nodded and it was she who was the first to follow him as they left the house.

Querilous Fitch looked up from his notes as they brought the prisoner into the room. This time the thing did not fight against its restraints as it was bound into the chair. Its head lolled against its chest and the pitch black of its eyes had faded to a dark, milky grey.

"Good God! How much sedative did you give it?" Fitch asked one of the warders.

"Not enough. Bloody thing near tore off Mitchell's arm when we went to fetch it. Took three of us to hold it down while we administered the needlereed. Ask me, the creature should be in chains twenty-four seven."

"Yes, well it's a good thing that the treatment of the prisoner isn't down to you then is it? I don't think that you realise the importance of the Chadassa to the Anointed Lord. You may go now, if I need you I'll call."

The guards left the room and Querilous turned up the lamps before wheeling his tray of instruments to the side of the restraining chair.

After its outburst of a few days earlier the creature had been stubbornly uncommunicative. However, in that time – and through his various techniques and manipulations – Querilous had learnt a great deal.

The Chadassa male currently in his custody was hundreds of years old and one of a race of many, although it was nowhere near as populous as that of the humans who dominated Twilight. The creature's natural habitat was the sea, though it could survive on land for short periods, which went some way to explaining why the Chadassa's attack on Turnitia a few months previously had been brief.

Through Querilous's sorcery he had managed to open a psychic link between the creature and its brethren beneath the waves. Now his questioning could touch not just on the knowledge of their prisoner but the knowledge of all the Chadassa. All without them being able to detect the human mind amongst them.

Sometimes, Querilous thought, *I am quite quite brilliant.*

He extracted a small measure of fluid from a vial and injected it into the creature with a needlereed.

Slowly, its eyes began to darken and its head rose from its chest. Querilous doused the creature with salt-water as it regained consciousness. Crouching before it he then looked for any sign of recognition, but the thing stared at him just as blankly as before.

"Oh, you can remain as coy as you like, but you'll find it very difficult to escape my touch this time."

Fitch pulled the creature's head back and tightened a strap around it. He checked that the restraint was secure before running his hands over the dark, scaled scalp. Where he had cut the spines from the creature's skull they had started to grow back and as Querilous filed down the stubs, the thing in the chair let out a low growl.

"Ah, it makes a sound! Good to know that you're still with us. Now, just relax, this won't take long at all."

Querilous's fingers sank through the scalp of the creature and into its mind. He felt it try to fight back but, this time, the Chadassa was no match for Fitch. Hearing the repetitions of an ancient mantra in his mind, Querilous pushed through the creature's resistance and suddenly he was surrounded by the whispers of its brethren as the psychic barriers fell away.

... all burned... He comes... half-breed... half-breed... lost... final cycle... Brood...

Words and images crowded Querilous's mind but in the storm of sensory information he recognised a familiar phrase.

"The half-breed, what is that?"

Again the creature tried to push against his questioning. It tried to reach out to its brethren, warn them that there was an alien mind amongst them but Querilous tightened his grip and the creature howled in pain.

"I think that you'll find challenging my talents is a bad idea. Do it again and I'll boil your brain in your skull. Now, let's try again. What, or who, is the half-breed?"

Querilous could feel a ripple run through the collective minds now open to him and an image began to form. He recognised Nürn immediately. How could he forget that shabby little coastal town where he had once holidayed with his mother? There was a fishing boat approaching the harbour and the image swam to focus on the man leading the craft to shore.

Half-breed.

"Him? That man is the half-breed that is so important to you?"

Half-breed. Lost.

"Lost? How? Show me."

Again, the image in his mind began to swim and this time the sounds of screaming and the roar of fire accompanied it.

Nürn was awash with the Chadassa as they smashed apart the town, eviscerating anybody who got in the way. By the docks Querilous could see the 'half-breed' surrounded by more of the fish demons. A woman was standing near to him and the ancient creature with the staff that he had seen before in the prisoner's thoughts loomed over the fisherman. Suddenly there was an explosion of magical energy and the ancient one was flying across the harbour as a boat rushed towards the shore. At its helm was a face Querilous recognised very well.

"Kelos!"

Querilous watched as Kelos rescued the fisherman and the woman before turning the boat away from the shore. Soon they were cutting across the waves with a supernatural swiftness.

Half-breed! Lost!

Querilous was buzzing with excitement now. He had found a lead to one of their ship thieves and, if his reckoning was correct, he thought he knew where Kelos's rescue boat had been heading.

LOST!

Suddenly there was an immense screech of psychic noise and Querilous's hands jolted as his flesh began to burn. He tried to pull away from the voices and images that crowded his mind but the maelstrom of sensations held him in its grip. He could feel the creature in the chair thrashing against its restraints and there was a peculiar smell. It reminded him of the sea but there was also an odour of burning to it. Querilous suddenly found himself blind and he gritted his teeth as he forced his mind against the barrier that had been thrown up against it.

Suddenly he was free, and he reeled across the interrogation room, he palms throbbing with pain.

Once his surroundings had stopped spinning Querilous looked down at his hands. They were blistered and peeling, as though they had been plunged into a pot of boiling water. The odour that he had smelt earlier was stronger now and he realised that it was coming from the prisoner.

Looking over at the thing in the chair he could see steam rising from its skull.

Querilous cautiously approached and was appalled to see two gaping holes in the Chadassa's head where he had hurriedly torn his hands free.

Querilous may have found a lead to their fugitives, he considered, but how was he going to tell Makennon that he had killed one of their most valuable prisoners?

CHAPTER SEVEN

Silus marvelled at the beauty of the Sarcre archipelago as they glided over the crystal blue water. He had never seen the sea so calm. The formation of the islands here broke apart the angry water that surrounded Sarcre, channelling it into the clear cool channels that separated the islands. Silus looked over the side of the boat and could see all the way to the seabed. The water glittered with life. If he and Katya lived here, he considered, they could make a very comfortable living. He wouldn't even need a net; he could just reach over the side of the boat and pick the fish from the sea.

At the oars Dunsany sweated in a heat that was even more intense than it had been that morning. The rest of them sat crowded into the boat; Emuel looking forlornly into the distance as though searching for a lost love, Jacquinto and his compatriots steadily drinking from hip flasks, Father Maylan beaming a smile as though he were rather enjoying every moment, Kelos looking eagerly ahead to the approaching island and Katya, sitting with her arms folded, her look a warning to anyone on whom it happened to settle.

The quietly smoking cone of a volcano dominated the small island towards which they were heading and Silus watched its approach with some concern.

"I don't suppose that there's any risk of that thing blowing its top is there?" He said.

"Oh, you mean Maladrak's Cauldron?" Kelos said. "Well, of course there's a risk but it hasn't erupted in living memory. So I wouldn't worry too much."

"Well that's reassuring," Katya said.

As they drew closer Silus recognised the regularly shaped standing stones that ringed the island a short distance from the shore. He'd noticed similar monoliths surrounding several of the other islands in the archipelago, though he'd never seen any of them up-close before.

Dunsany took the oars out of their loops as they drifted to a halt on the pebbles of the beach, while Kelos leapt out to secure the boat.

As Silus stepped ashore he could hear a strange low buzzing, as though a vast colony of bees were somewhere nearby. He turned to look at the rest of the crew but none of them seemed to have noticed anything out of place.

"Can you hear that?" He asked Katya.

"What am I listening for?"

"I don't know. It's sort of a weird buzzing."

"I don't hear it."

Trying to shake his head clear Silus followed the rest of the crew. As he drew closer to the standing stones, a pressure began to build up behind his eyes and a sharp pain gripped his head. Feeling nauseous and dizzy, he reached for Katya's hand.

"Silus, what's wrong?"

Ahead of him the stones swam as though in a heat haze. Gentle whispers filled his head and the monoliths began to glow.

"Silus?"

He staggered past the line of stones and fell to his knees, splattering the ground with vomit. Silus took deep breaths and, slowly, his head began to clear. He looked back and the stones stood silent, the air around them untroubled.

"What happened?" Katya said, kneeling beside him.

"I don't know. The stones, they filled my head with this awful noise."

"Are you alright old chap?" Dunsany offered his hand and helped Silus to his feet.

"I'm fine, I think. Those stones, what are they for?"

"No one knows," Kelos said, joining them. "But from what I have noted of the markings they probably held some religious significance for the early islanders. The minerals from which these rocks are carved are fascinating. I haven't seen anything like them elsewhere. They may even be unique to Sarcre. Why do you ask?"

"I seem to have an adverse reaction to them. Or maybe it's just the heat?"

Kelos looked at him with some concern, before Dunsany linked his arm in his and marched with his friend towards the volcano.

"Onwards team," Dunsany said.

"Where exactly is this ship of yours anchored?" Jacquinto said. "This is a pretty small island and I can't see this mighty vessel that you've been enthusing about."

"Ah, but the *Llothriall* isn't anchored at *this* island." Dunsany said, leading them to the foot of the volcano, where a cave opened up in the dark rock.

"Come on Dunsany, this is ridiculous!" Silus said. "You're leading us on some sort of merry chase now."

"Actually, this *is* the right way to the *Llothriall*." Kelos said. "It may seem strange but you'll understand the reasoning behind it soon."

"He's quite the showman," said Father Maylan. "Dunsany, I don't suppose you've ever considered the priesthood have you? I'm sure that a man with a flair for the dramatic such as yourself would fit right in."

"Funnily enough," Dunsany said. "It's not a vocation that I have ever considered," and he led them into the side of the volcano.

As the darkness closed around them Kelos summoned a light to his palm. It burned with a steady glow that revealed their surroundings perfectly.

They had to stoop as the roof of the cave angled down, but the tunnel soon widened as it turned sharply to the right and descended. There was a powerful smell of sulphur and steam rose from fissures in the walls, coating them in moisture and making their clothes cling clammily to their limbs. Silus felt for Katya's hand and gave it a reassuring squeeze as they followed the crew. He was wondering how much more of the stifling heat they could take when the tunnel levelled out and the temperature dropped.

The stone that surrounded them now gave off a pleasant coolness and the smell of the sea permeated the passage. The crash and susurrus of waves echoed around them and Silus wondered what kind of harbour they were being led to, so far beneath the ground.

It was hard to measure the passage of time as they walked along the tunnel, but Silus thought that at least half an hour had passed before Kelos extinguished his light. It took Silus a moment to understand where the new source of illumination was coming from, but then he noticed that the dark rock of the walls had given way to pale stone and it was through this that a soft marine glow filtered into the passage. Ahead of them the light increased and, as they continued, Silus was no longer looking at the walls, he was looking *through* them.

Dunsany and Kelos glanced back at the crew expectantly, trying to gauge their reactions to this new marvel.

"We're underwater. How are we underwater?" Katya said.

"Incredible isn't it?" Dunsany said. "And, I must add, completely safe."

"I confess that it's making me rather dizzy." Father Maylan said.

The rock of the tunnel walls was now completely transparent and Silus fought a nauseous feeling of vertigo as he stood, staring at the ocean that surrounded them. The seabed lay twenty feet below their boots and the surface was twice that distance above, shafts of brilliant sunlight cutting through the churn of the waves. Deep blue water flanked them on both sides as far as the eye could see and Silus gazed into the depths in wonder. Shoals of beautiful fish – the likes of which he had never seen– played through the tall fronds of emerald weeds. A fish the size of a dinner plate, covered in scintillant diamond markings, swam close alongside and Silus put his hand to the wall that separated them. The piscine eye followed the movement of his fingers for a moment before the creature darted away. Along the seabed below scuttled crustaceans the size and shape of large boulders, their bulk somehow supported on dozens of spindly legs. Eyes dotted the craggy surfaces of their shells at seemingly random points and long, many-jointed arms reached into narrow crevices in rocks to retrieve lime green worms, which they fed into dark openings in their chitinous sides.

"Believe it or not," Dunsany said. "There are yet more wonders to behold. Not far now and you will see the *Llothriall* herself."

Silus and the rest of the crew stared at Dunsany for a while, looks of wonder obvious on all their faces. Silus gazed back at the view of the ocean for a moment, reluctant to leave behind the breathtaking panorama, but then he followed. After a short while, the dark rock of the tunnel returned and they started to ascend.

The thunder of breakers greeted them as they stepped out of the tunnel and onto a pebble beach. They blinked in the intense sunlight for a few moments before the scene in front of them resolved itself. Sheer cliff faces flanked them on two sides, covered in screeching gulls and heavy with the stink of guano, while in front of them churned the angry sea. Silus could just see across it to the northern tip of the Sarcre archipelago. The water that separated the northernmost province of Twilight from where they now stood was wine dark and violent.

"And this," Dunsany said. "Is why Makennon's lot will find it impossible to discover our hiding place. No regular ship can cross that stretch without being destroyed. For the *Llothriall* though, the angry churn out there is nothing."

Dunsany led them through a narrow gap in the cliffs and Silus saw that the centre of the island opened out into a wide, deep lagoon. In this natural harbour sat the most beautiful ship he had ever seen.

Dunsany led them to a launch and, with the aid of this, they boarded the *Llothriall.*

The two fugitives from the Faith had clearly done a great deal of work since hiding the ship and it seemed to be stocked with all that they would need for a substantial voyage. On deck everything gleamed and not just with newness, some of the shine that emanated from the wood was due to the magic that gave the *Llothriall* its power. Silus looked up at the masts that towered above him and wondered at the strength of the sails that were furled there. He had a difficult enough time on his own small fishing vessel fighting the wind with a bit of canvas. Silus dreaded to think how the vast sheets above them would fair against the fierce winds on the Twilight seas. Surely they would be torn from the masts within seconds of being unfurled?

"Have you noticed the sheen on the material?" Kelos said, following his gaze.

"Sheen? No."

"Well the silk that makes up those sails came from the X'cotl."

"And what are the X'cotl?" Katya said.

"A sort of giant spider. They're said to exist in our reality only some of the time."

"So you guys must have a lot in common."

Kelos chuckled. "Hoist by my own petard. You mock Katya, but I just know that you're warming to the charms of this beauty of the sea."

And the *Llothriall* was both charming and beautiful. Below the main deck the ship was opulently attired. Each cabin was comfortably equipped and Silus reckoned that the sleeping quarters would be more than adequate for a high ranking officer in the Vos navy, never mind the ragtag band of thieves and renegades currently on board. There was also a vast dining room, a well equipped and impressively stocked galley, a hold big enough to contain the largest of treasures and an array of gleaming canons, well oiled and with a ready supply of ammunition.

"There is a lot more to the *Llothriall* that you can't see. The elf magic has been seamlessly integrated into the design of the vessel. This empowers many of the ship's unique abilities; its ability to negotiate the angriest of maelstroms, or its ability to sail beneath the sea, for example." Dunsany said. "And talking of elf magic..."

Emuel had joined them and Dunsany put a hand on his shoulder, smiling. The tattooed eunuch returned the mage's expression with a weak smile of his own.

"Emuel, would you like to show us to the gem room?"

Emuel nodded and led them down a short flight of steps and into a room buzzing with magical energy. The hairs on the back of Silus's neck rose as he entered and there was a sour taste in his mouth.

The stone sat in its housing in the centre of the room, veins of power rippling across its surface. The slightly cowed expression on Emuel's face was replaced by a look of affection as he ran his hand over the surface of the gem, almost as though he were stroking a much-loved pet.

"And this is why we need Emuel," Kelos said. "It is his song that unlocks the power within the stone and enables the *Llothriall* to handle the roughest of seas. This power will enable us to sail through the Storm Wall unharmed. Entire elf fleets used to venture forth in ships such as this. Unfortunately we have found no record of what they discovered."

"A good reason why we should set out on a voyage of discovery ourselves." Father Maylan said. "Why, we could map anything we find and sell copies to the highest bidder on our return. We could become very wealthy men."

"Ah, but this voyage is not just about money, Father." Dunsany said.

"Speak for yourself," said Ignacio.

"We are going to be paid, right?" Jacquinto said, his hand dangerously close to his dagger.

"Gentlemen, of course you will be paid." Dunsany said. "Have I not already given you a little taster? But, trust me, you will gain so much more from this than a full purse."

Silus led Katya to the main deck, leaving the rest of the crew to argue it out amongst themselves. They stood at the prow of the *Llothriall*, looking towards the mouth of the lagoon and beyond to where the angry ocean stretched to the horizon. The masthead of the ship followed their gazes, the violet eyes of the wooden elf maiden reflecting and somehow enhancing the glow of Kerberos. The wind blew strong and fresh in their faces and the ship swayed gently in its natural harbour.

"I remember that look," Katya said, turning to her husband.

"What look?"

"It wasn't just for me was it, that first night beneath the gaze of Kerberos on the subterranean lake? I know how you dream."

Silus embraced her. Sometimes he regretted the fact that he was so easy to read. "Katya, you know that I love you."

"I do know, Silus. But something like this... it's not going to happen every day. You deserve this, no matter how much I'd like to just return to our old lives."

"But what about our child?"

"We'll be safe enough, safer when you guys set sail. Then our son or daughter won't have to be born in the company of fugitives from the Faith. Besides, I have a friend on Sarcre who will look after me and I would rather not give birth in the confines of an inquisition cell or on a ship. So you see, it's probably for the best." Katya looked back up at the sails. "And she *is* a beautiful ship. When you return we can go somewhere quiet, live off the money and you can raise our son or daughter on stirring tales of the sea."

"You know that that this voyage is probably going to be dangerous?"

"Yes, but you face danger every day, out on the *Ocean Lily*. There's something about you Silus, Kelos was right. I think that your veins run not just with blood but also seawater. Like I said, you can't take the sea out of the boy. And nor would I want to. It's who you are."

"I'm worried Katya, worried about what I may be becoming. Those creatures called me half-breed and Kelos seems to think there's something unique about me, but what? Why did those standing stones seem to scream at me? Why do I suddenly feel like a player in a game I don't understand?"

Katya didn't answer, instead she put her arm around her husband.

The *Llothriall* seemed to be straining beneath them, towards the horizon, and – despite his fear – Silus felt that same tug himself, deep within his breast.

After their tour of the ship they returned to the tunnel, following it back to Maladrak's Cauldron.

Before they reached the cave that led out of the side of the volcano, Dunsany put a hand out to them, gesturing for them to stop. Kelos joined his colleague at the head of the group, straining to hear whatever it was that had brought them to a halt.

After listening for a moment he ran his tongue over dry lips and said: "There's no mistaking that taste is there?"

Dunsany shook his head.

Behind them the rest of the crew exchanged confused glances. Silus thought that he could hear a repetitive thumping sound, but that could have just been the waves crashing against the island.

"What's happening?" he said.

"Someone up there is using a lot of rather powerful magic." Kelos said. "Can you not taste that strange metallic taste?"

"Is it the Faith?" The panic in Katya's voice was clear to everybody and they too began to feel an edge of hysteria creeping up on them in the dark confines of the tunnel.

"No, it's not their style." Dunsany said.

"Well, in that case it's probably just some dabbler in the esoteric arts. You do tend to get the odd mage on the Sarcre archipelago." Father Maylan said. "Apparently the peace of the islands is conducive to magical practice."

"Whoever it is, it pays to be careful." Dunsany said. "Those with weapons, I suggest you ready them."

A short distance from the mouth of the cave, a shimmering blue light painted the walls. The taste that Kelos had detected earlier was now heavy in their mouths, drying up their saliva and making it difficult to swallow.

Jacquinto and his comrades drew their swords and pushed past Dunsany and Kelos to look out.

Silus didn't like the expressions of sheer terror that contracted the faces of the smugglers or the way they stumbled back, but something else, something like the siren song of the sea-maidens of legend, made him push his way past them.

The entire island was cloaked in the sheets of indigo fire that poured from the standing stones, creating a dome that extended far above him. Silus realised that it was shielding the island from the creatures which stood on the shore, their wet scales reflecting the light of the magical barrier that crackled and hissed only metres before them.

The Chadassa were chanting something in their guttural language and each syllable, echoing in Silus's mind, made him take another step towards them.

Behind him he was vaguely aware of the sounds of more weapons being unsheathed and his hand strayed to his own sword, a part of him screaming its awareness that now was the time to fight.

But the chanting blocked out all thought and his hand fell away.

At the centre of the line of Chadassa stood Belck. The gem at the tip of his staff burned with an angry scarlet light and the creatures that flanked him were gesturing with their hands as they tore into the magical energy of the barrier. There was a sound like the heart of a thunderstorm and a hole started to open up in front of Belck.

Silus saw Kelos rush past him. The mage reached into a pocket in his jerkin and threw a handful of glittering shards into the air. These raced towards the barrier and began stitching lines of fire across the gap that was rapidly widening there.

Belck raised his hand and the arcane threads crumbled.

From behind the ancient creature, a Chadassa twice as wide and at least a foot taller than he stepped in front of Belck and thrust a misshapen, trunk-like arm through the hole in the barrier. The warped limb ended not with a clawed hand, but with a hole from which dripped strands of green slime. Two fleshy sacks on the underside of the arm collapsed as something erupted from the barrel of the creature's limb.

Kelos staggered back under the force of the impact and looked down at the thing that was now embedded in the flesh of his chest. It pulsed there for a moment – emitting a sound like a small animal being tortured – before it suddenly contracted, hundreds of thread like filaments whipping out of its body and around the screaming mage. Dark red lines crisscrossed Kelos's torso as he fell, the threads seared into his flesh. Dunsany and Father Maylan rushed over and started to tug at the thing attached to their friend.

As the two of them struggled, Silus watched with only mild interest.

In front of Belck the hole in the barrier continued to widen and he began to speak, his gaze fixed on Silus.

"The Chadassa have long awaited your coming, Silus. Stories of you were told to me when I was barely a hatchling, tales that I have told my own broodkin. We all know of the half-breed. And you know, Silus, that your place is amongst us. You know that it is your seed that will produce the Land Walkers. You know that this reality needs to be bathed in the waters of the Great Flood. Only then will we be able to swim the oceans of time and space together."

Katya stepped into Silus's line of vision and he smiled briefly at her – as though he were imparting a greeting to a passing friend on the street – before returning his attention to the Chadassa ancient.

Silus remembered the vista that had greeted him through the transparent tunnel walls, how the ocean there had seemed so endless, stretching away into the midnight blue of the distance. He wondered what it would be like to swim there.

"You could swim forever with us, Silus."

And he would swim forever with his brethren. Entire worlds would turn, suspended in the waters of the infinite ocean. They would be masters of all life, all matter.

Katya was shaking him now, but he barely felt her touch. Beyond her Dunsany had begun to pry the strange creature free of Kelos.

The hole in front of Belck was now almost big enough for the creature to step through, or for Silus to step out of.

"Come to us Silus. Be with us."

Silus could see tears running down Katya's face. The words that she was saying failed to reach his ears. All he could hear was Belck.

Kelos sat upright, pulling the last of the vicious tendrils from his flesh. He was pale, sweating and covered in blood but he still managed to regain his feet with Dunsany's help.

And even though Belck's words began to fill his mind once more, Silus didn't fail to notice Kelos's finger pointing his way.

A cacophony of sound rushed in on him and Silus flailed back at the aural assault.

There was Katya screaming his name as she repeatedly pummelled his chest with her fists; Kelos's words of power pounding through his consciousness; the growl of rage from Belck as he realised that his hold had been broken, and a sound like a thousand summer storms as the barrier surrounding the island began to fail.

Silus's hand went to his sword as he looked at Katya's frightened face. She stepped back from him, as though expecting him to lash out, but when he put a hand on her arm she saw that he had come back to her.

With a gibbering scream something leapt through the hole in the barrier. It was smaller and faster than any of the Chadassa Silus had seen so far, and it launched itself at Katya with a feral cry. Silus was quicker, however, and the edge of his blade caught the thing across the skull as Katya fell back behind him.

The creature howled in pain but quickly found its feet and came after him instead. This time it cleared the arc of Silus's blade and was about to rake its talons across his face when Dunsany barrelled into it from the side, bringing the creature to ground.

The pinned Chadassa thrashed wildly beneath him as Dunsany gripped its skull. Silus could see the strain in his arms as he prevented the creature struggling against his grasp. Then, he wrenched the thing's head violently to the side and it stopped moving as its neck broke.

Kelos, panting with the strain of his injuries, rushed over and helped Dunsany to his feet.

Silus looked back to where Jacquinto and his comrades were cowering in the mouth of the tunnel, Emuel just visible behind them. They caught his gaze for a moment and seemed to be about to steal themselves to advance when the chanting of the Chadassa stopped.

"I suggest that we go, *now*." Father Maylan said, already backing towards the cave.

But before they could begin their retreat a shiver passed through the stones surrounding the island and the ground seemed to sway beneath their feet.

With a noise like a great door slamming the curtain of magical energy fell. Belck raised his staff and cried out a word that no human mouth could ever have formulated as the standing stones began to explode, one by one.

As burning fragments of rock showered them, the crew turned and ran for the shelter of the tunnel, Silus shielding Katya's body with his own, crying out in agony as shrapnel scored his shoulders. He saw Kelos turn and start to gesture with his hands as he attempted to weave the beginnings of a defensive spell. But when the Chadassa started to swarm across the island towards them, he too turned and fled.

Dunsany and Father Maylan were the last to the tunnel and, turning, they saw that the Chadassa were closing the distance to them fast.

"Kelos, is there anything that you can do?" Dunsany shouted, above the roar of the advancing creatures.

"Get clear of the entrance." Kelos said, his hands on the rock walls, his fingers seeming to sink into the stone. "*Go!*"

Dunsany joined the rest of the crew as they fled and, as the darkness of the tunnel swallowed them, a great wave of force slammed them to the floor as the roof of the cave collapsed. They covered their heads as a hot wind rolled over them and the sound of falling rock filled the tunnel.

And then the thunder of stones stopped and there was just the creak and groan of rock settling into new configurations.

For a moment they lay in absolute darkness, listening to each other's breathing. Silus reached out and found Katya's hand, a sigh of relief escaping his lips when she returned his grasp. Behind him he could hear Jacquinto and his friends swearing as they checked themselves for injuries. Emuel was sobbing to himself and muttering prayers.

"Kelos?" Dunsany called.

And they all listened, hoping for the sound of footsteps that would tell them that the mage was safe, but Dunsany's voice echoed away into emptiness.

"Kelos?" Dunsany called again, the threat of tears now in his voice.

From out of the darkness a light bobbed towards them and Silus was reminded of the corpse lamps that haunted the swamps on the borders of Nürn, for the face that the unreal glow illuminated certainly seemed to be that of a ghast or revenant. The lined features that drifted down the tunnel were a spectral white and a groan escaped from the cracked lips of the unholy vision. An icy chill touched Silus as the ghastly creature drew near.

"Dunsany?" It said, and a pale hand reached out towards him. "Water."

Dunsany handed the pallid vision his flask and, as it poured the water over its features, the rock dust was washed away and Kelos stood before them, shaking.

Dunsany embraced him with a fierce hug.

Kelos smiled weakly and sipped from the flask. "The tunnel entrance has been sealed. I'm afraid that leaves us with only one means of escape."

"The *Llothriall*?" Dunsany said.

Kelos nodded and the crew began to prepare themselves for the voyage.

The Final Faith ship was skirting Sarcre when a thunderous boom echoed through the channels of the archipelago. Brother Philip noted that the dome of magical energy that he had observed covering one of the smaller islands had come down.

He passed the telescope to Inquisitor Mandrias and signalled for the First Mate.

"Can you ask the Captain whether he can take us closer to the island with the volcano?"

"I'll relay your instructions at once Father, though some of the channels here may be too narrow for the ship."

"I'm sure that men of your calibre will be able handle it." Brother Philip said before turning to the short, dark haired man at his side. "You think that the disturbances point to the source of our fugitives?"

"I wouldn't be surprised." Inquisitor Mandrias said. "Fitch's investigations suggested that it was towards Sarcre that Kelos was last seen heading."

The ship groaned as it leaned hard to starboard. As it cleared a jagged bluff the island came fully into view and Mandrias leaned into the side of the vessel as he strained forward with the telescope.

Even without the aid of the glass, Brother Philip could see a multitude of dark shapes swarming across the island and he thought he knew what they were. He had seen such creatures before, observed them tearing into a band of thieves at the Turnitia docks. It had been Brother Philip who had helped to secure one of those same creatures for the Faith's dungeons at Scholten.

"Chadassa?" he said.

"Yes," Inquistor Mandrias breathed. "A lot of them. But why on earth would they be going after Kelos and Dunsany?"

"It seems that they have made more enemies than just the Faith."

There was another explosion and the side of the volcano spat out a cascade of rocks.

Inquisitor Mandrias passed the telescope back to Brother Philip. "It looks like the Chadassa have them trapped. Should we call in the attack ships? We can pick off the creatures and then go after the fugitives. The *Llothriall* must be somewhere nearby. We could have this all wrapped up by evensong."

As Brother Philip considered his options there was the sound of claws on wood as something clambered up the side of the ship. Above him the rigging creaked and he saw a dark shape leap from one rope to the next. He turned as a shipmate screamed, his cry cut off by a wet gurgle as dark claws punched through his torso. The mariner's body fell as the creature behind him rose to its full height. An overpowering smell of rotting fish and sulphur washed across the ship as more Chadassa stepped onto deck, their clawed feet gouging rough channels into the wood.

Neither Brother Philip nor Inquisitor Mandrias had time to go for their swords before the creatures were upon them.

CHAPTER EIGHT

Emuel closed his eyes and opened his mouth. His lungs filled with air and then his throat contracted as he hit the note. He held the delicate pitch for almost a full minute, during which time the gem shuddered, threads of magical energy pouring from its many facets and through the channels of power woven through the *Llothriall*. At the height of the note Emuel took a short breath before segueing into the cascade of lyrical resonances that formed the first verse of the ancient elf song.

The ship shuddered in response, like a lover in the first throws of an orgasm or as one touched by the voice of the Lord of All, as Emuel had been when he first heard the call in a tiny chapel in the foothills of the Drakengrat mountains.

Even though the song he sung was that of an ancient heathen race, Emuel couldn't but help be moved by its ethereal beauty, and it was this that he offered up to his Lord; hoping that He too would see to the heart of the music and the sincerity of Emuel's soul.

Two decks above, Dunsany rejoiced in the feeling of the wheel in his hands. Too long a time had passed since he had been in control of a ship. You never forget your sea-legs, that's what he'd learned as an apprentice sailor and as the boat began to roll gently beneath him, he instinctively adjusted himself to its pitch.

Above him, the smugglers – Jacquinto and his comrades – moved through the rigging. They had taken to the ropes immediately, moving between the masts with the surety and grace of those well used to a life at sea. The sails billowed around them, the shimmering cloth moving with a supernatural silence as it caught and played the winds. As they left the shelter of the lagoon and entered the fierce seas, Dunsany worried that the smugglers would be hurled from their nests, but the *Llothriall* was calm and graceful, effortlessly cutting through the churning waves.

Silus paced the main deck, appalled at the apparent lack of concern from the rest of the crew in response to their hurried flight. He threw a worried look back at the island, urging the ship onwards, as, with a surreal calm, the *Llothriall* entered waters that hadn't seen a manned vessel for thousands of years.

Still, he constantly scanned the waves, wondering whether the Chadassa would burst from them at any moment and claim him for their own. And would he go willingly? Part of Silus thought he would, remembering how easily he had fallen under Belck's enchantment. Was this because Belck was correct and he truly was one of the Chadassa?

As they moved further away from the peninsula, Silus felt a sudden yearning for home. It was true that he had always dreamed of voyaging beyond the known seas, but now that they were actually cutting through the waves towards an alien horizon, he felt that perhaps the reason the human race had never ventured this far was because they weren't meant to.

However, it was too late for such doubts and, turning to

look back, he saw that the island where the *Llothriall* had been sheltered was rapidly becoming a speck in the distance.

Nestled in a comfortable bunk on the deck below, Father Maylan had no such worries. He had finally freed himself from the shackles of the Faith and become, in effect, a heretic. This was a role that suited him just fine. He had grown tired of kowtowing to Katherine Makennon and her cronies, sick of playing the politics of the church and as a heretic he was in good company.

His uncle Stel had been branded an apostate when the Faith had first declared its interests on Sarcre and had been burnt for his sins in the town square. Even as the flames had consumed his flesh Uncle Stel had railed and sworn against the occupying church.

Maylan had been five and was a long way from receiving the mantle 'Father'. He stood with his family, who had been forced to watch the cleansing of the unbeliever in their midst. But even though Maylan was appalled at the spectacle of his uncle's fiery death, he was still inspired by the flames of Stel's passion as he preached one last sermon. Those words, bellowed over the crackle and hiss of human flesh cooking, had never left him and when Maylan became Head Diviner of the Many Paths twelve years later, it was his uncle's lessons that had driven him on. If the Faith ever discovered his heresy he would have been proud to burn for his beliefs. But they never did and when the Eminence of the Final Faith church on Sarcre died, Maylan put himself forward for the role, claiming miraculous visions.

At first the Final Faith were wary of his claims – the apostasy in his family had not been forgotten – but, like his uncle, Dunsany was a first class performer. He claimed to have been struck down by the Lord of All as he was fishing one day and made to see the error of his ways. A great light had shone down from Kerberos and Maylan had been shown that there were not many paths to the truth, but one and one alone. Now that he had been shown the straight and narrow road to God, he was inspired to preach the way to his fellow man.

As Maylan had revealed this to the board of Archimandrites at Scholten he had even begun to speak in tongues, just for good measure.

The robed hierarchy had clearly been impressed because, after intense training, Maylan was given the title 'Father' and put in charge of the Faith's one and only church on Sarcre. Conveniently for him they then left him to his own devices. The islanders had no interest in the ways of the Faith and Father Maylan never tried to preach the dictates of the Lord of All to them. Instead he continued to be the Head Diviner of the Many Paths while paying lip service to the rituals of the Final Faith.

This island-wide conspiracy had now been in place for many years but Father Maylan had begun to tire of the charade, and after the brutality displayed by the Faith in the last conflict between Vos and Pontaine, he no longer wanted to even play along with the pretence. So, when Dunsany had offered him the chance to become a full time heretic and discover the wider world, he had taken it without hesitation.

Without him, the islanders would be able to carry on as normal, having learnt to hide their day-to-day heresies with tact and skill. When the new Eminence was installed at Sarcre they would no doubt listen to his sermons and follow the rituals, but behind the doors of their own homes, their offerings would not be to the Lord of All. It was true that there were people that Father Maylan would miss, but he would never again have to wear the robes with the crossed circle and he would never again have to give benedictions that he didn't mean, and for that he was grateful.

As the *Llothriall* began to roll he was lulled into sleep and, as he dreamed, a gentle smile lightened his features.

It was magic that gave the glow to Kelos's face. Emuel was just finishing his song as he entered the gem room and as the last notes were sung, the light pouring from the stone increased until it was almost blinding.

"Thank you Emuel, that should keep us going for quite a while. You can rest now."

Squinting against the harsh glow of raw magic, Kelos manipulated the threads that diverted the worst of the winds away from the ship and stabilised the vessel.

He exulted in the powers that he was channelling, knowing that these were the least of the ship's abilities. The possibilities unlocked by Emuel's song were something that no mage of his ability would ever have dreamed they could control. After years of intense study Kelos had only just begun to understand the smallest part of Old Race magic. The mysteries of the elves and the dwarves had remained mainly in shadow, yet here he was, controlling what surely was one of the crowning achievements of the elven empire.

This was why he had entered into a life of esoteric study in the first place, not just so he could put wards on war ships and equip fisherman with cantrips to better their hauls. Magic was supposed to be wielded in the pursuit of the extraordinary and with the *Llothriall* they were opening up Twilight's ancient legacies.

Something of Emuel's song still resonated within the gem room and as Kelos listened to its echo he felt it reaching back, harmonising with the voice of a distant and fascinating past. The secrets of the millennia old forces now at his fingertips overwhelmed him for a moment – these songs that had never before been sung by a human, these magics woven from a tapestry so rich that not even the highest mage on Twilight had the barest inkling of its complete design – and his concentration was masked, for just a moment, by his awe at the power surrounding him.

The ship lurched suddenly to starboard and Kelos was shaken from his reverie to bring the magic back under control, righting the vessel.

Then he smiled to himself, shook his head and reached out to the threads.

It was just a small lurch but on the deck above Katya groaned as she staggered down the corridor. Their flight from the Chadassa had left her feeling nauseous and weak and the knowledge that they were pursued by enemies fanatical and demonic made the impending birth of their child seem all the more overwhelming. She mounted the steps to the main deck and, as she emerged into the sunlight, Silus held out a hand to steady her.

"Come on, the fresh air will make you feel better."

"What would make me feel better is not being on this bloody ship. You know, I never imagined that our child would be born at sea."

"If it's any consolation, Father Maylan has performed the duties of a midwife before and we have enough supplies to sustain us for quite a while. I'm sure that we'll find land soon."

"Really? And what if all of the rest of this world is just one great ocean? Had you ever considered that? What if the reason that there are no records of what the original elf ships found is because there was *nothing* to find?"

As Katya raised her voice there was laughter from above her and she looked up to see Ioannis enjoying their little dispute. The look that she shot him soon had him scrabbling back up the rigging and out of sight.

Looking back at Silus, Katya's anger softened as she saw the hurt in his eyes. After all, she considered, none of this was really his fault. They had been swept up in a maelstrom of events out of their control and Katya didn't think that any of them could have done anything differently.

"I'm sorry," she said.

There was a gentle kick then and she put a hand to her belly.

"Are you alright?" Silus said.

"Yes, I just think we may have woken someone up."

Silus put his hand over Katya's.

"Feels like our child is going to be a fighter."

"Then he or she will take after the father."

Katya smiled and the infant kicked again.

CHAPTER NINE

For five days they saw nothing but rough seas; the iron green waters rising and falling around them like a range of wild and constantly changing hills. Rain lashed the sails while lightning arced down to discharge itself into the water. Through all of this the *Llothriall* remained the one calm point, the deck remaining steady beneath their feet.

The ship sighed and sang as it made its way through the maelstrom. The magic that flowed through the *Llothriall* warmed it so that the temperature on board felt always like a balmy summer afternoon. On top of the subtle incense-like scent of the warm timbers was a stronger odour, like the musk of an ancient book or bales of perfumed cloth.

Kelos had told them that each strand of magic had its own particular smell and that sometimes they combined to produce heady, otherworldly scents. Ioannis was of the opinion that these otherworldly scents were more to do with the strange weed that Father Maylan was in the habit of smoking.

On the sixth day the sea calmed a little and Dunsany postulated that they had broken through the Storm Wall, the first vessel manned by humans ever to have done so.

That evening they celebrated and Ioannis introduced them all to a variety of sea shanties that Katya was grateful her child was not yet born to hear. The drinking would have continued well beyond the point where the majority of them were comfortably drunk, had not Dunsany pointed out that they probably didn't want to exhaust their supplies this early into the voyage.

And so, the crew offered their goodnights. The only one not to do so was Emuel, who had retired long before.

In their cabin Silus admired Katya as she slept, impressed that she had managed to hold court with as much élan as the drunken men who surrounded her. He kissed her as she sighed in her sleep, she didn't need drink to be witty or to be persuaded into song. Silus watched her for a moment more before leaving the cabin.

On the main deck the wheel held steady, set to a course that Dunsany and Kelos had decided between them. The boards of the deck steamed slightly as the recent rains dried and Silus enjoyed the touch of this gentle mist as he lay down.

Kerberos seemed to hang lower and larger in the sky than usual and he wondered whether the seas they were traversing would prove to be a path to the seat of the ancestors. (Father Maylan had told him that all paths lead to Kerberos, but Silus didn't fully understand what he meant). Taking a telescope from a pocket he trained it on the azure orb and watched the play of clouds that covered its surface. He wondered how many times he had sent entreaties into those impenetrable vapours. How many times had he asked a blessing of the ancestors who resided there, or cursed the unknowable sphere for some imagined bad luck or malady?

Silus put the telescope down and closed his eyes. Below him, the deck pitched gently and, for the first time during the voyage, he felt calm, though always there was the fear that the Chadassa would find them.

The susurrus of the sea and the touch of a gentle wind conspired with the alcohol in his blood to take him into sleep, and he gave up consciousness gladly.

He was falling towards an endless sea of clouds. On the horizon the first rays of a rising run sent shards of light across the slowly evolving landscape below. Flickering tongues of lightning erupted from hills of vapour, heavy with the threat of thunder while clouds parted to open up on great amethyst pools, their depths endless and hungry.

Far above him hung a blue-green sphere and he knew that it was from there that he had fallen.

He drifted down into the purple sea and the clouds parted only briefly to mark his passage.

He had no way of measuring the speed of his descent. On all sides he was surrounded by slowly rolling thunderheads, skeins of mist and great valleys and peaks that constantly shifted and changed.

A shadow passed him and he saw that there were other travellers in the storm.

He noted the look of serenity on the faces of those that fell past, arms outstretched, before they faded from view. Others rode the columns of cloud that boiled up from the depths below. He recognised one man, rocketing towards him, as Pandrick, the owner of The Necromancer's Barge. Windmilling his arms, he managed to get out of the way before Pandrick collided with him. He shouted a greeting to the publican, but any response that he may have called was eaten by the howling winds.

He only had a moment to consider what lay below him, on the other side of the clouds, before he was through and he saw for himself.

Silus was thrown out of sleep, across the deck and into the side of a locker as the *Llothriall* came to a sudden halt.

He struggled to regain his breath as, with a clatter of footsteps, the crew rushed up from below.

"I though that you said nothing could stop this ship." Jacquinto shouted.

"Yes, well I wasn't counting on running into the tip of a bloody great spire out on the open seas now was I?" Dunsany snapped.

Nursing the large bruise that was beginning to blossom on the small of his back, Silus got to his feet and joined them at the prow of the ship.

There, rising above the masts, was a tapering column of stone. Looking over the side of the ship Silus could see a ragged hole where they had collided with it.

"Bail! Now!" He shouted, starting to move. But Kelos put a hand out to stop him.

"No Silus. The *Llothriall* will provide for herself. Look."

Silus followed the direction of Kelos's pointed finger and saw a membrane forming over the hole. With a wet *pop* it quickly closed up, re-sealing the ship.

"In time she'll even grow a new skin of wood. Now, what do we have here?" Kelos said, the excitement of discovery evident in his voice.

Silus began to relax as he realised that they weren't about to sink and he took in the strange vista before them.

The structure that they had run into was just one of a ring of six towers, rising from the waves. Gulls called to each other as they swooped around the delicate spires or nested in niches in the columns of brightly marbled stone. None of the towers rose any taller than the one which had stopped the *Llothriall*, though several were grander in design. Intricate carvings had been wrought into three of them. From where Silus stood it was difficult to make out many details, but on one he thought that he could see the design of a figure riding a whale, surrounded by smaller creatures that may have been mermaids.

"Gods, what is it?" Katya said, joining them.

Silus slipped a hand into hers and with the other he shielded his eyes against the glare of the sun.

"It looks like the towers of a cathedral or castle." He said. "But who would have built such a thing out here?"

"Not the Chadassa?" Katya said, her grip on Silus's hand tightening.

"I don't think so," Dunsany said. "If it was I'd expect them to be swarming all over us by now."

There were starting to drift away from the towers and Dunsany signalled to Jacquinto to secure the ship. He scurried up the foremast with a rope, Ignacio in his wake, while Ioannis shouted guidance from below. With a dexterity and grace that Silus would not have expected of such weathered brutes they managed to loop the rope over the stone column before pulling the ship in close.

"Well I told you that we'd discover something soon enough didn't I?" Kelos said. "Ah, Emuel, you're awake. What do you make of this?"

The ship's eunuch emerged from below deck, looking so pale that he positively glowed, the tattoos that marked his face and hands standing out starkly against his flesh. He looked at the circle of gull-covered stone, his hands idly toying with the hem of his robe.

"The towers of a cathedral perhaps?" He said.

"Which means that there must be more to see below." Dunsany said.

"Emuel are you okay?" Katya said, noticing the perspiration that beaded the eunuch's forehead.

"Oh, don't worry about him," Ignacio said. "He always looks like that. He'll be pining for the Faith."

"I... I had an unpleasant dream. I'll be okay."

Katya put a hand to Emuel's forehead. The flesh there was hot and clammy.

"You're not well. Come on, let's get you some rest." She led Emuel below.

"Good idea," Dunsany called after them. "Make sure that the poor chap is comfortable and we'll explore that which lies below. By the way, does anybody know where Maylan is?"

"Still lost in the clutches of the weed," Ioannis said. "Not even running aground managed to rouse him."

"Then would you mind trying to wake him? He won't want to miss this."

Ioannis nodded and followed Katya and Emuel below.

"Dunsany, how are you proposing that we explore underwater?" Silus said. "We don't know how far down these towers reach and we're not going to be able to hold our breath for long enough to make anything out."

"As the *Llothriall* was being built there were several alchemists and mages working on a sort of suit that allows for underwater exploration." Dunsany said.

"And have these 'sort of suits' been tested?" said Jacquinto.

"Well, actually no." Kelos said. "Because Dunsany and I stole the ship before they could get that far. But we have eight of the suits below and there's very little doubt in my mind that they will work."

"To be honest I'd prefer no doubt to very little, but I suppose we should see for these things for ourselves." Silus said.

They descended to the lowest deck and were joined there, in a low square room, by a bleary-eyed Father Maylan and a fresher looking Ioannis.

"Ioannis tells me that there's something to see out there." Maylan said.

"We have run into a tower," Kelos said.

"Right, I'll give you a hand readying the boats."

"No need. We have everything we require here."

Kelos slid back a wall panel to reveal a row of eight identical suits.

A domed hood with large ovals of glass set into thick material sat on top of a baggy one-piece garment made of what appeared to be heavily waxed cloth.

"Those things are far too big." Silus said. "How do you expect us to move around in them down there?"

"Each of these suits will fit the wearer perfectly. Perhaps you would help me demonstrate?"

Silus struggled to get his arms and legs into the rumpled suit and, when he did, the material sagged around him in folds and crinkles.

Jacquinto laughed. "Could it be that the elves were considerably fatter than the legends state?"

"These suits weren't taken from elven design," Kelos said. "Believe it or not they were actually put together by the Final Faith themselves. Anyway, as I said, the suit will fit the wearer perfectly. Note the disk of metal on the chest? Watch."

Kelos took an identical disk from a drawer and touched it to the one attached to the suit. Instantly the material came to life, contracting around Silus until it fit him like a second skin.

"It's water tight and also protects against the cold. Now, the hood attaches like so."

Kelos placed the hood on Silus's head and it sealed itself to the suit with a sound like an indrawn breath. Silus stared out of the eyepieces, the glass throwing everything into perfect definition.

"Right, and how are we supposed to breathe down there?" He said. "There's a hole where my mouth is but I presume that you're not expecting us to inhale water?"

"Ah, now this is the really ingenious part. The secret is worms."

"Worms?" Father Maylan said. "He's going to breathe worms? Tell you what, I think I'm going to go back to my bunk. Let me know how you got on with that worm breathing thing on your return."

"No, of course he's not going to breathe worms. The worms are going to provide the air. Look."

Kelos opened a compartment and took out a gourd-like object. He unscrewed the bottom half to show an empty base. Opening another compartment he took out a box, which contained a writhing mass of midnight blue worms.

"These creatures were first discovered in the World's Ridge Mountains. When fed a certain mineral they will actually fart out, if you'll pardon the expression, air. So, we're going to need a couple of scoops of you fellows." He spooned the worms into the base of the gourd, "and then we sprinkle two measures of the mineral powder over the top." From a vial, Kelos poured a dark powder onto the worms before sealing up the two halves of the gourd. "Then we just give it a quick shake to get the process going."

"That reminds me of a cocktail I once had at Here There Be Flagons," Dunsany said. "It actually made me go blind for half a day."

Kelos screwed the narrow end of the gourd to the mouthpiece of the hood.

"Now Silus," he said, raising his voice, "you should be able to breathe. Give me a thumbs up if all is okay."

Silus felt a moment of claustrophobia as he heard Kelos's muffled voice through the thick hood. There was a strange taste in his mouth that reminded him of rock dust and honey but when he took a breath, the air was cool and pure.

He raised his thumbs and nodded.

"Excellent." Dunsany said. "Right, I suggest the rest of you get suited up and then we can have a look at what's out there."

CHAPTER TEN

They descended roped together, each carrying a glowing stone to light their way. When they entered the circle of towers Silus looked down and tried to see through the gloom below them, but whatever awaited them there was hidden for now.

Behind Silus trailed the three smugglers, followed by Father Maylan. Watching them climb into the strange suits had been a comical affair. As Jacquinto had pulled the suit over his legs he had leaned on Ignacio, knocking his brother into the renegade priest. Maylan had then stumbled into Ioannis and the two of them had tumbled to the floor. Katya had come to see the men before they ventured forth and, despite her tiredness and the worry that lined her face, she managed a chuckle at the sight of them in their various states of disarray, looking like some strange new race of sea creature in their bizarre garb.

"Any sign of danger, any sign of the Chadassa, I want you out of there," she said.

"Of course," Dunsany replied. "Don't worry, we'll be perfectly alright."

Katya had then touched her forehead to the hood of Silus's suit, mouthing *I love you*, before watching him follow the crew through the portal in the side of the ship and out into the sea.

The sudden cold that Silus had expected on entering the water didn't come. Instead there was just the warm embrace of the suit as he swam away from the *Llothriall*, his breath echoing hollowly and the beat of his pulse amplified by the confines of the hood.

Silus followed Kelos and Dunsany, the glow of the stone in the mage's right hand bobbing ahead of him like a will-o'-the wisp. Fish and other marine creatures swam in close, attracted by the illumination; some responding with their own bursts of light, briefly defining strange piscine forms in the darkness.

As the crew were rounding the curve of one of the towers they were suddenly confronted by the reflection of their glowstones in the pupils of an enormous fish. It opened its mouth and inflated to twice its original size, its gullet a dark tunnel lined with barbs. Pseudopods extended from the brow of the creature to paw the water around Kelos, one exploring the hood of his suit. Silus hoped that the probing tentacle wouldn't puncture the material, but the creature clearly didn't regard Kelos as prey as, after a moment's exploration, it swam away.

Kelos made sure that it was out of sight before giving the hand signal to proceed.

They followed the towers down and soon the surface was lost to view. Silus wondered how far below them lay whatever supported these mighty columns, or whether there were just the towers themselves, leading to unfathomable sunless depths.

He was beginning to think that this was indeed the case when the glow from their lightstones finally revealed dark shapes beneath them.

The towers rose from a vast mound of rock, its sides dropping precipitously away. There was no hint of design or purpose to the mound and the only thing to show that hands other than nature's had shaped the stone were the magnificent pillars rising from it.

Silus was beginning to wonder how they were going to find a way in when he saw what he took to be a window in the side of one of the towers. Signalling to the others to follow he swam in close, but could make out only his reflection and nothing of whatever lay inside. He put out a hand and tried to clear the glass, but instead of coming up against a solid surface it passed straight through. Silus cautiously flexed his fingers, but could feel nothing on the other side. He withdrew his hand and looked at it, but it didn't appear to be any different.

The others had now clustered around him and, giving them a nod, he held out his lightstone and thrust himself into the side of the structure.

Silus's stomach turned over as he dropped, but it was only a short distance to the floor and he did little more than bruise his knees. His hands left wet prints in the thick dust covering the floor as he raised himself to his feet and looked over his shoulder. The others floated there beyond the window and he was about to give them the signal to proceed, when he realised that they couldn't see him. So, instead, he gave a tug on the rope that let them know that it was safe to enter.

All seven of them took a moment to look around after they stepped inside, their breathing and the drip of seawater from their suits the only sound in the musty chamber. Father Maylan crouched over something in the corner of the room and removed his hood in order to get a better look.

"Did you even stop to think that the air in here might not be breathable?" Kelos shouted, after removing his own hood.

"It's perfectly breathable, look." Father Maylan said, and demonstrated by taking a deep breath. "I wonder what manner of creature this is?" He said, indicating the skeleton before him.

The skeleton was propped against a wall. The skull that sagged against the chest was larger than that of a human and had an oval hole for a mouth instead of a hinged jaw. Behind the broken ribs the spine was a single piece of bone that tapered down to just above the ankles. The legs were much like those of a human, though there were only three toes on each foot, while the creature's arms were – like the spine – each a single piece of tapered bone.

Silus saw an object lying near the body and picked it up. From a metal handle emerged eight thick strands of a material that looked not unlike squid flesh.

"I'd be careful with that if I were you," Dunsany said. "It may be a weapon and you don't know how what it does."

As Silus looked at it more closely, he tightened his grip on the handle and the strands came to life, swaying like the fronds of a sea anemone caught in a gentle underwater current. When they began to twine around each other and crackle with small tongues of lightning he dropped the strange flail and stepped away.

"Whatever this creature was, it clearly went down fighting." Dunsany said.

"Fighting what though?" Silus said.

Apart from the creature's corpse and the strange weapon, the chamber was empty.

Kelos took a moment to untie each of them from the rope that joined them together, before they ventured through an archway in the far wall.

As they exited the room they were hit by a strong blast of wind, whistling down the tower from above. On it Silus thought that he could just make out the call of gulls.

"These towers must act as ventilation shafts." Kelos said.

"If they needed air to survive," Jacquinto said, "what did they go and build this place underwater for?"

"Most aquatic mammals need air. Consider dolphins, for example."

"What, dolphins built this place?"

"I believe that Kelos was only using dolphins as an example," Silus said. "The architects who designed and built these towers were clearly far more complex creatures."

The wind at their backs dropped briefly and, in the lull, Silus thought that he could detect a bitter odour rising from below. It reminded him of the smell of a cold range in the morning, the phantom of smoke that wafted from the grate as the ashes were shovelled out.

Ahead of him Dunsany stumbled as he tripped over a broken step and Silus saw that the stone there was cracked and charred.

Streaks of soot began to mark the walls as they continued cautiously down, the stone in places bulging and glassy as though a fierce heat had once attacked the tower. When they reached the base of the tower the walls were almost entirely black and they had to hug the outer curve of the spiral to negotiate the last few shattered steps.

"Gods, it's a bloody charnel house!" Silus heard Dunsany gasp.

When he reached the bottom, Silus saw for himself what had so taken his crew-mate aback. Behind him there were similar exclamations as the rest of the crew joined them.

They stood at the entrance to a massive circular room, the floor of which had been gouged by deep, blackened rents. Above them the ceiling shimmered and through it they could see the six towers rising to the surface far above. Fragments of scorched bone and broken skulls were scattered across the floor, but it was not these that had evoked Dunsany's exclamation. There were three entrances into the chamber, besides the one through which they had entered, and each one was piled high with bones.

The smell of burned bone intensified as Silus approached one of the arches. The skeletons piled there – like a jumble of blackened twigs – had been fused together by the fire that had consumed the flesh that had once clothed them. Silus reached out to touch the edge of a leg bone and the whole pile shifted suddenly as it crumbled, a small avalanche of dry remains tumbling into the room.

"What in the name of Kerberos happened here?" Father Maylan said.

"A massacre." Silus said.

"Perfect! So, we discover a new race, only to find that it has already been killed off?" Kelos said. "Who'd want to be an adventurer?"

"It beats languishing in a Vos prison," Jacquinto said. "Trust me."

Beyond the archway, Silus could see through to where a flight of stairs descended.

"We could clear a way through this," he said. "Maybe we'll find some clues as to what happened here."

He unsheathed his knife and started to cut a path through the brittle skeletons. It wasn't a particularly difficult task as the majority of the bones crumbled as soon as he touched them. Black flakes rained down on him as the pile shifted and creaked. He paused for a moment but the mound of the dead held and he continued to tunnel towards the stairs.

The crew looked at each other, then at Silus sawing away, and – after only a brief hesitation – followed him through the charnel mound.

The quantity of bodies didn't lessen any as Silus approached the top of the stairs. The glow of his lightstone revealed yet more skeletons crowded into the scorched tunnel sloping away from them. Some were wrapped around their companions, as though the creatures had been seeking solace in their final moments. Others, towards the top of the pile, had arms outstretched and heads thrown back. Silus imagined them scrabbling across a pile of their already dead brethren, only for them to be annihilated by a roaring wall of flame.

"Do we really want to find out what did this?" Dunsany said from behind him. "I mean, I've seen the old battle fields in the Anclas territories but this... gods, it's just..." His voice caught for a moment and a sob escaped his lips. "Horrible."

Kelos put a hand on his friend's shoulder and Dunsany covered it with his own.

"I think that whoever did this is long gone," Silus said. "There's no more threat here. Just a tomb."

"It could be haunted." Ignacio said, from further behind him. "Places like this are always haunted."

"No, I feel nothing." Father Maylan said. "This place is just... dead."

Descending the stairs took them longer than Silus had anticipated. The bodies were packed in more tightly around them here and it was hard to see where each step fell. Twice Silus had to tell the group to back off so that he could work out the best route through.

As he was pulling bones away from the wall of the tunnel he heard a sound like a whisper and looked up.

A skeleton hung spread-eagled above him, its empty eyes seeming to observe him with contempt. Silus thought that he could see a glint of something deep within one of the sockets. The glint resolved itself into a more definite form, as a spider crawled from the hollow and skittered across a cracked cheekbone. With a dry rattle, the skull shifted slightly to the side, almost as though the dead creature were cocking its head at him.

Then, with a sound like the breaking of a thousand dry branches, the walls of bone shifted.

Silus ducked as a cloud of desiccated remains erupted around him, the vicious dust scouring his throat and making it difficult to breathe.

"Get back!" He shouted. "It's coming down!"

But Silus didn't have a chance to see whether his friends fled to safety, as he was swept away on a wave of bone.

The clattering avalanche that enveloped him sounded like the chattering voices of the dead. Wicked shards scratched his face and the lightstone was knocked out of his hand as he tumbled head over heels. And then, there was nothing below or above him as he fell into empty space, only to land with a thud that punched the air from his lungs.

From somewhere nearby there was the thud and crunch of living bodies impacting with long dead ones, as Silus's companions tumbled after him. He scrabbled his way to the surface and, looking around, he could see where some of their lightstones had fallen. Silus crawled his way to one of them and, raising it, he could just make out his friends, struggling to their feet.

"Well, I suppose that was the quickest way down." Father Maylan said, wading towards Silus. "Gentlemen, shout if you're amongst the living."

All answered and soon they had picked themselves up and were peering into the darkness that surrounded them.

This room felt bigger than the one from which they had descended and, as their eyes adjusted, they began to make out rows of columns rising to a roof far above them. The glow of their lightstones was thrown back by their smooth, reflective surfaces and Silus realised that the columns were made of glass.

Within them, cloudy liquid moved sluggishly.

"What does this do, do you reckon?" Ioannis said, and before they could stop him he had turned the wheel he'd found attached to one of the columns.

A massive *thunk* echoed through the room and a rain of dust sifted down from above. Then, with a rumbling hum that rattled the bones on which they stood, the liquid starting rushing through the vast columns, gradually clearing as the cloud of particles that muddied them were sucked up through the ceiling. A soft glow began to infuse the room then, starting at the base of each column and working its way up as thousands upon thousands of tiny, glowing creatures were pumped through the mighty glass cylinders. Silus moved his face closer to one of the columns and could see that each creature was no larger than a mayfly, composed of a glowing, rapidly beating heart surrounding by hundreds of cilia.

"Gods, this place is huge!" Dunsany said, and Silus turned to see that the light had banished the shadows, revealing the full extent of the room.

As he looked around him there was a sudden, searingly painful flash of insight and Silus knew the nature of the death that had come to consume this underwater citadel.

Silus was amongst them as they stormed through the tunnels, threading their way through the under-levels of the citadel. In their hands they held staffs with glowing ruby gems set in their tips, the burning hearts of the stones pulsing with the fire barely contained by their facets. Ahead of them Silus could hear the first wave of their brethren laying waste to the outer defences and they soon piled into their rear of that skirmish, burning or slashing any of the mongrel creatures that made it past their brothers. The yards of tunnels they passed through were soon decorated with the bodies of their enemies; some burnt to a crisp, others gored beyond recognition.

They flooded into the great hall and the wave of their attack washed over the creatures milling there in panic, some with their young hugged to their chests as they made to flee to the upper levels. But they were soon overtaken and added to the pile of their dead, already several layers deep. Some fought back and some took down their assailants, but the sheer number of their attackers prevailed in the end.

And Silus stood amongst the growing mounds of the dead, covered in blood, the battle cries rising around him like some hideous chorus. The creatures that poured from the mouths of the tunnels fought with a joyous ferocity, never once pausing between kills. Even in the black pits of their eyes, Silus could see the terrible lust that possessed them, and he felt some of that same hunger himself.

Looking down Silus flexed his claws. They had yet to be baptised in the blood of his enemies but that would soon change.

For Silus did know the nature of the death that had come to the citadel of the Calma, because he was, himself, part of that terrible horde.

With a guttural, animal cry he launched himself at the creature cowering before him and knew his own name.

Chadassa!

CHAPTER ELEVEN

Querilous Fitch hated the way this place smelled. No matter how thoroughly they cleaned the chamber, the stench of burning heretics still clung to the walls. For a while they had tried adding aromatic oils to the naphtha used to incinerate the accused, but all that had done was add a cloying perfume to the odour of cooking human flesh. Still, Querilous considered that one wasn't supposed to enjoy the atmosphere here. The suffering of a soul being purged should not be pleasing, no matter how much it gladdened the heart to see a heretic dispatched to the judgement of the Lord of All.

A door opened in the far wall and Brother Sequilious – the Final Faith's head sorcerer – entered, followed by Katherine Makennon. Sequilious acknowledged Querilous with a nod as Makennon held out her hand to be reverently kissed. The Anointed Lord was not surrounded by her usual entourage of acolytes and personal assistants this evening, as the business that they were to conduct here was not to be common knowledge amongst the faithful. The use of Old Race sorcery wasn't forbidden as such, but the magic that Sequilious was about to weave within this soot-stained room would be considered heretical in some quarters. This was why Makennon had to be in attendance, to absolve the sorcerer of the sins he was about to commit.

Brother Sequilious entered the circle of cages in the middle of the room and stood at the centre of the black spiral painted on the floor. Each soot stained cage mimicked the basic form of a human and stood at just over seven feet tall. In several places carbonised flesh still clung to the bars. A pipe rose from the top of each cage, juddering and steaming where it entered the ceiling, filling the room with a muggy warmth from the heat of the naphtha that flowed within.

As Sequilious closed his eyes, Makennon took a small silver sprinkler from her robes and anointed the sorcerer with holy oil while chanting the rites of absolution. After the ceremony was complete Sequilious bowed to Makennon and she exited the circle. When he looked up at Querilous there was a cruel glint in Sequilious's eyes, as he indicated to him to bring in the heretics.

The seven men that were led into the room by Querilous's assistants had been discovered on Sarcre. They were members of the cult of Many Paths, a heathen religion that Querilous had thought long since purged from the archipelago. It seemed, however, that the cult was very much a part of island life. In the light of this Querilous had suggested that a detachment of the Order of the Swords of Dawn be sent to Sarcre on a purification mission as soon as possible. The islands may be of little military or commercial interest to the Faith, but that was no reason why they should be allowed to lapse into the old heathen ways.

The heretics were in various states of distress. The youngest had fought against his bonds and screamed so much in his cell that Querilous had had to administer a strong sedative, and now the man drooped against the bars of his execution cage, a thin line of drool swaying from his stupidly grinning lips. Several of the other heretics were praying loudly to their ancestors, others were singing and one man stared at Sequilious with such intense hatred that the sorcerer was forced to look away. Final

Faith protocol required that each prisoner be read a list of the charges brought against them and offered the chance to confess before the purging began, but Querilous didn't deem it necessary in these unusual circumstances. Besides, he considered, it was unlikely that these souls would be winging their way to the clouds of Kerberos once the spell was completed.

"Before we start," said Katherine Makennon, "are you sure that this will render the eunuch useless?"

"Indeed, your Eminence," Querilous said. "Once the magic has been woven, the crew of the *Llothriall* won't be going anywhere."

"Excellent, do please proceed."

Querilous went to stand behind a steel screen set into the floor a short distance from the cages. It rose to a height of just over six feet and there was a reinforced glass viewing port set into it at head height. Behind the screen an array of levers extended from the floor and Querilous pulled one of these towards him.

There was a thunderous *clank* from somewhere in the ceiling, and then only the loudest of the prisoners' cries could drown out the sound of the naphtha rushing through the pipes.

The heat in the room intensified and Querilous looked through the viewing port to see Sequilious making the passes and muttering the incantations that marked the beginning of the spell.

As Sequilious sketched a dwarven rune in the air with his left hand and the black spiral upon which he stood began to glow with a maroon light, Querilous pulled on another lever.

The pipes were silent then for the briefest of moments and the only sounds in the chamber were the muttering of the sorcerer and the cries of the heretics, before the valve at the top of each cage squealed open and naphtha rained down.

As flesh began to sizzle under the onslaught of burning oil and the screams of the condemned men rose to an almost girlish pitch, Querilous pulled another lever and the fans set into the walls began to suck the human smoke from the room. It would rise through the many levels of Scholten cathedral to pour from the great chimneys that extended high above the church. Pilgrims making their way to prayer would pause and think that this smoke was from the incense of Makennon's devotions, and give thanks that they had witnessed the smallest part of such a holy rite.

The naphtha did its job quickly and the heretics were soon silent. However, their part in the ritual was far from over. Querilous began to manipulate the levers and the cages in which the heretics burned began to revolve around Brother Sequilious. The flames reached high as the cages spun faster and faster, adding their light to the glow of the magic that suffused the sorcerer. Sequilious threw up his arms and his pupils were suddenly full of the azure light of Kerberos. Threads of dark energy began to extend towards him from the circle of flame and, as they touched him, a strange cry filled the room, like the whimpering of whipped dogs. A dark aura began to weave itself around Sequilious and he was soon lost in the folds of a strange black caul.

Querilous pulled another lever and the spinning cages came to a sudden stop, the blackened bones within rattling against the bars.

The black aura surrounding the sorcerer began to grow until there was a dark column reaching to the ceiling. As it towered above Querilous it seemed to lean forward and he was suddenly fearful that it would fall on and consume him. But then a shudder passed through the column as the air in the room was sucked toward it with a great rushing of wind.

Above the keening of the maelstrom Querilous could hear the beating of his own heart and, as he struggled to breathe, he prayed to the Lord of All that the spell would soon be over. Through the blur of tears, he saw the dark column give a great shudder before it exploded outwards, bringing with it the smell of burning stone and cherry blossoms.

Querilous would have expected Sequilious to be flattened by the force of the magic he had just woven, but he stood in the last flickers of the dissipating energy, untouched. Brushing down his robes he stepped from the circle and bowed before Makennon.

"Anointed One, it is finished."

"Are you sure that it has been effective?"

"Oh yes. Somewhere on the Twilight seas Emuel will be in a great deal of pain."

Emuel cried out as Katya applied the wet cloth to his forehead. The ship's eunuch had collapsed shortly after the rest of the crew had departed, convulsing as he frothed at the mouth, his eyes rolling so far back in his head that only the whites showed. Katya had managed to bring him out of the seizure gradually, but now he was burning up and the skin that showed in the gaps between his tattoos was deathly white.

After putting him in his bunk Katya had thrown open the porthole, hoping that the fresh sea air would help cool him down. But now it seemed that all she could do was wait for him to ride out the fever.

Emuel arched his back until only the back of his head and heels were in contact with the bunk. Katya held his hand as the eunuch screamed, but he didn't return her grip, conscious as he was of nothing but the pain that wracked his body. She began to undress him, hoping that, out of his clothes, Emuel would be a little cooler and more comfortable.

As she unbuttoned his shirt, the extent of his tattoos became clearer. Katya had been aware that the cryptic patterns and swirls of elvish script covered most of Emuel's body but, up to now, she hadn't realised to what extent.

Katya removed his shirt and gasped at the sight of the living script that ran over the arches of his shoulders to cascade down his chest. Every time she thought that she had picked out a recognisable shape in the dark morass it would shift and warp, flowing into the indecipherable calligraphy that surrounded it.

Katya felt dizzy just looking at Emuel's illustrated flesh but it wasn't this that most disturbed her, it was the sound that the tattoos made.

It was so low that she had to still her breathing to even attempt to make it out. When she did, however, the soft murmur would disappear, and it was only when Katya shook her head and told herself that she had been imagining things that it would return;

sounding like someone talking low, yet urgently, in the next room.

No wonder Emuel looked to be constantly on the verge of panic, Katya considered. He had to cope with this maddening background chatter every day.

Katya dropped Emuel's shirt on the floor and began to remove his breeches. She stopped after she had tugged them halfway down, unable to take her eyes off the ridges of scar tissue that covered the wounds of his emasculation.

"Oh Gods Emuel, I'm so sorry."

The wounds had healed but the flesh there still looked red raw. Katya wondered at what manner of boy Emuel had been, to trust so much in his faith and the church that he had let them do this to him.

Katya closed her eyes and sent up a prayer to the ancestors, calling on them to send their blessings and guide the eunuch through the ravages of this vicious fever.

When she opened her eyes there was a strange glow emanating from the tattoo on Emuel's chest. The black spiral that was inked there glowed a deep maroon and she could feel an intense heat rising from it.

Emuel tried to scream but only a desperate keening hiss escaped his mouth. He looked at Katya then with eyes full of frightened panic as his flesh began to burn.

After Silus had collapsed, Dunsany and Jacquinto had carried him back to the room in the tower through which they had entered the citadel. Silus had raved about the Chadassa until a few slaps from Jacquinto had roused him from his waking nightmare. Silus had got unsteadily to his feet and Kelos had suggested that they return to the *Llothriall*. Silus had feared something rising from the depths to overtake them as they ascended to the ship – some spectre of the death that had befallen the citadel – but they made it back on board without further incident.

Their sense of relief, however, was soon shattered by the sounds of Emuel's pain.

Kelos was the first to the eunuch's cabin, with Silus close behind, rushing to the side of his wife as she tried to comfort Emuel. There was a smell like cooking meat as they entered the room and Silus noticed thin skeins of smoke drifting through the shaft of light pouring in through the porthole.

As Kelos went to the eunuch the boy fell back onto his bunk and was silent. The mage felt for a pulse on his wrist and then looked more closely at the maze of tattoos that covered his torso.

In the centre of Emuel's chest, where there had previously been inked a black spiral, there was now a patch of burned flesh.

"We're in trouble." Kelos said.

"Trouble how?" Dunsany said, entering the room. Behind him the three smugglers and Father Maylan crowded into the doorway.

"The script is broken. Emuel won't be able to sing to the gem anymore. Therefore, we're stuck; with no way to negotiate these stormy seas, no magical defences and no invisibility shield."

"If it helps, I know how to do tattoos." Jacquinto said. "In fact, I did all of Ignacio's myself. All I need is a needle, a candle and some ink."

"And you know how magical tattoos work do you?" Kelos snapped. "Familiar with the elven runes of power are we?"

"I was just trying to help!"

"Well you're not!" Kelos's voice rose to a shriek and Emuel woke up again and began adding his own cries to the cacophony.

Kelos barged his way out of the room only to barge his way back in several seconds later. Muttering a few words he broke what looked like a silver bird egg over the eunuch's brow, sending him into an instant, deep sleep.

"He'll be out for several hours and he won't be in any pain."

"Who did this?" Katya said.

"I've been stupid." Kelos said. "Very, very stupid. I should have realised that the symbol on Emuel's chest was not a part of the script that covers his body. It must have been inked there to ensure that if the eunuch ever fell into the wrong hands – for example, ours – then the Faith would be able to render him useless through the use of remote magic."

"So, how can we fix him?" Dunsany said.

"I'm afraid we can't. It looks like the voyage is over."

CHAPTER TWELVE

Findol snapped out of his reverie and raced for the stairs.

Behind him the five other Chadassa that had made up their circle began to wake, the sharp ozone tang of their meditation fading as they came to full consciousness.

In the library Belck was transcribing a set of symbols from ancient metal tablets. He didn't look up as Findol rushed into the room. Instead, he held up one finger as the Chadassa youngling made to speak, forestalling the news that he was clearly so desperate to relate.

Once he had completed the final symbol Belck looked up from his work.

"My lord. The humans' vessel has been sighted."

"Where?"

"Moored above Fandor, my Lord."

"The Calma citadel? That one was sacked before your time, I believe. It was a most joyous battle. Remind me to relate it to you one day. For now, I think that a visit to the ruroth pens is in order."

The Chadassa ancient rose to his feet with the aid of his staff, waving away Findol's attempts to help. As Belck straightened a tight band of fire seemed to encircle his waist and he waited for the pain to pass as he regained his breath. He knew what it meant, of course. He only hoped that he would live long enough to see his God's will done and the Land Walkers striding victorious over the human realm.

Belck let Findol lead the way to the enclosures. As they neared the creatures' pens the rumblings of the ruroth thundered down the tunnels towards them. Occasionally there would be a plaintive, keening cry as the creatures called to one another, but these were quickly silenced only to be replaced – seconds later – with screeches of pain.

Belck and Findol entered an enormous circular chamber ringed by the portals that led to the leviathans' pens. These shimmered as the handlers moved through them, providing the diffuse light that danced about the room.

Belck was pleased to discover that Throot – the Chief Handler – had already picked up on the news of the sighting of the humans' ship and had begun to prepare one of the deep water juggernauts.

As Throot and Belck talked, a handler burst through one of the portals and fell at Belck's feet, his blood misting the water around him. Throot quickly dragged the battered Chadassa to his feet, only to throw him down again before the ancient one.

"Apologise for your interruption!" Throot barked.

The handler managed to mime apology, before expiring.

"I can assure you, Throot, that that wasn't necessary." Belck said. "However, it does show that the creature is in a most agitated state. This is good. I presume that it knows not to harm Silus or his woman?"

"Indeed, my Lord. They will be taken unharmed."

"Excellent, perhaps we can see the ruroth?"

"Of course, follow me."

Together with the Chief Handler, Belck stepped through one of the portals.

They stood at the bottom of a deep shaft, far above them a pin prick of sunlight filtered through the surface. In front of them, held in its stone pen by the will of the Chadassa that moved slowly across its hide, lay the vast form of a ruroth.

Long before the Chadassa, the ruroth had been the rulers of the sea. Though they were not as populous as some of the other marine animals, their size meant that they had very few predators. The creatures had once been peaceful grazers, who spent most of their time trawling the seabed, but the Chadassa had turned them into weapons.

Despite their gargantuan size, the ruroth possessed an almost child-like intelligence and, because of this, the Chadassa had found it easy enough – through psychic manipulation – to bring their aggression to the fore.

The result was a devastating weapon that could break through the strongest of enemy defences.

Belck swam up to one of the great eyes that peered from the creature's head. Looking at the dark pupil, he saw beyond his reflection to where the leviathan's rage boiled. He basked in the heat of its anger.

The handlers swam away from the leviathan after removing its restraints, but Belck remained where he was. The calls of the other ruroth around him stopped then and a tense stillness pervaded the corral. Belck could see the creature's pulse increase as a great vein throbbed in its temple.

And then, it raised its head and let loose a long, ululating cry. Around it, its brethren responded with their own calls and the leviathan rose quickly to the surface far above, buoyed by the song of its kin.

Belck was caught up in its wake and he rode the current until the ruroth was lost from sight, marvelling all the while in its raw animal power and the fact that such a thing was in their control.

CHAPTER THIRTEEN

Emuel's fever finally broke, but without his song to empower it the magic of the gem waned and the stormy waters began to take hold of the *Llothriall*.

Dunsany rushed to the main deck to cut the rope that still moored them to the tower, fearing that a sudden wave could dash them against the stone. Once he slashed the tether the ship drifted into the centre of the ring of towers and Dunsany watched as the jagged stone peaks swayed threateningly around them. But then the *Llothriall* was beyond the towers and caught up by a current that bore it quickly away.

Dunsany staggered below before he was thrown from the deck by the next strong surge.

In the galley Maylan was throwing up as he tried to steady himself against a wall. When he looked up Dunsany could see that his features were ashen.

"Gods Dunsany, what are we going to do?" The priest managed to say, before another spasm gripped him and his shoulders heaved.

"I don't know. Where are the others?"

"Emuel is still in his bunk, but the rest of them are in the day room."

As Dunsany made his way up the corridor the ship gave a sudden lurch and there was the sound of plates smashing in the galley, followed by Maylan's cries of pain and then retching as his sea-sickness gripped him once more.

The lamps suspended from the day room ceiling were swaying wildly as Dunsany entered, throwing shadows spinning around the room. Waves crashed against the ship with a sound like the beating of a vast drum and spray exploded across the windows.

"We're fucked." Ioannis said as Dunsany managed to hold down a chair long enough to sit on it.

"Now, let's not panic quite yet." He said.

"Well, what do you suggest we do?" Silus hissed. "Without Emuel we can't empower the stone and without the power of the stone this ship's no better than a ragged merchant barque trading out of Allantia."

"Actually, that's not quite true." Kelos said. "As you know, the *Llothriall* has remarkable healing abilities. Despite the rough ride we are currently having, the hull is unlikely to be breached."

"Yeah, but one of us *is*. How many days of being thrown around in here do you think we can cope with? Have you seen Maylan? He already looks not long for this world and I don't think that the rest of us are going to fair much better."

As if to illustrate Silus's point one of the lamps suddenly snapped from the ceiling and caught Ignacio's head a glancing blow, before shattering on the boards. Dunsany rushed to stamp out the flames as Ignacio dabbed at the blood now trickling from his scalp.

"Are you alright?" Kelos said.

"I think so. I've suffered heavier blows to the head, believe it or not."

"I believe." Dunsany muttered under his breath.

"Look, Kelos," Katya said. "Is there really no way to restore Emuel's abilities?"

"When the tattoo on Emuel's chest was burnt away it broke the flow of the songlines that cover his body. With the design broken his song will now have no effect on the gem and I'm afraid that I just don't know enough about elven runes to restore the design. "However, there may be another type of magic that can help us here."

"Which is?" Silus said.

"Silus, we were determined to get you on this voyage for a reason. Not only because we needed another man to help crew the ship, but also because of the extraordinary talents that you possess."

Silus remembered his vision in the bone strewn chamber of the underwater citadel, and the feeling of pure joy as that distant battle had raged around him.

"When I observed you in Nürn," Kelos continued, "I remember being taken aback by the way you handled that fishing boat of yours."

"There's no secret to that. There have been fishermen in my family going back generations."

"But there *is* more to it than that Silus. It's as though you have a sixth sense when it comes to the sea. Think for me here, has there ever been an occasion when you have surprised yourself with your abilities?"

Silus thought back to the time when he had got his foot caught up in the anchor rope; how his vision underwater had been crystal clear and how it had taken a long time before he had struggled for breath.

When Silus related this to Kelos he smiled and said: "There, you see. You have a deep-seated magical affinity with the ocean."

Jacquinto laughed. "Fish man! Really Kelos, I've heard you spin some wild tales but this one really takes the bait."

Kelos was pleased to see that none of the other crew members shared in Jacquinto's joke and, once the smuggler had composed himself, said: "Are you done? Good.

"Silus, I believe that I can help you channel your power in order to get us out of this mess."

"But I didn't even know that I had any of these powers before you pointed them out. What is it you expect me to do exactly?"

"You are going to call for aid."

"How?"

"I want you to speak to one of the denizens of the sea. I believe that, with my help, you will be able to achieve this."

Silus looked around the table at his companions' faces and hoped that the trust he saw there would not turn out to be misplaced. A great shudder passed through the *Llothriall* and several of the crew members cried out in panic, as though they were expecting the sea to rush in at any moment.

Silus got to his feet and gestured to Kelos.

"If we're going to do this, I think that now is the time."

Kelos nodded and together they staggered to the stairs leading above.

As Silus raised his head above the hatchway he was slapped in the face by a stinging blast of salt water.

"I don't think that this is going to work." He shouted to the mage, but Kelos pushed him out onto the deck, before securing the hatch behind them.

In the gaps when water wasn't being whipped into his eyes, Silus saw vast hills of sea rolling all around the *Lothriall*. He clung to the mainmast and his feet were tugged out from under him as a surge of water rolled across the deck. As the ship rose to the crest of a vast wave all he could see was sky, before the horizon tilted dramatically and they were hurtling down into a dark, roaring hollow.

Silus turned to look behind him, convinced that Kelos would already have been dashed into the maelstrom, but the mage stood perfectly sure footed on the bucking deck. He face was creased in concentration as he tapped two emeralds together, while speaking words in a language that Silus didn't recognise.

After a moment he put the stones away and looked up at Silus.

"Take your hands away from the mast," he shouted.

"Are you mad? It's the only thing keeping me on the ship!"

"Trust me."

Silus looked at the calm expression on Kelos's face and did as he had been told.

Even as the ship was tossed from wave to wave, Silus stood firm. A motionless point in the chaos that surrounded them. He laughed and held out his palms to the mage.

"No hands!"

"No hands. And have you noticed that we no longer need to shout? The field that we're contained in means that we don't have to compete with the wind."

"Okay, what now?"

"Now we need to put you in the right state of mind. Hold my hand."

Silus did so. When Silus looked at the mage's eyes there was a soft glow there, like the sky just after a summer sunset. He couldn't hear the angry ocean at all now and could barely feel the boards beneath his feet.

"This power is within you Silus." Kelos said. "I want you to move away from the *Llothriall.* Hover out over the water like an albatross borne on a gentle wind. Just let your mind drift out."

Silus felt himself moving away and he looked down, expecting to see his reflection moving across the water, but there was just the sea, and he followed its ever changing contours, accompanied by Kelos's voice.

"Move into the sea now, Silus, and, as the water surrounds you, send your mind out and sense the touch of the many creatures that dwell there."

Silus hadn't expected it to be so noisy beneath the waves. As soon as he let his consciousness into the water he was surrounded by the music of thousands upon thousands of voices.

There was the blast of what sounded like a full church chorus as a shoal of shimmering gemfish exploded around him, their harmony changing with each turn of their glittering mass through the dark waters. Then there were the longer notes of the larger creatures; the passing of a ray sounding like a bow being slowly drawn across the strings of a cello; the flash and dart of a marlin like the hollow musical breaths played on a sailor's conch. And then further down – much further – the great bass notes of the vast creatures that moved along the sea bed.

"There. Call to them Silus."

For a second Silus seemed to expand until he *was* the ocean and he called out to the leviathans that moved through the depths. The voices that surrounded him fell silent as he waited for a response, as though those smaller creatures were waiting with Silus. And then there was a great bass rumble as a leviathan responded and began to move towards him.

"Yes, yes. I have it!"

"That's right Silus, now bring him towards the *Llothriall*."

Silus couldn't see the creature yet, but he could certainly sense it moving in the darkness, building up momentum as it rose towards the surface. He retreated before it, feeling the pull of his body as he rushed back towards the ship.

When he snapped back inside his head he turned to look at Kelos and there was triumph in his eyes.

"It's coming."

"Excellent. We can use the creature to guide us towards the nearest land."

"What have we called?"

"It's a distant relation to the whale. Quite peaceful I can assure you. You can sometimes see them from the northernmost tip of Sarcre. I was taking something of a gamble that they would graze this far out, but it seems to have paid off. Here he comes now."

A huge ridge of bone broke the surface and cut swiftly through the water towards them. The wind screeched across the crest of the creature as two vast flippers – looking like barnacle encrusted oars – rose from the spray, followed by the grey bulk of the leviathan. Its long, ululating call shuddered the air as it neared the ship. Then it was gone, the sea closing in over the spot where it had dived.

Silus closed his eyes and could sense the creature moving somewhere beneath them.

"Should I try to call it again?"

But, before Kelos could respond the ship lurched and – even with the field of magical energy containing them – the two men were knocked to the deck.

Silus pulled himself to his hands and knees and looked down

the vertiginously sloping deck, into the eyes of the leviathan as one of its huge flippers crashed into the side of the ship.

"Why is it attacking? I thought I had control." He shouted.

"I don't know. It doesn't make sense."

Silus concentrated as hard as he could – despite the blast of foetid breath that wafted towards him as the creature opened its maw – and tried to send a wave of calm towards the leviathan.

The creature responded by pushing its bulk against the ship, sending it slamming into the side of a wave that had just begun to rise above it.

Silus lost his footing completely as a wall of water hit him. For a moment he feared that he had been swept overboard – then a hand grabbed his and he found himself dangling just below the ship's rail, looking up into the face of Jacquinto. Beyond him Silus could see Kelos. The mage's hands were wreathed in fire as he sent bolts of energy into the flank of the creature. Despite the howls that accompanied his strikes, Kelos's attacks seemed to be having little effect.

Jacquinto pulled Silus back on board and handed him a sword. Ignacio and Ioannis charged up the stairs onto deck, their own weapons already drawn.

"Where's Katya?" Silus said.

"With Father Maylan. Don't worry, she's safe," Ioannis said. "Holy gods! Is that thing part of the plan to save us?"

"Something went wrong."

"Obviously. Hey, look out!"

Ioannis barrelled into the side of Kelos, just as one of the creature's flippers came crashing down. The mage tumbled to safety but Ioannis didn't get out of the way in time and his legs were smashed into the planks. He screamed out as bones splintered and he tried to pull himself away as the creature loomed above him again.

Jacquinto was already rushing to his comrade's aid and he pulled Ioannis free before the leviathan could strike. Silus tried not to look at the shapeless mess of Ioannis's legs or the blood that now stained the deck.

"We're never going to be able to fight that thing. We're going to have to outrun it." Ignacio said, and before Silus could stop him he was climbing the rigging.

The sails had been furled to prevent them being pulled from the ship by strong winds, but now Ignacio was hoping to use that wind to get them away from the creature.

The mizzenmast sails unfurled with a great snap and the ropes that had held them in place whipped away from the ship, catching the creature across its flank with a noise like the cracking of a bull whip. The creature reared and the *Llothriall* began to move out of its shadow.

"That's it." Jacquinto called to Ignacio. "It's working."

The ship leaned hard to starboard as the first of the unfurled sails took the wind and Ignacio scuttled along the ropes and leapt nimbly to the mainmast. The ropes holding the sails here were thicker and Ignacio unsheathed his knife, hoping to save time by cutting through them. He looked nervously behind him as he worked and saw that the creature was already gaining on them.

The first thing to catch up with the ship was the great bow wave that the creature pushed through the water before it. Ignacio was almost thrown from the mast as the crest hit and the ship's bow dipped sharply, the masthead disappearing into the water. There was the sound of splintering wood as the creature's snout nudged the stern and, for one terrifying moment, it felt like the *Llothriall* was going to capsize.

Ignacio redoubled his efforts and was almost pulled from his perch as the shimmering silks unfurled.

The ship crashed down as the mainmast sales filled with wind. Ignacio saw part of the day room tearing free with the snout of the creature but was relieved that none of his comrades tumbled after the wreckage.

The leviathan bellowed as they sped away from it, but the unpredictable currents of the Twilight seas were already begin to pull them in several directions at once. Ignacio realised that he had only brought them a few minutes at best and dropped back to the deck.

Ioannis was sitting propped against a chest while Kelos crouched over him trying to stem the flow of blood, without much success. Ioannis looked like he was wearing a pair of scarlet breeches. Jacquinto and Silus were looking towards the stern, expressions of impotent panic on their faces.

There was a thunderous splash and Ignacio turned to see that the creature had disappeared beneath the waves once more.

"It's gone," he said, breathing a sigh of relief. "It's okay. It's gone."

"No," Silus said. "It's going to come back and this time there will be nothing we can do to outrun it."

"What are we going to do?"

"Something is controlling that thing," Kelos said. "Silus, you'll have to break through its conditioning."

Silus nodded, watched the wake of the creature and waited.

There was a sound like the creaking of an ancient and wind blown tree as the stern of the *Llothriall* began to knit itself back together, the residual magic spending itself in repairing the vessel. Soon the hole where the day room had been was covered by an uneven patch of rough wood, but the ship hadn't resealed itself perfectly and one end of a table and the legs of several chairs now protruded from the stern. However they were no longer taking on water and while Silus awaited the creature's next attack he was very grateful for this.

He looked down at the water as the wind fought with the ship. The silks above him were already showing signs of strain and a tear had appeared in one of them. Every so often the direction of the wind would change, pulling the ship violently onto a new course with Silus having to hang on to avoid being pitched over the side.

The crew had retreated below. Both Ignacio and Jacquinto had wanted to stay and fight, but Silus had convinced them that he needed to be on his own for what he was about to attempt.

Kelos had agreed. "Anything that interferes with his concentration could lose us this fight."

Gulls had begun to congregate on the water not far from the *Llothriall*, picking through the detritus that had been scattered by the creature's attack. As they took to the air with a cacophony of shrieks, Silus drew his sword.

There was a moment of quiet then before the sea erupted.

The leviathan's body left the water, arcing high – its jaws opening to catch the gulls that were too slow to escape – and Kerberos itself was eclipsed by its bulk, a vast shadow falling over the deck of the ship.

Silus shielded his eyes and could see a mass of tentacles lining the creature's underside, just before it crashed back down, throwing up a wave that pushed the ship rapidly to starboard.

Silus lost his footing and his sword skittered out of reach.

He stumbled twice before he managed to regain his feet and he snatched up his weapon just in time to sever the tentacle that slithered towards him. Dark purple ichor sprayed into his eyes and Silus didn't have time to clear his vision before another tentacle snaked in behind and lifted him from the deck.

A deep lowing sound came from the creature as it drew him near and the pupils of several of the vast eyes that dotted its head dilated as they studied him. Silus saw his image repeated in those dark pools and he willed himself to relax as he saw beyond them.

There were Chadassa crawling all over him, their thoughts an incessant buzzing chatter as they communicated with each other. From somewhere in the distance he could hear the call of his brethren and he tried to respond, but a bolt of white hot pain was driven into his mind when he lifted his head. He tried to buck against the onslaught of the creatures, but found that it was their will alone that held him; a horrendous buzzing that itched at the back of his mind.

A Chadassa with a barbed spike swam into view and drove the weapon deep into his side. The anger that he felt at the injury was fed back to him by the other Chadassa – a continual loop of rage – until it became so acute that it was almost painful.

He cried out and his call echoed from the depths of the canyon that fell away a short distance beyond him.

And then the Chadassa were swimming away and he suddenly found that he could move.

He could feel the lightless depths of the canyon calling to him, where more of his kind grazed and bred and reared their young in peace.

It wasn't peace that was burning through him now however; just the pure and hateful anger that the Chadassa had instilled in him. He could still feel them somewhere out of sight, feeding his rage. Nurturing it.

Four of his kind swam into view; a male and female adult and, behind them, two calves.

The group called to him as friends.

He shot them a warning response – this much he could just about manage – but they didn't recognise the change that had been wrought in him, they only saw one of their kind and they continued to approach.

The young darted ahead of the group and he went for them.

The calves were easily broken and soon the water was clouded with their innards. The female of the group tried to flee but he lashed out with his tentacles and pulled her in close, before gouging at her side with his teeth.

Even as the male barrelled into him, he closed his jaws and killed his mate.

There was the rich iron taste of blood in the water as he turned on the last surviving member of the group.

The whispering of the Chadassa increased in volume as he squared off against his opponent. The male was bigger than he, the crest of bone that rose from his back marked with the many striations of age. He only hoped that with that age had come frailty, but the vast form that now barrelled towards him showed no sign of weakness.

They grappled and, as he managed to force his opponent to the lip of the canyon, he could see the Chadassa swimming into view as they moved in to observe the fight.

He disengaged and backed out of range of his opponent's

tentacles before rushing forwards, barrelling into the side of the enemy, taking him over the edge of the canyon and smashing him into the far wall. Great chunks of stone crumbled away and fell slowly into darkness.

Bellowing his victory he smashed into his opponent again and this time there was the rending of flesh. His opponent was fading in and out of consciousness now and, before he could regain his faculties, his tentacles encircled his body and squeezed hard.

He could feel the great heartbeat of his opponent close against him, echoing through his own body. It was an almost relaxing, reassuring sound but, still, he squeezed with all his might until that beating slowed and then stopped.

He let his tentacles drop away and watched as his dead brethren sank out of sight.

He had killed four of his own kind but it wasn't enough.

The anger still boiled within him –

– and he lashed out.

There was a scream and someone called his name. But that wasn't his name, was it?

"Silus, help!"

A tight band encircled his waist and he struggled against it before realising where he was.

The creature maintained its hold on Silus as it lifted Katya from the deck of the *Llothriall*. Ignacio and Jacquinto, leaning hard against the rail, tried to make a grab for her, but succeeded only in snatching the shoe from her right foot.

"Katya, try not to struggle." Silus shouted.

As the creature drew her close, Katya reached out and – for just a second – their fingertips touched.

"Silus, what's happening?" Katya called.

"This creature is being controlled by the Chadassa. They sent it after us. If I can – "

Out of the corner of his eye Silus noticed Ignacio knocking an arrow to a bow.

"No, don't hurt it, otherwise you'll get us both killed!"

It seemed that the wind was strong enough to carry his voice, as Ignacio lowered his weapon.

The creature brought Katya closer then, more tentacles coming to bear as it examined her. One explored the mound of her belly and Silus prayed for the leviathan to be gentle.

"I'm going to try to break through the Chadassa's control, Katya. Stay as calm as you can."

Silus looked into the creature's eyes again and he could sense the taint that lay over its will, like a diseased caul. He moved beyond this and called to the creature in friendship and in peace. He spoke to it of the lightless depths, the abundance of life that moved through the canyons and of the comfort and companionship of its brethren. Silus could feel how the creature yearned for these things and he focused this desire through his will, until it was keen and strong. Then he broke through the mental restrains that the Chadassa had put in place.

There was a rumbling sound from the leviathan and its grip on Silus suddenly relaxed.

He landed on damp grey flesh and grabbed hold of the ridge of bone that rose from the creature's back. Then, as the creature rose up in preparation to dive, Silus's feet went out from under him. Only his urgent mental calls prevented both he and Katya from being drowned.

The creature settled back down, expelling a jet of water from its spout along with a great sigh.

Silus stroked its flank as he spoke and soon Katya was lowered to stand beside him.

Holding his wife close, Silus spoke again and the leviathan slowly carried them back to the *Llothriall*, all the time filling Silus with waves of joy in thanks for its newfound freedom.

CHAPTER FOURTEEN

After the creature had guided he and Katya back to the *Llothriall*, Silus spent some time communicating with it. The creature responded to him with peace and gratitude, thankful that it was finally free of the Chadassa yoke. But, before it could go and join its brethren in the depths of the deep-sea trenches, Silus requested a favour.

They needed to find land, and soon. Without Emuel, without the full power of the stone that was the heart of the *Llothriall*, they were stranded. It would only be a matter of time before the Chadassa launched another attack and Katya was getting dangerously close to her full term. And so, Silus, asked the leviathan to guide them to land.

For a while the creature hadn't responded and Silus contemplated the possibility that there just wasn't any land nearby; that they'd ride the seas until they died of thirst or starvation. Years from now, they'd wash up on some Allantian shore, an unusual ship manned by a crew of skeletons. Perhaps somebody would even write a sea shanty about the mystery of the sepulchral travellers.

But then the creature replied and Silus breathed a sigh of relief.

The crew's enthusiasm and gratitude, however, were tempered by their friend's recent death and when Silus tried to persuade the two remaining smugglers to help harness the creature to the ship, Ignacio refused. After all, this thing had killed his friend. But Silus reminded him that it was the Chadassa, and not the leviathan who had been responsible for his loss.

"Ignacio, this is probably our only shot at survival," Kelos said, coming to Silus's defence. "Don't let this voyage have been for nothing."

"The mage is right," said Jacquinto. "How do you think Ioannis would have wanted to die, Ignacio? Deep in the Citadel at Turnitia, tortured to death by the City Guard for running Sarcrean spice to low-life users? Or out on the open waters, battling with his friends and using his sword for something worth fighting for? This was where he wanted to be."

Ignacio looked at Silus, then at Katya cradling the curve of her belly and his features softened.

"Throw me a knife." He said to Jacquinto before scrambled into the rigging.

Soon they were moving at the creature's full pace and Silus communicated his thanks to the leviathan. It responded with a great, booming call that vibrated the planks of the deck.

Brother Incera polished the telescope's eyepiece before bringing his right eye to bear on it once again. He found that he hadn't been mistaken after all. The thing that looked like a small black dot moving across the face of Kerberos was not a flaw in the lens.

The astronomer noted the position of the dark spec on his charts before increasing the magnification and looking again.

The dot now resolved itself into a sphere, about an eighth the size of Kerberos, its surface a pure featureless black. He tracked its progress for a couple of hours before satisfying himself that it was not on a collision course with Twilight. Then he cranked the handle that lowered the telescope's cradle, stepped down from the seat and stretched to work out the kinks in his back.

In all his years as the Final Faith's head astronomer, he had done little more of note than track the movement of the stars and record the phases of eclipses. He had studied what few ancient astronomical texts there were, but they told him nothing he couldn't have found out for himself just by looking at the sky. It would seem that to the Old Races the heavens were just as much a mystery as they currently were to the humans. Yet the Final Faith still maintained an interest in the astronomical arts and this was why Brother Incera had occupied his position for the last three decades, tucked away in his dusty observatory in one of the highest towers of Scholten cathedral.

He had to admit that he was a touch alarmed at the appearance of the new moon. Katherine Makennon would have to be informed. No doubt she would be just as surprised at his continued existence as she would be at the news of the astronomical phenomena.

Brother Incera felt a little trepidation at the prospect of an audience with the Anointed Lord. It had been quite some time since he had last spoken to the leader of the Final Faith. In fact it had been quite some time since he had last spoken to anybody.

Carefully, he descended the spiral staircase that led from his garret down to the main levels, his arthritis burning deep in his bones. By the entrance to a bell tower he paused to catch his breath and managed to startle a passing Eminence who hadn't expected to see so pale or so elderly a figure leaning against a wall in this part of the cathedral. The Eminence hurried on, throwing glances behind him as though he wasn't sure that Brother Incera wasn't a ghost.

The astronomer muttered a benediction at the priest's back before descending into the main body of the cathedral.

Here he briefly basked in the warm, heavily incensed air that wafted through the decorated arches and aisles. In their stalls beyond the transept, the Eternal Choir's song heralded the approach of dusk, the last few rays of the sun pouring through the stained-glass windows painting the robed singers with vivid splashes of colour.

Brother Incera realised that this meant that it would be at least two hours before the next service and, in all likelihood, Katherine Makennon would currently be in her audience chamber.

He descended more stairs before being stopped at an ornately decorated door by two knights of The Order of the Swords of Dawn.

"State the nature of your business with the Anointed Lord."

"I... I." Brother Incera swallowed. It had been so long since he had spoken that his throat seemed to catch on each word. "I have important astronomical news that I believe the Anointed Lord will want very much to hear."

One of the knights disappeared into the chamber only to reappear a moment later to usher him into the hallowed sanctuary.

Brother Incera had forgotten how beautiful Katherine Makennon was and, for a moment, he looked in confusion at the bejewelled hand she held out to him. But then, remembering the seriousness of his news, he composed himself and kissed the symbol of the Final Faith before bowing low.

"Brother Incera." Makennon said. "What a pleasant surprise. It has been quite some time since we last discussed matters of astronomy."

In fact, Brother Incera was fairly certain that they had never discussed matters of astronomy. He had, of course, been introduced to Makennon at her inauguration, but since then she had shown as much interest in matters concerning the heavens as had the crumbling relics who had preceded her ministry.

"Forgive me Anointed Lord, but I had thought you wouldn't remember me. I am most honoured."

"Well of course I remember you, Brother Incera. I often think of you up in the heights of Scholten, gazing at the stars. I only wish I had time for such activity myself. You must feel so close to the Lord of All, looking up at His most holy and divine work."

"Oh yes, yes I do. The beauty of Kerberos never fails to move me."

There was the sound of someone stifling a laugh from one of the dark arches that ringed the chamber, before a skeletal man with a shaved head, wearing dark robes, stepped into the light.

"Ah, Querilous." Makennon said. "Have you met Brother Incera?"

They hadn't met but Brother Incera had certainly heard of Querilous Fitch. He thought, with some regret, that previous Anointed Lords would never have employed someone so enamoured of the sorcerous arts. Even in his garret he had heard rumours of the magics being employed by the Faith to further the aims of the church.

"We haven't. But Mr Fitch's reputation precedes him."

Brother Incera shook Querilous's hand and the sorcerer returned his weak grip with one that made his bones ache.

"And have you named a new star in honour of the Anointed Lord?" Fitch said, a not entirely pleasant smile on his lips.

"N-no. This astronomical matter is rather more serious."

The smile dropped from Querilous's face and he gestured for Brother Incera to continue.

"I have sighted a body of some sort moving across the face of Kerberos. It appears to be a black sphere. It's quite featureless and, at the moment, it holds a steady orbit."

"A black sphere? Has it come from Kerberos?" Makennon said. "Could it be a sign from the Lord of All?"

"I don't know, but I don't think so. What is more there was no warning or sign of its approach. It's almost as though it appeared out of nowhere."

"A dark sphere moving across the face of Kerberos." Querilous said quietly, almost to himself, and Brother Incera noticed that he had paled.

"Querilous. Do you have a notion of what it could be?" Makennon said.

"Just something that the... prisoner said before it expired. It may be nothing to worry about but I probably should take a look for myself."

"Very well. Brother Incera, I'm sure you will not object to Querilous accompanying you to the observatory?"

"Not at all, Anointed Lord. It will be an honour."

Brother Incera had almost forgotten how much he hated displaying false deference. One of the advantages of being so isolated in his work was that he very rarely had to tug the forelock to higher ranking church members.

As they ascended to his tower, he insisted that Querilous walk ahead. The thought of having such a one at his back sent a chill through him.

In the observatory he noted Querilous looking with disdain at the piles of charts and mouldering books, many of which were draped with cats. In a corner, on Brother Incera's rumpled cot, a ginger moggy nursed six kittens.

"Ah, my family. They keep me company and keep me sane. Feel free to pet them, I can assure you that none bite."

"Thank you, but I'd rather not. Now if you could show me this object that has so perplexed you, I would appreciate it."

Brother Incera showed Querilous how to position himself in the telescope's cradle before checking the magnification. Having made a few adjustments he gestured to the eyepiece. "Please."

He watched Querilous as he looked, the expression of haughty disdain on the inquisitor's face slowly disappearing to be replaced by something like fear.

As the last rays of the sun disappeared behind the azure giant, the dark sphere moved into the exact centre of the face of Kerberos.

"'With the dying of the light, our dark God comes.'"

"I – I'm sorry Brother Querilous, but I'm not sure I follow. Is something wrong?"

"Yes Brother Incera, something is wrong." Querilous descended from the telescope and fixed the astronomer with a determined, yet disturbed, gaze. "I will assign several advisors to work with you as we chart the progress of this... thing. You will report back to the Anointed Lord and I on a daily basis. And, if I were you, in the meantime, I'd make this place somewhat more habitable."

Querilous strode from the room, scattering cats in his wake.

Brother Incera listened to his footfalls as they descended the spiral staircase and knew that the thirty years of peace he had enjoyed were now over.

Ioannis's body rode the waves – a tiny barque on the fierce seas – before a sudden swell washed him under.

Father Maylan closed his well-thumbed prayer book and sketched the symbol of the Many Paths in the air with his right index finger. The words that he had said as Jacquinto and Ignacio had committed their friend's body to the sea had seemed to resonate with the two men and, for a while, they prayed together in silence.

Ioannis had died while Silus and Katya had been entangled in the grip of the leviathan. Kelos had desperately tried to help him cling to life, but there had been nothing he could have done. Ioannis's wounds were so severe that his bleeding couldn't be staunched, and what few medicines and poultices there were on board had proved to be next to useless.

Jacquinto and Ignacio watched the place where their comrade's body had been swallowed by the sea before emptying his tobacco pouch and hip flask into the water.

"Go well, my friend." Ignacio said.

Father Maylan placed a hand on his shoulder. "All paths lead to Kerberos."

Beyond the three men the rest of the crew stood at a respectful distance, having already said their goodbyes and not wanting to interfere in the intimacy of the ceremony. Silus held Katya close and, beside him, Kelos supported a pale but sufficiently recovered Emuel, while Dunsany stood with his head bowed.

They all looked up at the sound of a rope snapping and falling heavily to the deck.

Ignacio swore and raced to the prow of the ship, where he tried to stop the rope going over the side. He managed to catch it before it slipped over the rail, but his strength was as nothing compared to that of the creature on the other end, and his hands were badly burnt as the rope was jerked violently into the water.

"Silus, can't you do something?" Ignacio shouted, stuffing his sore hands under his armpits. "It's your bloody pet!"

Silus stood at the prow and looking at the leviathan that guided the *Llothriall* under harness, he urged it to slow its pace.

As the creature responded, the ropes that led from the ship to encircle it lost some of their tension.

"I can tell you now that I'm not going down there to bring that rope back up and re-secure it. It was painful enough the first time." Ignacio said, looking over the side of the ship. "Who's idea was it to use this creature anyway?"

Belck was not angry, though the manner in which Findol delivered the news of the ruroth's failure suggested that he expected some severe reprimand. But they had not failed, Belck considered. Not really. They still knew exactly where Silus and Katya were. The fact that Silus had managed to break through the conditioning of the ruroth and tame the creature showed that he was changing faster than any of them could have hoped. Their plan may have to evolve a little, but it had in no way been broken.

Besides, now was surely not the time to wallow in defeat, for their God had finally come amongst them.

Belck could sense the excitement of his kin as he donned his ceremonial raiment and made his way to the temple. In all the history of the Chadassa they had never been so close to the time of the Great Flood. The time when all reality would become the dark sea from which the Chadassa had sprung and to which the Chadassa would soon return. The Old Races were all but extinct and now it was the turn of the humans to follow their ancestors into the night.

That a human would help to bring about this new era wasn't entirely lost on Belck. Yet Silus was not human, not entirely. It was Chadassa blood that ran in his veins and it was his seed that would produce the new breed; the Land Walkers who would devastate Twilight.

Even through the thick stone doors of the temple, Belck could hear the song of his people, their voices raised in the complex tonalities of ancient song to welcome the arrival of their God.

As the last verse of the song faded away, Belck gestured with his hands and the doors of the temple swung slowly open.

As the congregation turned to watch him Belck realised that they were all relying on his guidance, his judgement for the days ahead. After all, he was the avatar of their God. The enormity of the task before him cowed Belck for a moment, but as he took to the pulpit and signalled his acknowledgment to the elders seated to either side he tried not to show his fear.

Raising his arms he allowed the hope of his people to strengthen him.

"He is the Great Ocean and he has come amongst us!"

"He is the endless sea." The congregation replied.

"He heralds the time of the Great Flood."

"And we will swim together, in eternity."

"Brothers and sisters we will indeed swim together for the Great Flood will soon be at hand. The half-breed will join in communion with our Queen and together they will give rise to the Land Walkers. This new breed of Chadassa will stride across Twilight, slaying all in their path and when they reach the mountains at the edge of the world they will tear open the very earth. Then the Great Ocean will pour its dark waters into the exposed heart of this world and unleash the power of the Flood! All reality will be bathed in the waters of the Great Ocean and the Chadassa's empire will know no ends."

For all the certainties contained in his proclamations Belck was somewhat dismayed that he still felt an edge of doubt. It was the same doubt he had felt at the summoning ceremony, when the dark face of their God had been revealed to them. In fact, he realised, it was a doubt that had been with him for a very long time.

Belck had studied the ancient texts. He had listened to the council of the elders and born witness to their testimony concerning the work of their God amongst them. But when they had started to talk about the purpose of the Great Ocean and His plans for the Chadassa, Belck had begun to feel a flaw begin to work its way through his faith.

After all, who were they to say what the Great Ocean's purpose really was?

In all the times that Belck had communed with the God he had sensed nothing to link him to that consciousness, nothing that said to him: 'I have created you for a greater purpose and for a greater glory.'

There was only that dark, terrible presence. Older than Belck could ever imagine, and unknowable.

Those who had led the Chadassa before Belck had accepted the presence of the Great Ocean without question. They praised him and expected nothing in return. They had spent their lives preaching from the ancient texts just as they had been set down and prophesying the time of the Great Flood, which they had known would happen long after they died. And so, they had never had to come face to face with the reality of the God himself. They had never had to stare into that dark and pitted surface and wonder what the realisation of the prophesies would bring.

But Belck let none of this doubt taint his proclamations.

"He is the Great Ocean. Brothers and Sisters, gaze upon the face of your God."

Above them the ceiling of the temple rippled, as though they were looking up at the surface of a vast pool. And then, they were staring into the face of Kerberos. Yet the azure disk was marred by a dark tumour and, as the Chadassa realised that this black sphere was the face of their God, they raised their voices in song.

As Belck joined his congregation, he wondered if any of them actually really knew what the Great Flood was. Whether any of them could say that they truly knew what the plans of their God meant for them.

Belck couldn't.

And that scared him more than anything.

Ever since Kelos had shown Silus how to open his mind to the creatures of the sea, he had been aware of the abundance of life that moved beneath them. But it was not the only life he could sense now and he soon realised that the urgent whisper that he had been hearing, that seemed to underlie everything, came not from the sea, but from Katya's womb.

Katya clutched Silus's hand as a contraction gripped her. It was the second in the last hour and he could tell that she was beginning to panic.

"Not long now and I promise that you'll have something more stable than the deck of a ship beneath you."

"I really hope so. I have a feeling that this one isn't going to want to hang around."

Silus knew. The urgent whisper had grown in volume. In fact, the voice was so clear now that he could tell that they were going to have a son.

Katya breathed deeply as the pain passed. She looked exhausted and Silus wished that he could take away the fear that he saw in her eyes.

"You should get some sleep," he said. "You've gone through more than any expectant mother should endure. But when our son is –"

"We're going to have a son? Silus, how do you know?"

"I... I can hear him. He's speaking to us."

"Like you could hear the creature that's towing the ship?"

"Something like that."

"What's he's saying?"

"It's not words I can hear, so much as the voice of his urgency. He's almost ready to come into the world."

"How can you hear these things Silus? Where did this power come from?"

"I don't know. It just seems to have been awoken somehow."

"You're changing?"

Silus thought of the vision that the Chadassa ancient had shown him and the vision of the battle at the underwater citadel, how he had felt the joy of the fight overtake him.

"I'm still me," he said and kissed Katya's forehead. "Still the fisherman from Nürn you fell for."

But something about the look that Katya gave him told Silus that she was no longer so sure.

Katya's waters broke on the third day after they had harnessed the ship to the leviathan, and Silus immediately went into a state of full-blown panic. Fortunately Father Maylan had helped deliver children in his parish on many an occasion and was fully conversant in dealing with fearful new fathers.

"First thing Silus – and this is very important – drink this."

Silus took the bottle of flummox and necked half the contents. Beside him Katya shot her husband a filthy look.

"In case of emergency drink first huh?" she said. "Great advice. I'd always wanted to give birth on a ship with a half-cut husband by my side."

"Now Katya, don't say anything you don't mean," Maylan said, before rolling up his sleeves.

"Okay, in that case I won't say I wished that Silus had never met Kelos and that I wished we'd never been forced onto this voyage."

Silus gripped Katya's hand and kissed her on the forehead. "I'm so sorry Katya. Father Maylan will see us through this. Don't worry."

Katya screamed as another contraction hit and Silus looked at the priest, urging him to do something.

Maylan knelt down and hooked a pair of spectacles over his ears. "Oh yes, all quite normal down here I can assure you. Nothing to worry about at all. Now Katya, I want you to start to push... now."

Silus cried out in pain at the same time as his wife, as his hand was crushed in her grip.

"That's it Katya. Breathe. Breathe. Breathe."

Father Maylan did something with his hands and Silus was alarmed to see him wipe blood off them a moment later. The priest caught the panicked look on Silus's face and shot him a reassuring smile. "Really Silus, don't worry. The blood is all part of it. You're going to have to get used to a certain level of mess. All part of the magic of childbirth."

"Magic!" Katya shouted. "I'm sure you wouldn't say that if you were in my position."

"Don't worry Katya. We'll soon be there. And another big push. One, two, push."

The sweat was pouring off Katya now and Silus brushed the hair out of her eyes. Every time she screamed out, every time she had to give another push his heart lurched and a terror gripped him that something would go wrong. He knew women who had died giving birth. Strong, healthy women. And here was Katya, miles out at sea with not a midwife overseeing proceedings, but a priest on the run from the Final Faith.

The ship shuddered and the light coming in through the porthole dimmed as the sun moved behind Kerberos.

"That's it, I can see the head. Another big push now Katya."

The ship lurched again and Maylan stumbled into the wall. Above them the lamp swung wildly on its fastening and the flame within died.

And then Silus and Katya's son gave voice to his arrival in the world.

Maylan got to his feet and staggered over to Katya. He reached between her legs, urging her to push one more time as the cries of the infant grew in volume.

"You've done it Katya," Silus said. "We have a son. My gods, we have a son!"

"You do indeed," said Maylan, a grin on his face, holding aloft the child, his arms coated in birthing fluids.

After cutting the umbilical cord he gave the boy to Katya. The child struggled in her arms for just a moment, until she helped him find her breast, and then the only sound in the room was the gentle, content sound of his suckling.

Silus looked at their boy and, instantly, it was love. In Katya's eyes was the self same look.

Father Maylan was the first to break the quiet.

"And have you thought of a name for the wee chap?"

Katya looked up at Silus and he said: "Zac. His name is Zac."

"Zac," she repeated as though trying it out. And then: "Yes. Zac."

"Congratulations. Both of you."

"Maylan. I really can't thank you enough." Katya said.

From above them there was the thunder of feet on deck. Silus heard ropes creak as somebody scrambled up the rigging.

And then there was the call they had so desperately been hoping for these last few days.

"Land Ahoy!"

CHAPTER FIFTEEN

The city sat atop a rock plateau, supported by the sheer walls of iron green cliffs rising from the sea.

As the leviathan drew them closer, Dunsany could see something moving down the cliffs. He focused his telescope and what he saw just didn't make sense

What he had taken to be walls of green stone were in fact the sides of a vast wall of water. The city was not supported by a series of cliffs but, instead, was riding on the crest of an enormous wave, frozen in the moment just before it would have fallen into an avalanche of frothing surf. And the things descending the wave, moving swiftly down its vertiginous sides, were ships.

The leviathan brought them to the foot of the wave and the ship keeled to port as they stopped side-on to the water. The creature gave a great shudder and expelled a plume of spray. As it let out a bellowing call, Kelos moved to the prow and looked down.

"It's time to part ways with our friend. Ignacio, Jacquinto, give me a hand with these ropes."

Together they unharnessed the creature from the *Llothriall*.

It didn't leave immediately. Instead, it regarded them for a moment with its many eyes, running its tentacles over the *Llothriall* – one briefly brushing against Kelos – before it turned and swam away. They watched as the creature submerged, its great tail the last to disappear in a crash of spray.

"It's a shame Silus wasn't here to say goodbye," Dunsany said.

"Goodbye to whom?" Silus said, emerging from below, followed by Maylan.

"The whale thing just swam away." Ignacio said. "It sends its regards."

"I have some news. Katya has given birth to our son. Zac."

"A healthy baby boy I'm pleased to say." Father Maylan said.

"Congratulations!" Dunsany said. "That's terrific. I'd propose a toast but I fear that we may not have time to drink it before those ships are upon us."

"What ships?" Maylan said.

"Look up."

"Gods! What is this?"

The ships were almost on them, sailing down the vertical drop as though gravity was none of their concern. There were four vessels, simple in design, looking much like Allantian trading ships.

As Dunsany watched their approach, his sense of perspective suddenly shifted and – for one vertiginous moment – he felt that he was about to fall out of the *Llothriall* and towards the ships. The horizon spun and he could no longer tell which was sky, sea or the ship beneath him. He closed his eyes and when he opened them again, he forced himself to look at the planks below his feet and – taking deep breaths – willed his world to be the right way up.

"Are you alright?" Silus said.

"Fine. Fine. It's just that you don't see something that doesn't make sense everyday."

"Ho there!" Came a call, and they looked up to see the prow of a ship not more than twenty feet above their heads. "What seas have you traversed to find yourselves at Morat?"

What seas? Dunsany thought. *What does he mean what seas? Surely there are only these seas?*

"The Twilight seas," he said.

"Twilight must be very far away indeed, for it is not a place I have heard of."

"You are on Twilight. This *is* Twilight."

"No friend, this is Morat."

"Look," said Jacquinto. "Wherever we are, our ship has been damaged and we need shelter while we try repairing her."

"Of course, tie on and we'll guide you to port."

A rope dropped down and Jacquinto and Ignacio secured it to the *Llothriall.*

"Sorry, one moment." Dunsany said, as they made preparations to unfurl the sails. "How are we supposed to follow them to port? I don't know whether you've noticed but we are at the foot of a vertical wall of water. How are we supposed to traverse *that*?"

"An interesting argument friend," said the man above them. "But to my eyes, it is *your* vessel that is clinging to the side of a sheer wall."

"You know what?" Ignacio said. "I think we should just go with this. If you begin to question it, it may hurt your brain."

"Okay. Okay." Dunsany said. "Bring us about."

As they brought the ship round to face the wall, the rope tying them to the vessel above pulled taught and Dunsany was convinced that they would be dragged into the wave, crushed beneath the weight of all that water. Instead, there was another moment of intense vertigo as the horizon tilted. Kerberos wheeled in an arc across the sky and, as it tumbled past him, Dunsany thought he saw a dark spec moving across its face. He closed his eyes against a sudden, dizzy nausea and when he opened them again, they were sailing across calm waters.

Ahead of them, he could just make out the headlands of the city. Behind them, stretching far above like an infinite wall of sea, was the rest of the ocean. Dunsany tried not to think about it, tried not to think about how they could be sailing up a frozen wave that was not a wave. Instead, he concentrated on the line of ships ahead as they guided them towards a bustling port.

As the ship guiding them docked, the *Llothriall* moored alongside and the captain of the vessel leaped across to greet them.

The man was dressed in dark clothes; a vest of black silk and leather breeches that were inscribed with a pattern of intertwined flowers. His ears and eyebrows were heavily pierced and Dunsany couldn't help but notice the ridges beneath his vest that told of more piercings on his torso. The captain held out a many ringed hand, the back inked with a tattoo that appeared to show the sun rising out of the shadow of Kerberos.

"Well, this is a surprise. And a pleasant one."

Dunsany took the man's hand. "I'm Dunsany, the captain of the *Llothriall*. This is my second-in-command and resident mage, Kelos. Behind us stands Silus, Ignacio, Jacquinto and Father Maylan. Below we have Katya and Emuel."

"And Zac." Silus reminded him.

"Yes, and Zac. Newly arrived in this world."

"A most diverse and unusual crew," the captain said. "I'm Winrush Searah Jaxinion, child of Kerberos and Archduke of Morat. But you can call me Win. May I ask how just the nine of you manage to crew such a vast ship?"

"Ah," said Kelos. "That's because this is no ordinary ship. It is based on ancient elf design."

"Yeah, but we sort of broke it." Jacquinto said. "Well, something broke our eunuch. Anyway, it's a long story."

"Indeed. Clearly you gentlemen are tired and hungry. I think that we can converse more easily over some refreshment and a decent meal. I'd be honoured to have you as guests at the palace."

"Palace?" Jacquinto said. "Now you're talking!"

"That's a yes then? Splendid. Follow me gentlemen. And welcome again to Morat."

As soon as Dunsany stepped off the gangplank and onto the cobbles of the Morat docks, his legs told him just how long he had been at sea. They felt filled with the water upon which he had sailed and on each step he overcompensated for the rolling deck that was no longer beneath him.

Kelos watched him lurch down the street for a moment, before supporting him with an arm around his waist.

"Come on, we can stagger like drunks together."

Behind them followed the rest of the crew with Silus at the rear, his arm round Katya, who was carrying a squealing bundle close to her breast. She looked more tired than any of them, and her footing was less sure. Dunsany only hoped that Win could provide a suitable bed at the palace for her.

They followed Win along narrow streets hemmed in by tall buildings. There was a face at every window and doorway they passed. Most turned away at the first glance though, expressions of disappointment on their features, as though they had expected the strangers to be more exotic, maybe even creatures of a different race. Dunsany understood and shared their disappointment. Here they were on a previously uncharted island and the people around him could have been his fellow countrymen. The buildings that towered above them looked as though they could have been built from Turnitia stone. When they had planned the voyage, he and Kelos has been full of visions of fearsome new lands, peopled by strange beasts and promising exotic treasures. But what they had found was merely more of their own kind.

Dunsany had to concede, however, the fact that Morat rode on the back of a vast wave really was impressive.

It took a long time to move through the outer districts of the city, as Win insisted on stopping every few minutes to shake the hands of his subjects and inquire after their well-being. It seemed that he knew almost everyone they passed on a deep personal level.

"This you must taste," he said, stopping at a market stall and handing each of the crew a small pastry, before paying the trader.

"For the love of – " Ignacio exclaimed after taking a bite. "Well, I think that I may no longer have any taste buds."

"My eyes are watering." Dunsany said.

"Indeed, it is a little bit tart," said Father Maylan, finishing his pastry in two bites.

"Fantastic aren't they?" Win said. "Worth stopping for I think. Anyway, onwards."

Eventually the narrow streets turned into wide thoroughfares which started to descend in a series of terraces. Win led them through a district where the buildings were lower and larger than those near the docks, each displaying a lavish garden, through which rang the sounds of children playing and water trickling.

"This is the education district," Win said. "There are many specialisations. That building there, for example, is the Institute of Mechanised Puppetry. And over there we have the School of Salinity Studies."

"Sorry, but are you saying there's a place where you can go to learn how to measure the saltiness of things?" Dunsany said.

"Well, yes. Of course." Win said, as though it was the most natural thing in the world. "There's a school for pretty much every discipline."

They carried on downwards, negotiating flight after flight of precipitous stone steps. Dunsany noticed that in a dark alcove beneath each were candles burning in front of what appeared to be shrines. On closer inspection he found that in each shrine there was a carving depicting Kerberos; most often with the sun edging out of its shadow, sometimes with the added symbol of a ship sailing away from the planet.

"You wish to make an offering to the Allfather before we enter the palace?" Win said.

"No. It's just interesting to see that Kerberos holds religious significance for the people of Morat. It is the same on Twilight, although I'm sure that your church is much less dictatorial than our own."

They were leaving daylight behind now. Even though the sun was still a long way from setting, very few of its rays reached this deep into Morat. They had descended to the city's lowest levels and the streets here were lit with torches that gave off a curious fragrance as they burned, reminding Dunsany of the Allantian spice markets. Fewer people moved through this district, and those that did were attired in clothes which marked them out to be officials of some sort.

"Welcome to the palace of Morat," Win said.

"Palace?" Jacquinto said, looking about him. "Where?"

They had stopped in front of a dark wood door set into an unremarkable wall, which followed the curve of the street on either side and stretched high above them.

"After you, honoured guests," said Win, opening the door.

The palace was as modest on the inside as it was on the outside.

They entered a damp stone corridor, lined at regular intervals with more of the aromatic torches. The only concessions to luxury were the rugs that lined the floor, but even these were threadbare and black in places with ground-in dirt. As the crew crowded into the cramped space Win closed the door behind them and then shouldered his way through the group – apologising profusely all the while – before leading them along the corridor.

They followed the curve of the wall round to the right, occasionally passing doors, from behind many of which they could hear voices raised in what sounded like theological or academic argument.

"Ah, the chaos of the ministries," Win said. "Politics was never my thing I'm afraid. Which I suppose may be deemed a bit of a disadvantage for an Archduke. But one can't help it if one is born into a role."

Extracting a key from a ring on his belt, Win unlocked a door and led them up a flight of stairs to the first floor.

Here, at last, there were windows, but instead of light they admitted a steady bitter draft and a host of pigeons. Feathers moved lazily in the steady wind that whistled down the corridor, while more crunched underfoot, along with a litter of tiny bones and bird carcasses.

"The rookery," Win said.

"Get off you feathered bugger!" Father Maylan suddenly exclaimed, trying to brush away the pigeon that had landed on his shoulder.

"I'm so sorry," Win said. "They're not used to guests you see. For her, you are just another perch. Come on my darling. Win can be your branch today."

The bird jumped onto Win's head and shat down his back. He chuckled as it flew off, like an exasperated but loving parent humouring a child.

"It's alright," Maylan said, composing himself. "It's just that I have this thing about pigeons."

"Then we shall hurry onwards and leave our feathered friends behind."

Eventually they came to another door and Win led them up another flight of stairs.

As they came out onto the second level of the palace they were hit by a wall of heat. From vents in the walls poured forth a muggy warmth, while pipes lining the ceiling shuddered and hissed out plumes of steam. Soon the crew's clothes were plastered to their bodies and Dunsany began to wish for a return to the icy winds of the rookery.

Win dug in a pocket and produced several handkerchiefs, which he passed out to his guests.

"For the mopping of one's brow." He explained. "It does get rather moist up here."

Dunsany was beginning to feel dizzy by the time they reached another door, and he was beginning to worry how Katya and Zac were coping with all the exertion. When he looked back, though, Katya sent him a reassuring but tired smile and Dunsany began to pray that behind the next door would be the dining room, rather than another surreal tour of the palace service tunnels.

A staircase spiralled down and when they exited at the bottom Dunsany had to suppress a growl of anger.

The corridor in which they were now standing was lined with dirty threadbare rugs. The door on the left was the one through which they had originally entered the palace.

"Excuse me, ah, Win. But isn't that the way we came in?"

"Yes it is. But the door there leads to my quarters, and we couldn't possibly have approached it from an anticlockwise direction."

"No, no indeed." Father Maylan said. "Where would the logic have been in that?"

"Quite so, my friend." Win said, completely missing the sarcasm in the priest's voice. "Quite so. That just wouldn't have made sense."

When Win opened the door, Dunsany was relieved to see that what lay beyond was not another corridor. Instead, they followed the Archduke into a room that was warm and inviting.

A fire burned in an ornate grate in one wall, while the opposite wall held barnacle-encrusted sculptures in niches, candles placed around them filling the room with a gentle light. In the centre of the room was a low table surrounded by cushions and laden with food, all of it smelling utterly wonderful to the exhausted and famished crew.

"Please, eat." Win said, gesturing to the feast. "Do not delay on my account."

They didn't.

Only Katya held back. After taking a couple of mouthfuls of bread she turned to their host.

"Win, would you have somewhere where we can rest for a while? I'm afraid that I'm beyond exhaustion."

"Of course my dear. Please follow me."

Win led Katya, Zac and Silus from the room, returning a few moments later.

"I'm glad to see that you are enjoying the food." He said. "The palace chefs are really second to none."

"It's wonderful," Father Maylan said. "Trust me, we would get nothing like this back home."

"And where is home?"

"A land far from here. I must say I was rather glad to leave it."

"Oh really, why was that?"

"There was a conflict of faiths, let's put it that way."

"It is strange that we have never come across your land on our travels."

"Yes it is." Dunsany said. "Your entire city rides on the back of an enormous wave. There can't be any stretch of the sea that you haven't explored."

"We follow the path that the Allfather has laid down for us. But yes, there is another place. There is the Isle of the Allfather where, once a year, the path leads us, so that we may speak with Him more directly in the hope that He will call us back to His bosom."

"Well, I don't know about you fellows. But I'm confused." Jacquinto said. "Emuel, does this make any sense to you? You're pretty weird after all."

The eunuch had remained silent ever since they had disembarked from the *Llothriall* which, in itself, wasn't that unusual. What was unusual, however, was that he had a smile on his face.

"The songs are here." He said. "Can you not hear them? The beautiful songs."

"No," Jacquinto said. "That would be just you I'm afraid."

"Win, tell us of Morat." Dunsany said. "I would really like to hear the story of your people."

Win filled his glass and, after having drank, began his story.

The Allfather – or Kerberos – had once been the home of the Moratians. But, many generations ago, some great sin had been committed against the Allfather and the people were sent out in exile from the cradle of their civilization. As to the nature of this sin, not one of the Moratian legends spoke of its origin. Maybe the shame of the ancestors was such that they had sought to erase all memory of their trespass. All the Moratians knew was that the anger of the Allfather had been so great that it had flung them into the airless gulf between worlds.

But the Allfather's anger hadn't been so great that he had abandoned his people with no hope of survival. For he had sent them out with a part of himself, an immense stone that enabled them to survive the ravages of the void.

And so – after many years of travel – they came to this world of storms and endless water.

Here the stone of the Allfather continued to guide them, shaping the waters surrounding Morat, bending the environment to the will of the people while drawing them along the decreed paths through the angry seas.

All the while the Allfather looked down on the people of Morat and his implacable face was a constant reminder of their guilt.

In their ceremonies the high-priests channelled the remorse of the people; crying out to their creator in prayer and song, their hunger to return a fire that burned at the centre of their worship.

Once a year, the path that Morat followed through the dark waters brought it within sight of a small island. The Allfather seemed to hang lower and larger in the sky over this land and some people claimed that they could even make out his true face. So, it was decided that here they would build a temple in his name.

Slowly – year after year – the stones were laid. The masons worked only four days at a time, which was as long as Morat remained within view of the island, and when the temple was completed the builders had to return swiftly to their home, before it disappeared out of sight over the horizon.

The people of Morat then had to wait a whole year to christen the temple with their praise. A whole year before the currents brought them again within sight of the island.

On the first Festival of the Allfather the gathered people looked up – up through the great round hole in the temple roof that seemed to cradle their God – and sang their praises and their lamentations. And the high priests, through the use of a certain sacred lichen, freed their souls from their bodies, so that they flew through the Allfather's endless clouds where they could commune with him more directly.

But the Allfather still did not call the people of Morat home.

Yet they did not despair, for they had found a place where they could be closer to their God. Therefore, every cycle, the Moratians strove to improve themselves and each other by building a strong, just society where education and fellowship came first. And then, when they next came within sight of the island and the Festival of the Allfather was once more upon them, they offered up not just their guilt but the fruits of their labours and aspirations; showing the Allfather how his people in exile had improved, showing him how they were indeed worthy of his mercy and his love.

It was true that the Allfather still had not brought them back to their ancestral home, but for each year that the people of Morat built on their achievements they moved themselves closer to the day when they would ascend and be forever in his care.

And so, the high priests had come to realise that the Allfather had not sent his people out in exile merely as a punishment, but also as a way to reveal to the Moratians what they were capable of, to prove the glory of his creation.

"So, the Moratians believe that they come from Kerberos?" Dunsany said.

"It is not a question of belief," said Win. "The Moratians really *do* come from the Allfather, doesn't everything?"

"For many of us on Twilight, Kerberos is indeed central to our faith." Father Maylan said. "It is commonly held that when we die our souls fly to Kerberos, there to be joined with the Lord of All, to spend eternity in his glory."

"See?" Win said. "We both share that desire to return."

"The similarities between our beliefs are striking," Dunsany said. "Something else that you mentioned also interests me. You spoke of this stone of the Allfather that enabled the original exiles to exist in the void between worlds and which enables you to weather the Twilight seas. It is clear that the power of this stone is considerable and I believe that the stone that sits at the heart of the *Llothriall* must be composed of the same material."

"Were you given this stone by the Allfather?" Win said.

"No. I'm afraid that our stone was found by somebody else. We sort of had to steal it. Believe me, the people we took it from wouldn't have used it for so noble a purpose."

"We are fellow travellers are we not?" Win said, refreshing everybody's glasses. "Journeying to the glory of the Allfather."

"Well, some of us I suppose," said Jacquinto. "Ignacio and I are only in it for the money."

Win laughed and proposed a toast.

"To the glory of the Allfather."

"The Allfather," the crew echoed.

"So what now for the *Llothriall*?" Win said. "Where shall be your next port of call?"

"Well the problem we have is that we can't get our stone to, um... work." Dunsany said. "You see, Emuel used to be able to unlock the power within the stone through song. But the elven runics that enabled him to do that have been broken by sorcery."

"My friend, I'm afraid that this talk of elven runics makes no sense to me. Are these the marking on your friend's flesh?"

"Yes." Kelos said. "They are elf songlines."

"May I examine them more closely Emuel?" Win said.

Emuel looked up from his plate. He was humming to himself and the beatific smile that Dunsany had noticed earlier was still on his face.

"The songs are here," he said. "The singing is all around us."

Jacquinto leaned in close to Emuel, as though he was talking to a nearly deaf elderly relative. "Emuel. The nice man wants you to take your shirt off. Can you do that?"

"Yes, of course Jacquinto," the eunuch said. "There's really no need to shout."

Win gasped as Emuel took off his shirt and moved to run his hands over the text covering the eunuch's torso.

Jacquinto raised his eyebrows at Ignacio but said nothing.

"It is the holy text," Win said. "Emuel, your flesh is covered in the scripture of the Allfather."

"But that's not possible," Kelos said. "Those are elf runes."

"And this scarring on his chest, is where the text was damaged?" Win said, pointing to the still painful-looking wound.

"Yes, with the songline broken he no longer has access to the power of the stone." Dunsany said.

"It is possible that the high priests may be able to do something for your friend. They will certainly want to meet him."

"That is good news," Dunsany said. "The only other thing that you may need to know is that when we came to Morat, we were fleeing from some rather unpleasant creatures."

"Well, I really wouldn't worry about them. With the power of the Allfather, there is no way that they can trouble you here."

CHAPTER SIXTEEN

No one in the Final Faith knew what the planetary body now hanging before the face of Kerberos signified. Nowhere within the holy texts was there mention of the coming of the moon. But the biggest challenge the Faith was now facing was not this sinister new conjunction, but the increasingly panicked questions of the laity.

The people couldn't fail to notice the dark spec on the face of Kerberos and many were taking it upon themselves to proclaim it to be a sign of the end times. It didn't help that some of the clergy, in the more rural parishes, were going along with this assessment, preaching services full of the threat of damnation.

It was decided that, in order to staunch the panic before it spread to every community and began to destabilise the Faith's hold on their flock, there would have to be a proclamation from Katherine Makennon herself.

When the next Tenthday rolled around, therefore, Makennon stood on a high balcony at the cathedral at Scholten and –

looking down on the mass of people gathered in the great square below – made her pronouncement.

These were not the end times, she proclaimed, starting with at least a small note of comfort. This was, however, a time to be afraid, for the dark manifestation on the face of Kerberos was the eye of the Lord of All. He was gazing down on Twilight and taking stock of his people, for their morals had become lax and their behaviour questionable. Any man, woman or child the Lord of All found lacking would be judged with the full force of his fury. So, the people should look up at Kerberos and take it into their hearts to change their ways.

Much to Katherine Makennon's relief the proclamation seemed to work. Sometimes, she considered, the best panacea for fear was fear itself, because through wielding it one could control the people.

Over the next few days, reports coming in from every major city in the Empire showed a fall in crime across the entire region. There was also a fall in the number of heresies being committed. There were even stories of heretics willingly giving themselves up to the cleansing fires of the naphtha gibbets, claiming that now they could see the face of the Lord of All, they had come to realise the true horror of their sins.

All in all, Makennon considered, the arrival of this new planetary body had turned out to be no bad thing. Church attendance was up, collection plates brimmed with coin and the masses submitted to even the harshest decree.

This renaissance of faith, however, was not to last.

Days after the dark moon had moved into conjunction with Kerberos, the attacks on the coast began.

From every major port in Vosburg, reports flooded in of creatures walking out of the sea and launching vicious assaults on the populous. The military were stretched almost to breaking point defending the maritime provinces, and the channelling of resources away from the in-land cities meant that crime rose steeply in these areas. The Final Faith were forced to bolster the Empire's troops with detachments of the Order of The Swords of Dawn and, as a result, some heresies were now going unpunished, as all available Faith troops were put to use against the Chadassa menace.

The fighting was intense and casualties on both sides were high. For a while it seemed that some of the major ports would fall. But Freiport suddenly joined the conflict – briefly allying with a nation that they had openly spurned for years – and, with a last desperate push, the creatures were driven back into the sea.

Some of the smaller coastal settlements, however, had not had the might of the Empire to back them up and entire generations had been slaughtered, villages reduced to rubble before the sea demons – their hunger apparently sated – had withdrawn.

But not all of the creatures had escaped. A special cadre of the Order of The Swords of Dawn – under the supervision of Querilous Fitch – had managed to capture a handful of prisoners. And now that the Final Faith had the Chadassa back in residence at the dungeons in Scholten, they would use all means at their disposal to discover the true nature of their plans.

Silus sat and watched Katya and Zac sleep.

The bedchamber to which Win had taken them was opulent but dusty, though Katya hadn't complained and she was asleep almost as soon as her head hit the pillow. Beside his mother, Zac had burbled and cooed for a while before joining her in slumber. Silus would have joined them himself but, even though he was more exhausted than he had ever been, he couldn't sleep. Instead, he sat in a chair by the window and watched his wife and child, the soft light of a torch burning outside playing across their faces.

With a pang of regret, Silus wondered what he had brought upon his family.

His son had been born in exile and his wife was no longer sure just who her husband was, or what he would become. And then there were the Chadassa, determined to tear Silus from the people he loved and use him as a pawn in their unfathomable plans.

Katya stirred in her sleep, a hand coming up to weakly paw before her face, as though trying to ward off whatever phantom was haunting her dream.

He could just give himself up to the Chadassa, Silus considered. Maybe if he surrendered himself to the fate they so clearly thought was his destiny, then they'd leave Katya and Zac alone. Kelos had shown him how he could communicate with the denizens of the sea. All he had to do was reach out with his mind and find their song.

Silus closed his eyes and concentrated on the sound of his breath, on each inhalation and exhalation.

He left behind the three people in the bedchamber, he left behind the city riding on the back of its vast wave and then he was out over the water, listening to the songs of the creatures who moved below.

Silus searched for the call of the Chadassa but as he began to detect a whistling roar amongst all the other songs – sounding like the howl of wind through an abyss – another more urgent cry reached his ears.

This cry was filled with a dreadful and urgent need. At its core was a fear of loneliness that Silus couldn't ignore. He followed it back over the water to find himself back in his body, staring at Zac as he wailed and wailed.

Silus picked up his son and the child's cries stopped. Zac's body against his own was warm and he could feel the rapid beat of his son's heart as he pressed him to his chest. It soon slowed as Zac settled against him and Silus swayed him from side to side.

"Shhhhhh. Shhhhhh. It's okay. It's all okay now."

And as Zac's small fists bunched in the folds of Silus's shirt and those large, tearful eyes looked up into his own, he made a decision that when it came to it, when the Chadassa came for him, he would stand and fight with everything he had.

The next day, the crew accompanied Win as he led them to the centre of Morat.

They had risen early and, after a hearty breakfast, followed the

Archduke as he descended the narrow stone steps leading from the palace. When they reached the bottom Silus looked up and he could just make out the sky far above, as though he stood at the bottom of a deep well. The dark speck that they had noticed on arriving at Morat still marred the face of Kerberos.

"A sign that does not bode well, I fear." Win said, following Silus's gaze.

A domed building stood at the centre of Morat and across its surface, picked out in delicate curlicues and flourishes of stone, was the same script that decorated Emuel's body, and it burned with a vivid illumination.

"This is the seat of Morat. The engine house of our city. Gentlemen – and lady – welcome to the house of the Stone Seers. The text covering the building is the holy scripture, taken from the Book of the Allfather."

"The songs," Emuel said. "My Lord, the songs!"

"Win, this holy text of yours? Do you know who wrote it?" Kelos said.

"It was a gift from the Allfather. He sent it out with his people."

As they walked over the threshold, the song suddenly rose around them and Silus wondered whether this was what Emuel heard every time he communed with the stone on the ship. Silus had never heard anything so beautiful. He turned to Katya, to see tears rolling down her face. In her arms, Zac squealed with delight and clapped his hands.

Inside, dozens of robed people hurried through a wide hall, looks of deep concentration on their faces. As they passed Silus noticed that they sang softly to themselves. On their robes was the same script that covered the exterior of the building.

"The Stone Seers," Win said. "These are the men and woman who maintain the ancient song and make sure that its rhythms never fail."

They moved across the smooth, highly polished floor to a set of double doors framed by a vast arch. The doors stood four times as tall as any of the crew and looked as though they had been carved from bone. Into the yellowing material had been worked the story of Morat.

At the centre – and overlapping the two doors – was Kerberos, the clouds that covered its surface picked out in delicate folds and arches of bone. Below this, dozens of humans were depicted falling away from Kerberos, expressions of anguish and remorse on their faces. A great stone rode in their midst and linking them together were lines from the holy text. These travellers through the void were heading towards the city of Morat, which rode its great wave at the base of the doors.

Win put his right hand on the fresco and, with a click, the doors swung open.

The song increased in volume, rolling out of the chamber on a breath of warm, perfumed air. The room into which Win now led them was dominated by a vast stone sphere, its summit almost touching the ceiling. But for its size, it was identical to the *Llothriall's* stone. Veins of magical energy played across its surface and out across the walls, where it illuminated the lines of the holy text that had been worked into the stone. Around the circumference of the cradle supporting the stone was a ring of eight lecterns. At these stood more robed figures, their voices raised in the ethereal song that filled the room with its powerful resonance. Around the edges of the room stood more of the Stone Seers, waiting to take over from any of the singers who tired. Maintaining the song clearly involved considerable exertion, for those who were led away from their lecterns to be replaced with others of their kind were often pale and drenched in sweat.

"It is crucial that the song never falters," Win said. "For if that happens, Morat would be truly lost. It is the power of the stone that leads us on the path the Allfather laid down for us, and shapes the sea to carry us."

"And are all your stone seers eunuchs?" Kelos asked.

"Well no, why would they be?"

"Emuel, our seer, was emasculated in order that he would be able to attain the correct pitch in which the song is to be sung."

"How can somebody be so cruel? It is the rhythm, the cadence that is essential to maintaining the song. Pitch has nothing to do with it."

"I notice also that your Seers are not tattooed like Emuel."

"I must admit that I was wondering why the holy text had been needled into his flesh."

"It is a magical mnemonic," Kelos said. "The tattoos allow the song to flow through Emuel. It is this that enables him to unlock the power of the stone on the *Llothriall*. As you have seen, however, his flesh has been marred and the songlines broken."

"But the song can be learnt. Anybody can, theoretically, be taught how to become a Stone Seer."

"You mean," Emuel said, "that none of what I have been through was necessary?"

Silus noticed that the eunuch had his fists clenched and his shoulders were shaking. He had never seen Emuel so gripped by anger and he took a step back, putting himself between Katya and Zac and the eunuch.

"I'm afraid not," Win said. "Who was it who did these dreadful things to you?"

"My faith did this to me. Those who taught me the lessons of the Lord of All and who nurtured me from acolyte to Enlightened One, did this to me. I gave them my soul and my flesh and they used me. And to what end?"

Emuel's voice had risen to a shout. Some of the seers at their lecterns turned towards the disruption. Noticing the look of concern on their faces, Win began to usher the crew towards the doors.

"Emuel, I think that perhaps any arguments are best saved for outside. We don't want to disturb the Stone Seers."

"Yes, come on Emuel. It's not all bad news." Kelos said. "Win has said that the song can be taught. That means you can learn it again. They can fix you."

"Fix me? Fix me!"

"I – I mean heal, obviously."

"You don't care, do you Kelos? None of you really care what happens to me. I'm just a useful object to you people. You know, I was happy in my Drakengrat parish. My congregation loved me and we all shared in the glory of the Lord of All. But then I had to go and give myself to Makennon's cause when she came a-calling, only for her sorcerers and alchemists to turn me into a walking blasphemy! And then, you had to go and kidnap me, taking me on this dreadful voyage which is likely to kill us all!"

"Emuel, come on. Calm down." Dunsany put a hand on his shoulder.

"Get off me!" Emuel shouted, and shoved Dunsany hard in the chest.

Dunsany fell against one of the Stone Seers, sending him crashing to the floor, his lectern falling beside him.

For the first time the song faltered.

A great shudder passed through the room and a fine rain of dust fell from the ceiling. Silus felt his ears pop as the air pressure suddenly dropped. Immediately, several of the stone seers rushed to help their colleague to his feet as another of their number quickly took up his part in the song.

The walls groaned and Silus could have sworn he saw one of them begin to sag, as though it were melting. But, with the harmony of the song restored, the room began to stabilise and Silus saw Win breathe a sigh of relief.

Dunsany brushed himself down and walked over to Emuel, holding out a conciliatory hand. But the eunuch shot him a murderous look and stormed from the building

"I think that it's time we left," Win said.

Back outside there was no sign of Emuel.

"Perhaps one of you should go and look for him?" Katya suggested.

"No, I think that it's best if we leave him to work it out of his system." Dunsany said. "I don't think that anything any of us could say would calm him down right now."

Win nodded and gestured to a passing Stone Seer. "Arklyn, would you see to it that our friend is okay? Perhaps you could speak to him of the song. It does have many healing properties."

The seer nodded and set off in the direction Emuel had taken.

"Do not worry my friends," Win said, turning back to the crew. "Emuel will be in good hands. Now, shall we return to the palace for refreshments?"

Later, as they sat down to lunch, Emuel returned. He was considerably calmer than he had been before and he was humming a tune under his breath. Kelos offered him a drink but he refused and, instead, went to his room, saying that he wanted time to pray and consider what he had learned.

"Well, it's certainly been an eventful day," Kelos said, sitting down and helping himself to a hunk of bread.

"Win, I'm curious to learn more about Kerberos, the Allfather," Silus said. When I was a young man, I often wondered what it would be like to fly through those azure clouds and see whether anything more lay beyond them. Ever since I was a child I've heard its call."

"Silus, if you ever feel like remaining on Morat, I'm sure that we can find you a role amongst the priests of the Allfather," Win said. "You certainly talk like one of them."

"Yes," Kelos said, "he is a most unique individual."

For a moment Silus glared at Kelos, afraid that he was about to tell Win of his burgeoning powers and his link to the Chadassa but, instead, the mage smiled and poured himself another glass of wine.

"I'd like to meet the priesthood, certainly," Silus said. "For many nights now I have been dreaming of Kerberos. I would have dismissed these dreams as nothing but fantasies, but they've come to me night after night."

"But dreams don't necessarily mean anything do they?" Katya said. "I mean, we all have them."

"Yes, but it's almost as though Kerberos itself is trying to tell me something."

"Oh, here we go," Jacquinto laughed. "Apparently, fish boy here is the chosen one."

"No, don't mock," Win said. "Visions are just one of the ways the Allfather communicates with us. Perhaps a visit to the temple would not be such a bad idea after all."

"If you think it will help I have no objections. Unless – " Silus looked over at Katya.

"No, it's fine. Go."

Win nodded. "Good. We'll finish our meal, then if you and Kelos would care to accompany me, I'm sure the priests will be happy to talk to you."

As they ascended the terraces to the Temple of the Allfather, the sky began to open up around them once more. Silus was glad to feel the warmth of the sun on his skin again. The cheer that it brought, however, was marred by the sight of the black canker that continued to blight the face of Kerberos. Silus hoped that it was just some natural phenomena that would soon pass, but the more he looked at it, the more he knew this not to be the case. Something unnatural was hanging over the gaze of the Lord of All, like a barbed mote in His eye.

The Temple of the Allfather was spread over two levels and, from it, they could look down on the palace and the house of the Stone Seers. Its gardens were equal to anything they had seen since arriving and, as they approached, Silus could see several robed figures amongst the lush green ferns and flowers, sitting in attitudes of quiet contemplation.

The entrance to the temple gave on to a cool, marble hall festooned with hanging baskets overflowing with fragrant herbs and busy with the noise of the tiny birds that twittered from archway to archway.

A robed man greeted them as they entered.

"Friends, welcome. Win told me of your arrival. Indeed, I'm sure the whole of Morat is abuzz with the news of our guests. I am Bestion. I believe that we have much to discuss, so if you gentlemen would care to follow me?"

The priest led them down a flight of stairs and into an indoor garden. Above them, holes in the temple roof let in narrow shafts of sunlight, which fell on clusters of iridescent lichens clinging to dark boulders. Between the stones trickled a shallow stream, the noise of the water's play over the gravel beds amplified by the marble walls that surrounded them.

"The gardens are central to our work here at the temple," Bestion said, ushering them through a door and into a small room lit by oil lamps. "We use the herbs and lichens we grow here in many of our ceremonies."

Bestion seated himself on one of the cushions that were scattered across the floor, and gestured for his guests to do the same.

"Our friends here are curious to find out more about the Allfather," Win said. "Silus, in particular, seems to have a strong bond with Him."

"I have been fascinated by Kerber – sorry, the Allfather – for a very long time. Win tells me that you have a method of communing with Him," Silus said.

"Yes, through the sacred lichens we can leave our bodies for a short period of time and enter into His presence."

"I would very much like to do that, if you would be willing to guide me."

"Silus here has been having dreams concerning the Allfather," Kelos said. "Perhaps through this meditation he can work through some of his concerns and come to a greater understanding of our god?"

"With respect, Silus does not number amongst the priesthood."

"I understand," Kelos said. "But ever since I met Silus I have sensed a deep spirituality in him. It is my belief that he will increase our understanding of the Allfather. Maybe he will even be able to shed light on the dark speck that has so recently marred His face."

"Bestion, we do not pose a threat to your beliefs," Silus said. "We praise the same God you and I, just under different names. We all respect the sanctity of Kerberos, the Allfather.

There was a moment of uncomfortable silence then. Bestion stared at Silus intently, his gaze not unfriendly, yet piercing, as though he was searching for any sign of moral laxity in Silus's soul.

"If I am to guide you through the rites, Silus, you must do everything that I say, exactly as I say it," Bestion said. "The rituals are not to be entered into lightly."

"I understand."

"Win and I will return to the palace while you work with Bestion," Kelos said. "We will see you after your meditation."

"Very well," Bestion said. "Silus follow me to the sanctuary. I will inform the other members of the priesthood that we are not to be disturbed."

Bestion led Silus deeper into the temple complex. As they passed through more of the gardens, he saw men tending to the sacred lichens and herbs. He noticed that some of the priests had peculiarly iridescent eyes.

They passed through an archway and into a silent hall. No birdsong rang from the walls here and there was no trickling of water. Their footsteps made no sound. Bestion opened a door at the far end and they entered a room bathed in the light of Kerberos.

A stream ran out of an archway on the far side of the room, forming a moat around a stone dais in the centre of the chamber, before exiting through a second archway. On the dais four brass censers were set at the corners of a carpet woven with symbols not unlike the songlines that had been inked onto Emuel's body. Above the dais, a wide circular hole in the roof let in the light of Kerberos.

Bestion led Silus over the bridge crossing the moat and gestured for him to be seated on the carpet.

As he sat, Silus looked up and was reminded of that first night with Katya; how they had moored the boat on the subterranean lake beneath the gaze of Kerberos, how he had shared his dreams and fantasies with her. Now that he was actually to come into the presence of Kerberos more directly, Silus wondered whether any of his visions would turn out to be true.

Bestion poured a sparkling powder into each of the censers before lighting them. The smoke that poured from them was bitter and Silus choked as it wreathed itself around him.

"Don't fight it," Bestion said. "Otherwise this isn't going to work. Breathe."

The first lungful burned as deeply and painfully as a knife to the ribs and, as Silus fought a growing sense of panic, Bestion put his hands on his shoulders and forced him to be still.

"Breathe, Silus, *breathe.*"

Eventually, the pain subsided and Silus found himself able to breathe without gagging on each inhalation. There was a taste in his mouth that was vaguely metallic, but also sweet. Bestion sat opposite Silus and he noticed that the smoke didn't go near him. Instead, it seemed to be pouring from the censers and streaming directly into his nostrils.

When the censers were empty Bestion began to chant.

His voice was low and resonated deep within Silus's chest.

Silus didn't understand the words, but they seemed to be doing something to him. The taste in his mouth grew more pronounced and he felt as though he was going to be sick. He folded himself over the centre of his sickness – trying to hold it in – but a great shudder wracked his body, forcing him upright. When he opened his mouth what came forth, however, was not bile but smoke. It felt like he was being drawn inside-out. Silus tried to scream but he couldn't. The smoke pouring from his mouth felt like something solid, something living. He looked up and saw the column of smoke reach the hole in the temple ceiling, and he suddenly found himself following it. As he tumbled towards Kerberos he looked down and could see his body below, kneeling with its head thrown back. And as Silus looked at himself, he prayed to the Lord of All that he would be able to return so that life would once more shine behind those eyes.

CHAPTER SEVENTEEN

The sound of Bestion's chanting followed him as the thread tying him to his body unravelled.

Silus rose through the temple roof and, looking up, he could see the great disk of Kerberos expanding as he hurtled towards it.

As the last few words of Bestion's mantra faded away, Silus found himself moving over the azure planet, the clouds just inches from the soles of his feet.

This silence was bigger than himself, bigger than the stars that blazed above him like a multitude of jewels strewn across black velvet. Ahead of him, one jewel burned brighter than all the others – its blue-green light reaching him in brilliant cold shards – and Silus knew that he was looking at Twilight. It seemed so fragile, as though if he could reach out and touch it it would shatter.

Remembering his dream, he stared into the clouds below him, expecting to see the spirits of all those who had left Twilight behind, but there was nothing. Just the odd flicker of lightning gave life to the roiling mass.

Silus felt disappointed. He had expected this to be a profound, spiritual revelation but, instead, he had found that, even close-to, Kerberos refused to give up its secrets.

He felt anger burn through him. Below him the clouds darkened.

Lightning lit the planet from horizon to horizon in a blaze of blinding light.

Silus understood then that Kerberos had just blinked.

Tendrils of cloud rose up around him, caressing him as they drew him down towards the surface.

Silus closed his eyes and sank into Kerberos.

Silus wasn't sure how much time he had spent in Kerberos's presence before he found himself rising back up, but he felt as though he might have been conversing for hours. However, he found he could remember very little of what had been said. All his questions and doubts had been replaced with new questions and doubts. He was no more aware than he had been of who was right about the nature of the azure giant; the Final Faith, the followers of the Many Paths, or the priests of the Allfather. In a sense he knew that there was a grain of truth in all of their beliefs but, at the same time, he realised that they all had a long way to go before they could claim to truly know Kerberos.

Silus rose into the void and looked towards Twilight. To his left the sun blazed away, great geysers of fire shooting out into the eternal night. Twilight caught the light and reflected it back and, feeling the pull on his body, Silus moved towards home.

However, something was rising over Kerberos's horizon. Something that Silus only began to see as a deeper darkness moving against the sea of stars. Then, as it rolled towards him, he could see that it was a pitch-black sphere. It was about an eighth the size of Kerberos and utterly featureless, its smooth surface reflecting the light of the sun like polished onyx.

This was the blight that marred the face of Kerberos.

There was a sudden sense of disorientation and Silus found himself looking down on the black terrain of this strange new world, with Kerberos now looming above him. He tried to will himself towards home and his body, but the dark moon dragged him down until he came to rest on its surface.

He sensed movement behind him then. Silus turned to see an arm reaching up through the ground. No, that wasn't quite right, he decided. The arm was in fact forming itself *from* the ground, the very terrain shaping itself into the semblance of a limb. Another arm rose beside it and then the ground between them bulged as a head, and then a torso, pulled themselves free.

The thing looked up at him as it coalesced, and its face was as smooth and featureless as the dark moon itself. As it rose to stand over him, the only thing to define it against the night-black background was the reflection of the stars on its obsidian flesh.

Silus prepared to defend himself before realising that there was nothing for the creature to attack. He had no body.

"What are you?"

The thing's blank face began to form itself into his own.

"Please, don't do that. You don't know me."

There was the sound of the ground breaking behind him and he turned to see another figure pulling itself together from the surface of the moon. This one coalesced into Katya's form. Something crawled out of the ground beside her and when she picked it up, he saw that it was a mockery of his son. As Zac looked at him with its eyes of pitch, fear overtook Silus and he desperately tried to find the link to his body, but when he reached out, there was nothing.

"What do you want with me? What are you?"

We are the Great Ocean. The three figures said with one voice. *We are the endless sea. We are the father of the creatures you call the Chadassa. The creatures whose blood run in your veins.*

"But I don't understand what you want with me."

Silus, your birth was the start. You are the herald for a new age of the Chadassa. The time of the endless ocean.

"How? Look, you have driven me from my home. You have caused the deaths of people I care about deeply. You owe me an explanation."

We agree. Too much has been hidden from you. It is only right that you are made to understand. Maybe then you will submit to us with gladness when you realise just how important you are.

"How can I be so important?"

Look, said the Katya facsimile, holding out the thing that looked like Zac.

Silus didn't want to look at the thing. It wasn't his son. But when it smiled and said his name, he found himself falling into the bottomless pits of its eyes.

As Silus was dragged far into the past he tried to scream, but he had no mouth.

It felt as though he fell forever, but he didn't fall far.

As he came out of his tumble, he saw that Kerberos still turned slowly above him and Twilight still sat against its blanket of stars.

Something *was* different though and it wasn't just that the dark moon was no longer there to cast its shadow on the face of Kerberos. Something made Silus feel that he was further away from home than he had ever been.

Then he had it. He had fallen not through space, but time.

As Silus wondered why the creature that called itself the Great Ocean had dragged him into the past, there was movement at the edge of his vision and the dark moon drifted towards him. This time, however, it paid him no heed. Instead, it came to rest before Kerberos, hanging in the void.

As Silus began to wonder what great revelation it was that he had been sent here to witness ripples passed through the surface of the moon. The black orb convulsed and a great rock erupted from its surface to go spinning towards Twilight.

Silus was dragged into its wake, following it as it sped towards his world.

After the endless silence of space the booming concussion that the rock made as it entered Twilight's atmosphere was deafening. Fire erupted from fissures in the stone and gas vented from cracks to surround Silus in billowing steam.

The clouds broke and Silus saw that they were hurtling towards the sea, the water coming up to meet them at a sickening speed.

He braced for impact but the scene changed suddenly, and he found himself beneath the waves rather than falling towards them.

Silus was standing before a beautiful citadel, much like the one he had explored with the crew of the *Llothriall*. But whereas that city had been broken by war and time, this one shone in its perfection. Great towers reached from the seabed – linked by arches that looked like they had been formed from polished quartz – while domes of glass nestled amongst forests of seaweed, the green fronds alive with the play of brilliantly coloured fish. Shafts of sunlight filtered down through the surface, moving slowly over the scene, picking out the smooth green stone of the buildings one moment and shining from the glass domes in dazzling coruscations the next.

As Silus looked more closely he could see tiny lights darting through the city like fireflies and when a shaft of light moved to rest on one of them for a moment he saw that they were attached to strange creatures.

They were humanoid in appearance, though thin silvery tails propelled them quickly through the water and small globes of light hung from either side of their jaws, looking much like the lures of anglerfish. Their heads were larger than an average human's, with great dark eyes staring from above a circular mouth lined with hundreds of needle-like teeth. At the ends of their hands were not fingers but fronds, not unlike those of a sea anemone.

These are the Calma, the voice of the Great Ocean said. *A simplistic and mongrel race.*

The creatures moved through the city with a balletic grace that was a joy to watch. As Silus saw two of their young race each other to the surface, he realised where he had seen such incredible beings before. His vision in the broken citadel. He had seen himself killing the Calma. He had revelled in their deaths while standing knee-deep in their fallen.

There was a commotion above the city then and Silus saw a

host of Calma rushing away from the surface, as though fleeing from something there.

Panic overtook the city as a great shadow fell upon it.

Silus wasn't sure what had happened but he was suddenly surrounded by a thick cloud of debris. Dark shapes moved past him in the murk, and he could just make out chunks of broken rock and the tangled masses of shredded corpses tumbling through the clouds.

Then as rapidly as the cloud had rolled over him it was gone, and Silus now found himself looking at the ruins of a shattered city.

The scene before him blurred, light strobing erratically across it, as though the sun was racing through the sky far above.

Eventually the light stabilised and Silus could see survivors crawling through the ruins.

At the centre of the broken citadel sat the great black rock that he had followed into Twilight's skies. Dark tendrils were reaching out from the burnt and pitted stone, and where they touched the Calma survivors a horrible and violent change wracked their bodies.

The sheen of their scintillant scales darkened to a pitch black, while the fronds of their hands retracted and stiffened, razor sharp claws bursting from the flesh of their newly forming fingers. The process looked agonisingly painful and the screams of the creatures confirmed the torment they were in.

The creatures got stiffly to their feet as they changed, their toes elongating and sprouting vicious-looking talons that dug into the seabed; their jaws shattered and then slowly reformed, their mouths now lined with long sharp teeth. As the glowing nodes fell away from the creatures' faces, Silus knew exactly what he was looking at.

Chadassa.

The newly birthed Chadassa moved through the rubble, dispatching any of the survivors too weak or gravely wounded to make the change. As they experienced their first kills, Silus could sense their joy. Part of him – for the briefest of moments – even shared in it, but he bit down on this dangerous lust, burying it deep.

See the birth of the emissaries of the Great Ocean. See the first tentative steps of your kin.

Silus wouldn't have called their steps tentative. The Chadassa strode through the broken city killing anything that was not their own kind.

Now witness the rise of the Chadassa.

A great war followed, a wave of destruction wrought across the ocean by this fledgling race, Calma city after Calma city falling to their relentless onslaught.

But there *was* some resistance. Through necessity the Calma had to learn the art of war, but such a talent did not come naturally to a race who had lived in peace for most of their lives. Mistakes were made, more of their cities were lost and by the time they began to fight back with anything like success, their populous had been decimated.

Some Calma, in their desperation to save themselves, crawled onto land. But they soon found their hides drying out and cracking under the onslaught of the merciless sun.

The inhabitants of Twilight decided to take mercy on them.

Silus saw the shores of Nürn strewn with the bodies of Calma. Moving amongst them were lithe figures with pale skin and almond eyes the colour of Kerberos. Silus realised that they were elves – that ancient and beautiful race that had been dead for millennia – and, as the creatures of legend began to sing, he saw the birth of the human race.

Under the influence of the elven magic the Calma began to change where they lay. Their scales lost their sheen, gaining the soft pastel colours of flesh, their limbs shortened as hands and feet began to form, their tails withdrew into their bodies, their gills closed up and their jaws realigned as hair sprouted from newly shaped skulls. All along the Twilight coast the human race took their first breath and, looking up at Kerberos, they let loose their first cry.

With the change wrought, the elves sang one last song. The song of forgetfulness.

All knowledge of their brethren in the sea was lost to the human race. They forgot the Calma – their legends and culture – and began to form their own communities. In saving them, the elves had severed their roots. But they were satisfied that they had at least partly turned the tide of genocide. Only the few Calma who remained below the waves knew the truth concerning the human race and they guarded the secret as they continued to evade the attentions of the Chadassa.

However, it didn't take long for the Chadassa to find out the truth.

Silus watched as the sea demons built their empire on the ruins of the Calma's, growing in strength and breeding with an alarming rapidity. From infants, their growth to maturity took only a couple of years, and they began to reproduce almost as soon as they had shed their youth. Soon they ruled their submarine world with a ruthless efficiency, exploiting the ocean's resources, devastating whole swathes of seabed in the building of their cities.

As the centuries passed, the Chadassa began to feel that the conquest of Twilight's seas had not been enough. Jealously regarding the land that had been denied to them, they began to mobilise for an invasion.

As they strode from the waves, however, the Chadassa found that the humans had lost the Calma's propensity for peace, and they fought with an unbridled ferocity that matched the Chadassa's own.

There was, however, an even greater impediment to the Chadassa's plans for conquest of land.

As the Chadassa fought on the surface they soon found themselves sickening. They tried to fight on, but after only a brief time their bodies' shortcomings forced them to retreat back beneath the waves.

For generation after generation my creations brooded on their inadequacies, but despite their pleas to me I could not intervene. The voice of the Chadassa god told Silus. *For my act of creation I was banished beyond the void, where not even the stars shine, by the being you call Kerberos. But in my absence my children had begun to put a great plan into action.*

The Chadassa reasoned that just as their bodies' inadequacies were as a result of the adaptation of the Calma physique, then these same inadequacies could be remedied by taking on more of the physical attributes of the humans. They resolved to breed a new race of Chadassa.

They choose a human female – your ancestor, Silus – and in her they planted the seed of what was to come. Her child was born with Chadassa blood in his veins, but it was weak. And so, the Chadassa waited and observed. Through each generation of your ancestors the thread strengthened until, in you, we finally saw evidence of its burgeoning powers.

It is with your seed that the Land Walkers will be born and my children will take Twilight. Already they have pulled me out of exile through the power of their will and soon everything you know will become the one Great Ocean. The time of the Great Flood will be upon us all. All reality will be flooded with my dark waters until there will be only the Chadassa.

Silus found himself back on the surface of the dark moon, the three facsimiles standing before him.

The thing that looked like Katya reached out and took his shoulder.

The Great Ocean will bring about the end of death. The end of wars and suffering.

It would be the end of everything. Zac would never grow up to experience the joys of living. Silus would never grow into his dotage alongside Katya, would never see the seed of the family they had planted bloom and flourish. If this thing had reckoned that it would persuade Silus to side with the Chadassa, then it had failed. The blood of those creatures may run in his veins but it was his humanity that would overcome it.

"You already know my answer. I will never join with you."

But you really have no choice Silus. I didn't bring you here just to share my vision with you. I brought you here as a diversion while the Chadassa finally caught up. It's already too late, there is nothing that you can do.

The Great Ocean let him go.

As Silus began to tumble back towards Twilight, his prayer was that he would be in time to save Katya and Zac.

There was an intense darkness for a moment, but then Silus opened his eyes and saw Bestion standing over him, his arm on his shoulder and a look of alarm on his face.

Around them the temple shook, fragments of stone beginning to crumble from the walls.

The door at the far end of the room burst open and an acolyte hurried in.

"Brother Bestion come quickly, something is destroying Morat!"

CHAPTER EIGHTEEN

It took Silus a moment to realise that what was happening was not a part of his vision. The floor below him really was swaying like the deck of a storm-tossed ship and the masonry that was beginning to break away from the ceiling really would crush him unless he moved now. In the end Bestion made the decision for him, dragging Silus to his feet before hurrying him out of the room.

In the cloisters the walls shook and the sound of breaking stone was almost deafening. When they stumbled out of the temple and into the courtyard they could see that the city was shaking itself apart.

People were fleeing from their homes as they fell around them, some having no choice but to scramble from windows to drop to the street two stories or more below. Not all of them managed to drag themselves to safety before they were buried beneath falling stone.

A strong wind blew down towards them from the upper levels

of the city, bringing with it a foul stench.

A panicked tide of acolytes and priests flowed around Silus and Bestion. Most chose to head to the upper levels of Morat, fleeing towards the docks, but some went running down the terraces to the lower levels; throwing frightened glances behind them while trying to dodge the detritus that rained down around them.

"We must get to the docks." Bestion shouted. "The only safety will be out on the water."

Silus's first thought, however, was to the safety of Katya and Zack. They were still at the palace and, if the rubble from the collapsed buildings continued to tumble into the centre of the Morat, they'd soon be buried in the avalanche.

Silus made for the steps but an explosion threw him to the ground as the remains of an inn collided with the side of the temple, demolishing the cloisters. He got to his feet and was about to battle onwards when – through the thickening fog of brick dust and debris – he saw his wife struggling up from the lower levels, Zac clutched to her breast. Behind her followed the rest of the crew.

"Thank the Lord." Silus said, embracing Katya. "We have to get to the *Llothriall*. Bestion, follow us."

But when Silus turned to address the priest, there was no sign of him. He only hoped that he wasn't amongst the tangled corpses trapped in the temple ruins.

There was no time to check, however, as the tremors that had besieged the city intensified. The stairs leading to the upper levels cracked as they raced up them. Silus looked back once to see that Morat had become a vast landslide; its beauty lost in a vortex of tumbling stone.

As they crested the last terrace, Silus almost stumbled as he saw what lay ahead.

"Holy Lord! What is that?" Win said.

A dark wall of flesh rolled across Morat, consuming everything in its path. Already the docks had disappeared into its black gullet and as it ate it made a horrendous sound. The sun reflected from its wet hide and Silus wondered what manner of creature the Chadassa had called to their aid.

There was no escape. Behind them the city continued to fall apart and ahead of them it was being consumed at an alarming rate. Silus had just a moment to consider what had become of the *Llothriall* before the creature was upon them. He reached out and took Katya's hand, but his grip was wrenched away as he fell into darkness.

His pulse was loud in his ears as he awoke. Something damp covered his head like a hood and when Silus opened his eyes all he could see was a weak, milky glow filtered through a web of veins that beat in time with his heart. His throat burned. Something was holding his jaws apart. He bit down on an obstruction that felt like bone encased in gristle and a bitter taste filled his mouth. Silus tried to raise his hands to pry away the hood, but found that they had been encased in something that felt like warm, moist flesh.

He wasn't sure how much time passed before the tube in his throat was withdrawn and the hood was peeled away.

Silus found himself in a room that was made entirely of flesh. Great bony ridges supported the ceiling and the floor beneath him rose and fell as the walls pulsed. To either side of him sat several figures, their hands sunk to their wrists into the floor and their heads covered in fleshy hoods that grew from the walls. Fat, ridged pipes extended from the walls and into the hoods, suspended from which were veined sacs that hissed and wheezed as they contracted and inflated. Even though their faces were covered Silus recognised Win and the crew of the *Llothriall*. Katya and Zac weren't amongst them.

Silus tried to pull his hands free of the grip of the floor but the more he pulled, the tighter the grip became, until the bones of his wrists began to grind painfully together.

"Dunsany! Kelos! Wake up."

A portion of the far wall flexed and dilated open like a vast sphincter. A Chadassa stepped through the opening and into the room. The door folded closed behind it with a sound that made Silus's guts turn.

"What have you done with Katya and Zac?" he shouted, pulling against his restraints, a fresh surge of hatred for the Chadassa flowing through him.

"Belck has them now. They are no longer of your concern. I am to prepare you for the Queen."

"I'd rather kill myself than breed with your kind."

"If you resist us then the things we do to your woman and her grub will make this seem but a pleasant dream." With that the Chadassa put its hand against the wall and barked several words in a harsh, guttural language.

The hood encasing Win's head contracted and the Archduke cried out, thrashing against his bonds. The hood was so tight now that Silus could see Win's features clearly through the taut material. The expression he saw was one of uncomprehending terror. Blood trickled down Win's neck as the bones of his skull shifted and cracked.

His screams quickly fell silent. The hood relaxed its grip. Win slumped against Dunsany.

The Chadassa turned to Silus. "Now come, follow."

Silus's hands were released and he got numbly to his feet. The sphincter-door peeled open and the Chadassa was already halfway through when Silus tore the pipe free from Win's collapsed hood, his fingers almost slipping on the bony ridges. He ran at the Chadassa and encircled its throat with his left arm, before jabbing the pipe into its right eye, the black orb giving way easily to the jagged edge.

The creature screamed and scrabbled against Silus's hold, its claws tearing shallow trenches into his arm. Silus ignored the pain and rammed the broken pipe into the Chadassa's eye again and again until it dropped to the floor, its cries loud in the confines of the flesh chamber. Silus knelt on the creature's chest and, leaning down hard, he pushed the pipe as far into the Chadassa's eye socket as it would go. There was a loud crack and the pipe met with little resistance as it entered the soft meat of the Chadassa's brain.

Silus remained crouched over the creature for a moment, listening for the approach of more of its kind. But there was no sound of footsteps and, so, Silus got to work freeing the prisoners.

The hoods did not peel easily away from their heads and Silus was careful less he harm his companions in any way, but soon he had the first of them free. He gently extracted the breathing pipe from Dunsany's mouth, stepping back when he vomited copiously onto the ground.

"Am I dead? Is this the seven hells that the Faith used to threaten us with?"

"No, Dunsany, I can assure you that we are very much alive."

Dunsany noticed the corpse of the creature, and then Win's body.

"That... that's..."

"Yes, it is. Now help me get your hands free before they have a chance to do the same to the rest of us."

Using a section of broken pipe, they managed to dig Dunsany's hands from the floor. As he tore at the flesh of the room, Silus thought that he could hear squeals of protest coming from somewhere distant. When he peeled the hood from Jacquinto's head the chamber shuddered. Pores began to open up in the floor and through these oozed a sticky clear substance, while the door to the room began to shrink.

"Come on, we're leaving now!" Silus shouted, giving the crew no time to orientate themselves.

The hole of the door was almost too narrow to struggle through as the last of them left the room, and Kelos and Silus had to pull Father Maylan through the folds of flesh that had begun to close around his body. He tumbled through as the door sealed itself behind him and soon the chamber was lost behind a wall of unbroken flesh.

"I feel strangely reborn," the priest said, getting to his feet.

The corridor in which they now found themselves was made of a material that looked like raw steak. Above them, arches of bone supported the ceiling where thick red cables ran through the flesh, pulsing to a steady beat that echoed down the passageway. Silus put his hand to a wall and it twitched away from his touch.

"Wherever we are," he said, "this place is alive."

"We need to get out of here quick." Jacquinto said. "We have no weapons and there are bound to be more Chadassa on us at any moment."

"What if we *made* weapons?" Silus said.

He went to where a ridge of bone emerged from the wall and kicked it as hard as he could. For a moment it didn't look as if it was going to give, but then a hairline crack ran up its surface and Silus redoubled his efforts until the bone gave way. He then tore at it before turning to his companions, holding a vicious looking shard.

"It's not much, but it's better than nothing."

The crew of the *Llothriall* pulled and kicked at the walls until they had variously armed themselves with scimitars of bone and thick cords of flesh. Only Emuel refused to arm himself. "If it comes to a fight, and it is my time, then it is my time." He reasoned.

"And I'd argue that you were being a stubborn idiot if we actually had any time," Silus said, "but for now I think that we should start running."

Behind them the walls of the passage had begun to close up. As they ran Silus had a moment to wonder whether the collapse was as result of their damage to the walls, whether the organism through which they fled was trying to limit the harm they had inflicted upon it.

They turned a corner only to find that the passage came to an end. Behind them the corridor continued to contract.

Father Maylan closed his eyes and began to pray.

"Maylan, shut up! That's not helping." Silus said.

Silus pushed against the wall blocking their escape and it gave easily under his fingers. When he tapped it, it thrummed like the taut skin of a drum. Using his bone fragment, he cut into the barrier and it tore with a hiss of escaping air.

"Follow me," Silus said, before pushing his way through the gap.

He fell to the floor on the other side and, for one vertiginous moment, he thought that he would keep on falling. All that separated him from the surrounding sea was a thin, translucent membrane. The whole room was made of the same clear substance and Silus barely heard his companions tumbling into the chamber behind him as he stared in wonder.

The clear hemisphere in which they now stood protruded from an expanse of dark, scaled flesh. Through the side of the chamber and far to his right Silus could see a vast tail slowly fanning from side to side and he realised, with shock, that he was looking down the flank of an enormous creature.

Kelos ran his hand over the wall, a look of excited confusion on his face.

"Extraordinary. Thin as a bubble but utterly resilient"

"I think that we're *in* the thing that attacked Morat," Silus said.

"And I think that you may be right. Gods, I thought that the leviathan we encountered on the *Llothriall* was big, but this is something else entirely."

"There really is no hope then is there?" Dunsany said.

"What do you mean?" Silus said.

"We can't cut our way out of here because we'll drown and we can't stay where we are because the Chadassa will find and eviscerate us."

"I think that if they were going to eviscerate us they would have done so already." Kelos said.

"And what about Win?" Dunsany said.

As they stood in uneasy silence, Silus began to search about them for another exit, but it was a futile gesture.

"What is that?" Father Maylan said, from where he was crouched near the floor.

Silus dropped down beside him and saw a large shadow directly beneath them. As it unfolded a lance of green fire erupted from it and slammed into the flesh just beyond the chamber wall. A great cloud of blood immediately boiled into the water. In it, they could see the corpses of several Chadassa. Another lance of energy punched into the flesh further to the right and this time the floor of the chamber shook as a screech of pain rang through the walls.

"What is that thing?" Father Maylan asked.

"I don't know," said Silus.

And he was no closer to knowing as it suddenly lurched out of the darkness and pressed itself against the chamber walls.

Katya awoke to find herself lying on a strange, spongy bed with two Chadassa females standing over her. One of them held Zac to a pendulous breast and she was horrified to see him greedily tugging at the teat, his face flushed with the warmth of the milk he was drinking. When she snatched him away from the creature he began to cry. Katya tried to calm Zac by holding him to her own breast, but he refused to drink and instead beat against her chest with his tiny hands.

She tried to run then, but the room she found herself in had no door and when she started scrabbling around the moist, fleshy walls, desperately trying to find an exit, one of the Chadassa females grabbed her by the hair and dragged her back to the bed.

The thing pulled Zac out of Katya's arms and his cries were silenced as he began to feed once more.

Katya closed her eyes and refused to open them until one of the Chadassa hauled her from the bed and marched her from the room. Mercifully Zac was placed back in her arms then and he had looked up at her with a happy little smile.

As they entered a large chamber that looked out onto the sea, Belck turned to greet them. He reached out for her son and Zac was soon crying again as one of the Chadassa took him from her and placed him in the ancient creature's arms. Zac squirmed, his face wrinkled in a red grimace of distress. The Chadassa chuckled and cooed at the infant, increasing the volume of his cries.

Katya looked on helplessly as she was restrained by one of the Chadassa females. Her claws dug painfully into her wrists and she could feel her hot breath on the back of her neck.

"Ah yes," Belck said, "the bloodline may be even stronger in this one. It is a pity he is not of an age where he could be useful. Still, he is something of a prize. You may take him now."

The other Chadassa female took Zac from him.

"Leave him alone!" Katya screamed.

"And so to the mother," Belck said. "What to do with you I wonder?"

"You harm Zac and I will – "

"You'll what? What can you do Katya?"

It was true of course, she could do nothing but watch. Tears welled in her eyes and she quickly blinked them away, unwilling to show these foul creatures any sign of weakness.

"Yes, I thought so," Belck said. "Still, I believe that you can be of some use and Zac is still an infant. It would be wrong to separate mother and child at this delicate stage, don't you think?"

The Chadassa female came over to them, Zac curled against her breast, his eyes closed and his chest calmly rising and falling as he slept.

"If we give him back to you Katya," Belck said, "will you be more cooperative?"

She made a grab for her son and the Chadassa stepped away, Zac stirring briefly as he was jolted by the motion.

"No Katya," Belck said. "I asked you a question. Now, will you cooperate?"

A vicious, jealous hatred burned in her as she looked at her child sleeping in the arms of the creature, and she swore to herself that if she broke free she would kill the mongrel bitch that held him. But for now, her fury was of no use to her son, and so she held out her arms.

"Yes, I'll cooperate."

"Good. That was what I was hoping you'd say."

Zac was placed back in her arms and Katya was relived that he did not wake or struggle against her.

"What have you done with my husband?"

"Silus is being prepared for our Queen." Belck said. "His seed will be the herald for a new age. Aren't you proud to be even a small part of that?"

"Silus isn't one of you."

"So you have told us."

A sudden tremor shook the room and sent Belck stumbling away from her. Katya would have laughed at the look of confusion on his face if she weren't so preoccupied with keeping her own feet.

Across the room a door dilated open and a Chadassa male raced in.

"Ancient one, we are under attack. We have sealed the right flank chambers but we are already taking more hits."

"Podrol, what exactly is attacking us?" Belck said, as he steadied himself with his staff.

"I've never seen anything like it before, but Utral says that it is a Calma vessel."

Belck looked not only confused now, but Katya thought that she saw something like fear creeping into his face, though on features so alien it was hard to tell.

"Where is Silus?" Belck snapped.

"I'm afraid that he has escaped his bonds. However, he will still be somewhere on the ship. I have dispatched my best soldiers after him. For now, I suggest we get you to safety."

"No Podrol."

"I'm sorry ancient one, I don't follow."

"Get the woman and her child away from the ship first. I will stay and fight. If it really is the Calma they will not stand up long against the might of our warriors."

"Very well." Podrol approached Katya and she flinched away from his touch. "It is for your own safety."

There was nothing she could do to resist and she knew it. If Katya attempted to fight they would like as not take Zac away again and have her killed. The fact that she was being allowed to nurse her son was perhaps the only thing keeping her alive. She had to hope that Silus would win through and come and rescue her but, in the meantime, she could only numbly follow the creature that led her from the room and down a narrow corridor. Through the thin walls Katya could see what looked like a network of veins. Through each one flowed a dark fluid and, not for the first time, she wondered just where she was.

At the end of the corridor another door peeled open and she was led into a small spherical chamber. Podrol gestured to where a stump of knotted and bloody material grew from the floor.

"Sit." Podrol said, before leaving the room, the door dilating shut behind him.

Katya sat and rocked Zac back and forth, singing him a song that her mother had taught her, the lyrics telling of the glittering seas of Long Night and the creatures of light who danced there. She hoped that they would not have to wait long before Silus found them. The room was stiflingly warm and the light that illuminated it was sickly.

Suddenly there was a falling sensation in the pit of her stomach and she cried out, holding Zac tight. He woke with a squeal and began to struggle in her arms. Pale filaments grew from the walls, quickly wrapping the two of them in a tight, sticky web. Katya fought against them for a second, but as the room began to spin she found that she was glad of the restraints.

The walls of the room glowed before becoming translucent and now Katya could see where she had been imprisoned.

As she tumbled through the sea, away from the Chadassa craft, she wondered at just how they had managed to make their fortress inside an enormous fish.

CHAPTER NINETEEN

With a sound like a great sheet being torn in half, the Chadassa ship was breached and Silus saw the Calma in the flesh for the first time.

As the thing stepped through the rent in the chamber wall, Silus could see beyond it, into the interior of its craft. Like the ship they had found themselves imprisoned on it seemed to be entirely organic.

The Calma looked at Silus for a moment before raising the flail in its hand. Dunsany threw himself in the way, his bone sword raised to defend against a blow that never came.

Instead of attacking the Calma made its way to the tear through which Silus and the crew had entered the chamber. There it touched its flail to the wall and the flesh peeled back as sparks of energy crackled across it.

"What is that thing Silus?" Dunsany said, staring at the Calma.

"They're called the Calma. Don't worry, they are no friend of the Chadassa."

The collapsed walls of the corridor beyond opened up under the flow of energy from the flail and Silus looked down the passage to see two Chadassa racing towards them.

The Calma let out an almighty yell that filled the heads of the crew with a sharp pain. The Chadassa, though, seemed to feel it even more acutely because they dropped to their knees, bent almost double in their agony.

As the sonic assault died away, the Calma turned to Silus. "You will board our vessel and wait for us to return."

"Who are you?"

"My name is Seras."

But beyond that the creature was clearly going to tell him nothing. Instead it inclined its head and gestured towards the breach in the chamber wall as more of its kind poured from their ship.

"No, I'm coming with you." Silus told the Calma. "The Chadassa have my wife and son. We're not leaving without them."

From the corridor came the sound of fighting as the Calma and Chadassa clashed, strange inhuman cries and ululating screams echoing toward them.

"We're coming too." Dunsany said.

"I appreciate it, I really do." Silus said. "But you've done enough for me as it is. Risked enough. This is my fight."

"This is *our* fight," Jacquinto said. "Remember that the Chadassa are responsible for the death of Ioannis. If there's a chance that we can take them down, we should take it."

"For Ioannis," Ignacio agreed.

"And the people of Morat." Father Maylan spoke up. "Those abominations destroyed that beautiful city."

"And for you Silus." Emuel said. "For you, Katya and Zac."

"Okay," Silus said after a moment. "Okay. But if things get too dangerous there will be no dishonour in you retreating to the Calma ship. Stay well back and let the Calma do most of the fighting. If you see any sign of Katya and Zac, let me know at once."

With that Silus ran after the Calma warriors. Behind him he heard the footfalls of his companions and he felt momentarily buoyed up by their bravery.

This, however, was short-lived as he started to come across the first casualties of the battle.

The burns on the torso of the first Chadassa corpse he saw were so deep that they revealed the ruptured organs within. Ahead of him the walls of the corridor had been similarly scorched, and the floor was wet with the brackish fluid that poured from the wounds. The smell of cooking flesh was sour and Silus fought against a sudden, intense nausea. He realised then that in learning the art of war the Calma had also inherited something of the Chadassa's ferocity. As Silus pulled himself through a ruptured doorway, he saw another Calma take down a Chadassa. The Calma's flail wrapped around the creature's torso and tightened, the dark scales beneath the fronds splitting as they began to burn. The Chadassa tried to rake its claws across the Calma's face, but it died in agony before it could effectively retaliate.

Silus looked back and, seeing the expressions of appalled horror on much of the crew's faces, he started to search the room for an exit.

Three low tunnels led from the chamber in which they now stood, two of which were currently blocked by the entangled forms of Chadassa and Calma. The third remained clear and Silus gestured to his companions as he crouched to enter the passage. As he looked back to check that they were following, he saw Seras enter the tunnel behind them, followed by several more Calma.

He cursed under his breath but made no attempt to confront the creatures.

The tunnel widened as it sloped gently upwards and Kelos made his way to Silus' side.

"So, what's the plan?" He said.

"We find Katya and Zac and get out."

"And how do we get out?"

"I think we're going to have to rely on the Calma for that."

Kelos looked back to see Seras and his companions struggling to get ahead of the group. "They certainly seem keen to keep an eye on you."

Two Chadassa raced down the corridor towards them, wielding thin metal staffs. They stumbled to a stop when they saw Silus, seemingly unsure as to whether they should attack. Their indecision gave Kelos time to take a small ball of what looked like matted fur from his robe and throw it to the ground, shouting a many-syllabled word as he did so.

Silus experienced a moment of disorientation – an instance of pure darkness – before he suddenly found himself standing behind the Chadassa, further up the corridor from his companions. He didn't question what had just happened, instead he rammed his bone shard into back of the neck of the Chadassa on his right, before felling the creature on his left.

Kelos smiled as he stepped over the fallen bodies. "Just a minor teleportation spell. Thought that it might come in handy."

"I'd save your power for now," Silus said. "I think that the Chadassa have orders to capture rather than kill me and that's going to give us something of an advantage."

"Nevertheless," Seras said, finally pushing his way to the front of the group, "I would be happier if you would allow us to provide you with some protection."

They followed the Calma up the corridor. From close by they could hear the sound of battle and at one point they were thrown to the floor as the corridor shook.

"It seems that the first of the charges has been prematurely detonated," Seras said, regaining his feet. "I only hope this doesn't mean that Belck is attempting to escape."

Silus was more worried about the prospect of Katya and Zac being injured, but he said nothing as they left the corridor and entered a long low passage that reminded him of the cloisters of a monastery. Through arches of bone and sinew he could see more Calma and Chadassa engaged in battle. None of the combatants appeared to notice the humans led by the group of Calma in their midst, and they proceeded unchallenged to a huge set of labial double doors.

Seras used his flail on the barrier and the curtains of flesh withdrew slowly, strings of mucus dripping from the parting folds. Through them Silus could see into a vast chamber, one wall of which was entirely translucent, showing the underwater vista beyond.

"If you think I'm going through that slime, you've got another think coming." Jacquinto said.

At that moment another explosion shook the ship and a wall of black smoke billowed swiftly towards them, forcing the group into the room.

Silus immediately scanned the room for Katya and Zac, but the only occupants were two Chadassa. One stood not far from the door and did nothing to stop them, even appearing to view their approach with disinterest. He only looked mildly pained when Dunsany ran him through. The other Chadassa standing by the window only moved as his brethren fell.

As he turned, Silus recognised the gnarled and aged form of Belck.

"I'm afraid that you have missed her, Silus," he said. "When the Calma attack began I sent her away. You will not see her again."

With a yell Silus charged Belck. The creature gestured with a hand and the bone shard flew out of his grasp. However, this did nothing to slow his progress. If it came to it, he was willing to pummel this abomination to death with his bare hands. Behind him he was vaguely aware of his comrades following in the wake of his charge. But then there was a sensation like he had stepped through a sheet of ice-cold water, and the only sound he could now hear was the clicking of Belck's talons on the floor as he walked towards him. As Silus continued to rush forwards his legs grew heavy and he slowed.

Looking down, he realised that he wasn't moving at all.

"All this, and for what? A woman and child." Belck said. "I have seen how the human race have proliferated across Twilight, their numbers swelling each year, your cities growing more crowded. It always amazes me that you get so attached to each other when there are so many of you around and more are easily created. What's two lives amongst so many, Silus? They are nothing to you. You, however, are unique. Does that not give you a certain pride? Does that not make the lives of your family seem insignificant?"

Silus tried to speak, but he couldn't even move his jaw. His thoughts began to trickle away until he wasn't aware of any anger or hatred, any emotion at all. There were just Belck's words.

"Turn."

Silus did so. In front of him a glistening membrane divided the room, separating him from his companions. They tried to cut at it with their knives but failed to penetrate it. Even when Seras applied his flail nothing happened. In desperation they looked back at the entrance to the chamber, but a bone carapace had grown over the door, sealing them in.

"Ineffective creatures are they not Silus? Ultimately weak. And see where they have got you. All this pain and death is very much their doing. If they hadn't entangled you in their plans it would have been so much easier. If you had just given yourself to us willingly, then you would have had time to say goodbye to Katya and Zac."

Now that Belck mentioned it Silus could indeed see how foolish his companions were. Dunsany's face was flushed with rage and Kelos was trying to pull him away from the barrier as he pounded on it with his fists. Silus laughed at the look of frustration and concern on the mage's face. And there was Emuel, the boy's pale skin marked with the symbols of a forgotten, mongrel race; used like a doll, perhaps the most useless of them all.

Belck laughed along with Silus and Silus laughed until his chest hurt, disarmed by the sheer uselessness of it all.

"None of this matters, Silus. In the end not even I matter. Once the Great Ocean embraces us in its infinite waters, all will see the beauty of those endless seas. Reality will be remade to the glory of His name. Only you can make that happen. I have looked into those dark waters and the peace to be found there is everlasting. But there are those who do not share our vision, those who would make every single day a meaningless struggle."

Silus began to share in Belck's frustration. How pointless were these mayfly existences that drove themselves gladly onto the points of each other's swords to prove their god was the true god. How could Silus even have thought he was their kin?

"You aren't their kin Silus. You can feel what you truly are.

Even as you have fought it, it has begun to waken within you. That jagged anger that you feel, that's not for the Chadassa. That's for those you have, for so long, called your kind. Those who have held you back all this time from the realisation of your true potential."

The anger rose from the pit of Silus's stomach, burning like bile. He turned to Belck and saw himself reflected in the black orbs of the creature's eyes. In the darkness that surrounded his reflection he could feel the call of the Great Ocean; that wonderful infinite peace. And the thought of being denied that – being denied the chance to swim forever in those cool, dark waters – inflamed his rage and drove him, snarling, against the barrier that separated him from the humans.

"You are Chadassa, Silus. These creatures are nothing. Take them apart."

Silus's hands dug into the barrier and Dunsany started to reach for him, trying to help him break through. But when he saw the look on Silus's face he backed away. The slippery surface refused to give for a moment and this enraged Silus further. He started to scrabble furiously at the slick membrane, the growl in the back of his throat growing to an inhuman wail. He pushed his face against the barrier and it suddenly gave way.

Silus stumbled, but he used the momentum of the trip to take him barrelling into one of the Calma. He grabbed the glowing nodules that hung from either side of the creature's jaw and pulled as hard as he could. As they tore away a part of him wondered why their strange light didn't die. It was, however, a momentary distraction, and Silus tore into the struggling beast, marvelling at how easily its flesh gave way under his hands, appalled at the vivid blue coil of its guts as they fell to the floor.

He barely felt the flails of the other Calma as they brought them to bear. Something tickled, and there was the smell of cooking flesh, but then there were more bodies lying at his feet and those that he had called his friends were backing away from the spreading pool of blood.

Sera was screaming something at him, but he ignored the foolish creature. Instead, he turned back to Belck, seeking approval, but the Chadassa ancient was no longer there. The hatred that Belck had inspired in him, however, was.

"Silus, listen to me. Belck has placed some kind of glamour on you," said Kelos. "We're going to get you out of this but it's very important that you listen to me."

This ridiculous mage with his cantrips and charms, what good would they prove against the might of the Great Ocean? Silus wanted to hurt Kelos. But he didn't want him to suffer just physical pain, he wanted first for him to feel the torture of grief. Silus wanted the mage to taste that profound despair.

Dunsany held his bone shard before him as Silus approached, Jacquinto and Ignacio moved to flank him, their own weapons raised.

Kelos had seen the look in Silus's eyes and he realised what was about to happen.

"Silus, please don't."

"I'm warning you," Jacquinto said. "Don't make me have to kill you."

Silus's hand shot out, grabbed Jacquinto's face and pushed. The smuggler tumbled across the room and came up hard against a bone arch, his skull connecting with an audible crack. There was a cry of rage as Ignacio slammed into Silus's side, but he didn't shift, even under the weight of the heavier man. Instead Silus turned and twisted Ignacio's hand until he dropped his blade with a cry of pain. Then Silus turned back to Dunsany.

"Silus come back to us," said Father Maylan, but he didn't approach. "This isn't you."

Silus ignored the priest and looked into Dunsany's eyes.

Kelos ran at him and started pummelling him with his fists, but he knocked him aside and reached for Dunsany's weapon.

"You don't need this."

Dunsany's face was slack as Silus held his gaze, and he knew that the mariner was looking into the darkness that burned in his eyes, the call of the Great Ocean reaching out to him.

Silus ran his hand over Dunsany's head and cradled the back of his skull.

"This isn't so bad really, is it Dunsany?"

"No," Dunsany's voice was dead. "This isn't so bad."

"It's just like going to sleep really. It will be easy."

"Just like sleep."

Silus looked back at Kelos. The mage was picking himself up from where he had been thrown. As he gained his feet, Silus put the knife to Dunsany's throat. Then, when he was sure that Kelos was watching, he drew the blade across the flesh.

There was an explosion and spray hit Silus's face. It was too cold for blood though, and he soon found himself standing ankle deep in water.

Silus wondered why the bone shard in his right hand was covered in blood, and then he looked, in horror, at Dunsany choking as scarlet liquid welled from between his fingers.

Silus tried to reach out to his friend, help him staunch the flow, but the sea finally found its way into the Chadassa ship and pulled him into its cold embrace.

CHAPTER TWENTY

Silus tried to roll over on to his side as something tickled his stomach, but found that he was hemmed in. The tickling sensation continued and he brushed it away with his arm.

"Katya stop it. I'm trying to sleep."

Suddenly there was a sharp, jabbing pain and he woke up fully.

Silus looked down to see two giant trilobites crawling over his torso, probing the wounds that he had sustained in the destruction of the Chadassa craft. There was another burst of pain as one of them worked at a deep cut on his chest. Silus tried to drag the giant insect off, but it hung on tight as a limpet and pulling at it only caused him more pain.

All Silus could see from the confines of the narrow, coffin-like box he lay in was part of one wall and the moist ceiling above him.

"Katya? Dunsany? Kelos?"

There was no reply and he tried to climb over the side of the box. The trilobites stubbornly clung to him as he raised himself.

He staggered towards an archway before a rapidly approaching shadow drove him back into the room.

Belck caught Silus before he hit the floor.

"You shouldn't be up and about before the creatures have finished their work," the Chadassa said, helping Silus sit. "Ah, there you go."

With a high-pitched twitter, the trilobites scurried down Silus's torso and out through the archway. He looked down at himself and saw that the wounds that criss-crossed his chest had been expertly stitched shut. When he touched them they weren't even sore.

"We are not interested in hurting you, Silus." Belck said.

"What happened to Katya and Zac?"

"They are safe, but they need not concern you now."

"And the crew, my friends?"

"No doubt killed in the inept attack launched by the Calma."

Silus couldn't remember the attack. The last thing he remembered was following the Calma as they fought their way through the Chadassa ship.

"Those creatures, the Calma, you used them, changed them," he said. "The Great Ocean showed me how your race was grown from their kind."

"That is true, but we changed for the better. Just as you have been changing, Silus."

"What do you mean?"

"You really don't understand how different you are, do you?"

Silus struggled to his feet and shrugged off Belck's touch. He was sick of ancient prophecy, sick of being the chosen one to a twisted aquatic race that had done nothing but bring pain and death into his life.

"If I cooperate, will you let Katya and Zac go?"

"If you do, then they will be well looked after, yes," Belck said.

"And what will happen to me?"

"You are to be prepared for the Queen. By breeding with her you will father the Land Walkers."

"Will it hurt?"

"Your body will be consumed but you will find it to be a joyous and fulfilling experience."

The thought of his own death didn't move Silus in any way. In fact, he was so exhausted, so drained by grief and worn down by fear that he found it difficult to feel anything.

"Gods, what am I?"

"Let me show you."

Belck ushered Silus into a wide corridor. Stone arches covered with molluscs stretched away into the gloom, while the floor was slick with rotting seaweed. The walls were decorated with murals depicting, for the most part, the Chadassa battling the Calma. Whatever artist had carved these reliefs clearly delighted in cruelty, for the most intricately worked parts of the stone were the scenes depicting slaughter.

Other reliefs were more simple, portraying nothing more complicated than a vast black disk.

"Is that...?"

"The Great Ocean, yes. The father of the Chadassa. It is to His infinite waters that we shall soon return, when the time of the Great Flood is finally brought about and all reality is changed."

"What exactly is the Great Ocean?"

"I have told you, it is our creator, our god."

"And what is the Great Flood?"

"It is the time when the Great Ocean will change all reality so that it will be as the Great Ocean. Then we will swim together, forever in His infinite waters."

"You don't actually know what that really means though, do you Belck?" Silus said. "You sound like a member of the Faith, blindly following their god wherever they are told, even if they don't understand why."

Another Chadassa passed them and raised a hand to Belck in greeting. "The Great Flood be upon us," the creature said.

"I... I... yes, the Flood," Belck stammered, clearly thrown by Silus's interrogation.

Recovering himself, Belck gripped Silus by the shoulder and marched him into a room that was bathed in the diffuse light of the sea. Only a thin, translucent membrane separated them from the water beyond.

"Now, Silus, behold your natural habitat. We drained the

rooms you passed through so that the shock of the water would be lessened, but you, like us, can breathe water. I will show you how."

With his hand on the small of Silus's back, Belck pushed him through the membrane and out into the sea.

As the chill water gripped him, Silus instinctively closed his eyes and started to struggle for the surface.

Belck, however, held him firm.

Be still, his voice came. *Open your eyes.*

Silus had expected the sting of salt water, but he could see clearly and without pain.

Now, breathe.

Silus shook his head and tried to kick away from the Chadassa again, but he couldn't move.

Breathe, Silus.

Silus looked up and realised that he couldn't see the surface. Even if Belck let him go, he would drown before he could reach air.

After a moment it became clear that he had no option but to take a breath. As water filled his lungs, he fought panic. Even though he had prepared himself for death, when he was faced with its inevitability he still railed against it. He struggled against Belck as his chest tightened with the coldness of the water that was now inside him, but the Chadassa's grip remained firm.

This is what you are, Silus. This is what the Chadassa have made you.

Why had this creature gone to so much trouble to capture him only to bring him out here to drown? But then Silus was startled to realise that the water wasn't choking him, that the cold sensation of the sea moving in and out of his lungs was easing, that, in fact, he was breathing the sea as easily as if it were air.

What is this?

This is what we have been trying to tell you all this time, Belck said, releasing his hold. *You are no ordinary human.*

He truly was the son of the Chadassa. With the despair this brought, however, there was still a rush of excitement at the abilities that had been revealed to him.

Come, Belck said, swimming away from him, *let us experience the joys of the ocean together.*

Belck was rapidly dwindling from view now and Silus didn't think that he'd be able to catch him up, but then he sprang from the seabed. The weight of the water between him and the surface was vast, but he cut through it rapidly, revelling in the sensation of it rushing against his body, taking great lungfuls of the sea, feeling its invigorating power as it filled him.

As he spiralled up through the depths a school of dolphins surrounded him, calling to him with clicks and whistles. Beneath their chattering language, Silus could hear their true song. The song that was at the core of their existence, all existence. The song that Kelos had taught him to hear. Above him, Silus could even hear the song of Belck. It was a discordant and jagged tune, one that didn't belong in the great symphony that played here beneath the waves.

Silus began to close on the Chadassa. The soft glow of Kerberos was beginning to penetrate the water and life was more abundant this close to the surface. A great, roiling mass of glittering gemfish shattered as he powered through them.

Silus broke the surface and spray surrounded him like a multitude of glistening jewels. Contained within each individual droplet he could see the azure glow of Kerberos. Ahead of him Belck re-entered the water and Silus followed in his wake. He overtook the Chadassa, swimming down amongst the shafts of sunlight. One of these caught the edge of an arch of stone and, his curiosity piqued, Silus swam towards it.

The great bow of volcanic rock rose from the seabed far below and Silus followed its curve down. Belck caught up with him and swam alongside.

Let me show you what it is to know the Great Ocean, Silus.

Belck overtook him and Silus followed.

They swam for a long time. Finally, as the pressures of the deep began to make Silus's bones ache they arrived at the base of the arch. Even here, however, they didn't rest. Instead, Belck led Silus over the lip of a canyon and into a darkness more absolute than anything he had experienced before.

Belck reached out and took his hand. Silus didn't resist, even though he found the touch of the creature repellent. He was too afraid of being lost in the infinite darkness to let go.

He is the Great Ocean. He will come again, Belck began to chant.

As the Chadassa's mantra filled Silus's mind he sensed the walls of the canyon fall completely away.

Nothing surrounded them now. Silus couldn't even feel the water against his skin.

Now, Belck said. *Witness his coming.*

The Chadassa sent out his consciousness into the darkness, yet there was no response. Silus could feel Belck straining to make contact with his God.

He is the Great Ocean. He will come again.

The chant sounded more urgent this time, as though Belck was pleading.

After what seemed like a long time, it became obvious that the Chadassa's god was not going to grace them with its presence.

The doubt and anxiety that Silus had sensed in Belck earlier began to boil over into anger. The Chadassa's grip on his hand suddenly became painful and the canyon walls rushed past them as he was dragged up through the depths.

Soon they came into sight of the Chadassa city and Silus only had a moment to take in the enormity of the terrible architecture before Belck shoved him out of the sea.

He fell to the floor of the chamber and began to cough up the water that filled his lungs. It burned as it flowed out of him and Silus found himself shivering uncontrollably as an intense weakness overtook him.

He looked up to see Belck standing over him, his dark eyes regarding him dispassionately.

"Get up."

But Silus couldn't stand and, with another great shudder, he coughed up more saltwater. He cried out as Belck wrapped his claws in his hair, dragged him to his feet and threw him across the room to land in a heap before another Chadassa.

"Take this one to be prepared for the Queen," Belck said. "It is time."

After Katya had been ejected from the belly of the Chadassa craft she had fallen through the depths – cradling Zac to her as he screamed and screamed – convinced that they were going to die. For a moment the sphere they were in stabilised, gently swaying, rather than spinning in all directions, and Katya looked up at the bizarre vessel they had left behind.

There was a flash of intense light and then they were tumbling again like some circus act from Miramas, as the shockwave from the explosion caught up with the sphere.

The water around them boiled with clouds of debris and within them Katya could see the broken corpses of dozens of Chadassa. For a moment she thought that she could make out a human face in the morass but then, with a violent shudder, the sphere was snatched away from the scene as they hurtled down along some unseen current.

Katya closed her eyes as her stomach somersaulted. Zac, however, had begun to enjoy himself and his cries turned to squeals of laughter.

There wasn't much to see outside of the sphere now, other than the occasional pulse of fluorescence from the delicate creatures who grazed on the plankton fields that seeded the depths. Katya gently shifted Zac into her lap before leaning over and pulling on the fleshy protuberances that grew from the sphere floor. She had hoped to be able to take control of the strange craft in this way, but her ministrations did nothing to alter their course.

Something caught Katya's attention then. A pale shape moving just at the edge of her vision.

It emerged from the darkness, its long body stretching far behind it, seeming as though it would never end. Its eyes were a blind milky white, yet the pits of its angular nostrils seemed more than sufficient to smell out any prey that entered its territory. It scooped up the creatures grazing on the plankton in its great jaws, but this didn't seem enough to sate its hunger because it headed straight for the sphere.

Katya closed her eyes and braced herself, with Zac held tight to her breast. There was a flash of light and an intense smell of ozone filled the sphere. When she opened her eyes, the creature was falling away from them, its vast length entangling around itself as streams of bubbles rushed from its slack jaws.

Katya saw the creature crash into the side of a jagged peak of stone that appeared to be part of a building of some kind, before it impacted with the seabed in a cloud of silt.

The sphere followed the creature down into the city, descending at a much more sedate pace. As the towers and strange mound-like structures rose around them, Katya breathed a sigh of relief. She had thought that they would fall forever, to die in some lightless, airless abyss. Instead the sphere rotated on its axis before heading towards a hole that had opened up in the side of one of the buildings.

Absolute darkness enfolded them then, the bottom of the sphere rising up slightly beneath them as it settled onto a solid surface.

All that Katya could hear was her and Zac's breathing and the soft drip of moisture falling from the ceiling. The drip became a trickle and then a torrent as the sphere melted around them.

Katya rose to her feet, holding Zac, shivering as the thick film of slime that covered them rapidly cooled. From somewhere there was a deep rumble and hiss before a shaft of light broke the darkness, making Katya throw up a hand to shield her eyes.

Silhouetted in a doorway stood the form of a Chadassa, though it seemed taller than any Katya had seen before, the crest of spines that ran from the small of its back to the top of its skull more prominent than that found on most Chadassa. As it stepped into the light Katya saw that it was a female, heavy breasts swaying as it strode towards them, flapping against a distended belly that could only be swollen by the presence of a child.

When the creature saw Zac in her arms it made a strange crooning sound and its crest shivered with a dry rattle.

Katya backed away, only to come up against a wall.

In her arms Zac made no sound. He held her eyes with his own and in them she could see no awareness of the danger they were in.

Before Katya could do anything, the Chadassa snatched Zac from her arms and retreated back through the doorway.

The shaft of light was extinguished as the door closed behind them and Katya dropped to her knees, howling as she was left in the darkness without her child.

The Chadassa's name was Snil. She had mothered twenty-five younglings and her belly was taut with three more. Her fertility was legendry and her spawn were highly valued for both their martial and leadership skills. When Belck had told her that they had come into possession of the half-breed's son she had fervently hoped that she would be picked to nurse the child. And Belck had not disappointed her, picking Snil, out of all the potential Chadassa mothers, to hold the extraordinary being in her arms.

She only wished she could have nursed him in the sea, but Belck had said that though the child may well have inherited his father's abilities, it was best not to risk drowning the wee one.

And so, Snil sat in a drained but damp chamber, as the infant struggled against her scaled hide, kicking against her belly with his tiny feet. She held him up before her and crooned a sing-song sound. What was this creature's name? What was it that his mother had screamed as Snil had spirited the child away?

Ah yes, Zac.

"Zac," she said, just about managing to vocalise the word. Snil hadn't the proficiency with the human language that some of the older, more learned, Chadassa had, but she eventually got the hang of the infant's name. "I like you Zac," she giggled and shivered the spines of her crest. The sudden rattling sound made Zac pause in his protestations and stare at her with wide, deep eyes.

Such eyes and such colour! The dark pits of his pupils were surrounded by a vivid blue. It reminded Snil of the play of light through the shallows, reminded her of the time she had stood right on the edge of the human lands, just beneath the waves, and marvelled at the warmth of the sun on her face.

Snil rattled her crest again. Zac responded with a bemused smile and brought up his hands as though to grasp at the quivering quills. But she didn't want him to cut his delicate hands on her spines. "No, no." She chided, holding the child against her chest.

Snil knew exactly what Zac really wanted and she offered him a breast.

In momentary shock he pulled away from the vast dark nipple that she thrust at his face. But then, as her viscous milk started to leak from the swollen dug, Zac clamped a hungry mouth onto her and began to feed.

He was so much more tender than any of the children that had sprung from her loins, almost considerate. He closed his eyes and made sounds of satisfaction deep in his throat as he fed, his small hands raised, clenching and unclenching. Snil stroked the top of his downy head until Zac pulled away from the touch of her rough hand and began to cry.

"Shhh. Shhh," Snil soothed, guiding him back to her nipple.

She realised now that she'd be unable to comfort Zac in quite the same way she would one of her own. Snil knew so little about the humans. She only knew that the Chadassa were supposed to hate them and covet their mastery of land. But she found it difficult to hate something as perfect as the creature in her arms. In comparison to her own kind it would seem that humans were a far more subtle and complex race, created for a greater purpose than to merely breed and kill.

Zac looked up at her and enclosed one of her fingers in a fist. She could feel a fierce heat emanating from his palm and a flush of warm contentment was beginning to spread across his face.

As he fed, Zac held her gaze and Snil felt that she could look forever into those deep blue eyes.

Suddenly Zac's hand tightened its grip and he gave a sound like a violent hiccup. His teeth clamped down on Snil's nipple and bit through, her dark blood washing over his face. She tried to pull him away but, with a growl, Zac strengthened his hold. All the time he held her gaze, the darkness at the heart of his pupils growing to eclipse the brilliant colour of his irises until his eyes were a deep, uniform black.

Somewhere Snil thought she could hear chanting.

He is the Great Ocean.

He will Come Again.

In her womb, her unborn children began to writhe, the pain as they twisted around her guts and kicked and punched filled her belly with a raging fire.

The chant grew louder until it was all that Snil could hear.

The child in her arms, however, would not allow her to draw her eyes away from his dreadful stare. Snil could see beyond Zac's eyes, to something vast. Something that approached from an incredible distance, yet drew swiftly near and filled him with its midnight taint.

He is the Great Ocean.

He will Come Again.

There was an agonised mewling sound coming from somewhere and, with a growing sickness, Snil realised that it was the call of her unborn children. There was an intense, clawing pain and her belly began to distend as they pushed against the wall of her womb.

Pale tendrils emerged from Zac; from his eyes, nose and mouth. These wrapped themselves around Snil, sinking into her flesh, laying down lines of white-hot fire where they touched, until Zac was securely bound to her.

The pain was so intense now that she couldn't help but cry out and Zac added his voice to the cacophony as the flesh of Snil's belly finally ruptured.

With the hideous screech of the unborn, three partly formed Chadassa heads thrust themselves into the air and joined in with the chant that echoed all around her.

He is the Great Ocean.

He will Come Again.

Snil looked down at the twisted progeny that clung to her ruined torso. The darkness that filled the creature that had been Zac flowed from him and into her, enveloping her in an impenetrable night.

All that Snil could sense now was the endless chant as something ancient and evil rushed into her body.

Belck had told them all to look to the coming of the Great Ocean, to glory in his infinite presence, but now that Snil was filled with that dark and hateful water, she realised that the Chadassa had pinned their hopes onto nothing at all.

Belck stood at the edge of the canyon and stared into the darkness. Behind him, the water shimmered with the heat rising from the great mound of the Queen. The mass of flesh shivered and twitched in anticipation of the union that would make her eggs sacs teem with life. Belck should have felt joy at the prospect, but instead a fierce doubt ate away at him.

What exactly is the Great Ocean?

The truth was that Belck didn't know the answer to Silus's question. Even after all these years of indoctrination into the mysteries of the faith, Belck felt no closer to his god. Even having stared into the face of the Great Ocean itself, he felt no bond with the Chadassa's creator. Yet, because of his lineage, Belck had been chosen to lead his people towards the time of the Great Flood. And just what great new age was it that he was supposed to be the herald of anyway? Belck had spoken of it often, had even stirred up crowds of Chadassa into rapturous religious frenzy with prophecies concerning the arrival of the great event, but in all that time he had never truly understood what it was.

Once all reality was as the Great Ocean what then? What would there be for the Chadassa to do? Swimming together through infinity, all time and space being one vast sea may be a wonderful image with which to empower a sermon but it meant nothing to Belck when he thought of the Chadassa's future.

He sensed movement behind him and turned to see something striding towards him from the encroaching gloom. It looked like another Chadassa but there seemed to be something wrong with the creature, for as it advanced it moved with a shuffling gait, occasionally going down on one knee as though it had only just learned how to walk, kicking up clouds of silt as it did so.

How can you, who have seen my true face, doubt the plan that I have for your people?

The gait of the creature was growing more confident with each step it took and soon it was approaching him with purpose.

Belck could now see that the creature was Snil, the nurse that he had assigned to look after Zac, but the voice that had spoken was not hers. As she drew closer, the terrible change that had been wrought upon her made Belck take a step back, closer to the edge of the trench.

Snil, what happened to you?

Do you not recognise your god? said the malformed infant that clung to her breast. Belck realised that it was Zac, though, somehow, his flesh had become fused to Snil's.

He is the Great Ocean, He will Come Again, chorused the heads of the Chadassa infants that thrust from the ragged hole of her belly.

You have failed me Belck. Your doubts speak louder than your praise. Your prayers are not expressions of your joy and awe in my presence, but expressions of your fear.

With an encroaching fear, that threatened to break out into full blown panic, Belck realised that he may not know his god, but his god certainly knew him. Belck looked at what had been done to Snil and knew that the Great Ocean would use them all just as ruthlessly.

You possess none of the fire of your forebears, Belck. You are a disgrace to their memory.

The thing that had been Snil reached out and laid a hand on his shoulder, the pure black of her eyes had misted into the milky white of the dead. Zac, hanging in his fleshy webbing, looked up and smiled. But it wasn't Zac and, in his eyes, and the eyes that stared from the ruins of Snil's womb, Belck saw the same thing.

Nothing.

This oblivion was not what he desired for his people at all. This was not the glory that the Great Ocean had promised them. Belck realised then that he had to let them know, otherwise they would all march blindly into the abyss.

He shook off the thing's touch and started to hurry back towards the city.

Zac's mouth snapped opened and a thick tendril of flesh erupted from it, to wrap itself around Belck's neck and bring him crashing to the seabed, a cloud of silt rising around him as he landed. Belck struggled against the creature's hold but it tightened its grip and soon he couldn't move at all.

He looked up into the eyes of the Great Ocean and his god stared down at him without pity or remorse from behind the Chadassa's dead eyes. Then, the unborn creatures crawled free of Snil's womb and kicked their way towards him. They landed on his chest and, for a moment, the cord that still joined all three of them to the womb prevented them from progressing any further. One of the infants bit through the rope, however, and severed the connection. It seemed all that they wanted now was affection, because they started to nuzzle against Belck, their mewling sounding like a plea for the milk he could not give them.

But the creatures were not nuzzling. Instead, they were looking for a vulnerable area of Belck's flesh. Finding it, they began to burrow into his hide. Even though they were tiny, they had none of the weaknesses of the unborn and were soon gnawing their way towards his heart.

Belck screamed and begged his God to make the pain stop, and his God obliged.

The Great Ocean placed its clawed foot on his head and pressed down with all its strength.

As his skull shattered, Belck got a taste of the oblivion that would be brought to his people and all reality, before it overtook him and he was no more.

CHAPTER TWENTY-ONE

Kelos realised that something Dunsany had once told him was wrong. Drowning was not easy.

There was no feeling of soporific calm as his lungs filled with water, no sense of sinking gently into an eternal sleep. Instead, he thrashed his limbs and clawed for the dim light far above as a deep cold gripped him.

Then, as consciousness began to slip away, there was anger and despair. This was not how it was supposed to end. Kelos had wanted to reach a fine old age, living out his retirement on some sun-kissed island with Dunsany. There they would be far from the Final Faith, the politics of a divided nation and – more importantly – the rest of the human race. He had wanted to die looking up into Dunsany's eyes as they wished him a last goodbye, not consigned to a watery grave like some anonymous mariner.

But all that wasn't to be, so Kelos let go.

Seconds later, or so it seemed, he found himself kneeling on a stone floor, throwing up an apparently endless stream of water. Emuel knelt beside him, a look of concern on his face as he rubbed Kelos's back.

"Let it come. You're safe now."

Once the nausea had passed, the eunuch helped Kelos to his feet and he saw his new surroundings for the first time.

They were in a glass dome, beyond the walls of which moved the same creatures that had attacked the Chadassa vessel. Kelos watched their graceful forms as they darted between the towers and over the domes of a glittering citadel. The Calma shared some of the same features as the Chadassa, being bipedal creatures of roughly the same size. But where the flesh of the Chadassa was dark-scaled and rough, these creatures' hides shimmered in the diffuse light trickling down from above. Thin, silvery tails grew from the small of their backs, with which they propelled themselves swiftly through the water. From either side of their jaws hung small globes of light, reminding Kelos of the lures of anglerfish.

"The Calma," Emuel said. "They saved us when the Chadassa vessel was blown apart."

Kelos began to remember.

The expression on Silus's face as Belck's influence began to take hold.

The shard of razor sharp bone in Silus's hand.

Dunsany's blood trickling between his fingers as he clutched at his throat.

"Dunsany, where is he?"

"The Calma are taking good care of him, though he is still weak," Emuel said. "He lost a lot of blood, Kelos."

"I need to see him."

Emuel led him through a series of tunnels, each linked by more glass domes. On the way they passed several Calma and, at one point, Kelos thought he heard the raucous laughter of Jacquinto and Ignacio coming from a chamber.

"Sounds like somebody else is being well looked after too," he commented.

"The Calma have been most hospitable."

They reached a small, dim room. Through the glass ceiling Kelos could see the fronds of fern-like plants moving in a gentle current. Fragrant lamps burned in niches on the wall and in the centre of the room, on a low mattress, lay Dunsany.

He was pale and his breathing was uneven. The scar at his throat was the dark red of raw liver. As Kelos and Emuel stood over their friend a Calma entered the room.

"Your friend is in a deep sleep," the creature said, "but we have made sure that he is not in any pain."

"When will he wake up?" Kelos said.

"At the moment, we don't know."

Kelos bit back the tears that threatened to come and knelt beside his friend. "You stupid bastard. Look what you've gotten us into now."

Kelos had never seen Dunsany looking so frail, it was almost as though it wasn't him lying there but some poorly realised wax replica. Dunsany's hand was cold and when he squeezed it there was no response. The tears came then and the grief that they brought was massive and debilitating. Kelos didn't think that he'd be able to contain it. When he looked up, Emuel and the Calma had gone, leaving him alone with his friend.

Had he the magical knowledge to reverse the damage and pull Dunsany out of his deep sleep, he would have performed it in an instant. But such a thing was beyond him. Instead, Kelos took a fragment of tree bark from the pouch at his belt and lit it from one of the lamps. He let it burn for a while before blowing out the flame. Intoning the words of a spell he blew the smoke towards Dunsany's open mouth where it insinuated itself between his lips. Dunsany's breath caught and he gave a small cough, but then he was breathing easily again and the lines of tension were smoothed from his face.

Even though Kelos was unable to free Dunsany from the clutches of his unnatural sleep, he knew that whatever dreamscape his friend was now traversing, he was doing so holding Kelos's hand.

"Sleep well, my friend. Look for me in your dreams."

Kelos stayed by Dunsany's side for a while longer, before leaving the room to look for the rest of the crew.

All Kelos had to do to find his companions was follow the sound of Jacquinto and Ignacio's laughter. He entered the room to find them practically bent double with hilarity. Clearly the scabbed-over wounds that they sported were no longer bothering them as Jacquinto was just reaching the punch-line of a particularly filthy joke and Ignacio was begging him to stop. Sat around a table, in the centre of the room, were the rest of the crew. Without Silus, Katya and Zac the gathering now looked somewhat diminished. Father Maylan was slowly sipping from a glass and watching the two smugglers with a bemused expression and Emuel was conversing with the creature at the head of the table. This Kelos recognised as Seras, the Calma who had led the attack on the Chadassa vessel.

When Kelos sat down and the smugglers saw the expression on his face, they immediately brought their jocularity to an end.

"I'm sorry about Dunsany," Jacquinto said. "We're all praying for him."

"But try not to worry too much, eh?" said Ignacio. "The Calma will have him fixed up in no time and then they'll take us all home, right?"

"No," Emuel said. "We have to rescue our friends. We can't just leave them behind."

"Silus tried to kill Dunsany," Kelos said.

"Besides," Father Maylan said, "we don't even know whether they're still alive. We only just managed to survive the explosion as it is."

"They're alive," Seras said. "The Chadassa would not allow their greatest prize to perish and we must not allow Silus to remain in their hands."

"Silus tried to kill Dunsany," Kelos said again. "He almost succeeded. I don't know whether I can bring myself to face him again, I'm sorry."

"But that wasn't him. He was under Belck's influence, you saw that," Emuel said.

"And if we do go and rescue him, what state do you think he will be in then?" Kelos said. "You know what power he has. He could kill us all. I'm sorry but we're out of this fight Emuel."

"You are not out of this fight," Seras said. "None of us are. If Silus is not rescued then it will mean the end of everything."

"The end of everything how?" Father Maylan said.

"When Silus mates with the Chadassa Queen it will give rise to the Land Walkers. This new breed of Chadassa will lay waste to your land, killing every human in their path. They then plan to perform a dark ceremony in the World's Ridge Mountains that could alter reality irrevocably. Everything we know would be destroyed."

There was silence around the table for a moment then.

"That bad huh?" Jacquinto said.

Ignacio tried to bite back his laughter but he couldn't contain it.

"I'm sorry. I'm sorry. It's just the look on Maylan's face!"

"This is not a fucking game!" Kelos shouted, rising from his seat.

"I'm sorry," Ignacio said, with more sincerity this time.

"And how do the Calma fit into all of this?" Father Maylan asked Seras. "A few days ago we weren't even aware that there was another marine race like the Chadassa."

"We are not like the Chadassa! They are a corruption of our form. They are alien to this world." Then, seeing the reactions of the crew to his outburst, Seras calmed. "I apologise, but the Chadassa and Calma have been at war for millennia. Much of that time we have spent in hiding – the citadel here is almost all that remains of our civilisation – but when news of the Hybrid reached us, we knew that we had to intervene."

"Sorry," Kelos said, "did you say 'hybrid'? Who is that exactly?"

"The one the Chadassa call the half-breed. The one you know as Silus. The one for whom, for countless years, the Calma have waited to join us and banish the Chadassa threat for all time, leading us in a new era of peace."

"Correct me if I'm wrong," Kelos said, "but I thought that it was the Chadassa who saw Silus as some kind of 'chosen one'?"

"To the Chadassa, Silus is merely a pawn to be used to bring about the terrible wrath of their god, this thing they call the

Great Ocean. But to the Calma he represents hope. After all, it is our blood that runs in his veins. Our race who helped to bring about his birth."

The crew were looking at one another now with confused expressions. Jacquinto appeared to be about to say something but Kelos raised his hand to silence him before he could begin.

"And how are you going to rescue Silus?" Kelos said. "After all, the Chadassa seem to be a formidable force with greater numbers than yourselves."

"It is true that our numbers are not what they once were, but it is imperative that we at least try. The alternative is unthinkable."

"Just what is the alternative?" Father Maylan said.

"The end of everything. All will be as the Great Ocean, an infinity of nothingness."

Seras sounded weary and already half-defeated. Kelos realised that he had little hope that the Calma would succeed against the Chadassa. His heart sank as he looked around the crew. All were exhausted and demoralised, though some – like Jacquinto and Ignacio – were managing to hold back any outward signs of distress. Kelos himself tried to put aside his hatred for Silus and what he had done to Dunsany. After all, as Maylan had pointed out, he had been under the influence of Belck at the time.

"Seras, if we could help you we would," he said, "but I don't think that five men could make much of a difference. If we still had the *Llothriall* then maybe we could be of some help, but all we have is ourselves."

"Actually," Emuel said, "the *Llothriall* may not be lost."

"But it would have been destroyed in the attack on Morat, surely?" Ignacio said. "I mean, that thing swallowed a city *whole*. It would have obliterated a simple ship."

"And yet the song remains," Emuel said.

"Gods, you can still hear it?" Kelos felt an edge of excitement now and, with the hope it brought, he began to see some sort of future for them all.

"On Morat," Emuel said, "the Stone Seers showed me that there are many paths to the song. Many ways to open yourself up to its influences. The Faith may have thought that they destroyed my connection to the stone but that's because they only understood a part of its magic. But now I am beginning to hear the call of the *Llothriall* once more."

"Do you think you will be able to lead us to it?" Kelos said.

"I think so, yes."

"Excellent." Kelos turned to Seras. "How long can you wait before you attempt the rescue?"

"Not long, three days at most."

"Emuel?"

"The song is close. It shouldn't take us long to find its source."

"Seras, will you be able to help us? If we can find our ship then you will have powerful magic at your disposal which could secure your victory."

"I can provide a vessel that will speed you to your destination, yes."

"Then I suggest that we leave right away. The sooner we find our ship then the sooner we can rescue Silus and bring this to an end."

CHAPTER TWENTY-TWO

Sleep didn't come easily. Especially not with the sound coming from the cell next door. Silus didn't know what manner of creature the Chadassa had incarcerated there or what they were doing to it, but its cries shook the walls of the tiny room in which he lay.

The sound of voices approached, raised in song. For a moment they overrode the cries coming from the neighbouring cell before silencing them completely, as though the creature residing there had forgotten its agony to listen to the strange hymn. Then there was the sound of bolts being drawn and then a jagged shard of light leapt into the room, startling Silus and making it difficult for him to define the shapes standing in the doorway.

A Chadassa male stepped into the room, its hide marked by the symbols of ritual scarification. "It is time for the Queen to receive you."

Silus felt the last traces of hope burn away then. The crew of the *Llothriall* were dead, his wife and child incarcerated somewhere in this gods-forsaken place and now he was going to be forced to mate with the Chadassa's queen.

Silus looked at the creatures that had crowded their way into his cell, still singing that seductive, yet horrific, song. Desperately hoping for an ally, he looked for Belck amongst the throng.

"Belck, tell your people what the Great Ocean really desires for them, for all of us. Tell them Belck, you must have realised the truth, I saw it in you."

"Belck is not here," the creature standing over Silus said. "He too will be preparing for the ceremony."

Silus held his body rigid as the Chadassa tried to drag him from the cell. He wasn't going to make this easy for them and twice his captors dropped him. As he was manhandled down the corridor, the screaming from the neighbouring cell started up again, this time with more vigour as though to protest at the song being taken away.

Silus and the Chadassa choir descended the spirals of the prison tower until, passing through a membrane, they entered the water. Again, Silus's first instinct was to fight against the sea that filled his lungs, but soon he was breathing easily.

They passed through chambers carpeted with seaweed and lit by the glow of strange minerals until they came to a wide tunnel, sloping down into darkness, seemingly cutting through the bedrock of the ocean floor. A cold current rushed over them. Ahead, Silus could hear more voices raised in song and, as the two choirs neared one another they reached a complex harmony that was so exquisite it brought tears to his eyes.

The two groups of Chadassa emerged on either side of a large chamber and formed a circle around Silus as he was shoved into the centre of the room.

The cavern was warmed by the heat that was rising from a hole in the centre of the room. Silus looked down and, within, he could see the writhing forms of hundreds of fluorescent thread-like worms.

The choir fell silent and the Chadassa who had spoken to Silus in his cell stepped forward.

"To prepare yourself for the Queen, you must first be cleansed."

Silus looked at the creatures that surrounded him. There was nothing that he could do but obey.

Silus stepped towards the hole in the floor and a strong current suddenly grabbed him and pulled him down. As he was dragged into the warm darkness, the fluorescent worms shivered over his body before burrowing in through his pores, the pain like a thousand needles suddenly piercing his flesh. Soon, however, a great sense of calm and wellbeing overtook him and he found himself falling into a vast cavern, lit by the gelatinous forms that moved slowly across the floor. The worms that had entered his body left him then, erupting from his flesh in brilliant threads of coloured lightning. As the last of them swam out of sight, Silus realised that he felt better than he had in a long time, purified, even.

He came to rest on the carpet of glowing creatures that undulated across the cavern floor. They supported him on a bed of tentacles while passing him slowly across their bodies. Silus glided towards an archway at the far end of the room. Where the gelatinous creatures touched him his very flesh felt energised, buzzing with a new life and power. Silus wanted to stay down here forever, wanted this state of bliss to never end. He was surrounded by light and gentle caresses and soon all memory of his previous travails were erased.

His state of euphoria was shattered as he saw three Chadassa females hovering in the archway at the far end of the hall.

Though they were as fearsome in aspect as any of their brethren that Silus had met, their approach was gentle and considered. Instead of rushing in and grabbing him as he had expected, they beckoned to Silus to follow them.

Beyond the archway the water was cooler, the light softer.

Silus looked for the Chadassa females but they were nowhere to be seen.

There was a touch then, a palm gently stroking the back of his head and Silus turned only to catch the briefest glimpse of something swimming swiftly away. He moved deeper into the room and then there was another touch. Fingers lightly grazing his nipples, sending an inadvertent shiver of pleasure down to his groin.

Again Silus turned. Again, the merest hint of a shape.

Before he could proceed there was another touch and then another.

Another.

Lips briefly against his own.

A tongue.

The sensation of scale moving against his inner thigh.

A talon running swiftly down his spine, laying down a line of incandescent pleasure.

The touches and caresses surrounded him now and Silus tried to turn and see the source of this frenetic pleasure, but unseen hands held him firmly in place, carrying him onwards. He didn't fight it though part of him realised that he should be feeling revulsion, horror – even a deep guilt that he was allowing the caresses of these things while Katya was still captive somewhere within the citadel – but he burned with arousal and he let the Chadassa maidens and his lust carry him onwards.

They came to a flight of stone stairs, ascending towards a light. Silus's feet didn't even touch the steps and, as the light rushed towards him, he felt as though he were about to be reborn, as though he were about to come face-to-face with his god.

And, in a sense, he was. For as Silus was raised into the temple, standing before him was the Great Ocean incarnate, this terrible power now clothed in Chadassa and human flesh.

For the briefest of moments Silus was overjoyed to see his son again, but as he saw what had been done to Zac his mind railed against the horror.

The infant fused to the breast of the Chadassa smiled when it saw Silus. The half-formed foetuses that dwelt in the corrupt cavern of the creature's womb chattered in their imbecile language and the misted eyes of the Chadassa host wept a viscous, putrid fluid as it opened its jaws.

As one, the creatures playing host to the ancient and evil mind said, "He is the Great Ocean. He will come again."

Silus couldn't breathe. He tried to shut his eyes but one of the Chadassa maidens forced his head back, while another pried his eyelids open with her claws.

"Say it," she hissed into Silus's face.

Silus didn't know what she meant at first, but as the eyes of the Great Ocean bore into his, he finally understood.

"He is the Great Ocean."

The Chadassa maidens released him and returned below.

Behind the Great Ocean Silus could see that the temple was filled to capacity, the Chadassa's awe at seeing their god made flesh obvious in their humble and prostrate forms.

"What... what have you done to Zac?" Silus said.

"There is only the Great Ocean." The thing said, the congregation repeating its words just a fraction of a second later so that they echoed from the temple walls.

"And Belck?"

"His doubt undid him."

The Great Ocean took Silus's hand and turned him to face the congregation.

"Behold your salvation! The father of a new generation of Chadassa that will lead us all into a brave new era. No longer will we have to share this world with the humans. No longer will we have to remain beneath the waves. Soon all will be as the Great Ocean."

The congregation raised their voices in thanks and praise and, as they looked at him standing there, Silus could sense the weight of their need and the hope that they had placed within him. Despite himself, he felt a surge of pride and anticipation. That just one human could bring about such a transformation was astonishing. But then, he considered, he wasn't really human. The Chadassa were as much his people as they had been Belck's.

When the Great Ocean joined the congregation in the words of an ancient litany Silus closed his eyes, trying to picture his wife and child as they had been at Zac's birth, hoping that the image would shake him free of the creature's thrall. He tried to remember the fierce love that he had felt as he held Zac in his arms for the first time, and the look of happy exhaustion on Katya's face. He asked for their forgiveness.

The voices in the temple fell silent and the great double doors at the far end of the hall swung open. Silus realised that his time had finally come.

Weakly he submitted to the Great Ocean as it handed him to its acolytes. He didn't fight as they raised him up and carried him forth.

As they proceeded from the hall and out into the passage beyond Silus looked at the murals that decorated the walls as they scrolled slowly past. Scenes of conquest and icons of Chadassa leaders had been chiselled into the stone, some with surprising finesse considering the creatures behind the art. One face he saw looked familiar and as they neared the mural Silus realised why this was. He was looking at himself. The likeness may not have been painstakingly accurate but whoever had worked the stone had certainly managed to capture his essence. This was not a new mural either, the stonework was worn in places and covered with sea lichens. Looking up at himself, as he was passed from hand to hand, Silus realised then that this final act really was his destiny. This was where he was supposed to be. It had been foretold.

He had fought and fought, drawing his family and friends into an unnecessary conflict when he should have given himself to the Chadassa when they had first called.

The regret that Silus felt at this, however, was dispelled as he was brought by acolytes of the Great Ocean before the Queen.

The powerful musk of the creature rolled towards him on a warm current and Silus inhaled the scent deeply, letting her perfume fill him with a fierce arousal, of which the touch of the Chadassa maidens had been but the merest taste. The great mound shivered as he drew near and, the folds of flesh gently parting before him, the Chadassa Queen blossomed.

Silus didn't hesitate to enter her embrace.

After all, his destiny had been written in stone.

CHAPTER TWENTY-THREE

Querilous Fitch removed his sodden shirt and threw it into a corner where it hit the floor with a wet splat. For a moment he considered removing his trews also – anything to allow the air to get to his clammy skin – but that, he thought, would be a step too far and not an act befitting the dignity of the Final Faith's Head Inquisitor. His predecessor hadn't been so coy by all accounts, in fact it had been said that Master Mullens sometimes used his nakedness to facilitate his acts of torture. Querilous, however, preferred to perform his duties clothed, even in the overpowering heat of this particular dungeon.

Here they were too far below ground for the light channelled by the cathedral's sun traps to reach the chamber. Instead the room was illuminated by the torches that ringed the walls and the glowing coals of braziers.

Above one of the braziers hung the Chadassa prisoner. Querilous had suspended the creature above the fire until its scales had dulled and cracked, and even then it had refused to struggle or make a sound. It wasn't that the thing was unconscious, it just appeared to be particularly obstinate. The Chadassa hadn't made a sound since it had been captured and Querilous's mind probes had been unable to elicit any useful information. That was why he had brought the creature to the deepest dungeon in Scholten Cathedral, for it was here that some of the more arcane torture equipment resided.

As the usual methods had failed him, it was time to turn to the knowledge of the Old Races.

Querilous lowered the specimen to the floor and doused it with a bucket of water. With the help of his assistants he then carried the creature to the equipment that dominated the far end of the room. Querilous had helped build this particular device himself, working to dwarven plans that had been painstakingly translated by Faith scholars. The design for the equipment came from the age when the Old Races had been at war, and it would appear that it had originally been intended to torture elves. Querilous, however, had altered the construction so that it could accommodate any type of prisoner. The machine had been used only a handful of times so far and two of those occasions had been test runs, utilising subjects who had volunteered from among the Faithful; righteous masochists happy to give their lives to a holy cause.

Querilous didn't understand such people. He himself had experienced some of the incredible pain the machine was capable of delivering and that was only because he had accidentally touched one of the contacts during the powering-up process. He couldn't imagine anyone putting themselves through such suffering voluntarily.

The prisoner was strapped into place and Querilous's assistants opened the valves that allowed the flow of arcane energy to suffuse the frame of the machine. The inquisitor donned a pair of smoked-glass goggles. He had no such protection to offer his assistants. However, their ensuing blindness would be the insurance the Faith needed to avoid them accurately describing the mechanisms of this wondrous toy to any potential Brotherhood spies. Sadly such impostors were everywhere.

The power of the machine rolled from it in cool waves, goose-pimpling Querilous's skin and making him wish that he had kept his shirt on. There was a raw mineral smell in the air and the hairs on his arms started to prickle. The crystals embedded in the frame glowed a deep umber, gradually changing into an intense lavender as the power levels rose. The torches on the walls flickered out and Querilous found himself momentarily deaf as the air pressure in the room increased. But then his ears popped and the roar of the device at full power came at him.

Querilous turned one of the valves attached to the frame and the webbing holding the Chadassa in place started to glow. And now he really did see a change in the prisoner's attitude for, as the smell of ozone intensified, something like fear glittered deep in the creature's eyes.

"Now, will you talk?" Querilous shouted, the howling of the machinery almost drowning out his words.

The Chadassa reached for him, its talons weakly opening and closing just inches from his face.

Querilous smiled and removed a crystal from the frame.

A jagged shard of lightning arced between the creature's shoulders and it cried out.

"What, what was that? I can't hear you."

Querilous knew that he wasn't supposed to enjoy the act of torture – it was a holy rite, a spiritual duty to be treated with the appropriate reverence – but sometimes he allowed himself just the merest hint of pleasure.

The creature did now appear to be about to say something and Querilous powered down the machinery so that he could make out its words.

"Mercy. I said mercy. I'll talk."

The prisoner broken, Querilous loosened its bindings, allowing some respite before sending for a scribe to take down the monster's statement.

Several days later, in a cove not far from the bustling port of Turnitia, lay the fleet of ships the Faith had prepared to deal with the Chadassa threat. It was true that none of the vessels were as magnificent as the *Llothriall* or would be able to weather the tumults of the Twilight seas for long, but then not one of the ships would be returning. Each vessel was manned by a crew consisting of a selection of the most fanatical and devoted members of the Faith. These men and women did not care that, moments after they had delivered their deadly payloads, their bodies would be broken on the rough seas. In fact, their faith burned so fiercely within them that they considered this sacrifice the least they could offer up.

Katherine Makennon was a little in awe of such martyrs, even some of the highest-ranking Archimandrites would be hard pressed to equal their levels of devotion. In turning themselves into holy weapons they had assured their passage to Kerberos. Makennon couldn't believe that she hadn't considered the use of such martyrs on the battlefield before. Such suicidal devotion may have shortened the last war between Vos and Pontaine considerably and may even have seen the destruction of the Brotherhood. Once this foray was over she would certainly look into the benefits of a programme of radicalisation.

Katherine looked down at her feet as the iron floor began to vibrate. She was standing in the lamp room of a lighthouse, the entire structure of which had been converted to accommodate the magical equipment that would teleport the fleet. In the centre of the room a tangle of hair-thin wires rose from the floor. Katherine watched as a mage poured a tray of metal balls into the steel web. As they fell they emitted sparks where they came into contact with the wires, before falling through a trapdoor in the floor. Katherine could hear their progress beneath her as they raced through the interior of the lighthouse, crashing through more trapdoors, setting off cantrips and making the wires sing with arcane energy.

Beside her, Querilous Fitch was talking to a mage as he polished the great lens that stood before the equipment, the circumference of which was inscribed with runes and lines of prayer.

"Brother Querilous, you are certain that the fleet will be transported to location of the Chadassa citadel?" Makennon said.

"Oh indeed, Anointed One. I broke through the prisoner's lies and truly did I see the seat of all their blasphemies."

"And the weapons aboard the ships will work?"

"A fire that burns underwater and cannot be extinguished. It will destroy their city entirely and Twilight shall be free of their kind."

Katherine hoped that they would also soon be rid of the black sphere that had been plaguing Kerberos. Brother Incera had still not discovered anything further concerning the planetary body and it was beginning to affect the morale of her flock. It had even been rumoured that a cult had sprung up near the Drakengrat mountains, dedicated to the worship of this aberration. Makennon would make sure that they were put down by the Swords before she delivered her next address at Scholten Cathedral.

"Anointed One, the equipment is ready if you would like to make a blessing?" one of the mages said.

As her attendant lit a censer Katherine sketched the symbol of the Faith in the air. Those gathered before her bowed their heads as they prepared to receive the blessing.

"Lord, send these ships to enact your will. Remove from the face of our blessed seas this unnatural scourge and call into your arms these brave holy warriors. Amen."

"Amen," chorused the Faithful.

"Anointed One, it will be safer if we leave the tower," Querilous said. "There is a slight risk of backlash and we wouldn't want to put you in any danger."

Katherine followed Querilous to a bluff that overlooked the cove where the ships were readying themselves for the voyage. She was pleased to see that each of them had raised the flag of the Faith, the sight of the crossed circles snapping in the wind instilling within her the fervour of hope.

To their left the room atop the lighthouse began to blaze with a light so intense it was as though a new sun had appeared in the sky.

A jagged crack ran up the side of the building and there was a rain of crumbling mortar.

"Querilous," Makennon said, as stone began to grind against stone, "I think that something is wrong."

"Don't worry Anointed One, the structure has been reinforced, it won't topple."

As the lighthouse began to sway Katherine wondered what it was like, at that moment, to be one of the mages in the lamp room. The light above them intensified even further, bathing the cove in a startling brilliance that threw the shadows of the ships far across the waves. There was a sudden cold wind and then the ships were following their shadows across the sea; though as Katherine watched it was almost as though they weren't moving at all, rather it was she who was rushing away from the fleet. She got the impression of a sky heavy with boiling clouds above a landscape of mountainous waves, but then she blinked and the vision was gone, along with the ships.

The wind died as suddenly as it had risen and the light above them winked out. Katherine found herself plunged into absolute darkness. She was beginning to fear that the spell had backfired and she had been transported to the void when she detected the soft sound of the waves.

The cove and the lighthouse gradually emerged from the gloom, bathed in Kerberos's glow.

"Anointed One, are you okay? You appear shaken."

"I must admit, Querilous, that sometimes magic scares me." Katherine sketched the symbol of the Faith in the air before taking the Inquisitor's arm. "Back to Scholten I think. I wish to spend time in prayer while we await the news of our glorious victory."

CHAPTER TWENTY-FOUR

Bestion's pen skidded across the page, digging a shallow trench in the paper as another tremor struck the ruins of Morat.

In the aftermath of the attack that had seen the majority of the city devoured, the power of the stone of the Allfather had been utilised to draw together the remains. Bestion sat at the centre of this tiny archipelago of ruins, working in a chapel attached to the house of the Stone Seers.

He had set himself the unenviable task of documenting the last days of Morat – for already the power of the stone was waning – and he had finished his account of the attack and was now moving onto his recollections of the strangers. In particular, the extraordinary individual Silus.

Bestion had been astonished to discover one with such a strong link to the Allfather – especially one who was not from Morat – and for a moment he had even contemplated the possibility that Silus was the herald of their God, sent to lead them on the journey home. If anything, though, he had turned out to be a portent of destruction. Yet Bestion had been with Silus as his soul had left his body to commune with the Allfather, and he had sensed no malice within him. Bestion would have given anything to know what Silus had learned during the ritual, but the stranger had taken that knowledge with him.

However, the visitors had left something behind. The magnificent vessel they had arrived in – the *Llothriall.*

The ship lay anchored near the ruins of the palace and Bestion had visited it often, mainly to study the stone that sat at its centre. This was clearly the sister of the stone of the Allfather. Indeed, it had begun to respond to the death song that now emanated from the temple, harmonising with that melancholy hymn as though in sympathy. Bestion had contemplated taking the *Llothriall,* loading up the survivors and leaving Morat. But while the stone of the Allfather still sang he could not leave his home, not while there was the merest chance that He would call them into His arms. For surely the Allfather could see the suffering of His people, surely they were now worthy of His forgiveness? Bestion was beginning to wonder, however, whether the Allfather cared at all.

The room shook and Bestion was thrown out of his chair and over the desk. He rolled across the floor, the pages of his journal fluttering around him, before coming to rest at the foot of the altar. A crack appeared in the chapel wall and through it Bestion could hear the churn of the angry sea. He closed his eyes and waited for the water to find him. But then he heard the song of the stone, and this time it wasn't a song of death.

"Bestion, Bestion!" It was Joseph, one of the Stone Seers. "The stone, Bestion! It's calling to something. Something is coming."

Maybe this was it. Maybe the Allfather had heard their prayers after all. Suddenly Bestion felt ashamed for ever doubting his god.

He followed Joseph and saw that something of the former brilliance of the stone had returned. The grey veins that had begun to marble its face were filling with a glow like the gentle fire of sunset.

"When did this begin?" Bestion said.

"Just a moment ago. The song suddenly changed. We believe that it is a call."

"To whom, the Allfather?"

"We don't think so."

"Then who?"

"Captain Tyron has spotted something approaching Morat from the east."

Bestion felt a chill grip him then as he remembered the maw that had risen from the sea to devour them. Joseph noticed his pallor change and placed his hand on Bestion's arm. "If Morat was in danger from this thing, I can assure you that the cadences of the song would be far different. Come on."

Bestion followed Joseph out of the temple and across to the next island in the archipelago.

The fragments of the broken city now orbited the power of the stone, each small island linked by a hastily constructed bridge. Bestion looked around him at what they had lost and wondered how much longer they could survive.

Six islands away from the house of the Stone Seers Captain Tyron stood on an outcrop, watching the approach of a strange mound that moved swiftly through the water towards them, sending up plumes of spray in its wake.

"I spotted it on the horizon not long ago," the Captain said as they approached. "And when I trained my glass on it, I saw what appeared to be a human riding on its back. Look."

The Captain handed his telescope to Bestion.

There was indeed something riding the mound of grey-green flesh, a figure with its arms outstretched and head raised. Bestion adjusted the magnification and the tattooed face that sprang at him out of the mist of spray was instantly recognisable.

"My God, it's Emuel. The strangers are returning! They must be the ones the ship's stone is responding to. Maybe they have brought Silus with them, maybe there is hope after all."

The *Llothriall* sat not far from where Bestion and the two men stood and as the strange mound neared Morat, he could have sworn he saw the ship shudder, the wood of its hull briefly flaring with lines of magical fire.

The mound slowed as it drew alongside the small island and a hole dilated open in its surface. Through this scrabbled Kelos,

Father Maylan, Ignacio and Jacquinto. Bestion got Captain Tyron to lower a rope and soon the visitors were before them.

"Gentlemen, I had thought I'd never see you again," Bestion said, taking each of their hands in turn.

"And we had not reckoned on seeing Morat again," Kelos said. "I had thought it destroyed."

"It may as well have been, as you can see. Sadly, what little we have won't hold together for much longer. It is only through the stone that we have managed to save this much and there have been few survivors. How did you find us?"

"We followed the song." Emuel said. "We sought the *Llothriall*."

"Well you've found her and your vessel has certainly faired better than our city. Anyway, after your journey you must be hungry."

"Starving," Kelos said. "But time is not on our side. Silus is in great danger, as is the rest of our world."

"At least spare a moment to tell me your tale. Perhaps we can help?"

Kelos looked unsure, but at the urging of the rest of the crew he finally relented.

When they had finished their story, Morat finally began to fall apart.

Bestion and his guests only just managed to flee the chapel before it fell down around them and Jacquinto took a glancing blow to the head from a falling shard of masonry. The most appalling thing about the death of Morat was not the scale of the destruction or the sound of buildings tumbling into the sea, but the silence coming from the house of the Stone Seers.

As Bestion rushed into the building, not willing to believe that which he could no longer hear, Kelos raced after him.

"Bestion bring whoever you can find, we need to get out of here now."

The cradle that had supported the stone for millennia shattered, shards of rock skittering across the floor as dust filled the air. For a moment the stone remained where it was, gently rocking from side to side. Then it dropped through the floor and into the sea below, a huge plume of water erupting from the hole it left behind.

Bestion and Kelos raced from the building to find the crew standing outside, trying to decide on the best route back to the ship, aware that they had only moments left before the whole of Morat sank.

The many islands that made up the ruins of the city were now beginning to drift apart, ropes snapping as the bridges that had connected them were torn in two.

"For Gods sake what is wrong with you lot? Don't just stand there, *go*! Get to the *Llothriall*!" Kelos shouted.

Following the crew Kelos all but carried Bestion across the first of the bridges, the supporting ropes beginning to unravel even as they raced over the planks. At one point Ignacio's foot went through a rotting board, shards of wood gouging into his ankle. Emuel tore the smuggler free, supporting him across the remaining span. As the crew cleared the bridge the island they had left behind cracked into two huge pieces and rapidly sank.

Bestion stared at the place where the house of the Stone Seers had been and then started to turn as the wave thrown up by the sinking island rushed towards them.

The island on which they now stood was suddenly shoved forwards by the wave. One of the Moratian survivors who fled with them stumbled as he tried to clear the gap to the next island, only to fall between the two islands just as they clashed together. Bestion looked away as a geyser of blood fountained into the air, but he could still feel the warm rain on his skin as they made it to the next rock in the chain.

Bestion looked towards where the *Llothriall* was anchored and realised that they were rapidly running out of stepping stones. As they leapt over the gap between one chunk of rock and the next the sea was already beginning to lap at their heels. He could see the strange, mound-like vessel that had brought the crew to the island skirting the scene of the tumult, as though it was searching for a way in to help them. However the sinking islands were packed too tightly for it to reach them.

The next island they leapt to lay just below the surface but, with a lurch, it suddenly rose from the water. And then Bestion saw the next island rising also, and the next, creating a clear path of stepping-stones to the ship.

"What's happening?" he shouted to Kelos, but then he saw.

Emuel was singing.

The stone of the Allfather may have died but it was now the stone on the *Llothriall* that was forging them a path as Emuel reached out to it. Ahead of them the ship blazed with the power of the song. Bestion gestured to those remaining survivors who were close enough to follow as they made their dash towards safety.

Kelos and Father Maylan were first on deck and they hurried to get the ship ready for departure as Emuel continued to weave his spell. Bestion held back for the moment, helping any of those who had escaped the tumult leap onto the ship. Beside the crew there were pitifully few survivors. He counted only a dozen or so before the eunuch's song began to lose hold and Morat finally sank below the waves.

The *Llothriall* was borne up on a sudden swell that whipped it into a spin, those on deck reaching for the handrail as their feet went out from under them. Above them all Jacquinto and Ignacio barely managed to hold on to the rigging as they worked at the sails. But then, with a crack, the silks unfurled, throwing rainbow swirls of light across the deck as they caught the sun.

They rode the crest of the wave thrown up in the wake of the sinking city. Bestion looked back but could see nothing to mark the place where Morat had been. He finally found his legs, managing to stand as the ship stabilised beneath him. He left the rest of the crew and survivors behind him and moved to the prow of the *Llothriall*. There he looked up at the Allfather and, closing his eyes, he reached out in prayer. Yet this time he did not ask for forgiveness, or offer up thanks for his safety. Instead, he directed his anger at the azure sphere and offered up his rage to the god who had abandoned them.

Eventually the wave upon which the *Llothriall* rode lost its power and soon they were calmly negotiating the hills and troughs of the Twilight seas once more.

Emuel had sung the last verse and was now helping Father Maylan tend to the most severely injured of the Moratian survivors. Jacquinto and Ignacio were spending their time either up on deck, in the rigging or scanning the horizon for any signs of danger. Bestion, meanwhile, had found the darkest corner of the hold in which to lose himself; refusing offers of food, drink or friendship.

To starboard followed the Calma vessel that had brought Kelos and the crew to Morat. Kelos had yet to introduce the survivors to the aquatic humanoids, reasoning that now was not the best of times to reveal this strange new race to the Moratians. But time was something of a luxury and so, once enough of it had passed for the passengers to have at least begun to compose themselves, Kelos called a meeting.

He didn't think that the hollow-eyed survivors who stared at him from the edges of the cramped day room were ready for war, but that was precisely the reality they would now have to face up to. It didn't stop Kelos from feeling like an utter bastard, however, when several of the Moratians broke down and cried after he had explained the situation.

"If we allow the Chadassa to see their plans come to fruition then it will not just be Morat we'll have lost but the whole world," Kelos said. "I understand that now is not the time you want to be dragged into a conflict you did nothing to create, but if we lose Silus we lose all hope. The Land Walkers must not be allowed to march."

"The Allfather has abandoned us," Bestion said. "What does it matter if we die?"

"Look, it was the Chadassa who were truly responsible for the destruction of Morat," Jacquinto said. "Don't you want revenge for that?"

"And after we have taken our revenge what then?" said a thin woman. "Once we rescue this Silus, won't the Chadassa just come for us again?"

"If we stop the Land Walkers from being born, then the Chadassa won't be able to effectively attack Twilight," Kelos said. "Then, with the Calma's aid we will have our chance to regroup and put the Chadassa down for good."

"And then maybe once this has all blown over we can search for new land," Father Maylan said. "Help you to build a new Morat."

"So, you want to sail us into enemy territory, put our lives at risk," one of the few remaining Stone Seers said, "while you attempt to rescue a man most of us have never heard of, let alone met?"

"Believe me," Kelos said, "the *Llothriall* is one of the safest places you can be in that situation. This is no ordinary vessel."

"Yes, surely you have heard the song?" Emuel said.

The Moratians didn't look convinced, but Kelos didn't have time to string out the argument any further. Already a deadly new army could be gestating in the vast womb of the Chadassa Queen.

"In order to persuade you that our course of action is the correct one," Kelos said, "let me show you something of the *Llothriall's* abilities. Emuel, I'll need you in the stone room. The rest of you follow me."

The only one not to follow him onto deck was Bestion. Jacquinto and Ignacio offered to go and fetch him but Kelos told them to let him be for the moment.

The deck shuddered beneath them as Emuel began a new song. In a perfect circle, surrounding the *Llothriall* for about a mile, the sea suddenly became still, its surface now as smooth as a mirror.

"Are you sure this is going to work?" Jacquinto said as Kelos prepared himself. "I mean, have you actually tested whether the *Llothriall* really can sail underwater?"

"No, but have faith. Go, do your thing."

Jacquinto and Ignacio hammered free the heavy wood bolts that were threaded through the base of each mast. Kelos then called up a light breeze that lifted the sails and furled them tightly around each one. He then brought his hands up sharply, like a conductor calling for more volume, before bringing them down just as suddenly. As soon as he did this, the three great masts dropped, telescoping into themselves with a soft hiss, until they were flush with the deck.

Behind Kelos, the men and women watching him drew closer to one another as they found themselves standing on a vast ship without sails. The sky all of a sudden seemed that much wider and deeper above them.

But the transformation of the *Llothriall* was far from complete.

Kelos raised his arms again and brought his palms together. He said a word that had no meaning to his audience but which seemed to whisper deep inside their minds, eliciting a shiver from each individual as they felt the magic now working around them. The *Llothriall* began to grow, the wood of the hull to either side flowing above them, each edge curving towards the other before joining together, closing above them like a clam shell, sealing them in what many now felt to be a huge, lightless coffin. But Kelos coughed and said "my apologies," and then light began to filter in as organic portholes blinked open down the length of the ship.

"The beauty of the *Llothriall*," Kelos said as his audience rushed to the windows, "is that she is as proficient at sailing *beneath* the waves as she is upon them."

There were gasps from those looking through the portholes as the *Llothriall* began to sink. No, not sink, Kelos thought, that would suggest that they were trapped in some kind of shipwreck. What the *Llothriall* was actually doing was submerging, the magic that now suffused every part of the vessel taking her into a gentle descent. Kelos couldn't help a huge grin plastering itself onto his features. He had wanted to try out this ability of the ship ever since he had first read of it.

There was the hiss of air being pumped through the great chamber in which they now stood and the light filtering through the portholes soon faded to a deep aquamarine.

"Ladies and gentlemen," Kelos said, "welcome to the world beneath the waves."

It was so quiet.

The only sound that reached Kelos as he sat reading in the

dayroom was the low murmur of Father Maylan's prayers. Usually there would be the sound of Jacquinto and Ignacio calling to each other from the rigging or playing dice, but tonight it was almost as if Kelos and the priest were the only ones on board. The rest of the crew and passengers had decided to get some sleep.

Kelos was too restless to sleep. He kept thinking about Dunsany. The prospect of his closest friend never waking up again scared him almost as much as facing the Chadassa in battle. He had tried to distract himself with books, but he'd been reading the same page on Brotherhood beliefs and heresies for the last hour and it was doing nothing to keep his mind off things.

He didn't realise that Father Maylan's litany had come to end until a knock at the door made him jump.

"Come in."

It was Bestion. "Mind if I join you? I couldn't sleep."

"I'm surprised that anybody can. Of course not, please."

Bestion gently closed the door before taking a seat opposite the mage. For a moment he didn't say anything. Instead he sat looking down at his hands. However, when he looked up and glanced over Kelos's shoulder his expression changed.

"My God, what are they?"

Kelos had forgotten about the Calma ships surrounding the *Llothriall*. He supposed that, in his worrying, he had become numb to their beauty.

"They are the Calma, or rather their vessels."

Bestion went over to the window. Kelos, deciding that he wasn't in the mood for reading, joined him.

There were about ten Calma ships visible from this side of the *Llothriall*, but Kelos knew that at least twice that number followed in their wake. Shoals of gemfish surrounded the ships – drawn either to the lichens that encrusted them or their lights – making it difficult to discern their shape. If Kelos had been pressed to describe their appearance, however, he'd have to say that they looked like nothing so much as giant starfish.

"It was in one of those that we came to Morat," Kelos said.

"You never realise quite how big your world is, do you,"

Bestion said, "until you're forced to leave home?"

"Quite, and I can assure you that the crew of the *Llothriall* know what it is to be exiles. If we ever returned home we'd be tried and executed for heresy."

"Your church would do that?"

"It isn't *my* church."

"But you believe in the one god, just as we do?"

"In my own way, yes, though I don't think that we can say that we really know Him. Or Her. Or It, for that matter."

"I know what you mean," Bestion said. "I always thought I knew our world and our god but then you came along. Our world fell apart and our god abandoned us." Not hearing it in Bestion's voice, Kelos looked for any sign of anger or hatred on the priest's face but all he saw there was exhaustion. "And this fight, is it worth it?"

"You've met Silus. I know that you've sensed how extraordinary he is. Would you say that he's worth fighting for?"

Bestion watched the Calma armada as it followed them, the great limbs of the ships propelling them slowly through the darkness.

"You know," he said, "I'm not quite sure why I believe this but yes. Yes, I'd say he's worth fighting for."

CHAPTER TWENTY-FIVE

The Great Ocean stood with its followers, watching the twitching and trembling of the Queen. The heat rising from the great mound was so intense that it instantly cooked any of the sealife that came within a mile of it. The Chadassa themselves were standing at a safe distance, not wanting to join the litter of dead fish and marine mammals that radiated out from the great mound.

Silus had entered the embrace of the Queen only hours before and, already, the process was near completion. The birth of the new race had taken millennia to prepare yet only moments to realise. Soon the Chadassa would leave the sea behind, there to call forth a much greater ocean; one that was infinite, untainted and pure.

The ground shuddered and cracked. Vents opened up around the Queen, spewing black jets that bubbled high before solidifying into thin, twisted ebony sculptures. The heat suddenly died away and a cool tide rolled over the gathered Chadassa.

There was silence then and the Queen was still.

The Great Ocean could feel the expectant stares of the congregation. The elders clutched at their robes, willing forth the progeny of their god. The creature that had been Zac twisted and thrashed, while the Chadassa younglings hiding within the hollow of the Great Ocean's torso chattered in their idiot language.

The Queen sagged, the walls of flesh bowing outwards, rolling towards them a little way before coming to rest. Then she ruptured; a thick soup of amniotic fluid and shredded flesh boiling into the sea. As the cloud rolled over them the Chadassa tried not to gag on the nauseating stench that flooded their gills. They could see nothing of the Queen now. Some of them tried to make their way towards the mound, but the Great Ocean called them back, knowing that it would mean death for those who wondered into the path of what was about to emerge.

A pale light suffused the fog of debris and low, dark shapes could be seen within, shambling towards them. They grew in stature as they neared, looking much like the Chadassa themselves in outline, but when the first of the creatures stepped out of the cloud the differences in the new race were more marked than the similarities.

The Land Walkers stood twice as tall as the Chadassa and whereas the Chadassa were dark and scaled, these creatures had smooth, pale hides. The same vicious, quills ran from the top of the skull but they did not stop at the base of the spine. Instead they ran down the length of a long, thick tail that trailed behind, dragging along the seabed. The arms were shorter than the Chadassa's but well muscled, with hands almost human in appearance. Though these creatures had lost their brethren's talons they had developed a more powerful jaw. The snout was long and lupine, lined with razor-sharp teeth and crowned with wide, deep nostrils that looked capable of smelling out the smallest of prey. The eyes were entirely human in shape, only the night black pupils, flecked with gold, spoke of their alien ancestry.

The Land Walkers ignored the Chadassa before them – despite

their calls of praise – and strode away from the citadel. The Great Ocean knew that if they tarried beneath the waves for long they would die. The sea was not their home, instead they would become the new masters of land and bring death to the human race.

The Great Ocean looked up to where the faintest glimmer from Kerberos pierced the waves.

A long time ago, before Twilight even existed and when just a handful of planets hung turning in the void, that azure globe had given birth to the Great Ocean. For a while the Great Ocean had worked in perfect harmony with the rest of the universe, but it had soon grown envious of creation. And so it had come here, to the best loved of all the worlds, and seeded it with creatures of its own imagining. For that the Great Ocean had been exiled to the very edge of the universe, where the roaring nothingness was barely held back by the fabric of reality. Over the millennia, though, it had begun to hear another sound. The call of its children. A plea no parent can ignore.

When the Chadassa had grown sufficiently in power they had pulled their god out of exile, drawing it across the universe with the force of their will. As the Great Ocean had phased into orbit with Kerberos it had thrown a blanket of silence over the planet, so that none would hear its call. Now it was time for the Great Ocean's children to leave the cradle and remake reality in its name. It understood now something of the pain Silus had gone through when his child had been taken from him. The pride that the Great Ocean felt in the creatures that marched towards land was so fierce that it regretted the brevity of the lives it had given them.

The ground shook as the birthing process accelerated. The Chadassa continued to gaze in awe at the rank upon rank of Land Walkers that marched past them. But these wonders were the smallest part of what they would soon behold. Soon, all of creation would ring with the songs of their praise and the Great Ocean would be all and all would be the Great Ocean.

Not far from where the Great Ocean stood, two Land Walkers dropped, their flesh burning. They made no sound as they fell and for a moment the god didn't understand what had happened, but then it saw a flash of light at the edge of its vision.

The ships unfolded from the darkness, glittering with light as they discharged their weapons. The Great Ocean had only a second to call a warning before the citadel began to fall apart.

Something was pushing down on Silus, smothering him as it closed over his face like a wet blanket, pulling him out of his warm, safe slumber. He scrabbled at the thin membrane, tearing it away before it could suffocate him, and fell to the sticky floor when the webbing that had held him in place gave way.

Something was wrong with the Queen.

All around him egg sacs were bursting as they putrefied, spilling out half-formed and aborted Land Walkers. One creature cracked as it hit the floor, its eye sockets empty and dry. Another crawled towards him dripping mucus, a fat black tongue lolling from its wrinkled jaw. Silus backed away from the abominations only to be dragged to the floor as a large wet hand closed over his face. A Land Walker that was little more than a torso squirmed over him and clamped its mouth on a nipple, futilely trying to suckle. When Silus pushed it away his hand sank into a skull that tore like wet paper, the brain beneath a sponge that crumbled beneath his touch.

There was a dull thud then and the chamber shook. Silus noticed the rent in the wall just a second before the sea rushed in.

He flailed in the darkness, a multitude of limbs brushing up against him as he tumbled through a nightmare of grotesques. A hand made a grab for him and he struck out, only to find his wrist clamped in a firm grip.

Silus turned to see what had grabbed him and found himself looking at his reflection in twin disks of glass. It took him a moment to realise that he was looking at someone wearing one of the underwater exploration suits from the *Llothriall*. Above the figure hung the ship itself and it gestured towards the vessel urgently. Spurred on by the sounds of fighting, Silus followed.

On board, when he saw who was within the suit, Silus gave him a fierce hug.

"Kelos! Gods, it's good to see you. Where's Dunsany?"

From the pained expression on the mage's face he could tell that something bad had happened.

"What? What is it?"

"Silus, you tried to kill him."

A chill ran through him. Silus tried to think of something to say, but there was nothing.

"I had no idea, really Kelos. You have to believe me. I remember nothing."

"The Chadassa within you was driven on by Belck," Kelos said. "He made you open Dunsany's throat. I thought we'd lost him. I thought we were all dead. But the Calma rescued us."

Kelos gestured with a hand and a part of the hull became translucent. Through it Silus could see the chaos that had come to the Chadassa city.

Things that looked like giant starfish moved over the citadel; some emitting brilliant beams of light that seared the flesh off any Chadassa they touched, others wrapped themselves around the coral towers until rubble rained down on the fighting below.

"Calma attack ships," Kelos said. "Their footsoldiers are in the city below, taking on the main Chadassa forces."

Silus saw that though the Calma were outnumbered they were quick and vicious as sharks. They would dart in, their silvery tails rippling, and wrap the tentacles of their flails around their enemy before darting away again, leaving a charred corpse rolling in their wake. For all this though, the Calma were being slowly whittled down and it would be only a matter of time before they were overwhelmed.

"The Calma think of you as their chosen one," Kelos said. "That's why they helped us rescue you. While one force attacked the main defences, we freed you from the Queen. We managed to kill the majority of the Land Walkers and interrupt the birth, but some of the creatures still escaped. I only hope that the forces on the peninsula will be sufficient to stop them."

"And what about Katya?"

"The Calma will bring her safely to us," Kelos said. "Don't worry, we can trust them."

There was a flash of light and when it faded they saw that part of the citadel had disappeared. In its place now was a vast area of scorched seabed over which fell a slow rain of corpses; Chadassa and Calma alike.

"I have to find her," Silus said, before adding, "I'm sorry about Dunsany, Kelos. Really."

Kelos reached out to him but, before he could say anything, Silus stepped through the membrane in the side of the ship and into the sea.

He breathed deeply, energised by the cold burn of the salt water in his lungs.

Belck had made him embrace his Chadassa nature and use it against his friends, but now he would use it against the Chadassa themselves. As he thought of Katya, trapped somewhere within the city, and of what had been done to Zac his rage intensified.

Ahead of him four Chadassa were tearing into a single Calma, oblivious to him in their killing frenzy.

Silus barrelled into them, grabbed one by the head and squeezed until it came apart. He didn't feel the blows of the other Chadassa as they fought him and when he turned on them they came apart just as easily. One of them he left alive, but only as long as it took him to peer into its mind and find out where Katya was being kept. After that he slammed the creature into the ground again and again, his fingers dug deep into the flesh of its throat. The Chadassa flopped in his grip like a rag doll as a strange, high-pitched keening made his skull ache. It took Silus a moment to realise that the sound was coming from him. It shocked him out of his fury and he stood in a cloud of sand and viscera, wondering just what he was becoming.

Kelos had taught him that he was special and the Chadassa had shown him that he was a monster. Silus knew that he was both.

He kicked away from the seabed, darting into a forest of weeds when he was spotted by more Chadassa. He lost them amongst the fronds, only to be startled by a shoal of gemfish that exploded around him as he swam into a clearing.

Ahead of him lay the centre of the citadel. Its dark coral towers swarmed with the Chadassa as they tried to defend them against the Calma ships. One of the towers fell; fortunately, Silus saw, not the one that Katya was imprisoned in. However, he didn't have long. Already several of the Calma ships had fallen – great clouds of sand and silt marking their impact sites – and more Chadassa were boiling up from beneath the city all the time. Silus even thought he saw the twisted form of the Great Ocean amongst the chaos, but couldn't be sure.

He looked for a way in, but knew that to wander into the centre of the fighting would mean death. Somehow he had to make it to the prison tower unseen.

A flash of neon caught his eye and he knew what he had to do.

Silus called the gemfish to him and soon he was hidden within the glittering shoal. Together they moved into the heart of the conflict. Several times, when they ventured too close to the fighting, the shoal threatened to break apart, but Silus reasserted his will and kept the gemfish close. To those caught up in the chaos it would merely seem that a school of fish had come to feed on the detritus of the battle.

But there were bigger scavengers than the gemfish around and soon a gaggle of razor dolphins had closed in on them, picking off the glittering fish and picking apart Silus's carefully constructed shroud. Realising that his cover was rapidly disintegrating he tried to bind the razor dolphins to his will; however, their minds were slippery and soon they were darting away again in search of more food.

Silus floated, isolated in the middle of the conflict, wondering how long it would take for the Chadassa to spot him.

It wasn't the Chadassa who noticed him first, however, but the Calma.

Gesturing to its four comrades, one of them swam towards him, the light shimmering on its gossamer tail as it approached. The last time Silus had been this close to the Calma, he had been killing one of their kind, driven on by Belck's manipulations. Something of that bloody hunger must have been obvious in his eyes now as the Calma suddenly hesitated in its approach.

A Chadassa riding a giant, horned eel swooped in, spearing the Calma through the chest with a barbed javelin and scattering its brethren in the wake of its mount. The Calma soon regrouped, however and, as the eel turned for another pass, they brought their flails to bear.

Amazed at the Calma's bravery Silus moved to join their defensive line.

The eel coiled around a tower and out of sight and, for a moment, Silus thought that it had moved on to other prey, but then – with a terrifying screech – the sinuous beast was amongst them.

The rider lashed out with its javelin, only for one of the Calma to wrap its flail around the shaft and pull. The weapon slipped out of the Chadassa's grasp and started to fall towards the seabed. Silus snatched it up before it could disappear and turned in time to see another Calma entangle its flail around the wrist of the eel rider. Within moments, however, the Chadassa had unsheathed a knife and severed its own hand, freeing it of the Calma's hold. Dark blood boiled into the water, throwing the eel into a frenzy that jolted the rider about in the saddle, but it soon had its mount back under control.

The eel opened its jaws and rushed another of the Calma, only to find Silus barring its way. The creature came to a sudden halt, jerking its rider forward in the saddle, its long, slim tail coiling behind it. A stream of bubbles slowly rising from its nostrils, the eel's eye slits narrowed as it considered this new thing now before it.

However, Silus didn't give it long to calculate its next move. He lunged for the eel, wrapped one arm around its thick neck and drove the barbed point of the javelin deep into its mouth. The eel let out a shriek that sounded like sheet metal tearing before rapidly ascending, taking Silus with it as he continued to cling on to the shaft of the weapon. The Chadassa crouched low over its mount's skull as it urged it on, trying to shake Silus off with rapid twists and turns.

As the towers of the citadel rolled dizzyingly around him, Silus saw that the remaining Calma were following in the eel's wake. He urged them back, not wanting any more of their blood on his hands but, despite his gestures, they closed on the beast.

One of them latched onto the eel's dorsal fin and tore into the ridged flesh, causing the creature to buck and writhe as it attempted to dislodge its attacker. Another Calma descended on the rider and tried to pull it from the saddle, but this attack met with less success and soon the Calma was tumbling away from them, blood gushing from its throat.

Silus's arms were beginning to ache with the effort of maintaining his grip on the javelin. Blood was pouring freely from the wound in the eel's mouth and the strong oily taste of it, as it clouded the water around him, was beginning to make Silus dizzy and nauseous.

They were not far from the surface now, but instead of launching itself from the sea, the eel began to slow. Thinking that it was finally succumbing to its wounds, Silus loosened his grip on the javelin and looked up to see how the Chadassa was responding to the imminent death of its mount.

But the creature didn't seem at all perturbed; instead it dug its heels sharply into the eel's temples and placed its remaining hand on the top of the creature's skull.

There was a flash of light and it felt as though a vice had suddenly closed on Silus's heart, as though he had been slammed into a brick wall at speed. One moment he was preparing himself to deliver the killing blow, the next he was falling, wracked with pain and paralysed. The water around him sparkled with electrical discharge and a dead Calma drifted down towards him, lazily turning, its eyes the white of cooked fish.

The eel coiled down from above and tore the creature in two, hungrily gulping down the innards that burst from its sundered flesh. But the Chadassa didn't give its mount long to feed and soon the eel was hurtling towards Silus once more.

He willed his limbs to move, he even attempted to reach into to the eel's mind and turn it on its rider, but all he could do was watch as death came to claim him.

He was about to close his eyes and offer up a final prayer to the ancestors, when a Calma ship closed around the eel.

The Chadassa was thrown from its saddle only to be cooked in an instant when a thin beam of emerald energy lanced from the ship. Riderless now, the eel coiled itself around the strange vessel and tried to close its jaws on the flesh-like hull, but the ship was clearly tougher than it looked. The eel worried at it in vain, rapidly becoming more and more enraged by its impervious prey. The ship withstood its futile scrabblings for just a moment longer, before suddenly flexing its limbs and pulling the eel apart.

As the sundered chunks of flesh fell slowly past, feeling began to return to Silus's extremities; but not quickly enough for him to get out of the path of the ship as it closed on him.

A thin, translucent tentacle unfurled from the centre of the craft to wrap itself around his waist. He knew that the Calma were on his side, but he couldn't help but feel afraid as he was pulled into the red, gaping maw that opened up at the vessel's core.

The mouth closed behind him and Silus was deposited into a small domed room that began to rapidly drain, leaving him on his knees, coughing up the seawater from his lungs. Once he was breathing normally again he managed to stand, though his legs shook with the strain and he had never felt so tired or so cold.

With a sound like lips moistly parting, a door dilated open above him and a hand reached through. Silus knew that hand and when he looked up, sure enough, there stood Katya. She helped him scrabble up into the ship's control room, where several Calma were busy piloting the vessel.

Silus and Katya didn't say anything as they embraced.

With his wife's arms around him, he realised just how long it had been since he had last held her. All the things he had taken for granted – the smell of her hair; the warmth of her skin – suddenly seemed as though he were experiencing them anew, and when she said his name he began to cry.

"I'm so sorry. So, so sorry," he said. "What did they do to you?"

"They took Zac away and then left me. After that there was nothing. Have you seen him Silus? Do you know where Zac is? He's safe, isn't he?" The look in Silus's eyes told Katya that he wasn't. "No, please no. No, *please* Silus. Tell me that he's okay. *Please.*"

But no matter how much she pleaded with him, Silus couldn't tell her what she wanted to hear, so instead he continued to hold her, and when the grief overcame her and she sank to the floor, he went with her.

"Make them pay, Silus," she said, "promise me that you'll make them pay."

As they sped away from the Chadassa citadel, Silus promised.

Kelos waited until the remaining Calma ships surrounded the *Llothriall* before he began to cast the spell. The parchment he took from the battered leather tube had the rainbow sheen of fish scale and, indeed, the sheet had been made from the hide of an extremely rare marine creature. It had cost Kelos a considerable amount to acquire and would crumble into dust once the spell was cast, but he considered that such circumstances as they now found themselves in more than justified its use.

Kelos lay the shimmering material flat on the table before taking out a small bottle of violet ink and a quill from a pocket in his robe.

"Kelos, what the fuck are you doing? This is no time to draw a picture," Jacquinto said, as he peered over his shoulder, "those bloody things are almost on us."

"I am not drawing a picture. It may not look like it, but I am performing some extremely powerful magic. You should be impressed."

Kelos began to draw a diagram onto the sheet, the ink of the chasm squid sinking into the page with the faintest of crackles as he moved the quill.

The *Llothriall* shook as something ploughed into its side and the bottle of ink went skittering across the table. Jacquinto caught it just before it hit the floor and Kelos exhaled heavily.

"Thank you, you may well just have saved all our lives."

Kelos finished his illustration as the sound of the assault increased on all sides. Then, after blowing on the ink to ensure it was dry, he took the page and folded it into eight segments.

The *Llothirall* shuddered as the sea warped around it. Kelos closed his eyes as the geometry of the cabin ruptured, the scene before him breaking into a kaleidoscope of disparate fragments. He heard Jacquinto say something, but his voice seemed to be getting further and further away.

Kelos tied the threads of elemental power together, spoke the closing words of the spell and unfolded the sheet.

The noise of the Chadassa bombardment stopped suddenly and the quiet was only broken when Jacquinto dropped to his knees and vomited.

"What the hell did you do?" he said, after the last spasm had died away. "It felt like being turned inside-out."

"I simply brought our destination closer to us, thus facilitating a swift exit and avoiding the need for a lot of tedious sailing. We are now not far from the Calma's city. Look."

But through the porthole, they saw not the glass domes of the city but a pall of thick black smoke boiling swiftly and steadily to the surface. Above, they could just make out the keels of a fleet of ships, from which fell a steady rain of dazzling white fire.

"I thought that you said the *Llothriall* was the only ship capable of sailing the Twilight seas," Jacquinto said.

"It is."

"Then who in the name of the seven hells are they, and why are they attacking the Calma?"

CHAPTER TWENTY-SIX

The *Llothriall* surfaced and, at a gesture from Kelos, the covering that had enclosed the deck dissolved, bright sunlight washing across the boards as it fell away. He chose to keep the masts down and the sails furled for now, not wanting to attract the attention of the fleet of eight ships that sat some thirty yards from starboard.

Whatever Kelos had been expecting to see on breaking the waves, it certainly hadn't been the symbol of the Final Faith, painted in red on the white of the ships' sails. For a moment he thought that the Faith had managed to repeat the success of the *Llothriall*, but then he saw that these vessels weren't suited to the Twilight seas at all. Already several were sporting rents in their hulls where the waves had battered their way in and, as he watched, one of the ships took a sudden nosedive. The men and women who fell from the deck were sucked under in her wake.

This, however, did not detract the remaining ships from their task.

Gun ports stood open along each vessel and through these were being pitched weighted barrels that burned with a blinding light. Even as they sank the flames were undiminished and Kelos wondered what kind of fire burned underwater. His awe at this peculiar sorcery, however, was broken by the realisation that if they didn't act soon the Calma city would be entirely destroyed. More importantly, Dunsany was somewhere down there. For all Kelos knew he could already be dead.

Kelos raised his hands. The *Llothriall's* masts rose from the deck and the sails unfurled. He grabbed a speaking tube and shouted down to Emuel to begin the song. As the deck shuddered beneath him, Kelos brought the *Llothriall* about, swiftly cutting a path towards the Faith vessels.

He ran to the prow as they neared, raising his arms and shouting, "Stop! You're killing them!"

Perhaps it was Kelos's plea, perhaps it was the realisation that the Faith's fugitive ship was amongst them, but the bombardment finally came to a halt.

By the time the *Llothriall* reached the fleet, more of the Faith's ships had succumbed and only three remained. Kelos realised then that this must be a suicide squad of some kind, sent to enact Makennon's vengeance with no hope of returning.

As they came alongside, Kelos extended the *Llothriall's* protective field to encompass the diminished fleet, before leaping onto a neighbouring deck, only to be immediately seized by men in robes.

"Let go of me! What are you doing?"

"You are a fugitive of the Faith. We are detaining you in the name of the Anointed Lord."

"For god's sake, we're trying to stop you killing the Calma."

"The Calma? What are the Calma?"

As if summoned, a Calma vessel surfaced nearby. A door dilated open in its topside and out stepped Silus and Katya, followed by several of the creatures. The craft drifted towards the ship and the small party climbed onto deck.

"Those are the Calma." Kelos said, nodding towards the creatures. "Now why did Makennon send you to kill them?"

A man with the symbol of the Faith tattooed onto his face backed away from the visitors, his hand going to the dagger at his belt, but before he could wield it, one of his shipmates had knocked it from his grasp.

"No. Leave them. They're not your enemy, the Chadassa are."

"The Chadassa," Kelos said. "What do you know about them?"

"They have been attacking the Twilight coast. Makennon's inquisitor –"

"Fitch?"

"Yes, Querilous Fitch. Through his methods of interrogation he managed to get one of the Chadassa to give up the location of its base here. Makennon's mages teleported us in to destroy it."

"You'd give your lives for her?"

"Gladly, it is the most holy duty one can perform."

"Then I'm afraid," Kelos said, "that your colleagues have died in vain. The Chadassa citadel does not lie below you. It is the Calma who reside here and they are peaceful, no threat to Twilight. The Chadassa have tricked you, sold you a lie. As you have been destroying the Calma's home a new breed of the Chadassa are marching on Twilight."

"Lord of All, what have we done?"

"Is there any way of getting a message back to Makennon?" Kelos said. "If Twilight is pre-warned then they may be able to defeat the remaining Land Walkers."

"Spalding, our mage, should be able to help you reach her. Spalding?" The man with the tattooed face stepped forwards. "Take this man below. He wishes to converse with the Anointed Lord."

Spalding sketched the symbol of the Faith in the air, before nodding to Kelos to follow him.

An intense chemical smell emanating from the gun decks– a marriage of bad eggs and burning hair – hit Kelos as he followed the mage down a short flight of narrow steps. Compared to the *Llothriall*, the Faith ship was squalid and cramped. Kelos's shoulders brushed the sides of the narrow corridor, and twice he stumbled in the candlelit gloom, falling over ropes and thudding into crates. Eventually they reached a box room, the walls of which had been daubed with the symbol of the Faith. In the centre stood a pedestal supporting a bowl of water.

Kelos shuffled in beside Spalding and looked up at him expectantly.

"So, are we going to talk to her, or did you just want to get close to me?"

Spalding looked down at Kelos with something like contempt before waving his hand over the bowl.

A soft glow suffused the room and Makennon's face came into focus upon the water.

"Spalding, is it done?" Katherine Makennon said. "If so you have my blessings. May the Lord of All take you into his arms."

Spalding nodded at Kelos and the mage leaned over the bowl.

"Hello Katherine."

Shock briefly crossed Makennon's features only to be quickly replaced by her usual cold expression.

"Kelos. You're not dead."

"No, I'm not. Although your fanatics have been doing their best to rectify that."

"Do you still have my ship?"

"Yes, and we'd like to keep it if it's all the same to you. Anyway, this isn't a social chat Katherine. You have sent your suicide squad on a wild fish chase. The Chadassa aren't here, they've tricked you. Your boys have been killing the wrong creatures."

"Kelos, if you're trying to sell me on some– "

"No, listen to me for once! The Chadassa are going to launch another attack against Twilight, but this time with a new breed of creature. We managed to destroy the majority of them, but some got away. Now, if you prepare your best Swords you have a chance of defeating them, but you have to mobilise now. Drag Pontaine into this if you have to. The Land Walkers must not be allowed to reach the World's Ridge Mountains."

"How do I know that you're not spinning me lies?"

"Tell her Spalding, you've seen the Calma."

For a moment he thought that the fanatic wasn't going to say anything – was perhaps mute – but after staring at Kelos as though he were going to kill him, he leaned over the bowl and said, "It's true. The Chadassa are not here. There are... other creatures."

"Makennon – Anointed One – we can use the *Llothriall* to fight the Chadassa," Kelos said. "After all, wasn't that what the ship was intended for all along, to be a holy weapon? And we have some of your most fanatical followers to fight beside us."

Katherine Makennon's head turned to one side and Kelos could hear her speaking to someone out of view. After a moment she turned back to them.

"When you have defeated the remaining Chadassa forces you will return the *Llothriall* to us."

"Like f –" Kelos caught himself in time. "Of course Anointed Lord. We shall return directly to Turnitia once the battle is won. We shall, of course, be treated with leniency?"

"Goodbye Kelos."

The image in the bowl dissolved.

They were going to need a bigger boat, Kelos considered, as he ushered the remaining Final Faith fanatics on board the *Llothriall*. At this rate, if they picked up any more refugees they would have to sleep three to a bunk. He had no idea what they were going to do with them once the battle was over. Makennnon had demanded that he return the *Llothriall* to Turnitia, but Kelos had absolutely no intention of doing so. He had only warned her of the impending assault by the Land Walkers because he had dreaded the consequences otherwise.

As they descended in the *Llothriall* to the Calma city the last of the fires were dying out. Kelos almost wished that the shroud of smoke had remained, because now that he could see the extent of the devastation he realised what little hope they had against the Chadassa. All but a handful of the glass domes had been shattered – though Kelos's horror was somewhat alleviated when he saw that the dome Dunsany had been recuperating in still stood – while the rest of the city seemed to have melted into the seabed. Within the soot stained ruins he could just make out the few surviving Calma, pulling the dead and dying from the rubble. Silus was out there already, doing what he could to help. Kelos would have offered his own assistance but, as he pulled on an underwater exploration suit, he had thoughts for only one man.

Dunsany.

Once out of the ship he headed for the glass dome. There Kelos could see several Calma working on sealing a crack in the structure's side, a stream of bubbles steadily rising from the fissure.

He stepped through the entrance membrane to find himself ankle deep in water.

"Dunsany!"

There was no reply. The only sound was the steady trickle of the sea as it poured into the dome. Ahead of him the water was tinted with swirls of blood, washing from the entrance to a room. Kelos felt his stomach tighten as he splashed towards the doorway, but inside the room there was no sign of Dunsany, only five Calma corpses lying neatly side by side. Each room he passed held more corpses and he was beginning to lose all hope of ever finding his friend when he heard the splash of footsteps from up ahead.

"Dunsany?"

Dunsany was pale and his long hair was plastered wetly to his scalp. When he looked up at Kelos it seemed he didn't recognise him for a moment, but then a smile crept into his features.

"Kelos? You know, all through my dreams you were there. Every step of the way, even to the edge of death. But you led me away from that dark vale and here I am. Though I can't quite remember where here is."

Kelos wanted nothing so much as to hold Dunsany, but as he approached his friend there was a bang and a crack zigzagged up the wall of the dome. Beads of moisture began to leak through.

He held out the spare underwater suit he had brought from the *Llothriall*.

"I hope that you're not too weak to swim."

The drip had become a trickle by the time Dunsany suited up and the dome had begun to sing as more cracks raced across its surface.

"Thank you for coming for me, old friend," Dunsany said before sealing the suit's hood.

And then, as the dome came down around them, their arms found each other.

Katya stood in the Calma ship, watching Silus help with the rescue operation outside, feeling as though she were losing him all over again.

This man who flitted through the water as quickly as the Calma – more quickly in fact – and who breathed the sea as easily as air, surely this man wasn't her husband? In fact, he was barely human. Katya still loved him, but the part she loved was the fisherman from Nürn, not the strange creature he had become.

If Zac had lived would he have grown into *this*, she wondered. Would father and son have spent their time together exploring the world beneath the waves, returning to her with treasures from ancient wrecks and tales of mermaids, sunken cities and forgotten islands; things she could never experience, never share?

The thought of Zac sent a new shard of grief through her. Katya tried to hold it in, only for it to erupt as a high-pitched sob. The Calma looked up from where they worked, but made no move to offer comfort or sympathy. A few even stood staring at her, as though wondering what she would do next. In her embarrassment, Katya tried to hide her grief, but it was too big to contain.

When Silus stepped back onto the ship, naked and dripping, he went to her but she pushed him away.

"Katya, what is it? What have I done?"

But she couldn't tell him, couldn't explain to Silus why she was so repelled by his touch.

This was what it came down to. This was the place to which all of Dunsany's visions of adventure and discovery had led them; a ship full of disparate refugees arguing about the best way to fight a losing battle.

Dunsany thought that the fanatics of the Faith looked the most lost. Not only had they discovered that their holy mission had been for naught, but now they found themselves having to incorporate the existence of the Calma and the theology of the Moratians into their blinkered world view. Dunsany watched Bestion calmly explaining about the Allfather to Spalding, who was becoming increasingly agitated by the dissonance between their beliefs.

The Calma, of course, must be feeling the most acute sense of loss, though it was hard to read the creatures. The few that stood with them on deck silently looked out at their diminished fleet.

"Do you think I should say something before our friends from the Faith start executing heretics?" Kelos said.

"I think that may be a good idea."

"People, your attention please." Nobody was listening, so Kelos lit up the deck with a spell that made them turn and stare. "Thank you. Now, I understand that this isn't where we want to be, but we owe it to ourselves not to run."

"We should consider it a great honour to give our lives in the service of the Lord of All," Spalding said.

"Thank you for your thoughts brother, but I'm hoping that won't be necessary. No, this is something we *can* win. Already we have weakened the Chadassa and all but defeated the Land Walkers. We can do this."

"To die will be glorious."

"Yes, thank you again brother. It may be best if you didn't keep reminding us of that."

"I'm sorry Kelos, but we can't win this." It was one of the Calma. Kelos thought that it was Seras, the creature who had helped Dunsany recuperate. "When we still had a city we may have been able to help you, but now that we have nothing, no defences... I'm afraid that this is the end."

"Ah, but you have yet to see what the *Llothriall* is fully capable of," Dunsany said. "She has, at her disposal, a devastating array of magical weapons."

"It won't be enough," Seras said. "What we have faced so far is but a small part of the Chadassa's army and now, led by their dark god incarnate, they will fight with a conviction and ferocity that will ensure their success in wiping us out. I'm sorry Kelos, but the Calma can no longer offer their aid. We have to flee before the Chadassa once more."

"There must be somewhere we can make a stand," Jacquinto insisted. "Is there no land nearby? If we can fight the Chadassa out of water then they will soon tire."

"I'm sorry, but there's nowhere you can run to," Seras said.

"That's not true," Bestion said.

"Morat is gone, Bestion," said Kelos.

"Not Morat. The Isle of the Allfather."

"Do you even know how to get there? We have no charts for this area," Dunsany said.

"We don't need charts. We simply follow the call of the Allfather." Bestion raised a finger to Kerberos.

Spalding had had enough and he pushed his face into Bestion's before spitting his venom: "The only place that your blasphemies are going to lead us is the bottom of the sea."

"Which is exactly where you'll be going if you don't keep a lid on those convictions of yours," Dunsany said, steering the acolyte into the capable and firm hands of Jacquinto and Ignacio.

"Bestion, no offence, but how exactly do you expect us to follow this call?" Kelos said. "I hate to say it, but I can't hear it and I'm not sure that anybody else on board can either."

"There is somebody here who heeds the call quite clearly," Bestion said. "In fact, I'm almost certain that he has been hearing it all along."

"Is it... is it me?" Emuel said, stepping forwards. "Ever since I was taught to re-discover the song I have felt... something."

"No Emuel. The one who hears the call is the one who brought us all here."

Seras understood. "Silus."

"What is he talking about?" Katya said. "Is this what has been leading you away from me, Silus?" Silus chose not to answer, instead he turned to Bestion. "It's Kerberos, isn't it?"

"Ever since I led you in communion with the Allfather I have sensed your unique bond with Him," Bestion said. "You still hear Him, don't you?"

"Yes."

"Guide us to the Isle of the Allfather, Silus. If the Chadassa mean to fight us with their god, then we shall simply have to call on our own."

CHAPTER TWENTY-SEVEN

Silus heard the island before he saw it.

The music rose and fell with the warm breeze that moved across the deck, sounding as though it were being played on a thousand discordant pipes.

Above him, Kerberos sat so large in the sky that the rim of the great disk touched the horizon. If he were to step from the *Llothriall*, Silus could almost believe that he would fall straight towards those endless azure clouds.

"How much longer?" Kelos said. "At this rate the Chadassa are going to overtake us before we even reach the island."

"We're almost there, listen."

"According to Bestion you are the only one who can hear the call."

"No, not the call. The music. Can't you hear it?"

For a moment the only sound was the crack of the sails and the creak of rope, but when the wind strengthened the ethereal piping surrounded them.

"What on earth is it?" Kelos said.

"I think that it's the Isle of the Allfather."

A low dark shape could now be seen on the horizon, crowned with what looked like a host of crooked towers. As they rapidly closed the distance to the shore, the music grew in volume.

There was the thud of feet on the deck and Silus and Kelos turned to see Bestion racing towards them. "It's the Isle isn't it? I heard the music."

More people were coming up from below now, drawn by the strange melody.

Once they were close enough to drop anchor, Silus could see that what he had taken to be towers were in fact irregular pinnacles of stone rising from the bedrock of the island. These structures were not manmade; rather they appeared to have been sculpted by the wind which fluted through the many holes in the rock, producing the weird cacophony.

"Jacquinto, Ignacio – prepare the launches," Kelos said. "The rest of you, prepare to disembark."

Silus didn't wait for the boats; instead he dived over the side and into the blood-warm water.

The sand here was so white and the water such a pure sapphire blue that he was reminded of the paradise of the Sarcre Islands. However, it wasn't only the sea that reminded him of Sarcre, for as Silus surfaced and began to wade towards shore, a low incessant buzzing filled his head.

Ahead of him, the dazzling sands suddenly ended in a line of dark rock and there stood the monoliths, marching away along the coast as far as the eye could see. They were half as tall as a man and encrusted in lichens and salt. On their surface were etched runes.

Silus tried to fight against the nausea that seemed to emanate from the stones, but a sudden dizzy spell put him on his knees. As the darkness crowded his vision, he only vaguely registered that someone was standing beside him.

"They're the same as the stones on Maladrak's Cauldron," Kelos said.

"That... that's nice," Silus managed. "Just help me get past the bloody things."

He felt a hand under each armpit and then he was being carried forwards. As he drew level with the stones there was a second of intense pain before he blacked out.

When he came to he was lying on the ground and the sun was just beginning to edge into Kerberos's shadow.

"Well that is good news," he heard Kelos say.

"What is?" Silus said, getting to his elbows.

"The monoliths. They'll make the island a lot easier to defend against the Chadassa."

"More importantly," Bestion said, offering Silus a hand up. "They'll buy us time as we call on the Allfather."

Once the last of the *Llothriall's* passengers had reached the shore, Dunsany set about forming them into groups, which he then sent to scout out the island. It didn't take long for them to return, as they discovered that the island wasn't much bigger than the smallest of those in the Sarcre archipelago. The monoliths surrounded the Isle on all sides – even topping the sheer cliffs on the southern edge – and everywhere were the twisted stone spires, channelling the wind into the ethereal music that they had first heard on the ship.

In all, Silus considered, there wasn't a lot of land to defend, but then there weren't that many of them to defend it.

As Dunsany set about allocating tasks and forming up their defences, Bestion led Silus and Katya to the temple.

The low round building stood in a grove of trees whose perfume was almost as powerful as the incense sticks Bestion lit once they entered the cool interior. An anteroom opened into the main chamber where a bridge crossed to the island that sat in the centre of a wide, shallow pool. There, flanked by metal censers, stood a simple stone altar. Above them a wide circular hole in the roof let in the light of Kerberos, the azure planet entirely filling the aperture.

As soon as Silus stepped up to the altar silence fell on the temple. Not even the music of the wind reached them. He noticed that Bestion was looking at him with a kind of awed reverence. For a moment he thought that the priest was about to sink to his knees, but when he turned his full gaze on him, Bestion was frozen where he stood.

"What's happened to your eyes, Silus?" Katya said.

"What do you mean?"

"Truly He has touched you," Bestion said. "Truly you are His avatar on our world."

"What are you talking about? Katya, what's going on?"

But neither of them would answer him, so Silus knelt down by the water and looked at his reflection.

The light of Kerberos streamed from his eyes.

"You must be prepared to come into His presence," Bestion said. "His call has drawn you here and His call will draw you into His arms. Are you ready?"

"I didn't want this," Silus said. "Katya, you have to believe that I didn't want this."

"It is not for us to ask what we want, but what He wants." Bestion said.

"I want my son back and I want to go home with my wife. I just want this all to end now."

"And it will Silus. When you call on the Allfather."

"Katya help me." Silus reached out and she took his hand, though a long time seemed to pass before she was willing to look at him. "I love you," he told her. "Believe that."

"I believe."

"Silus are you ready?" Bestion said, putting a hand on his shoulder.

"For the gods' sake man, give me a moment!" Then he turned back to his wife. "Katya I love you and I can't tell you how sorry I am for drawing you into this."

"It's not your fault Silus, you're just different... *chosen*, I suppose. Just promise that you'll come back to me."

"I promise."

Beneath the gaze of Kerberos Silus took her into his arms, and this time Katya looked deep into his eyes.

In preparation for the coming battle Dunsany moved the *Llothriall* into the shelter of a shallow cave on the southern side of the island. The last thing he wanted was for it to be destroyed, leaving them with no way of escape. Then, he removed the gem that sat at the heart of the ship. Kelos had asked him to do this, saying that he and Emuel could channel the power of the stone for use in the defence of the island. It could also, the mage said, be used as a weapon if it came to it. Next, Dunsany distributed weapons from the armoury. He knew that most of his crew were handy enough with a sword – with the exception of Emuel – but he wasn't too sure about the Moratians or the Final Faith fanatics. Thankfully, the latter saved him the worry of what to do with them by taking to their ships and sitting not far from shore. Kelos's magic had ensured that the three remaining Faith vessels had reached the island intact, but his protection wouldn't be required for much longer. The disciples of the Faith planned to detonate their explosives at the first appearance of the Chadassa, taking down any in their path. It seemed that whatever happened they were determined to give their lives, and Dunsany had neither the energy nor the inclination to argue with them.

At least they should buy them some time, and time was very much what their success hinged on here. Now that they didn't have the support of the Calma they had little hope of defeating the Chadassa on their own. Instead they would have to rely on Silus successfully persuading whatever power resided in Kerberos to intervene. If he were interrupted before he could do this then their slim hope would turn into no hope at all. In truth, Dunsany thought that they were already doomed, but both Bestion and Kelos had persuaded him that this was the only path open to them.

"Silus has a unique relationship with the Allfather that I have never before seen, even in the most devout of our priests." Bestion had said. "If anybody can persuade the Allfather to intervene then it is he."

"Bestion may well be right, Dunsany," Kelos had argued. "Who knows what power Kerberos holds? Besides, the Chadassa are not just going to withdraw now that we have stymied their plans. They will want revenge."

"I have seen the wrath of the Lord of All with my own eyes," Spalding spoke up. "In the World's Ridge Mountains a great bolt of energy did fall from Kerberos and destroy the heathens and their vile den of iniquity."

There wasn't really anything Dunsany could say to that, and so here they stood waiting to take on an army from the sea.

Dunsany looked up at Kerberos. "Don't you dare fail us, you bastard," he said.

Silus lay back on the altar and gazed into the depths of Kerberos. The dark moon that plagued the planet's orbit clung to its face like a black canker. He could feel the cloak of negative energy it had wrapped around its host but, through it, Silus could also hear Kerberos's call. It was the same call that had plagued his dreams from the beginning, drawing him away from all that was safe and familiar and into a host of mysteries he still didn't fully comprehend.

The censers were lit and the smoke rose to the ceiling before settling over him in a choking shroud. The first few breaths were the hardest, but when Silus felt his body begin to lose its hold he relaxed.

He looked up at Katya, as though seeking her permission to leave. She nodded once and Silus let go.

Twilight dwindled swiftly below him as his spirit soared away from the temple, the words of Bestion's chanting following him.

Before he could fall into the lightning kissed depths of Kerberos, however, he was brought to a sudden halt, hanging before the dark moon.

He knew that this entity was the same as that which called itself the Great Ocean; the same being who had taken Zac from him, pouring its taint into the infant's soul. Silus stared into its implacable face, the pure black of its surface unrelieved by any flaw. It was like staring into nothingness itself and that, Silus realised, was exactly what the Great Ocean was. Nothing.

It no longer had any hold on him, and so he tumbled away from it and into Kerberos's arms.

Maybe the Chadassa aren't coming for us after all, Dunsany thought, *maybe it's over already*.

They had been waiting so long for something to happen that the gentle and repetitive sound of the surf breaking on the shore was beginning to lull him to sleep.

When the Faith ships exploded he dropped his sword.

The light from the blast left red ghosts flitting across his vision and he had to blink several times before he could see to where the ships had been.

A wave raced towards them, kicked up by the blast, crashing against the monoliths and soaking those who stood near the stones. Dunsany looked for Chadassa bodies in the wash but the only thing floating there was a human hand. On the index finger was a ring wrought in the shape of the symbol of the Final Faith.

Dunsany was beginning to wonder what had prompted the ships to detonate when something rose from the sea.

The giant ball of black spikes looked not unlike a sea urchin. It drifted towards the shore before coming to rest, bobbing on the swell. Dunsany had half a mind that this thing wasn't anything to do with the Chadassa at all, but rather was some benign seabed denizen which had been uprooted by the blast.

With a sound like a sneeze, a spike flew from the sphere. It pierced the chest of one of the Moratians standing further along the beach and exploded from his back, pinning him to the ground. He stood for a moment – knees slightly bent, back arched, gasping for breath – before sinking down the length of the spike, his blood a vivid scarlet on the white sands.

"Take cover!" Dunsany shouted as more spikes flew towards them.

Using the power of the stone from the *Llothriall* and Emuel's song, Kelos threw up a magical shield. However, it didn't encompass everybody and more spikes found their mark.

A Moratian woman ducked behind one of the stone spires, only for a spike to pierce both the rock and her. Another man was pinned to his friend as he turned to run; the spike entering the back of his head and continuing through his friend's right eye.

The barrage lasted no more than ten seconds and when it was over they had lost half their army and the survivors stood in a forest of shivering black quills.

"What the hell was that?" Jacquinto said.

"I suggest we fall back," Kelos said, as the sea began to churn.

"The monoliths should hold off the Chadassa," Dunsany said as he followed them in-land.

"Yes, but I don't know for how long and I don't want to be standing anywhere near the stones when they go."

"So what are we going to do?" Jacquinto said. "We can't just fight them all."

"We have to hope that Silus will come through for us," Kelos said. "Otherwise, gentlemen, it has been a pleasure sailing with you and I hope to see you in the next life."

There was nothing but clouds.

The first time that Silus had communed with Kerberos – in the temple on Morat – he had sensed something like a vast consciousness, a planet-sized intelligence that may well have been the planet itself.

Now there was only the storm.

As he fell through the lightning and the wind he called out to his ancestors, whose spirits surely resided here, but there was no response. In fact, it felt to Silus as though he truly were the only living thing here.

Then what had been calling to him?

"What are you?" Silus shouted.

"What are you?"

Just an echo, Silus thought. Though hadn't those last few words seemed to overlap his own?

"What are you?"

"... you... you... you... you..."

The single word echoed around him and kept on echoing, as though it had become trapped within the clouds.

This was pointless. Bestion was mistaken. There was no benevolent and just god here.

Silus began to search for the thread that would lead back to his body.

"... you... you... you... you..."

"Shut up! Bestion, help me!"

"... you... you... you... you...."

The thread wasn't there, but then something about the word cut through his panic and made him stop and think.

You.

You.

You.

There was something here. *He* was here. Silus had been looking in the wrong place. Even before the ritual had been completed – even before he had left his body – Kerberos had entered into him.

Silus reached out and the lightning arced around him in a nimbus of power that lit up the clouds for miles around. He reached even further and now he could hear the roar of Kerberos itself as it turned in the void, could feel the immense energies that held it together.

At the heart of the storm, at the centre of it all, Silus burned.

"... you... you... you... you..."

"Yes," Silus said, "*me.*"

Kelos watched the others nervously watching the shore as they took up their fallback positions.

The blue fire burst from the monoliths and a dome of shimmering energy closed around the island. Kelos felt the hairs on the back of his neck rise as, at his feet, the stone from the *Llothriall* began to pulse in sympathy with the magic. Beside him Emuel was singing, the tattoos that covered his body dancing to the strange rhythms he weaved. Along the line, the rest of the crew stood with their weapons readied. Only a handful of the Moratian refugees stood with them, the rest having fallen in the attack by the urchin thing. Kelos was impressed that the survivors had chosen to fight on, even as the blood of their comrades sank into the blazing sands.

There was still no sign of the Chadassa themselves, though

they must have been close else the monoliths' power would have remained dormant.

The sea began to withdraw then, as though the tide were going out, though no tide that Kelos had seen had ever retreated so rapidly. Already the sea was five hundred metres from where they stood on the beach, and thousands of dying fish lay flopping in the wet sand while crabs raced to keep up with the dwindling tide. Now seaweed draped rocks were uncovered, some the size of houses, and among them Kelos could see the wreck of an ancient ship.

Beyond that the water fell away even more swiftly, revealing the Chadassa army.

There were thousands of them and, at their head stood the Great Ocean, clothed in the ruins of Snil's flesh. Zac still hung from the Chadassa's torso, giggling as the dark god's energy coursed through him. Bringing up the rear, like a line of siege engines, was a phalanx of monstrous crustaceans.

"Gods, they're not leaving anything to chance are they?"

Indeed, Kelos considered, why did the Chadassa feel the need to put such a mighty force up against just a handful of humans?

Then, even in the face of such overwhelming odds, Kelos felt hope renewed. Because, if the Chadassa were leaving nothing to chance that meant the Great Ocean knew what Silus was doing at the temple, and feared that he would succeed.

When he saw the Great Ocean give the signal to advance, Kelos reached for the threads of elemental power before dropping to his knees and burying his hands in the sand. Channelling a thread of energy from the *Lothriall's* stone he spoke the words of an elven spell. It had originally been created to protect a coastal town against raiders. Whether or not it had been successful Kelos didn't know, as he'd never found the town on any ancient map of Twilight. That was the thing with practicing Old Race magic, he considered. Sometimes you only had a vague idea of the results you were going to get.

The spell cast, he looked up. The Chadassa hoard were even closer. Kelos spoke the last word of the spell again, borrowing yet more power from the stone, but nothing seemed to happen.

But then, with a dull thud, the sand beneath the first wave of the Chadassa army turned to liquid and they were quickly sucked under. Kelos estimated that he had taken down at least three hundred of the creatures.

A cheer went up from the line of human defenders, but they were far from out of the woods. Kelos's magic would only stretch so far, and once the power of the monoliths was breached they had only a dozen or so swords against thousands of wicked talons.

In a matter of seconds the Chadassa regrouped and the next wave came for them, this time with the Great Ocean itself at its head. The line of gigantic crustaceans launched rocks at the island as they followed. For one brief moment Kelos managed to pull the fallen missiles into the form of a rock elemental, which ground several Chadassa into paste before a counter spell from the Great Ocean took it down.

Above them, light strobed across the surface of Kerberos and it looked to Kelos as though the planet were beginning to turn more swiftly.

The magical barrier that protected the island was now screaming with the force of the Chadassa against it and Kelos could see several of their mages working to undo the power of the stones.

He remembered how swiftly the stones on Maladrak's Cauldron had fallen. On the Isle of the Allfather they fell in less than half the time.

Silus could no longer tell which part of him was Kerberos and which was his own spiritual essence. Even though he had no body, he felt each flash of lightning, each rumble of thunder as a deeply physical sensation.

When he looked down at the blue-green globe that turned below him a lance of energy erupted from his mass and struck the planet. He felt the deaths of some of the Chadassa as the bolt hit and a shockwave rippled through the dark moon in his orbit. Silus's laughter raced through the clouds as Kerberos began to turn faster and faster. He reeled drunkenly for a while, but he was careful lest he turn too fast and dissipate himself into space.

Silus slowed down, turned his face away from Twilight and stared into the star flecked void.

Wouldn't it be something, he considered, to just leave Kerberos behind? To send his spirit out as far as it would go. Perhaps he would find a new world more beautiful and less troubled than his own. He was almost tempted to let go, but as he turned to look back at Twilight he could feel the needs and fears of the people there, and he could feel the taint of the Chadassa that lay itself across all creation.

Silus gathered the storm within himself. For the first time in millennia Kerberos was perfectly still. He enjoyed the peace for a time as the turbulent energies built within him.

Then, Silus opened his eyes, reached down and touched Twilight.

They began to run, even before the first of the monoliths exploded.

Father Maylan was the fastest – his robes flying out behind him as he sprinted away from the shore – but then he was the least encumbered of them, carrying, as he did, only a lightweight dagger. Kelos's progress was rather less swift, as he had the stone from the *Llothriall* in his arms. There was no question of leaving it behind. Without it, their ship would be next to useless. He almost regretted asking Dunsany to remove it now.

The last to join the retreat towards the temple were Jacquinto and Ignacio. Ignacio even made a stand for a short time, side by side with one of the Moratians, throwing rocks at the swarms of Chadassa racing towards them. However, when a considerably larger stone than the ones they were wielding flattened the man from Morat, Ignacio decided to run.

"Emuel, try to keep up," Dunsany shouted at the eunuch, who was beginning to lag behind. Even as he ran Emuel was singing, though the song did little to protect him as a spear glanced off his shin. He stumbled and fell, but before the Chadassa could reach him, one of the Moratians threw himself in front of the eunuch. Emuel regained his feet and, as he fled, he tried to block out the sound of his rescuer being eviscerated.

Dunsany looked back to see that the Chadassa were gaining on them. The sound coming from the throat of the Great Ocean as it led the charge was like nothing he had ever heard. The long, ululating wail seemed to speak of the darkness of space, the emptiness of the void and the oblivion it would bring to their world.

Ahead of him, Dunsany could see the grove where the temple stood and from within he could just make out the sound of Bestion's chanting.

"Get inside," he shouted to his companions. "We may be able to barricade the entrance."

"That's a terrible idea and you know it," Jacquinto said. "Face it, we're done for."

"This is not a time for arguments," Kelos said, gesturing with his hands. Behind him the stone spires began to explode, showering the Chadassa with fragments of burning rock. However, it did little to slow their advance. "Silus will come through for us, you'll see."

"Well I have yet to see any evidence of his – "

Jacquinto fell silent. For a moment Dunsany thought it was because he had been struck down, but then he turned and noticed what had made the smuggler gaze in awe-struck silence.

The Chadassa had come to a halt, but clearly not at the Great Ocean's command. The god paced up and down the ranks, berating its soldiers. Though it killed several as a lesson to the others, none of the Chadassa even moved to acknowledge the deaths.

"Is this it?" Kelos said.

The Chadassa sank slowly to their knees, settling so gently on the sand that they didn't make a sound. Then, from every eye socket and from every mouth streamed the light of Kerberos as the Chadassa began to sing.

The sound was deafening but glorious.

"My God," Emuel said, "it's the song." Then he turned to the temple and shouted: "Bestion, it's the song."

The strong, high note washed over them all for a second more before falling in pitch and then ceasing altogether.

The Chadassa remained where they were, but now smoke rose from their empty eye-sockets and their open mouths. Gulls descended on the corpses, drawn by the smell of cooking flesh.

The Great Ocean howled at the death of its children, before turning its fury on the humans in its midst.

Far from the Isle of the Allfather, on the coast of Turnitia, the Land Walkers burst from the sea only to be faced with a vast army wearing the crossed circle of the Final Faith.

Though the army before them was formidable, the Land Walkers raised their voices and charged. They had advanced no more than halfway up the beach, however, when a pure, holy light blazed from their eyes and mouths and they dropped dead.

"Well done Anointed Lord," said one of the knights, turning to Katherine Makennon. "Truly such abominations are as like wheat to the scythe before your divine presence."

"Thank you Alonkin," Katherine Makennon said, "but, really, it was nothing."

The Great Ocean's howl was that of a parent bereaved, but Jacquinto didn't give the creature time for its sorrow as he swung his sword. The blade was caught before it could connect and the steel shattered in the creature's grip.

Ignacio, seeing the danger his comrade was in, followed with his own attack. This time the weapon connected, but when the smuggler drew back to strike again, the creature grabbed his skull.

Jacquinto was showered with his brother's blood as the Great Ocean brought its hands together, but he still managed to scramble out of the way when the creature turned its attention on him.

Kelos stepped into the monster's path and raised the stone from the *Llothriall*, speaking words from a long dead tongue as he channelled the power of the gem.

The Great Ocean stood its ground against the sudden gale that howled around it, before taking the stone from the mage's hands and turning it into dust.

Kelos stared in numb horror as hope blew away on the wind. Emuel was shouting something at him, but, though he could see the eunuch's lips moving, he couldn't hear his words.

The pitch black eyes of Zac looked up at him from where was he was fused to the monster's breast. "Give Silus to me now and your deaths will be painless," said the Great Ocean through the infant's mouth. "Otherwise, your agony will be ten times worse than this."

The Great Ocean strode towards Father Maylan, brushing aside a Moratian as he attempted to defend him. The creature reached towards the priest and the half-born foetuses scrabbled out of the ruins of its body, to swarm over him. Father Maylan screamed as the tiny creatures burrowed into his flesh. He tried to pull them away but they were too slippery and soon they were moving under his skin.

Kelos looked away as the aborted Chadassa fed. Emuel was tugging on his sleeve now and, this time, he could hear what the eunuch was saying.

"Run."

Silus felt the deaths of his friends as the Great Ocean took their lives and the storm gave voice to his sorrow. The Chadassa may have been destroyed but the father remained, the shadow of the black moon moving across Kerberos testament to this fact.

He searched for the sound of Bestion's chanting and when he found it the words seemed less sure of themselves, as though they were being spoken under duress. However, with them Silus regained the thread that would lead him back to his body.

But he didn't follow it home just yet.

Instead he left Kerberos and moved across the surface of the dark moon. Below him a ripple passed through the orb as it sensed his presence. This thing was as much his true father as it was the Chadassa's. When it reached out to him he didn't fight its embrace, even though he was repulsed.

Though the Chadassa had been everything he didn't want to be, Silus gave up a part of himself to their god.

The Great Ocean poured into him and when he felt himself beginning to drown, he fell back towards Twilight, carrying its tainted waters within him.

Dunsany and Jacquinto held the main entrance for a time but soon the Great Ocean had them backed into the temple.

Parrying a swipe of its claws Dunsany tried to push it into the pool in the main chamber, but it lashed out with its other arm, scoring a series of deep slashes into his chest. When the blood began to flow Dunsany decided to retreat, though there was nowhere to retreat to. Behind him Silus lay prone on the altar while Bestion chanted over him, lost in his devotions. Katya stood beside them and she had been the only one to look up as they barrelled into the temple, a howl of grief erupting from her when she saw what had happened to Zac.

"He is the Great Ocean," the child said, giggling. "He is the Great Ocean. Praise him."

"Katya, get out of here." Dunsany shouted, before bringing his sword down in a wide arc. The blow connected with a hollow sound before the sword was swept from his grip. The weapon skittered across the smooth marble floor, coming to rest at Katya's feet.

Dunsany closed his eyes as the god pressed forward, waiting for the killing blow, but the Great Ocean paid him no heed and instead walked towards where Silus lay.

The remaining members of the crew looked on helplessly as the monster approached. Kelos reached out to Katya as he saw what she was about to do, but it was too late.

She rounded the altar and charged the Great Ocean, Dunsany's blade held before her. The creature watched her come with a mild disinterest and didn't even cry out as the sword sank into its chest to the hilt. Katya kept her grip on the pommel and pushed until she was face to face with the creature.

The dead white eyes of the ruined Chadassa body writhed with maggots. Only a small trickle of blood covered Katya's hand where she held the sword. There was a tug on her chest and she looked down to where Zac was fused to the creature. She had thought her son dead, but somehow this was worse.

A wide smile split the infant's face as it looked up at her, but it wasn't a smile of recognition. It was a smile of malice, a smile that said it would bring death to them all.

Zac's small hand pushed her gently back, until she was bent over the altar with Silus beneath her. Foul smelling liquid gushed from the Chadassa's corrupt body to cover her.

"He is the Great Ocean. His time is now," said the voice coming from her son and, beneath her, Silus's body stirred. "He is the Great Ocean. Praise Him. Praise Him. Praise Him."

The chanting was so loud it overrode Bestion's own words. Katya looked up at the priest, pleading with him to break out of his prayerful meditations, but he did not stir, even with the presence of something so foul in their midst.

Then another voice joined with the Great Ocean's as Silus sat up on the altar.

"*I* am the Great Ocean."

Katya turned and when she saw the darkness that filled her husband's pupils she backed away in horror.

"Yes, that's right Silus," the Great Ocean said. "That's right, join with me."

"I am the Great Ocean."

The darkness streaming from his eyes, Silus reached out. His hands went to Zac and held him. There was a deep rumble of thunder and, above them, a sheet of blinding light suddenly washed across Kerberos. It was almost as though the planet had blinked.

As the echoes of the thunder died away the sound of a child crying filled the temple. Katya looked over at her son to see a pure azure light pouring from his pupils. The flesh that had bound him to the body of the monster melted away and Silus lifted him free from the hideous caul.

"Silus, what are you doing?" said the Great Ocean.

Silus ignored it and placed his son in Katya's hands. As he did so the light went out of Zac's eyes, to be replaced by the deep blue gaze she had first fallen in love with. This time when the child cried, it was with an entirely human voice.

"Silus, you are my son. We are the Great Ocean," The dark god said, doubt now tingeing its voice.

"No, *you* are the Great Ocean, I am something else. We were both born of Kerberos, yet you choose to seed this place with your own taint. A taint that I carry within me only to deliver back to you a thousand-fold."

Silus gripped the monster's skull and let the dark water of the Great Ocean pour back out of him. With it, though, came an energy more ancient, more powerful – that of Kerberos itself.

Silus maintained his grip as the creature dropped to its knees and he didn't let go even when it began to burn. Soon there were only ashes on the temple floor where the Great Ocean had stood.

Bestion's chanting came to an end and he opened his eyes.

"What happened? I heard the voice of the Allfather."

But Silus didn't say anything. Instead he went to Katya and Zac, knelt and put his arms around them.

Listening to his son cry, Silus thought that it was one of the most beautiful sounds he had ever heard.

Soon the Isle of the Allfather was awash with great buzzing clouds of flies as the Chadassa's bodies rotted. A nauseating stench washed over the island and made it difficult to venture anywhere other than the temple. When the supplies on the *Llothriall* ran low it was clear it was time to leave.

"Where are we going to go without the power of the stone?" Silus said. "The waters may be calm around the isle, but out there are currents that will rip apart the ship in seconds."

It seemed to him that they had escaped one disaster only to head into the jaws of another.

"There are a chain of smaller islands not far from here," Bestion said. "We could head over there."

"And what then?"

"I hadn't thought much further than that if I'm honest."

"Where's your sense of adventure?" Dunsany said. "The ship can hold her own for a while I'm sure. We don't need magic all the time after all." Kelos looked up at him and smiled. "Besides, if it gets too rough on board Silus can always swim alongside. Maybe he could call the creatures of the deep to our aid."

So, with the sales billowing they left the Isle of the Allfather behind. As they turned hard to starboard the sun was just coming out of Kerberos's shadow. There was nothing to mar the azure sphere now, the Great Ocean had vanished.

Silus held Katya tight as the shore moved out of sight over the horizon. In her arms Zac stirred sleepily. Silus wondered how much Zac had inherited from his father and, more, he wondered how much his time in the grip of the dark god would have tainted him.

Silus swore that as his son grew up, he would teach him to fight.

THE END

JONATHAN OLIVER

Jonathan Oliver is the Editor-in-Chief of Abaddon and Solaris. He has had stories published on both sides of the Atlantic in various publications, along with a handful of articles. He used to dabble in stand-up comedy before coming to the realisation that writing may be far less gruelling. He lives in Abingdon with his wife Alison and their cat Fudge. *The Call of Kerberos* is his first novel.

ACKNOWLEDGMENTS

Firstly, thanks must go to Alison, my wife, who had to sit through many an evening of me pounding at the keyboard, swearing at the computer and being wracked with self-doubt as the novel took shape. Your patience is amazing and I love you with all my heart.

A massive thank you must also go to Rebecca Levene, my editor on this project. Rebecca's advice and editorial guidance have been invaluable.

Mark Harrison – as ever – was master of cover duties and I couldn't be happier with how beautiful it is. Mmmmm... tentacles.

Pye and Luke are the design team who have made sure the book looks the biz. They both rock the kasbah and are design gods.

Thanks also to Mum and Dad, Jim and Anna, Chris and Antonia. the Bardsleys and all my family. Joel Lane, the NRFTers (Sam, Owen, James, Pete, Craig) who have fought many a fish demon and continue to provide friendship and dice-based hilarity, Rob Spalding, the *2000 AD* and Abaddon/Solaris teams, especially Jenni who proofread this, Kelly and Pat who have been reading my stories possibly longer than anyone, and Sam and Elaine who have sat through many stand-up gigs and tales from the ice-cream factory.

Now read the first chapter of the next exciting novel in
the *Twilight of Kerberos* series...

ENGINES
of the
APOCALYPSE

MIKE WILD

ISBN: 978-1-906735-37-1

£6.99/$7.99

COMING SOON

CHAPTER ONE

The world was plunged into darkness. There was a scream.

The scream in question came from one Maladorus Slack, entrepreneur and guide, hired only hours before by Kali Hooper after he'd approached her in the *Spider's Eyes* claiming to know the location of a forgotten passageway leading directly to the fourth level of Quinking's Depths. It was an audacious claim, and it wasn't every day that Kali trusted the word of some drunk in a backwoods tavern, but there had been something in the way Slack made it – with wariness, rather than greed, in his eyes – that had made her take a gamble on its veracity and hand over fifty full silver for the privilege of having him share it with her.

As it turned out, her money had been well spent. Slack guided her at twilight to a cave in the hills above the remote town of Solnos and deep within, pointing out an overgrown cryptoblock defence that he swore – once unlocked – would enable her to bypass the Depths' first three levels and find treasure of such value that she might, as he so colourfully put it, "come over all tremblous in the underknicks." Kali had had a word with him about this, pointing out that it was *her* business what went on in her underknicks and, far more importantly, that she didn't do what she did for the *money*. Most of the time, anyway.

She felt a bit bad now, about having pinned him against the wall. Especially considering the man's fate. Not that it was her fault – or his, really. For one thing, Slack's nervousness had threatened to make him come over all something else in the underknicks and he had stuck to her like a limpet even though she tried to shoo him away, and for another there was no way either of them could have anticipated what was going to happen once they had found what lay within the Depths.

Perhaps, though, she should have done. Perhaps the way things had gone she should have realised that the whole thing was going to go tits up.

"This cryptoblock," Slack had said as she had begun to work on it in the cramped conditions of the cave, "It is some kind of puzzle, yes?" He was crouched awkwardly between the skeletal remains of previous adventurers who had found their way there, trying to ignore the fact that every one of their bones was completely, utterly shattered.

"Not some kind of puzzle," she replied. "A very specific kind."

"You have seen such things before?"

"Once or twice. Cryptoblock defences are typical of an ancient race called the dwarves."

"The Old Race, you mean? With the pointy ears and bows?"

Kali sighed but took time to set him straight because Slack had at least heard of the Old Races, which was more than could be said of most people on the peninsula. "No, the other lot. The noisy ones with axes and blood pressure."

"Bows, axes, what does it matter?"

Slack sniffed the kind of sniff where you could hear the contents of his nostrils slop against his brain, and Kali grimaced in distaste. But as she once more felt his hot, alcoholic breath in her face, the man seemed to accept the truth of what she was saying.

"I remember. These dwarves were supposed to have been masters of deadly traps, yes?"

"Oh, yeah."

"Then this door is such a trap?"

Kali glanced at the skeletons on the floor of the cave. "Either that or these guys succumbed to a very bad case of the jitters."

Slack glanced fearfully around the cave, looking for hidden devices.

"You won't see a thing," Kali advised. "They were master engineers, too."

"Then I hope you know what you are doing!"

"Wish I did," Kali said. She was working on one particular area now, concentrating hard, tongue sticking out between her teeth between responses. "Trouble is, each cryptoblock is different... springs, balances, counterbalances... you just have to feel your way around." She suddenly pulled back with a gasp as something *sprang* inside the cryptoblock and one of its component parts snapped into place where she had delved a moment before. "Farker!" she cursed, shaking and sucking her fingers, then almost casually grabbed Slack's sleeve, pulling him aside as a solid stone fist the size of an outhouse punched down from the cave roof onto the spot where he had stood, reducing what remained of the skeletons to dust. With a grinding of hidden stone gears, the fist retracted, and Kali returned to her work, leaving Slack where he was, white-faced and with a small stain spreading on the front of his pants.

"Sorry about that," Kali said. "Getting somewhere, now."

She continued to work diligently on the puzzle for the next few minutes, Slack staring warily around himself, below and above all the while, flinching or emitting a little whimper each time there was the sound of something clicking into place in the cryptoblock. But at last there was a sound that was different to the others – somehow *final* – and Kali stood back with a sigh of satisfaction.

Slack regarded her and the cryptoblock with some puzzlement, because at first nothing seemed to happen. Then each part of the cryptoblock that Kali had repositioned retracted into another adjacent to it, which in turn retracted into adjacent parts. Other components of the cryptoblock automatically moved up or down, enveloping their neighbours or moving in or out. This reordering became faster and faster, the size of the cryptoblock diminishing all the time until Slack found himself staring at a small cube where the cryptoblock had been. For a second it simply hung there, and then Slack jumped back as it, too, retracted – this time, into itself. Nothing remained of the cryptoblock – nothing at all.

"I do not understand," he said. "It is gone. How can it be gone?"

Kali looked at him, smiled. Questions, always questions. "The corporeal stability of the cryptoblock has been transfeckled," she said, adding in response to his puzzled stare, "It's a dimension thing." She hoped it sounded convincing because, frankly, while having cracked a few of these things, she really hadn't a clue. There was no way, however, that she was going to let Slack know that.

Thankfully, Slack wasn't interested in deconstructing her statement too deeply, because his attention had been sidetracked by other things, namely the glittering ore in the wall of the passageway revealed by the vanishing cryptoblock. It was only triviam, all but worthless, but its glittering held the promise of greater things, and as Slack wiped sweat from his lips with his arm, Kali frowned. There was a growing air about the man that suggested while he'd been happy to guide her to the entrance, he'd never really expected her to *open it*, and now that she had was maybe having second thoughts about who deserved the treasure beyond. Her suspicions were confirmed as Slack raced ahead of her into the opening.

Cursing, Kali threw herself forward and grabbed his tunic from behind, just in time as it turned out. Slack was already skidding helplessly down a sharp incline and Kali fell onto her stomach with an *oof* as she was wrenched in after him. Her dark silk bodysuit tore at the waist and rough stone grazed her torso as she skidded down in his wake, but then she hooked and jammed her feet against the sides of the narrow passageway, tearing away loose stones and crying out with the effort as she applied pressure to slow their progress. They continued to slide for a few more seconds but at last came to a stop. Slack was now a dead weight on her arm, the man dangling above a dark and seemingly bottomless abyss into which the disturbed stones poured around him, clattering echoingly ever down.

Kali heaved him up. "Looks like I'm going to have to keep an eye on you in more ways than one," she chastised.

"I was – I was checking it was safe," Slack protested, breathlessly.

"Yeah, right," Kali said. She positioned herself on a safe part of the ledge, rubbed her stomach and cursed. "There are rules to this game," she added, "and rule one is watch *every* step."

A flash of resentment crossed Slack's face as he dusted himself down, but then he turned to stare into the dark, shaken by the end he had almost met with but staring with undisguised greed. Kali joined him at the edge of the abyss, wondering fleetingly whether it might be easier if she just shoved him off, but considering what it was they faced it was obvious Slack could do nothing without her.

As always, through her research, she had known roughly what to expect when coming here, but as always the expectation never quite did the reality justice. The two of them were staring into a vast natural cavern that must have extended beneath three or four of the hills surrounding Solnos, a huge expanse barred with immense stalactites and stalagmites with a pillar of azure twilight streaming down from somewhere above at its distant centre. The pillar of light was the only illumination in the darkness, and picked out an isolated column of rock, maybe six feet in diameter, the base of which disappeared into the abyss below. It was clearly unreachable by conventional means but it was nonetheless Kali's destination. She bit her lip and studied her distant goal. At this distance, she could not make out the details of what she knew lay there but her above average eyesight could at least discern the motes that slowly danced in the pillar of light in an almost dreamlike way, as if something beneath them was affecting the reality where they hung. Something that itself played with reality. Something magical.

Kali had no doubt that she'd found what she'd come for. All she had to do was reach it.

"There?" Slack observed incredulously. "But there is no way across!"

"Rule two," Kali answered, pulling a small object from one of the pockets in her dark silk bodysuit. "Plan ahead."

Slack stared at a small, carved piece of stone Kali held in her hand, then watched her move to the rock wall, brush away some lichen from a small area and then insert the stone into a niche revealed behind. She tightened her grip on the stone and then, with a grunt, turned it solidly to the right, to the left, and then twice to the right. Something grated behind the niche and then below, in the darkness, something rumbled. Slack watched in amazement as, continuing to rumble, a rock column rose slowly from the abyss, shearing thick cobwebs, dust and the detritus of ages from itself as it came. The top of the column stopped level with the ledge on which they stood, some hundred feet out into the void.

Kali withdrew the stone key from the niche and smiled. Slack, meanwhile, stared at the column and then Kali, regarding her quizzically.

"I still do not understand," he said. "That is still too far away to reach."

Kali nodded. The fact was, it was *just* too far away for a running jump, even for her. But even had she been able, she wouldn't have tried. Revealing her unique capabilities to a man who would, for the price of a shot of boff, tell all and sundry about a freak who could make such a jump was not a wise move. In a backwoods region such as this, such tales could easily reach the ear of some overzealous Final Faith missionary, and she had no wish to be dragged to a gibbet and burned as a witch. Luckily, however, there was no need to jump at all.

"Rule three," Kali said. "Be patient."

She smiled again as, from under the lip of the ledge where they stood, a scintillating layer of bright blue energy moved out towards the risen column, manoeuvring itself around stalactites and stalagmites to form a zig-zagging translucent bridge. More motes danced lazily in the blue, before freezing where they hung, trapped in what had appeared.

Slack squinted, frowned, and Kali realised he hadn't a clue what he was looking at. It was easy to forget that while she lived with such wonders on a day-to-day basis now, the average peninsulan, especially those out here, had never once encountered the threads.

"It's called magic," she explained.

"Magic?"

"It's –" Kali paused and contemplated. How exactly *did* you explain magic to a man like Slack? "It's kind of like using the world around you... a way of doing things with invisible tools."

"So, with this... magic, I could dig a cesspit with an invisible spade?"

Kali pulled a face. "Uh, yeah, I suppose," she conceded, thinking that she was the only one digging a hole around here. "Let's move on, shall we?"

A wary Slack dibbed his toe onto the bridge, clearly not trusting its solidity, and as he did Kali strode casually by him into the void, high-fiving stalactites and humming a happy tune. She reached the column and waited for Slack to catch up before she inserted her stone key into a second niche carved in its centre. This time she turned it left three times, right and then left again. There was another grating sound, and another rumbling from below.

"Six columns," Kali explained as another rose ahead of them, "six combinations. If all are entered correctly, they form a bridge all the way to where we want to go."

Slack sniffed, becoming over-confident once more. "That sounds easy enough."

"Easy?" Kali chided as she waited for the bridge to form and skipped onto the next stage. "You think I got this key from some bloody adventurer's corner shop? It's been crafted from separate components, six again, each one hidden in a site rigged to the rafters with every kind of trap imaginable. These past few weeks I've been shot at, scolded, suffocated, stifled, stung, squeezed, squished and squashed, so maybe, Mister Slack, you should rethink your 'easy'."

"And you say you are *not* doing this for the money?"

"Nope," Kali said. "Holiday."

"*Holiday?*"

"Holiday." The fact was, she was still reeling from recent events and revelations, so much so that she'd had to get away, from friends, from the *Flagons*, from all of it. Not that there were actually that many friends around right now – she'd barely seen hide nor hair of Merrit Moon or Aldrededor since she'd brought the *Tharnak* from the Crucible, the old man, whose shop was being rebuilt after the k'nid attacks, and the pirate spending all their time tinkering with the ship in Domdruggle's Expanse. Dolorosa had summed it up with a phrase that had brought a grin to her face – boys and their toys. There was a serious side to their tinkering, it had to be said – readying the ship for whenever and for *whatever* it might be needed – but a desire not to think about that was what had brought her here. Slowhand, too, was currently absent from her life – the archer making good on his promise to avenge the death of his sister. Not, of course, that she'd had time to miss Slowhand or the others – the holiday she'd taken, she'd chosen specifically to keep her on her toes, and she had lost count of the number of times she had barely avoided it becoming a funeral. In short, she'd had one hell of a time, and the acquisition of what lay ahead of her was the last challenge she had to face. Because what she had so far not told Slack was that forming the bridges was only half of it – and what would happen if you didn't input the codes directly. She debated keeping this aspect to herself but what the hells – it would do him good to know how much he needed her around.

"One wrong move," she said, "and the entire mechanism resets itself. The bridges behind and ahead of us would disappear and we'd be stranded on the current column. Not to worry, though – it's not like we'd starve to death or anything – because the column would then retract into the depths below – bang just like that. *That's* when we'd need to worry."

Slack peered warily into the black depths. "Are you saying there is something down there?"

Kali leaned over his shoulder, cheek to cheek, and whispered, "Something horrible. There's always something horrible."

With the even more restrained Slack in tow, Kali negotiated three more bridges, coming at last to the final one – the one to the resting place of the artefact. This time she wielded the key but hesitated as she held it before the lock, drawing a worried glance from her side.

"There is a problem?" Slack asked.

"No, no, no problem," Kali responded. Well, not much of one – only that at this point in the game it was most likely she'd get them both killed. The fact was that while her studies of the dwarven key had revealed a pattern to her, she'd been sure of all the combinations except this last. The combinations represented a really quite simple series of nods to the inclinations of the dwarves' multifarious minor gods – "lightning" equalling "from above," in other words up; sunrise, east, therefore right; sea, which from this point on the peninsula was to the west and so was left – and so forth. The problem with the last combination was that it contained a glyph for the god of wind, and frankly that one had left her stymied. Wind, after all, could come from any direction, north, south, east or west, down, up, left or right, so how in the hells was she supposed to know where it came from? In the end, she'd whittled the possibilities down to two answers – up, because the wind in this valley was predominantly northern, which was spurious to say the least, and down, or south, because... well, because.

Hesitantly, she inserted the key in the final niche, turned most of the combination, and stopped before the final twist. North now, or south? If she guessed wrong, the last thing she'd see would be Slack wetting himself, and she could think of better images with which to depart the world. She stared at the smelly man and decided. Because it had to be, didn't it?

She turned the key south, locked it into place. After a few seconds the bridge appeared.

Kali sighed long and hard, realising she'd gambled correctly. And on a dwarven joke. A crude but effective joke, much like the dwarves themselves. She could imagine them roaring with laughter when they had thought of it – hey, Hammerhead, how about this? *There's more than one kind of wind!*

Beside her, Slack whooped, and not about to tell him she'd just gambled both of their lives on a fart, Kali moved on without a word, setting foot on the reassuring solidity of the central column. And right in front of her was what she had come for.

The Breachblades. Legend had it they had been forged by the greatest of dwarven smiths from wreckage washed up on shore near Oweilau millennia before. No one knew the origin of the wreckage but many speculated it had been part of a machine of those said to live deep beneath the sea, themselves having forged it from a material from the skies capable of withstanding the pressures of impossible depths. Whatever its origin, the metal possessed unprecedented properties, a toughness that was as evident in its finest component parts as its largest. It had taken the finest dwarven tools to extricate a piece which could be worked but from it the smith had produced prototypes of weapons for use against the elves. The blades were said to be sharp enough to slice through anything – rock, metal, or, more relevantly, the impenetrable armour with which the elves had by that time garbed their warriors. For such was the armour's indestructibility that one elf was able to cut a swathe through hundreds of dwarven warriors before being felled, and their enemies were desperate to even the odds. The irony was that though the dwarves had planned to forge a thousand such blades, these Breachblades were the only ones ever made – the moment of their forging coinciding with a new found peace between the Old Races that, in itself, was to last for almost a millennium. They were, in other words, unique, a one of a kind artefact that Kali had had on her 'must have' list for as long as she could remember. The only sadness was that because of the need to protect Twilight from itself, she could never let anyone know she had found them, let alone sell them, which was irksome because with the money they'd raise she could rethatch the Flagons with *gold*. *That* was something she had planned to do with the money for the plans for the elven ship, the *Llothriall*, but the Filth had put paid to that when they had visited the tavern uninvited one night. The bastards.

Kali sighed and picked up the Breachblades from their resting place in the pillar of light, swinging them about her experimentally. Some sources said they were even capable of slicing an elf's soul from its body and, while she held little belief in the whole Soul-goes-to-Kerberos thing, she couldn't deny a certain aura about them as they cut the air with a sibilant whoosh. She weighed the weapons in her hands, feeling as if she were barely wielding anything, their metal as light as a feather...

Which was something that could hardly be said about the rusty, serrated blade she felt suddenly pressed against her throat. Kali sighed again, but this time with a weary resignation.

Well, *that* was a surprise.

"I will be taking those, Miss Hooper," Maladorus Slack said from behind her. His blade wasn't anywhere near as uncomfortable as the fact that he was pushing himself up tight against her, his other hand rubbing slow circles on the exposed midriff beneath her torn bodysuit. His breath was hot as he added, "Drop them to the ground."

"You sure about that?" Kali responded.

"What? Of course I am sure!"

"Only it's just," Kali went on, "that if I drop them to the ground then you'll have to pick them up, and while you're doing that I'll kick you in the nuts so hard people'll be calling you Four-Eyes."

There was a hesitant pause.

"I told you, Slack, plan ahead."

"Then pass them to me slowly, between your legs."

Kali drew in a sharp breath. "Or No-Nuts."

"Over your shoulder, then!"

"Mister Knife-head."

"Damn you, woman. You are toying with me. Buying time."

"Actually, no. I'd prefer to get this over with quickly. Have you any idea at all how much you *stink*?"

"I sympathise. But you will not be able to stink... smell me when you're dead."

"Don't kid yourself, swamp boy."

"*Give me the blades.*"

"No."

"No?"

"No."

Slack sighed in exasperation and Kali smiled, having waited for it. All you ever had to do was wait for the sigh of exasperation because at that moment you knew that whoever *thought* they had the upper hand was momentarily off guard. She took advantage of this subtle shift in his stance to elbow Slack in the ribs then fling his gasping form around in front of her, kicking his legs out from under him as he came. It was a manoeuvre that should then have enabled her to pin him to the ground with her much sharper blades at *his* throat, and that was exactly where they would have been were it not for the fact that at that very moment the entire cavern trembled violently, so much so that it almost spilled them off the column. Kali stumbled and dropped to her knees, the Breachblades skittering from her hands. There was another tremble and Kali looked upwards, thinking *what the hells*? She hardly cared as, with a cry of triumph, Slack grabbed the blades and ran for the bridge, then she remembered the hand on her stomach and with a grunt of irritation made to pursue him. But she abruptly stopped about four yards onto the bridge.

What the hells? she thought again.

The tremors, the quake, whatever the pits it was, seemed to be interfering with the energy bridges throughout the cavern and, as Kali watched, each faded or flickered dangerously on and off. In his greed, Slack seemed not to have noticed but the very surface on which his filthy little feet pounded was already beginning to sparkle with the very same pattern it had when it formed. For whatever reason, the magic seemed to be destabilising.

"Slack, come back!" Kali shouted, but the only response she got was a backward flip of a finger. "Fine, you idiot, run, then! Just get off that farking bridge!"

This actually had the opposite effect to what she intended, and Slack paused in his tracks, turning to face her with a curious glance. It was the worst thing he could have done. And as Kali suddenly leapt back onto the security of the central island with a startled yelp, Slack's perspective on his situation turned his mood from triumphant glee to undisguised panic. For as his gaze shifted from Kali down to his feet he saw that the bridge was flickering more rapidly now, blinking in and out of existence every half second, the rapidity of the transition the only thing that was stopping him from falling through. There was no guarantee that it was going to continue blinking in that fashion, though, and the sudden realisation that at any moment there could be nothing between himself and an abyss filled with *something horrible* galvanized the thief into turning and running for his life. Unfortunately, the exercise was pointless, the man having realised his predicament at approximately the half way point of the crossing, so whichever way he went he seemed doomed. And a few seconds after he began his run for his life Maladorus Slack found himself treading air, and then, with a whimper, a dog-eyed glance at Kali and a scream, he was gone, flailing into the abyss.

"No!" Kali exclaimed with a stamp of her foot, but couldn't help raising her eyebrows when she saw the Breachblades resting on the still-flickering bridge, still held in Slack's severed hands, amputated the moment he'd fallen through. As sorry as she felt for the prat, even if he'd brought his fate upon himself, at least the blades had survived. And if they remained where they were long enough, all she had to do was reach them.

Which led Kali to her current predicament.

Reaching the blades was not her biggest problem. The tremors that seemed to have disrupted the magic of the bridges were continuing, dust and small stones cascading down from above, coating her in a grey shroud and forcing her to occasionally dodge a fall of heavier rocks. Whatever was causing the tremors was powerful enough to have disturbed this sanctum of ages and there was no guarantee that the whole lot wasn't going to come down on her head at any moment. She had to get out of there fast. But that was going to be easier said than done considering the current status of the bridges – there was no order, pattern or meter to their flickering at all. They seemed simply to be responding to some unknown, outside interference, which meant she had no way of judging what was coming next. Still, what was the alternative? If all of the bridges vanished completely, she'd be spending the rest of her life taking very short, circular walks. All she could do was make a best guess with each bridge, starting with the first – and do it fast.

Kali studied the stretch of energy and crouched down, poised like an athlete in blocks, ready to make her move. The bridge went through a cycle of non-existence, translucence and then the half second fluctuations that had occurred before Slack had vanished. As soon as these began she burst forward, legs and arms pumping, until she neared the Breachblades. She did not slow to pick them up, instead performing a rolling somersault as she ran, grabbing a blade in each hand and tucking them under her arms, and as she came upright again swinging them forward and clenching them in her fists like batons, flashing at her sides. The Breachblades sliced the air as she continued to run, almost as if they were slicing away any wind resistance she faced, and she seemed to run faster.

But would it be fast enough?

Kali made the first column safely and kept running there, in a circular fashion, taking deep breaths while the second energy bridge reached a point in its fluctuation cycle that she felt stable enough to make a move, and then again she launched herself onward, reaching the second pillar just as the bridge behind her flickered out completely. This time, she did not continue running but stopped and narrowed her eyes, muttering a curse as she studied the remaining bridges. She cursed not because the state of the bridges had worsened but because a second spanner had been thrown into the works, namely that the columns themselves had begun to slam themselves up and down, as if someone had entered the wrong combination sequence in their niches. No one had, of course, it was just that whatever was causing this interference seemed to be affecting *everything*. And it was clearly worsening.

Now it wasn't just the across she had to contend with, it was the up and the down, too. *Of course, it had to be*, she thought, rolling her eyes. Gods forbid she ever encountered anything that was farking *easy*. Her mind raced, trying to think in three dimensions how each column acted with each bridge. If she went immediately, the bridge would vanish before the next column rose, if she went in a second she'd make the end of the bridge but by then the column would have dropped, and if she waited until each were half way up and half way over...

Gods, it was no good. It was like being in the middle of some kind of weird *game.*

The only decision she could make came to her unbidden. Fark it.

Kali roared and raced forward, jumping the insubstantial sections of bridge ahead, panting and running on the spot in those places where she needed it to cycle back to some state of stability, throwing herself onto the next column as it rose towards her. As it did she leapt up towards the next bridge, flipped herself onto it and pounded onward, making the next bridge with half a second to spare. Only one to go now, but it was flickering with greater and greater rapidity, but at least there was no dancing column at the end of it, only the ledge that led to the exit. Breachblades whooshing against the air, her own breath heavy in counterpoint, she began to pound along its length. She was going to make it. She was going to–

A rockfall obliterated the ledge and the exit. At the same time the bridge flickered out of existence about thirty yards ahead of her. Crap.

Kali didn't stop running, her mind racing for a solution, eyes scanning the cavern ahead of her for something, *anything* she could use. Then it loomed out of the darkness, and Kali knew it was her only hope. She continued to run and without hesitation leapt out into space towards it, arms and legs wheeling, hoping fervently that the Breachblades did exactly what they said on the tin.

She thudded into the stalactite with an *oof,* both of the blades held solidly in her hands embedding themselves deeply and effortlessly into the rock.

"Oh, yes!" she cried, elatedly.

Kind of. Because then the blades began to cut down *through* the stalactite, and she looked down the length of her body past her feet. Beyond, she saw the last of the bridge flicker away completely, and all around the cavern, the others, too, and beneath where they had been, all there was was the abyss. She was dangling in a blackness alleviated only by the shaft of light now some way behind her, but somehow it managed to pick out the broken body of Slack far below being consumed by something... well, by something horrible. *Okaaay,* she thought. I've done it again, haven't I? Leapt before I looked. But hey, look on the bright side – at least the sun seemed to be coming up.

The bright side dimmed somewhat as, while she hung there over the abyss, it illuminated her predicament rather too well. Muscles straining to maintain their grip on the Breachblades, they were continuing their work, slowly slicing their way down through the stalactite that had proven to be her saviour. The pressure of the blades in the growth was already proving too much for it and, above her, a half-inch crack suddenly appeared across the horizontal, making a loud, cracking sound in the silence and spewing streams of rock dust into her face. Kali swallowed. Clearly, she couldn't hang around here all day.

As the stalactite jolted and dropped above her – the half inch gap widening to an inch, about to separate at any moment – Kali once more looked up, working out a possible route to safety and determining that the hole through which the light streamed was her only chance. She said her goodbyes to Slack and then, taking a deep breath, folded her legs up so that the soles of her feet rested on the stalactite and then kicked herself off it, maintaining a tight grip on the blades as she somersaulted backward. The stalactite she had left behind broke away, turned end over end through the air and then plummeted to the cavern floor, and Kali grunted as the blades impacted with another, slightly higher stalactite behind her.

"Gahhh!"

It was a precarious series of moves but gradually the hole in the cavern roof drew closer.

Maybe when she reached it she'd be able to find out just what the hells was going on.

For information on this and other titles, visit
www.abaddonbooks.com

Abaddon
Books

WWW.ABADDONBOOKS.COM

Price: **£6.99 ★ $7.99**

ISBN 13: **978-1-905437-54-2**

TWILIGHT of KERBEROS

THE CLOCKWORK
KING OF
ORL

MIKE WILD

Price: **£6.99** ★ **$7.99**

ISBN 13: **978-1-905437-75-7**

Price: **£6.99** ★ **$7.99**

ISBN 13: **978-1-905437-87-0**

TWILIGHT of KERBEROS

NIGHT'S HAUNTING

MATTHEW SPRANGE

Price: **£6.99** ★ **$7.99**

ISBN 13: **978-1-906735-25-8**